W9-BYB-270

Alan B. Shepard High School

Praise for the Shadow Falls Series

"Hunter sucks you in . . . an amazing roller-coaster ride." —*RT Book Reviews*

"The Shadow Falls series belongs to my favorite YA series. It has everything I wish for in a YA paranormal series. A thrilling tale that moves with a great pace, where layers of secrets are revealed in a way that we are never bored. It continues a gripping story about self-discoveries, finding a place in the world, friendship, and love. So if you didn't start this series yet, I can only encourage you to do so." —*Bewitched Bookworms*

"Ms. Hunter handles this series with such deftness, crafting a wonderful tale that speaks to the adolescent in me. I highly recommend this series filled with darkness and light, hope and danger, friendship and romance." —*Night Owl Reviews* (Top Pick)

"Jam-packed with action and romance from the very beginning, Hunter's lifelike characters and paranormal creatures populate a plot that will keep you guessing till the very end. A perfect mesh of mystery, thriller, and romance. Vampires, weres, and fae, oh my!" —*RT Book Reviews* on *Taken at Dusk*

"An emotional thrill ride full of suspense, action, laughter, multiple love stories, and an intriguing variety of paranormal species. I could not put this book down and can't wait to start the next book as soon as I finish this review." —*Guilty Pleasures Book Reviews* on *Awake at Dawn*

"There are so many books in the young adult paranormal genre these days that it's hard to choose a good one. I was so very glad to discover *Born at Midnight*. If you like P. C. and Kristin Cast or Alyson Noël, I am sure you will enjoy *Born at Midnight*!" —*Night Owl Reviews*

"The evolving, not-always-easy relationships among Kylie and her cabin mates Della and Miranda are rendered as engagingly as Kylie's angst over dangerous Lucas and appealing Derek. Just enough plot threads are tied up to make a satisfying stand-alone tale while whetting appetites for sequels to come." —*Publishers Weekly*

"With intricate plotting and characters so vivid you'd swear they are real, *Born at Midnight* is an addictive treat. Funny, poignant, romantic, and downright scary in places, it hits all the right notes. Highly recommended." —*Houston Lifestyles and Homes Magazine*

ALSO BY C. C. HUNTER

Born at Midnight

Awake at Dawn

Taken at Dusk

Whispers at Moonrise

Chosen at Nightfall

Reborn

── SHADOW FALLS ✦ AFTER DARK ──

Eternal

C. C. HUNTER

ST. MARTIN'S GRIFFIN ⬟ NEW YORK

This is a work of fiction. All of the characters, organizations, and events portrayed in this novel are either products of the author's imagination or are used fictitiously.

ETERNAL. Copyright © 2014 by Christie Craig. All rights reserved. Printed in the United States of America. For information, address St. Martin's Press, 175 Fifth Avenue, New York, N.Y. 10010.

www.stmartins.com

The Library of Congress Cataloging-in-Publication Data is available upon request.

ISBN 978-1-250-04461-7 (trade paperback)
ISBN 978-1-250-05630-6 (hardcover)
ISBN 978-1-4668-4306-6 (e-book)

St. Martin's Griffin books may be purchased for educational, business, or promotional use. For information on bulk purchases, please contact Macmillan Corporate and Premiums Sales Department at 1-800-221-7945, extension 5442, or write specialmarkets@macmillan.com.

First Edition: November 2014

10 9 8 7 6 5 4 3 2 1

To Lily, who, if she's said it once, she's said it a thousand times, "Mawmaw, tell me a story."

I can't wait, young lady, until you can read Kylie and Della's stories.

Acknowledgments

To all the fans who write just to let me know that my stories keep them up at night and make them think about the value of friends, love, and laughter. Thank you for reading.

Here's to all the family and friends who make my life complete. You know who you are. And each and every one of you is a cornerstone in my life.

To my agent, Kim Lionetti, who encourages me to follow my gut. To my editor, Rose Hilliard, whose faith in me is inspirational. Thank you.

Eternal

Chapter One

Della Tsang swung one leg outside her bedroom window. The sun had risen but hung on the eastern horizon, spilling just enough light to paint that strip of sky a blood-red. The color had her mouth watering.

Her empty stomach rumbled. She needed blood. Later.

First things first.

She knew what she had to do—hadn't slept half the night because of it.

A blast of late-October air stirred her black hair in front of her eyes. The wind was cold on her face, but not cold like when she'd had the fever.

Since she'd woken from the two-day coma after being Reborn, which was an unusual second transition into being a vampire, all her previous flu-like symptoms had disappeared.

Pushing off the window ledge, her boots hit the wet earth with a squish. She paused right outside the cabin to see if the sound had awoken her Shadow Falls roommates, Miranda or Kylie, almost hoping for some company.

Only silence filled her ears.

They'd both stayed out late last night with their boyfriends. Della had seen Steve, too, but she'd pulled the tired card and called it an early night. She took a small step, still listening for any sign they were awake.

I don't need them. I don't. Della had to do this on her own. *Alone.*

That had been her mantra for the last week. Well, not exactly—more like: *Not with Chase.* The lying, conniving vamp whom she'd unwillingly become bonded to when he'd convinced Steve, Della's almost-boyfriend, to let him mingle his blood with hers to up the odds of her surviving the so-called rebirth.

Bonded. She recalled what little information Chase had explained. *It links the two vampires. They become almost a part of each other. It has been compared to the relationship shared by identical twins or perhaps soul mates.*

Pushing that from her mind, she glanced again at the dark woods, sensing something waiting for her . . . calling her. There was no turning back.

Reaching around, she closed her bedroom window. A twig snapped from inside the woods. Della turned and faced the trees, inhaling the air to catch anyone's scent.

Nothing but the wet, musky scent of a possum.

She started walking. As soon as she entered the woods, the night's noise vanished. Even the trees seemed to hold their breath. A carrier of the vampire virus, she'd been turned almost a year ago. This second turn, extremely rare, meant she was stronger, faster—meant she could really kick ass and ask questions later.

She'd give the power back in a snap if it would bring Chan back.

Perhaps she should be appreciative for what Chase had done, making sure she lived, but she would've preferred he'd done it for her cousin Chan. Burnett, the camp leader and another Reborn, had survived his rebirth without a transfusion; she probably could have as well. Plus, Chase had done it so secretively and had lied to her until the very end.

The real pisser was—he hadn't stopped lying.

She'd texted him the question: *Who sent you to check on me and Chan?*

His reply: *Don't know. Just following orders,* was bullshit.

He'd messaged her last night. *Five minutes . . . give me five minutes. I'm at the gate.*

She'd replied, *Until I get answers, I don't have five minutes for you.*

Not until he came clean. The guy had more secrets than a rogue werewolf had fleas.

If her suspicions were correct, and she'd bet her canines they were, he had information about her missing uncle who'd gotten turned and faked his own death as a teen. Who else would care about her? Who else would know Chan was her cousin? And if it was her uncle calling the shots, why hadn't he cared enough to save Chan, too?

Thinking of her uncle had her automatically thinking of her father and how easily he'd turned his back on her. Adding to her heartache was the discovery that he'd been suspected of killing his own sister.

Her mind couldn't wrap around that. Her father couldn't, wouldn't have done that.

She continued walking, her footsteps soggy. The night had seen its share of rain. Instead of sleeping, she'd listened to the sound of drizzle dancing on the tin roof of the cabin. But that wasn't the only sound of water she'd heard.

The roar of the falls had echoed in the distance. There was no way, even with her vampire hearing, that she could hear the falls from her cabin. Which meant the falls were calling her.

The falls, being that magical but creepy place where the death angels—mystical beings who stood in judgment of all supernaturals— were said to hang out.

The sound of the falls echoed louder.

"Don't worry. I'm coming." She wouldn't back out, and not simply because it called her—Della had never been one to come when called. She made this trip because she'd remembered something Kylie had once told her. *I go to the falls to find answers.*

If those death angels could answer Kylie's questions, then by damn, they could answer Della's. Never mind that last time she'd gone there after feeling called, someone . . . as in the death angels themselves . . . had clobbered her on the head with a rock.

A nervous tickle whispered through her, but she kept going. For the answers, she'd risk it.

But if it was the death angels that knocked her on the head, they'd best be forewarned. This time, she'd be a hell of a lot harder to take down.

As Della neared the falls, her tickle of unease evaporated, and a sense of well-being grew in her chest.

She stepped between the trees and caught sight of the cascading water. She turned her head side to side, wanting to take it all in. Trees circled the area. Their limbs arched above, almost hugging the area of the falls, making it feel like a special little alcove. The sun, still new to the morning, cast its first golden hue of light through the trees. The air smelled fresh, verdant, and peaceful. She'd never considered what *peaceful* smelled like, but she knew it now.

The ambience reminded Della of a Buddhist temple she'd visited in China when she was twelve. Without explanation, she suddenly knew the death angels hadn't hit her on the head.

"So who was it?" She muttered the question aloud, not the least bit paranoid to be voicing her question to the empty woods.

Just because she couldn't see them didn't mean they weren't there.

She wasn't alone.

She sensed it. For the first time since she'd woken up from that coma after being Reborn, she felt . . . less alone. Complete.

"Who was what?" The voice blended with the rush of the falls.

Her heart leapt and her gaze shot to a spot in the curtain of water that blurred as a figure emerged.

Recognition hit and Della's sense of peacefulness shattered.

"What are *you* doing here?" she asked.

"Probably the same thing you are." Chase's gaze whispered over her. "I kept hearing it last night."

"You followed me," she accused.

He smirked. "Now you're not even being logical. I was here first. If anyone was followed, you followed me."

"I didn't." Ambivalence rumbled around inside her, and had her clenching her fist. Should she hightail it out of here and continue with her vow not to speak to him until he told her the truth about who had sent him? Or should she cross over the water and go vamp on his butt to get the truth out of him?

She knew which one she wanted to do. Oddly, kicking ass—in a place where peace flavored the air—felt wrong. Decision made, she swerved around and started walking. Hopefully he'd follow her to a less than holy place and she could kick his butt then.

"Whoa! Stop!" he called.

She ignored him. Ignored the sound of the falls. She kept walking, her focus on the ground, the way the wet earth squished around the edges of her boots. Gaze still lowered, suddenly, another pair of wet leather boots appeared in her line of vision.

She stopped, but didn't look up. Didn't have to. She knew they were Chase's boots. Her heart did another tumble. His speed still awed her.

Am I that fast now?

She hadn't really had a chance to test her limits. Not with Burnett micromanaging her powers. Not with all her pressing issues.

But those issues didn't need her immediate attention, so she nudged those thoughts aside to deal with the problem at hand—or rather, the problem at her feet. Chase. Lifting her gaze, the visual details—Chase details—hit her at once. She stared, soaking them all in like a hungry sponge.

Details like how his wet, black hair clung to his brow. Like how his white T-shirt appeared shrink-wrapped to his upper body, showcasing every dip and curve of his muscular form. How he appeared buffer, or maybe she'd just forgotten how male-model perfect he was. She hated perfect!

"Hey." His one soft word seemed to float through the air as he inched closer. His nearness made her skin feel extra sensitive. Maybe she didn't hate perfect so much. Had he always had this effect on her, or was this just post-bonding crap?

She growled, annoyed at her own weakness. But for the life of her, she couldn't seem to move back. Look but don't touch, she gave herself one rule.

He grinned as if he could read her mind.

She growled louder.

"You are a sight for sore eyes." He reached out as if to pull her against him. She found the strength and lurched back, leaving skid marks in the wet grass.

The look-but-don't-touch rule would stand firm.

He stepped toward her. His scent, part musk, part mint, invaded her air. He lifted his hand.

She sucked cold oxygen between her teeth before speaking. "Your eyes aren't the only thing that's going to be sore if you touch me!"

He held up both of his hands, a sign of submissiveness, but his sexy smile signaled trouble. She would not, could not, give in to these crazy feelings. How could she when part of her heart belonged to someone else?

"Fine, I'll keep my hands to myself." He looked over her shoulder at the falls and then back at her. "But can't you see it's fate?"

A spray of sun shot through the trees and cast swirly shadows over his face. That's when she noticed the purple bruise under his eye. Considering vampires didn't bruise easily, that had to have been a hell of a lick.

"What's fate?" she asked, trying not to care that he'd been hit. Hurt. That he could have been killed.

Bonded.

"This," he said, moving his hands between them.

"What's this?" she asked.

"Us."

"Us what?"

"Us. Here."

She glared at him. "Did you forget how to use complete sentences?" she smarted off.

He half chuckled. "Come on. Doesn't it seem strange that we were both lured here?" He shifted slightly and the precious gold light touched his face. His hair, wet from his trip through the falls, appeared almost black, and his eyes, a light golden green, almost glowed with the sun on them. But noting the bruise again, she felt a sympathy pain under her left eye.

She had to remember not to let herself get lost in those eyes—in emotions she couldn't explain.

"I wasn't lured." Her heart danced around the mistruth as the sound of the cascading water hummed in the background. "I came here for a reason." That much was true. She stiffened her shoulders.

"What reason?" he asked.

"To find answers. Answers that you aren't giving me." Accusation rang in her tone. She pressed both her hands on her hips and stared up at him. Oddly, she'd forgotten how tall he was. He towered above her. She wasn't accustomed to feeling small or feminine, but his presence did that.

He tucked his hands in his jean pockets and tipped back on his heels. "What answers?"

She raised her chin and studied him, trying not to note the bruise or worry what he'd done to get it. "Who sent you to check on me and Chan?"

For a flicker of a second, he hesitated, then spoke, "I did answer that. The Vampire Council." But the sneaky vamp looked away as soon as the words left his mouth. And she knew he always did that when he lied.

"That's bullshit," she said. "You're still keeping something from me."

He glanced back at her. "It's not a lie. I got my orders from the council."

She studied him. This time he didn't blink or turn away. Did that mean he spoke the truth?

No, she didn't trust him. If he could learn to control his heartbeat when he lied—and he'd admitted he could do that—then he could learn to control his facial reactions. Surely by now he'd figured out why she constantly challenged his word.

"Did they also order you to let Chan die?" The moment the

question left her lips, she felt her resolve strengthen. It didn't matter that her strength came from her own guilt—she'd take it.

Chase inhaled and looked down at the ground, shifting the tip of his right boot into the wet earth. When he looked back up, she saw a flicker of emotion in his eyes.

"No. Letting Chan face the rebirth on his own was my decision. I told you, I didn't think he would survive, and if I'd tried to save him, I wouldn't have been able to save you."

"Do you have any idea how that makes me feel?" Her throat tightened. To save her, he'd let Chan die.

His shoulders lowered half an inch. Refocusing on his gaze, she spotted empathy in his eyes.

She hated empathy. It ranked right up there with pity.

She turned to leave. He grabbed her. Gently.

His thumb moved in small circles over her elbow. "I'm sorry. But I'm not responsible for his death any more than you are. We didn't make this happen. And I did what I thought was right. It wasn't easy for me, either. I liked Chan. But he was just too weak."

Her skin tingled where the tips of his fingers moved. Remembering her no-touch rule, she shook off his hand. "Which is exactly why you should have helped him. If two people are in a river, you save the one who can't swim."

"And let you drown?" he asked.

"I might have made it through the rebirth. Burnett did." The second the words left her mouth, she worried Chase didn't know Burnett was a Reborn, but his lack of surprise put her at ease.

A frown tightened the corners of Chase's eyes. "Burnett's an exception. Less than three percent of Reborns live. The odds weren't in your favor."

"I would have taken those odds if I'd been given a choice. But I wasn't. You didn't even tell me Chan was dead and you knew. You kept this whole Reborn thing and your being here to help me to yourself. And why? Because you knew I'd be opposed to it."

He kicked at a rock on the ground. The pebble soared through the air and hit a tree with a dead thump. "So I'm the bad guy for wanting to save your life?"

She leaned in. "You're the bad guy for not being up-front. And you're still doing it."

His mouth tightened, and he crossed his arms over his chest. "Okay. I didn't tell you everything. Be mad at me for that. But you can't just ignore me or the fact that we're bonded. You feel it. I feel it. You can't deny it."

"Watch me. I'm good at denying shit!" She seethed and darted around him to start back.

"God, you're stubborn!" he called out, then again appeared in front of her.

She came to an abrupt stop, slamming her hands on his chest to stop from falling face forward. He caught her by the waist. Gently. His touch sent her heart racing this time.

"Either tell me the truth or leave," she said, stepping out of his embrace. It was her last ultimatum. "Who are you working with besides the Vampire Council, and don't tell me no one, because my bullshit detector goes off every time you tell me that."

Chapter Two

Chase stood there, staring at her. She wished she could read his mind.

Della's patience finally snapped. "Leave! If Burnett finds you, he'll . . ." Then it occurred to her that Burnett should have already found him. The alarm would have gone off. Why wasn't the camp leader already here giving Chase hell and interrogating him? Something was up.

Chase's expression of confidence confirmed it. "He knows I'm here. I had a meeting with him." Honesty deepened Chase's voice.

She tried not to let her disappointment show, but her expression tightened. Was Burnett in cahoots with Chase again? Hadn't he been just as pissed as she was when he'd packed up his shit and disappeared?

"When we were done, I asked to come to the falls. I told him I kept hearing it." Chase shrugged. "Burnett's only rule was to not go near your cabin, and I didn't." He shrugged, almost guiltily. "Not yet, anyway. But I probably would have before I left. I needed to see you. He can get furious at me if he wants."

He took one step closer.

She took one step back. "Why were you meeting with Burnett?"

"The council sent me back."

"Sent you about what?" she asked.

He didn't answer.

Tired of playing games, she darted around him in a dead run, her only goal to get away from him—away from the temptation to lean against him, to find out what this bonding really meant. Or if it meant nothing, she thought, wanting that to be true.

This time he didn't follow. Good, she thought, ducking under tree limbs, moving fast. That's what she wanted. So why didn't she feel victorious? Why was she now hearing the falls louder? Was it the falls luring her? Or Chase?

They sent him about you. The words rang out.

She came to a sudden stop.

Where had the damn voice come from? She stood there, cutting her eyes east to west, then back again.

Did you hear me?

This time she knew the words hadn't come from her left or her right. They had come from within her. She recalled hearing similar internal voices. Chan? But he'd crossed over, hadn't he? She'd been sure of it. Or was he waiting until the FRU, Fallen Research Unit team—the FBI in charge of supernaturals—released his body and buried him.

You listening?

Yes, I am, Della answered, realizing the voice was female.

"Lorraine?" Della whispered the name of the murdered girl, the last spirit she'd heard in her head.

Yet hadn't Holiday assured her that Lorraine had moved on, crossed over?

So who the hell was this?

Did Della have another ghost hanging around?

"Crap!" she muttered.

Did you hear me? the voice repeated, as if taunting her.

"I wish I didn't." Della's heart thumped against her chest. She fought the panic swelling inside her. Inhaling, she tried to find a sense of calm. She'd done the ghost thing. First, communicating with Chan, then with Lorraine. It shouldn't freak her out.

Who was she kidding? Communicating with spirits was a rare talent, one that freaked out most supernaturals. And she was no different. Adrenaline chased goose bumps up and down her spine and then all the way down to her toes, which she curled in her boots.

The Vampire Council sent him about you, the voice repeated. *Aren't you curious?*

For the first time, she really heard what the voice said. "What does the Vampire Council want with me?" She posed her question aloud. And just like that, her fear was replaced with . . .

Hell yeah, I'm curious. It had to be about her uncle, damn it!

She swung around and started back—fast. Moving at a dead run . . . but hoping the dead didn't come with her.

The sound of her boots hitting the wet earth filled her ears and played like background music to the rush of the falls. As she neared, she saw Chase's figure disappear behind the wall of water.

Or, at least she thought it was him. In reality, it could have been anyone.

She didn't care. Curiosity and something else . . . something she couldn't explain, propelled her forward.

Bonded. The word echoed in her heart as an explanation, but she refused to believe it.

She kept running, her feet splashing through the stream. Her face hit the curtain of water—cool, but not cold. It spilled over her face, down her shoulders, soaking her clothes. The second she got on the other side, she saw nothing. A cave-like darkness swallowed her. She blinked and waited for her eyes to adjust.

One second.

Two.

No light. Nothing. Even the sound of the falls had been yanked away.

Something wasn't right.

Chapter Three

Trapped. Claustrophobic. Hungry. She sat on the cold ground.

Emotions whooshed through Della like a fire chasing kerosene. Then she heard it. Breathing.

In.

Out.

Air being pulled into another set of lungs.

She remembered she wasn't alone.

"Chase?" she whispered his name, but even as she said it, she knew it wasn't him.

It was Liam.

But who the hell was Liam? She didn't know any Liam, so how did she know his name? Her heart thumped a little faster and she tasted blood on her tongue.

Mo fo! What the hell was happening?

"You okay?" a voice asked, Liam's voice.

"No," Della said. *I'm pretty sure I'm losing my mind.*

"Here. Drink some more."

She smelled another vamp. Liam was a vamp. But she'd already known that. How could she know and not know something at the same time? An arm, a strong limb of flesh and blood, came against her mouth.

"Go ahead, drink a little more."

Knees pulled up to her chest, her empty stomach clenched as she realized what he was offering. Vampires didn't drink another vamp's blood. At least not the ones she knew.

"No." Della pushed the arm away, but as she moved the limb, her fingertips touched tiny wounds . . . wounds that felt like teeth marks.

When she rested her arm on her bare knee, she felt the same tiny wounds on her wrist.

"Do it, Natasha. Come on, I'm fine." His arm came against her mouth again, and she gently moved it away, holding on to him a second longer than necessary, needing the contact.

She started to tell him she wasn't Natasha, but it would have been a lie. She was Natasha. Somehow, someway, she was inside Natasha. Then she remembered this happening before, with Lorraine. But Lorraine was dead. Were these two . . . She blinked and tried to make out her surroundings. Only darkness filled her vision.

She was locked in a dark, dank place that smelled like wet dirt with a boy named Liam. The tangy taste of blood lingered on her lips. Then the realization hit. They weren't dead. Didn't feel dead. They were actually trying to survive. And to do it, Liam and Natasha were feeding off each other.

"Seriously, I'm fine," Liam repeated.

"I'm not hungry," she lied. She barely noted the skip of her heart, listening to the sound of her voice. Not Della's voice. Natasha's voice.

Who was Natasha?

Panic started to swell inside her chest. She buried her nails in the wet earth she sat on, and almost cried out from the pain. Obviously, she'd already tried to claw her way out.

And it hadn't worked.

They couldn't continue to feed off each other. She and Liam were going to die.

No, Natasha and Liam were going to die.

But the realization didn't make Della feel any better. A feeling, a need, to save Natasha and Liam, swept through her. No, not swept. It felt as if it was tattooed on her soul, as if it was part of her destiny. As if not doing it would mean death not just for Natasha and Liam, but for part of herself as well. Part of her soul.

Save her! Save her! The words echoed as if in the distance. The same voice she'd heard before she'd come inside the falls. A ghost? Maybe.

"You okay?" another voice, a deep male voice, snuck into her awareness and tickled her subconscious. "You okay?" the deep voice repeated.

It wasn't Liam this time.

The deep tenor carried an undertone of confidence that she recognized. A tone she admired, but wished she didn't. Another feeling swelled inside her, and one word resounded in her heart.

Bonded.

Chase.

She mentally climbed out of the odd kind of dream state that had sucked her under. Chase held her by the shoulders, and he gave her a slight shake.

"Hey. What's wrong?" he asked, his brow wrinkled, his lips almost white, he held them so tight. "Answer me." He touched her face. His palms moved down her arms. His touch . . . felt so right. It felt so wrong. "Della?"

"Stop fondling me." She slapped at his hand and took a step back, her gaze shifting around the cavern.

"I wasn't . . . what just happened?" he asked.

Her breath caught, wondering how long she'd stood here, lost in that other place. Or not exactly lost, but trapped. Trapped like Natasha.

She suddenly remembered what the ghost—or whatever it had been—had said to her about Chase.

The Vampire Council sent Chase here about you.

"What does the Vampire Council want with me?" she asked.

Chapter Four

A look of surprise entered Chase's eyes. "I didn't say they sent me here for you." He lowered himself and sat on a large rock. The filtered light from the falls cast shadows around him. Some of the light held tiny rays of color, like a mini light show.

"The truth, Chase. Please." The "please" sounded wrong. She shouldn't have to beg for the truth. And that was why she couldn't ever really trust this guy, she reminded herself.

He exhaled. "They want you to work a case." He let go of some air as if frustrated. "I'll get my ass chewed out by Burnett for telling you this, but that's probably a plus for you, isn't it?"

She ignored the ass-chewing comment and the slight hurt in his voice, and focused on the information he'd finally leaked. "A case? What kind of a case?"

"One you've already partially solved."

"What?"

"Supposedly, you captured and then led the FRU to that creep, Craig Anthony, who was enslaving new vampires and using a funeral home as a front."

Yeah, she'd stumbled across his organization when she'd gone to ask questions about Chan and her uncle's funeral, but . . . "Craig Anthony was caught, so what's the case about?"

Glancing back at the falls, Chase rested his hands on his knees. His jeans, still wet, stretched over his muscled legs. "Anthony was caught, but he isn't talking. Between the FRU and the council, we're pretty sure we've reined in most of his clients holding vampires. But according to some leads, there could still be as many as twenty or thirty fresh turns under someone's thumb."

"So the FRU and the Vampire Council actually compare notes?"

Chase frowned. "Not very often, and only when it benefits the FRU."

"Or the other way around," Della said. Then she remembered how sleazy Craig Anthony was and she had no doubt those new vampires were being treated terribly. Somebody needed to find them. Why not her?

"So, they want me to work with the FRU to find them?"

"Not quite. They want us to find them." He studied her face. "They want you to come and work for the council."

Della stared at the wall of water, trying to wrap her head around this piece of news. Ever since she'd learned of the council's existence, she'd considered them partly rogue. The FRU was the legitimate supernatural governing body. Knowing Chase was even halfway associated with the Vampire Council tainted her view of him.

She glanced back at him in his wet clothes. The idea of working with him, being with him, had panic swelling inside her again. "I'll have to think about it."

"Don't waste your time. Burnett already denied the council's request."

He denied it? "I'm sure he wants to talk it over with me," Della said, hoping she was right, but accepting she probably wasn't. First, she knew Burnett didn't trust the Vampire Council. Second, even with her new powers, knowing him, he'd still probably hesitate to let her work any case he considered dangerous. But shouldn't the decision be hers?

Hell yes, it should, the ghostly voice inside her shouted. *Find Natasha!*

And just like that, she knew the two things were connected. Natasha and Liam were victims of Craig Anthony. He may have been caught, but those he had imprisoned and enslaved were still out there.

"Burnett denied my request right out," Chase said with sarcasm. "He keeps you all on a short leash."

Pushing her latest thought aside to deal with Chase, she cupped her hands and considered his accusation about the camp leader. She knew what Chase said was true. She'd spent most of the last few months yanking on her leash, but her loyalty to Burnett demanded she defend him. "Not that short. We caught Craig Anthony, didn't we?"

"There is that," he said. "But I'll bet anything you did it while breaking some of his rules."

Right again. But she wouldn't admit it. She met Chase's gaze, noting the bruise under his eye. "Some rules are there for a reason. Like we're not supposed to reveal our Reborn powers. Is that how you got that black eye? Inviting trouble by showing off?"

"I don't invite trouble, but I take care of it if it shows up."

"Well, stop it. Stop showing off what you can do. Burnett's right. It'll invite all kinds to try to outdo you. Next time, instead of a black eye, you could have a broken neck."

A slow smile came across his face. "Careful, you almost sound like you care."

Damn it! She did care. *Bonded.* What the hell did that really mean? She almost asked him to explain it more, but why the hell would she trust someone who was full of nothing but secrets?

She turned to leave, but before she walked through the falls, he appeared in front of her.

"Don't go," he said.

She shook her head. "The only conversation I want to have with you is when you tell me who sent you to check on Chan and me."

"I told you already," he growled, frustration sounding in his tone. "The Vampire Council."

Della studied his face, realizing that this time he didn't flinch. Was he telling the truth? Did he not know who else was behind it? Oh, hell, she didn't know what to believe anymore.

"Then how did they know about me?" she asked.

"Della, I work for them, just like you work for the FRU. Do they tell you everything? Hell, no. Burnett didn't even tell us they sent other agents in when we were looking for that Billy kid."

The truth of his words had more doubt flopping around her head and her heart. She hated uncertainty.

And he seemed to sense it. "We belong together now." He moved closer, put his hand on her shoulder. "Why are you fighting it?" He studied her and a frown suddenly pulled at his lips. "Is it Steve? You still have feelings for him?"

She tilted her head back. "Yes, I care about Steve."

She wasn't going to lie. She and Steve were practically together now. This last weekend when he'd been here, she'd stopped pretending in front of everyone. Steve had even put his arm around her when they'd been walking to lunch Friday. And because she'd sensed it had been a test, she'd let him. Damn it, she hadn't wanted to fail that test.

She hadn't wanted to fail Steve. Yet there was a small part of her that worried she was destined to fail him. And all because of some stupid bonding with the guy standing in front of her.

"And this," she waved a hand between them, "*this* isn't the same thing." She reached deep inside to find something to explain it.

She saw emotions flash in his eyes. Disappointment, anger, maybe even jealousy.

"You even told me. This bond thing can be compared to the relationship shared by identical twins."

His eyebrow arched in complete disbelief. "So, you love me like a brother? That kiss last week—"

"Not exactly like a brother, but . . . but . . ." His words echoed in her head. Or, at least one word did. *Love.* "I don't love you, period." She gripped her hands. "I go back and forth on even *liking* you." Being attracted to him, caring if he got hurt, that was something different. Something she didn't want to think about.

Something she was working on denying.

He exhaled. "That's bullshit."

Suddenly feeling the urgency to deal with other issues—that didn't have to do with him—she glanced up at another rainbow of color dancing on the walls. "I gotta go." Turning on the heels of her boots, she stepped out of the cavern. The cold of the waterfall almost felt surreal. It washed down her head, seeping beneath her shirt. Immediately, she felt a sense of loss at leaving. *I'll be back.*

"Go to do what?" Chase was right behind her, but she kept walking. She refused to look back, and refused to acknowledge that the sense of loss had anything to do with him and not everything to do with the falls. Please let it be just the falls.

"What is it that you have to do?" He repeated the question when she didn't answer.

"Talk to Burnett," she answered, thinking about him denying

her the case—without even talking to her about it—and then she recalled the whole ghost issue and the crazy vision. "And Kylie and Holiday," she said aloud as she formed her own plan. If anyone could explain what had happened there, it would be them.

"Talk about what?" His question came at her ear. His closeness felt both wrong and right at the same time.

"About me working with the Vampire Council." Her mind raced back to Holiday and Kylie. "About finding Natasha and Liam," she muttered aloud, but more to herself than to him.

Remembering how desperate she felt when she'd been in that vision, she started running. The sun had crawled higher in the east. Yet the sky still grasped the golden hue of pre-morning. The warmth of the light felt good on her damp skin and she couldn't help but recall the darkness smothering Natasha and Liam.

As her footfalls sounded on the ground, she realized Chase no longer followed. She was halfway to the office when she suddenly became aware that Chase hadn't asked her who Natasha and Liam were. A crazy thought hit. Had he somehow had the same vision?

She was tempted to turn around, find him, and ask. But, no, that was crazy. First, because getting any answers from him was like pulling teeth out of an angry lion, and second, because . . . surely a dual vision like that couldn't happen. But she recalled how upset he'd been when she'd first awoken from that dark, damp place. Was his reaction from his distress for her, or had he shared the same experience that she had?

Slowing down to a jog, she snatched out her phone and dialed Kylie's number. The chameleon answered sounding a little sleepy, but concerned.

"What's wrong?"

"Nothing . . . really. I'm fine. I just have questions. Meet me at

Holiday's office, please." She hung up, confident Kylie would be there. Kylie would never let her down.

As she continued to the office, another thought hit. She'd come to the falls to get answers, but left with more questions. How was that fair? Why did the death angels answer Kylie's questions and not hers?

"That couldn't happen, could it?" Della sat on Holiday's office sofa, telling them about the voice, about the vision, and asking if they thought Chase could have actually been in the vision with her.

The fae camp leader sat at her desk, looking perplexed. Kylie, appearing almost as befuddled, sat beside Della.

"Wow," Holiday said. "You've had a heck of a day, and it's not even seven o'clock."

"Tell me about it," Della said, plopping back on the sofa, her heart heavy. "So what am I dealing with here?" Her thoughts shot back to Natasha and Liam. If Holiday or Kylie couldn't help, how in the hell was Della going to save them? She didn't have a clue how to understand any of this.

"Do you know a Natasha or Liam?" Holiday asked.

"No," Della said. "But . . . I think it might have something to do with the Craig Anthony case. Chase told me that there are still a lot of fresh turns that haven't been accounted for. What if Anthony is the one who imprisoned them?"

Holiday nodded. "That could be it, but . . . normally there's more of a connection."

"Maybe this one isn't normal." She tightened her hands.

"First, don't be frightened," Holiday said.

"I'm not," Della insisted, and then realized Holiday was reading her emotions. But the fae had it wrong. "I mean, yeah, I didn't like it, and when I first heard the ghost, I freaked out a little." Her heart rushed to the sound of a lie. "Okay, a lot, but I've sort of moved past that. What's scaring the shit out of me right now is that I won't get Natasha and Liam out in time. They can't live like that for long."

Della saw the way Kylie and Holiday looked at each other, as if they knew something she didn't.

"What?" Della asked.

Holiday stood up and sat next to Della on the other side of the sofa. The look on her face expressed pure empathy. The fact that she'd moved closer told Della that whatever she was about to tell her wasn't good. In fact, it was so bad that she knew Della needed some of her calm-inducing touch to hear the news.

When Holiday's hand came closer, Della shot up off the sofa. "No, don't touch me. Just tell me. What is it you think I don't want to hear?"

Chapter Five

Della heard Kylie sigh. The chameleon sighed when worried or stressed.

Della glanced at her friend's light blue eyes shimmering with concern and asked, "What is it? Just tell me already."

Kylie looked at Holiday and the camp leader nodded.

"Normally," Kylie began, "when you have visions, ones where you're actually the person, it's because . . . because they're already dead."

"I know, but this time they weren't dead."

"They might feel alive, but it's them showing you . . ."

"No." Tears welled up in Della's eyes. "Then why the hell would she show me that? If they're dead, what the hell can I do? That's wrong. It's sick. Why put me through that?"

Kylie nodded. "I felt the same way when it first happened to me, but—"

Holiday spoke up. "They do it because they want to be found. Because they want the person who hurt them to be stopped."

Della tried to get her head around that. But it hurt. It hurt too damn much.

Then she remembered the other vision she'd had—the one where she'd been the murdered girl, Lorraine, looking down at her bloody hands. Somehow in the vision, Della had sensed the girl was dead. But not this time.

"No, this was different," Della insisted. "They're alive," she said. "I felt it."

A tear slipped from Della's lashes, and it felt hot rolling down her cold skin. She wiped it away. Then she remembered the ghost's voice. *Find Natasha.*

"No," Della said again. "The ghost told me to find Natasha. The ghost wasn't Natasha."

Holiday stood up and took a few steps toward Della. "But, if you were in Natasha's body, it normally means . . ."

"*Normally.* You both keep throwing that word out there. But what's normal about any of this? I'm vampire, I'm not even supposed to deal with ghosts. Maybe I'm doing this whole ghost thing abnormally!"

Holiday pulled her long red hair over her shoulder and twisted it as if in thought. "I'm not going to say it's impossible, Della. You and Burnett are the first vampires I've known to be mediums. But I'm just telling you what I believe."

"But you know," Kylie added, and looked at Della as if she wanted to help, "Sara's grandma came to me to heal Sara when she had the cancer. So maybe this is a ghost coming to you to help someone."

"True," Holiday said. "But you were never in Sara's body, were you?"

"No." Kylie leaned back against the sofa and met Della's gaze.

Della looked away from the sympathy in Kylie's eyes. She understood they were trying to help and were just telling her what they thought to be the truth. Della just didn't believe it.

Or was it that she didn't want to believe it? Her heart gripped, and pain—real pain—filled her chest. She felt their empathy, and she tried to push the grief to the side with all her other issues to deal with later.

Later. She'd gotten really good at postponing her meltdowns.

Taking a sobering breath, she asked her next question. "What about the whole Chase thing? Him seeing the same vision I did?"

"That's possible," Holiday said. "Especially since you were at the falls. It's a magical place."

Della almost agreed with her, but remembering they thought Natasha and Liam were dead, she wondered how the place could be magical and deliver such devastating news.

Magical would have been if they were alive. Her having a chance at saving them. No, real magic would have been them never being put in that position.

Later, she told herself again, pushing back the emotion that tried to crowd her lungs.

Holiday gave her hair another twirl. "The fact that Chase was at the falls tells me he very well might have some of the same ghost whispering abilities that you and Burnett do. And that could be because . . ." The fae glanced at Kylie and stopped talking.

"Because of what?" Kylie asked.

"I don't know," Holiday said, shrugging it off.

Della knew what she was going to say. Because of them all being Reborns. Were all Reborns prone to being ghost whisperers? Della saw the puzzled look on Kylie's face. So far, Della hadn't told Kylie or Miranda about this. They still thought she'd simply caught a strange virus. She knew she couldn't keep it from them forever, but she was kind of hoping to get a handle on it before trying to explain it.

Della titled her head to the side. She heard someone walking up the steps of the cabin. She raised her nose. Correction. Two some-ones. Though only one set of footsteps moved in.

One of those someones was innocent and sweet, doused in baby powder. The other . . . the other was someone with whom Della had a bone to pick. And with all the angst stirring inside her, she had never felt more ready for an argument than right now.

Burnett walked into Holiday's office without knocking, his daughter, Hannah, on his hip. He looked from Holiday to Kylie and then Della. "What's wrong?" His gaze locked on Della, no doubt reading her pissed-off expression.

She didn't even have to answer the question—he did it for her.

Burnett growled out, "Damn that sneaky bloodsucker. I forbid him from—"

Hannah started to cry.

"See, even our daughter doesn't approve of your language." Holiday moved in. "I swear, if the first word out of my daughter's mouth is a curse word, I'm washing your mouth out with soap twice a day for the rest of your life." Her maternal tone rang loud.

Burnett, obviously not a soap lover, made a face. "Sorry," he said, pressing a kiss to Hannah's dark hair with a gentleness that looked almost impossible for the tall, dark vampire. "Don't talk like your daddy," he said to the child. After turning over the little package to her mother, his gaze went back to Della, and all of that tender, gooey expression vanished.

"In my office," he ordered, motioning for her to follow.

Della didn't hesitate. She started behind him, mentally prepar-ing herself for another head-banging, knock-down-drag-out fight with the stubborn, chauvinistic vampire. If he thought he was going to stop her from trying to find Natasha and Liam—even if they were dead—along with the other fresh turns who'd been forced into slavery, the next few minutes weren't going to be pretty.

. . .

Burnett silently positioned himself behind his large oak desk that took up most of the space in the small office. Unlike Holiday's office, which felt feminine and a bit magical, Burnett's office felt sparse. The only personal items in the room were the photos on his desk of Holiday and Hannah.

Della, arms crossed over her chest, dropped down into the chair across from the vamp, staring daggers at him. He stared right back at her as if to prove a point.

She'd decided to let him start the conversation . . . let him put his size-twelve feet in his mouth and try to talk around them. Unfortunately, he had more patience than she, and she finally blurted out, "Were you even going to tell me?"

"Of course I was going to tell you," he said in a voice much calmer than hers.

"But you didn't think you should tell me before telling them I wouldn't do it? Since when do I *not* get a say in what I do?"

He leaned in, met her eye in a calculated stare. "Calm down."

"I will not calm down. You denied—"

He thumped his hand on the desk. "Yes, I said no to you working for them. But I've already made a call, and am trying to contact someone to make a counteroffer. But, to answer your question, you don't get a say in the matter when I feel you're putting your life at risk." He hissed out air through his clenched teeth. "And before you start, it's not because you're a girl! I wouldn't have allowed anyone here at Shadow Falls to do that."

She unfolded her arms, hearing the honesty in both his tone and his steady heart. "What kind of counteroffer?"

"I'm suggesting they allow Chase to come work with us, and you two work the case." He held up a hand. "I might . . . *might* be willing to compromise and let him report to both of us, but only if they agree to my conditions."

"What conditions?"

"All assignments have to be cleared through me, and I have the right to have other agents shadowing you two if I feel it's needed."

"And if they don't agree to it?" she asked, thinking of Natasha and Liam.

"Then there isn't any reason why the FRU can't start our own investigation. We've already done the basic legwork."

"And you'll put me on the case?" she asked, needing assurance.

"It will have to be cleared by the FRU, but I don't see any reason why they wouldn't. You've already built a reputation with them."

Della relaxed back in the chair, liking the sound of that, but it brought little reprieve from the real problems. "Thank you."

He nodded, then frowned. "All this could have been avoided if Chase hadn't set out to stir shit up."

"You mean 'cause trouble,' or perhaps 'stir crap up,'" Della corrected. When he looked confused, she explained, "You can't cuss, remember?" A slight smile brushed across her lips remembering Holiday's soap-washing threat.

"Trouble," he said, correcting himself.

"And . . ." she continued, "honestly, Chase didn't set out to cause trouble. He just happened to be at the falls when I went there." Her heart did a little dance, because she didn't actually believe it was a coincidence. They'd been called there. But was it about her and Chase or about Natasha and Liam?

"But he still told you about the case," Burnett said, his tone deepened with anger.

"Not really. I mean, someone else told me and I just had him confirm it."

Burnett studied her, probably listening to see if her heart marked her words as a lie. "No one else knows," he said.

"Someone knows," Della said.

"Who?" His brow tightened and he leaned forward.

"A ghost," Della said, and felt the frown rise up inside her.

"What . . . ghost?" he asked, glancing around as if he expected it to be there.

She repeated what had happened at the falls to Burnett, told him about the voice, about the vision of two people feeding off each other. He picked up a pencil and rolled it in his hands while he listened. "Did you tell Holiday all this?"

Della nodded, her chest tightening as she grasped ahold of what little hope she had. "She thinks Natasha and Liam are dead."

"And you don't?" Burnett's pencil rolling stopped while he waited for her to answer.

"No. I think the ghost is someone wanting them rescued. She referred to Natasha by name. She didn't say 'find me.' "

Burnett leaned back in his chair, making it squeak. "She?"

Della nodded. "And oddly, she didn't mention Liam. It's as if she's more concerned about the girl."

Burnett gave the pencil another roll between his palms. "But most of the time when Holiday has visions like . . . like the one you had—"

"I know," Della said. "Most of the time it's the person who's dead. But I'm not Holiday. Maybe being a Reborn makes it different for me." She looked up at him. "For us. Have you had any visions where they weren't dead?"

He looked appalled at the idea of communicating with spirits, as if she'd asked him for a recommendation on which tampon to use. "I've . . . I've never had a vision. I just sense them when they're hanging around Holiday and can hear them sometimes. But I've actually only seen one ghost—Hannah, Holiday's sister."

"Lucky you."

"Yeah," he agreed, almost too wholeheartedly, but then added, "But it is because of you seeing and hearing ghosts that we caught the last killer and didn't arrest the wrong guy. Holiday insists it's a gift. And sometimes I can't argue with her."

"I know, and if dead people weren't involved, I might agree." A tickle of dread ran down her spine thinking about it. Was she doomed to be like Kylie now? Ghosts popping in all the time? But damn, she didn't want that.

Burnett shrugged and nodded at the same time as if he wished he could disagree, but couldn't. He leaned forward again. "Holiday also says when you get those kinds of visions it's normally someone you know or someone who is connected to you somehow."

Della nodded. "She told me that, too, but I don't know a Natasha or a Liam. And the ghost is the one who told me to find them. So maybe she knows Natasha, because I don't."

"Okay, let's say you're right and the ghost isn't Natasha. Do you think you might know the ghost?"

"I don't think so. I think she just chose me because I'm connected to the Craig Anthony case."

The room grew silent for a minute and Della's thoughts went back to the other issue. "Have you actually spoken to anyone on the Vampire Council yet?"

"I've called and they said someone will be in touch."

"In touch today, or this week?" Della asked, concern tightening her voice. If Della was right, and Natasha and Liam were alive, they needed help, and needed it fast. Or was Holiday—who knew her ghost stuff—correct, and they'd already met their fate?

Burnett adjusted his weight in the chair again. "The ball's in their court. If I try to push, it could have a negative effect. But I will go ahead and put in to start the investigation on our part. And I'll get someone to go through all the files we confiscated from Craig Anthony. Maybe we can find some info on a . . . Natasha and Liam. You wouldn't happen to have last names, would you?"

"No."

"Did you get anything else that might help us locate them?"

She let her mind return to the vision. "Nothing other than it was a dark place that smelled like dirt. Like an underground room." *Buried alive.* The thought sent chills down her spine. "But . . ."

"But what?" Burnett asked.

"I don't know for sure, but Chase might know something about it, too."

"How would he know?"

"It's just . . . I could be wrong, but I think he might have been connected with that vision, too. We were both lured to the falls for a reason, and I think that was it."

"You mean, he saw it, too?"

"Yeah, Holiday said it was possible." She hesitated. "Has he already left the property?"

"Yeah. Right before I came here."

She pulled out her phone and dialed his number. Burnett leaned on his elbows and drummed his fingers on his desk. The call went to Chase's voice mail. "Hey, it's me, Della. I . . . have something to ask you. Can you call me?"

When she hung up, Burnett studied her. "Does he return your calls?"

"I don't know, I've never called him." She'd been proud of not giving in to the urge. But this was different. She didn't need him for herself. She needed him for Natasha and Liam.

"My gut says he'll answer," she added, remembering how many times he'd messaged and called her before. Then again, she remembered one of the last things she'd told him. *I don't love you, period. I go back and forth on even liking you.*

Her words bounced around her suddenly tender heart, recalling the hurt in his eyes. Then, swearing not to get caught up in all that syrupy emotion, she made herself focus on other issues. She looked down at her hands for a second, a question looming in her head, but knowing the answer scared her. Yet not knowing wouldn't help anyone, so she asked, "How long? How long can vampires feed off each other and live?"

Burnett dropped the pencil and locked his fingers together, resting them on top of his desk. "Why don't we just try to find them?" he said. "Besides, if Holiday is right—then time . . ."

"But just in case I'm right, and they're alive. I need to know. How long do I have to find them?"

Chapter Six

Burnett gripped his hands tighter and his expression told Della he found her question as disgusting as she did. "Della, you've had a rough few weeks. Don't take on the worries of the world. It's Sunday, go enjoy being a teenager. Let's wait until we get the go-ahead to work the case, then we'll worry about—"

"Quit being difficult," Della seethed. "Just tell me!"

He let go of a gulp of air. "It depends. If they're careful not to deplete each other too much, they could hang on three weeks."

It was longer than she'd expected, so she tried to find comfort in that.

But the ugly truth remained. If they were still alive, and if Chase hadn't been in that vision, then the bulk of the responsibility of finding them lay on her shoulders.

Well, not entirely. There was the ghost. Della's stomach quivered ever so slightly. Who was the ghost? And why had she come to Della for help?

But more important than her identity, or any connection, was how Della could get her to give up some information. By God, if this uninvited spirit wanted Natasha found, she needed to get off her dead ass and give Della something to work with. A feeling of panic swelled inside her as she recalled Kylie telling her over and over again that ghosts couldn't be rushed or provoked to talk.

Wasn't that just what Della needed? Another unreasonable and difficult individual to deal with.

She glanced up at Burnett. He leaned forward. "I'm serious, you need to go and . . ."

"Enjoy being a teenager," Della finished for him. "I heard you the first time." How the hell could she enjoy anything with so many damn issues weighing on her mind, filling up her heart, and pressing on her conscience?

As she got up to leave, one of those issues surfaced. She stopped at the door and looked back. "Any news on when we'll get to bury Chan?"

Burnett's expression spoke of frustration. "I checked on that this morning. Still waiting to hear back."

Waiting. It seemed everything in her life was on hold.

After fretting for a few hours in her room, Della decided to give Burnett's advice a shot. Obviously, sitting in her room waiting for a dead person to drop in wasn't easy. Both Miranda and Kylie were out—probably with their boyfriends—so Della took off in search of her own "almost boyfriend." After abandoning him early last night, she wanted to spend a little time with him before he went off to work with the doctor and the doctor's daughter.

The thought of him working with Jessie, who had a crush on him, still rubbed her raw. But, considering she was probably going to be working with Chase again, she supposed she should shut her trap.

As she left the somber shade of the woods and spotted Steve's cabin, she saw Perry stepping off the porch. She got a few feet closer. Before he noticed her, she caught his expression: sad and troubled. "What's wrong?" she blurted out, and he jumped at the sound of her voice.

"Nothing," he said quickly. Too quickly, and Della heard his heart tango with the lie.

And there was only one reason for him to lie to her. She crossed her arms over her chest and studied him. "You know I like you, right?"

"Yeah," Perry said, as if unsure what she meant.

"Good, so you won't take it personal if the 'nothing' you've got going on hurts Miranda and I have to kick your ass."

He made a face.

"I'm just saying, I like you, but I like her better. And if you hurt her . . ."

He made a low growling sound. "Okay, let me change my answer to: It's none of your damn business. And if you think I'd hurt Miranda on purpose, you're an idiot."

Della watched the blond shape-shifter storm off, realizing how weird that was. Anger wasn't Perry's go-to emotion. He usually made some wisecrack comment, using humor to either cover up the real issue or to defuse the situation.

Which meant whatever was wrong must be bad enough to take a bite out of his sense of humor.

When she turned around she saw Steve standing at the door, waiting with a half-smile. Steve's half-smiles always looked sexy. It was the way his eyes tightened, and his lashes lowered over those warm brown eyes. His dark hair looked a little like he'd been sleeping. She always liked it a little messy. He wore jeans that hugged him in all the right places and a navy T-shirt that looked so soft she wanted to touch it. Oh, and he was barefoot. Even that got to her.

Her concerns for Perry and Miranda took a backseat to wanting to lean her head on his chest and feel his arms around her. To let the magic that was all Steve make her own issues feel less than. And if that made her less than, too, so be it. She'd pull up her big-girl panties later.

Besides, she was just following Burnett's orders. *Enjoy being a teen.*

When she stepped up on his porch, his half-smile faded. All her soft feelings vanished and she remembered seeing Chase and the craziness that had happened at the falls.

"What's wrong?" he asked.

Was her expression as sour as Perry's?

She opened her mouth, but didn't have a clue where to start. Or what all to tell him. Did she tell him everything?

That Chase had come to see her?

That the Vampire Council wanted her to work with them?

That she had a ghost hanging around again?

Did she tell him she thought there were a couple of vampires buried alive and it might be up to her to find them?

She had a feeling Steve wasn't going to like hearing any of her issues.

She frowned. "Can I just say 'everything' and leave it at that?"

"Hell, no." He reached for her and pulled her against him. Her head found the special spot she loved. After a two-second embrace, he turned and started inside his cabin.

"What's going on?" he asked after settling her on the sofa and sitting beside her. His warmth pressed close to her side, his arm shifted around her shoulders.

When she didn't just spit it out, he lifted her chin and made her look at him. "Why do I think it has something to do with Chase?"

Oh, hell. See, she was right, Steve wasn't going to like this.

"I went to the falls," she said.

"Why?" he asked, sounding like Miranda.

"Because I kept hearing it. Holiday says the falls call you. Anyway . . ." She swallowed and just said it, "Chase was there."

She felt Steve's muscles tighten and could swear his temperature actually inched up a few degrees. "Trespassing? Did Burnett grab him and teach him a lesson?"

"No, because he . . . he'd actually been here to see Burnett."

"Why?"

"The Vampire Council wants me and Chase to work on finding the missing fresh turns that the creep Craig Anthony sold into slavery."

"And Burnett vetoed that deal, right?" Steve's brown eyes grew a dark amber color as he waited for her answer.

"He's trying to arrange a deal where we will be working for the FRU and not the council."

"But you'll be working with Chase?" Steve asked, his tone tight.

She refused to lie. "If they agree to it."

"I don't like it. Seriously, you caught that Anthony creep, now let someone else do the rest."

She cupped her hands together. "I can't."

"Why not?"

Because it's the right thing, because . . . "A ghost."

"Chan?" he asked, his eyes widening just a bit.

"No, a new ghost. She's asking me to save a girl named Natasha."

"And you have to do what the ghost asks? What if she asks you to jump off a bridge or eat a bowl of—"

Della pressed a finger against his soft lips. "She somehow . . . gave me a vision, and I was Natasha. She's trapped, Steve, like in a tunnel, or a room underground, with another vampire and . . ." She had to pull in a deep breath to say it again, "She and another vampire are feeding off each other." Della's sinuses stung, remembering the horror she'd felt in the vision. "She's scared, no, she's terrified, and . . . and I know all this because I was her for a few minutes, in her body, and I felt it. I have to help her, Steve."

He stared at her, the color in his eyes softening back to its normal warm brown with flecks of green and gold. She knew he was accepting it—that he understood. She couldn't say he was thrilled about it, as his look was still frustrated, but he wasn't going to hold it against her.

He brushed a strand of hair off her cheek. "You always try to come off as a hardass, but honestly, there's nothing hard about you. You'd help your own enemy."

"Don't give me that much credit."

"It's you that needs to give yourself more credit." He exhaled deeply and continued to stare at her. "Okay, you told me why *you* have to work this case, but why Chase? Why does he have to work with you? Why couldn't I do it? Or Lucas?"

She hesitated before telling him, but then decided he deserved the truth. "The reason he was at the falls was because he'd been called there as well. I think he shared the same vision. For some reason, we're supposed to do this together."

He dropped against the sofa with a sigh. "I don't . . . I just don't like you being with him."

She looked him right in the eyes. "I don't like you being with Jessie, either."

"At least I'm not . . . bonded to her. Whatever the hell that means." He reached up again and tucked a strand of hair behind her ear. "And I know you don't like talking about it, and I'm trying really hard to respect that, but I could really use some reassurance here."

Oh, hell, what did he want her to say? That she didn't give a flip about Chase. That would be a lie. That she wasn't the least bit attracted to him? That would be a lie, too. That she wasn't afraid of what she felt? Another lie.

She was scared shitless. Scared of where all of this was going to end, but the one thing she knew, the one thing she felt certain of was . . . Steve. Of how he made her feel.

Safe.

Accepted.

Cherished.

He knew her and still liked her, still wanted to be part of her life.

He cared.

He looked at her. Waiting. Waiting for something.

Her heart ached from indecision and her need to offer him something made that pain increase. Finally, she found one truth. One truth that she could offer. "I'm here, aren't I?"

She lifted up and pressed her lips to his. It must have been enough, or at least enough for now, because he kissed her back.

Chapter Seven

Steve's lips were warm, his taste addicting. And the magic, the magic that was pure Steve, happened. Della let go of all her issues, all the heartaches, fear, and haunts from the past, and she let herself be pulled into nothing but the kiss. The wonderful feel of his lips against hers.

That feeling led to more feelings. Tingling. Wants. Desires.

It led to them shifting. Getting closer. To them reclining, side by side on the sofa.

In a few minutes, they were even closer. Their arms and legs entangled, their hearts beating together. Even at her vampire temperature, she burned . . . on fire from his hard body pressed against hers. Lost in how his soft breath felt on her neck.

His hand slipped under her shirt and she didn't stop him. She wanted this as much as he did. Not that she planned to let it go too far, but this . . . this was what she needed. This was following orders. This was being a teen.

But then she heard them. Voices. Voices and footsteps coming toward the cabin.

She gasped and caught his hand. "I think we're about to have company."

He growled and lifted his head from the sensitive spot he kissed on her neck. "Do you want to kill them, or do you want me to?"

She giggled.

When she met his sexy, hooded eyes and saw the heat and desire there, her breath caught and the same emotions filled her chest. If she hadn't heard the voices again, she would've caved and gone back to kissing him. This place, this wonderful place she went to forget things, could also make her forget her limits. Sooner or later they weren't going to be able to stop.

Was she ready to go there with Steve?

Oh, hell, she'd just found another thing to worry about.

After a good-bye kiss filled with with pent-up frustrations, Steve walked her outside through the back door to avoid the approaching company. "I'm heading out in about an hour," he said.

She nodded and laced her fingers with his. "Be good." An unwanted vision of Jessie filled her head.

"You, too," he said and she could guess what he was imagining.

He gave her hand a squeeze then leaned down and kissed her again. The birds and soft whisper of the breeze played background music.

That kiss was probably about as hot of a kiss as they should be indulging in, she thought, but then she found even that brief feel of his lips on hers to be alluring.

She only got a few feet away when her phone dinged with an incoming text. Her heart raced thinking it was Chase. But she didn't check it until she got in the mix of trees—pines, a few oaks, a maple or two—away from Steve's line of vision. The thought of hurting him sent a sharp pain to her chest.

And yet, if right now Steve was getting a text from Jessie, it would hurt like hell. If Steve cared even nearly as much about Jessie as she did Chase, Della would be damn pissed.

Shit. She had to be hurting Steve. But how could she fix it?

Two choices. Only two. Let him go or refuse to work with Chase on the case. Refuse to ever have anything to do with Chase again.

The realization tumbled around inside her like a ball of thorns. A few tears threatened to fall as her phone dinged again.

She looked at it.

Not Chase. Burnett. The message read, *Come to the office.*

She didn't hesitate.

When she stormed into his office, he glanced up. "I hope you were close—if not, you came too fast. I've warned you not to—"

"I was close," she said and it was only half a lie. She had been close, but she probably still came quicker than he would have liked. At least being Reborn came with a few perks, superspeed being one of them. "What is it?"

"I got a call from the Vampire Council."

"Are they approving Chase and me working together with the FRU?"

"No. One of the council members called to ask if we'd heard from Chase. He missed a meeting with them and isn't answering his calls. They say this isn't like him."

Della felt her blood pressure rise. "Do they think something happened to him?" She could still recall how he'd moaned when he'd taken her blood inside him during her rebirth. When he'd willingly done it, willingly taken on the pain to save her. *I don't love you, period. I go back and forth on even liking you.*

"No. He seemed more concerned that I'd convinced him to

work exclusively with us. When I assured him that wasn't the case, he insisted that you would know where he was. They said he's been obsessing over you lately."

Obsessing? She shook her head. "He hasn't called or texted me since we saw each other at the falls. If he had, I'd tell you."

"That's what I assured them," he said.

Della pulled out her phone again and typed Chase another message. *Worried. Vamp Council looking 4 u. U ok?*

She stared at her phone, her lungs tight, praying he would text her back.

When it didn't ding back in seconds, she looked up at Burnett. "Maybe I should go look for him."

"Where?"

"I don't know, but—"

"No. If you knew where he was, it would be one thing, but—"

Her phone dinged. She looked at the number. Chase's number.

"It's him." She read his message—to herself.

Worrying means u care.

She clenched her teeth.

"And?" Burnett asked.

She ignored Burnett and typed: *R u ok?*

His reply came back quickly. *Fine. Working our case. Later.*

Della looked up, drawing in air. "All he says is he's okay and is working the case."

She half expected Burnett to ask to see the texts. He didn't, and that showed a lot of trust on his part. She appreciated that more than he knew.

"Text him back and tell him I said for him to contact the council. We need him to stay in their good graces right now."

She did as Burnett said. They sat in the silent office for several minutes, waiting for his reply. Her phone didn't ding.

Finally, Della set her phone down. "What could Chase know, or the Vampire Council know, that we don't? How can he be working on the case?"

Burnett's expression hardened. "I don't know. My people are still going through the files that we got. I know that one of Craig Anthony's homes was torn apart before we got there. Maybe someone with the council found something. But I don't think so. We found most of our evidence in the files at the funeral home and on his phone and computer."

"I hate this," Della said, and this time it wasn't about her feelings for the crazy vamp, but for Natasha and Liam.

"I know, but right now there's nothing we can do."

All of a sudden, Burnett's cell rang. He looked at the phone. "I need to take this."

Della figured he meant he wanted her to leave, and she stood up.

As she took one step to the door, she heard the voice on the line. "It's Leo. I got the approval, but we're going in dark. We never got ahold of the owner. That said, we're good to move tonight. Three a.m."

What was going down? Did it involve Chase? The case? Okay, she didn't want to be rude, but curiosity bit. Bit hard. She took another step toward the door, but she didn't open it.

"Okay, I'll be there," Burnett's voice came.

Just as she reached for the knob, Burnett said, "Della?"

Crap. Was he upset that she'd been eavesdropping? She turned around, feeling guilty. It had been rude.

"I'm sorry, I should have left, but I thought maybe it was—"

"Sit down." He shut off the phone. His gaze met her eyes, and she saw it. That phone call involved her.

She didn't do as ordered.

"What is it?" She sensed his hesitancy and that could mean only one thing. It was bad.

"Sit back down," he repeated. "We need to talk."

The clock on Della's bedside table listed the time as 2:55 a.m. She had five minutes. She looked down at her clothes. She was ready.

Black.

Black boots.

Black jeans and a black fitted T-shirt.

All black, so she'd blend into the night.

It had been the first rule of thumb that her cousin, Chan, had taught her about being a vampire. How appropriate that the color was right for this event. Black for grief. Black for pain. Black for putting Chan's body into the ground and saying good-bye.

The call Burnett had gotten today while she'd been in his office had been about Chan. They had finally finished the autopsy and were releasing his body. At least now he'd be laid to rest. When she thought of him, she wouldn't think of his body in some cold morgue.

Burnett had tried to talk her out of going. They'd discovered the graveyard was owned and managed by werewolves, and they weren't answering their calls. But Burnett had been relentless that they needed to get Chan in his proper grave. After failing to survive being Reborn, other rogues had buried him in an unmarked grave in the woods to prevent his secrets from being revealed.

Now that he'd been found, he deserved one person at the burial who loved him. Even if she had to defy Burnett's orders, she'd be there to see them lower his casket.

For the second time.

Damn you, Chan! It should have been me. She swallowed the tightness down her throat, remembering his first funeral. The fake one. Not that she'd known it'd been fake. When he'd first been turned, he faked his death, like most vampires did to separate from their human lives. And Della had mourned him then as she did now. Only then, she hadn't felt the guilt.

Survivor's guilt, Holiday explained. Pointing out that Chase had chosen to save Della instead of Chan. Della didn't care what name you stamped on the emotion. She still felt like shit.

Inhaling, she went and stood by the window. A few stars twinkled down. A cloud crawled across the sky, hiding all but a small sliver of the half moon. She watched as the gray foggy formation inched by, reminding her of ghosts.

Not that she'd had one visit since the falls, but they hadn't been far from her mind.

Her phone dinged with an incoming message. She pulled it out of her pocket, hoping it was Chase telling her he'd gotten something on Natasha and Liam. She'd texted him again after leaving Burnett's office, but he hadn't returned her message. Was he not answering because he was upset about what she'd told him earlier?

Now wasn't the time to worry about trivial things. It might not feel insignificant, but when compared to life or death, it lost merit. Right now, all she needed from Chase was to find out if he'd somehow experienced the vision of Natasha and Liam. If he had, had he gotten anything from it that would help find them?

A heaviness stirred in her chest as she stared at the message illuminating her phone. Not from Chase. Just Burnett telling her he would be five minutes late.

She sent Burnett a "got it" message. Then, with her mind on Natasha and Liam, she pulled up the link to Chase's prior messages.

Sighing, she typed in, *Call me,* and started to hit send, but then added, *please.*

Still staring at the phone, the slight sound of mattress springs adjusting to another toss and turn sounded from behind Della's bedroom wall. Something was keeping Miranda, Della's witch roommate, awake.

Did it have to do with Perry, and whatever had put him in a pissy mood earlier?

She didn't really have time to check on the witch, Della told herself. Besides, between grief over Chan, the worry over things like visions, her own family and romantic issues . . . she shouldn't be trying to take on anyone else's problems. Then she heard the girl's sniffle.

Oh, damn, this wasn't just anyone else. It was Miranda. If it was Della in a pickle, the little witch would be here in a snap. Five minutes, she thought, walking out of her room and lightly tapping on Miranda's door.

"Come in," Miranda's voice came low, unsure.

Della stepped inside. "I only have a few minutes, but . . . is something wrong?"

Miranda sat up and pulled her blanket-covered knees to her chest. "Yes, but I can't talk about it."

"Why not?" Della moved in a few more steps.

"I promised I wouldn't mention it."

"Why would you go making stupid promises like that? We share everything." Even as Della said it, she knew she'd been keeping her own secrets from Miranda and Kylie. But not for long. She needed to tell them.

"I know we do, but . . . I can't." Miranda drew in a shaky breath.

Della took another step, hating the pain in her friend's voice. "Do I need to kick someone's ass? You don't even have to tell me why, just tell me who, and I'll do it. So, no promises will be broken."

"No," she said. "But I love that you'd do that for me."

"Is it Perry?" Della asked. If so, Della would totally kick his ass, but she was definitely the wrong person to offer up advice. Kylie was the relationship guru.

Kylie could fix almost anyone's romantic disasters. Well, except Della's. Her feelings for Steve, and yet her emotional ties to Chase due to the bonding—whatever the hell that really meant—was a mystery even for a relationship guru.

"I can't talk about it," Miranda said again and let go of another sob.

Did that mean it was Perry or wasn't? Della pulled out her phone and eyed the time. She needed to be going. "Can I get Kylie for you?"

Face it, Della wasn't the best sympathizer. But it stung just a little that Miranda wouldn't confide in her.

Miranda shook her head. "No." She wiped her cheeks. "But I could use a hug."

"Figures," Della muttered under her breath as she moved in and let the witch embrace her. Miranda's warmth reminded Della of her own core body temperature, something she hated thinking about. But for friendship's sake, she even patted the girl on her back ever so slightly—albeit, a little awkwardly.

"Where are you going?" Miranda pulled back, her large, watery green eyes gazing upward.

Della rubbed her palms on the back of her jeans. "We're burying Chan."

"Oh, my bad," Miranda said. "Here I am, asking you for a hug, when you're the one in need. Come here. Come here." She held out her arms and wiggled her fingers.

"No, I'm fine." Della even took a step back, but damn if her chest didn't grip with a reviving of the grief. That's what hugs did sometimes, brought everything to the surface. Some things didn't need to come up for air.

Miranda shot out of bed, her pink heart-covered nightshirt fluttering around her. "Why don't Kylie and I come with you? Wait." Miranda waved her hands in the air as if erasing the request. "Forget I asked, we're coming even if you don't want us. You shouldn't go to a funeral alone." She started for the door as if to go wake up Kylie.

"Nooooo." Della caught her by the arm. Damn it, she'd come in here to help Miranda, not to start World War III. And that's what every argument felt like lately with the witch.

"Why? Is Steve going?" Miranda asked.

Della's heartstrings yanked. Just hearing his name did that to her, and it came with a quiver of guilt. Guilt over what she felt for Chase. Not that she'd really defined what "that" was, but it was there. And denying it wouldn't make it go away.

"No, he's not coming," Della said the truth and the thought hit: If Steve knew about it, he'd want to come. That was Steve. He cared. She cared about him, too. But did she care enough to let him go? To stop hurting him?

Miranda gently removed Della's hold on her arm. "Just give it up, vamp. Because no way, no how, are you going alone. Kylie and I are coming." She even did that attitude shake of her head that reminded Della of one of those head-bobbing dog figurines some people put in their cars.

Frustration built in the pit of Della's stomach. "Put your broom down, witch!" she bit out. "You can't come. Besides, it's not a funeral," Della said, her tone getting tighter. If she showed up to meet Burnett with Miranda and Kylie in tow, Burnett would have a shit fit. And Della avoided Burnett's shit fits at all costs.

Seeing the determination and love in Miranda's eyes, Della held out her hand, seeking patience from both the witch and herself.

"Look, Burnett didn't even want me to come. They're burying Chan in the fake grave where he was supposed to have been buried earlier. So, it's a little dangerous, unearthing a casket, putting a body in it, and doing it without getting caught. Supposedly, breaking into graves can get you five to ten years in prison. And orange is not your color."

"I look just as good in orange as you do," the witch sassed back while twisting a strand of her multicolored hair. Then she frowned, and even got teary-eyed again. "Please. I still don't like you going alone. It hurts me right here." She put a hand over her chest.

Della's own heart took a blow at her words. "Burnett's going to be there," she assured her.

Miranda made a face, which included one of her signature eye rolls. "Like he'd give you a hug if you needed one."

Della didn't think Burnett would hug her, but she didn't doubt he'd offer his sympathy. And from one vamp to another, that was more than enough.

"I'll be fine." And she would, Della told herself. Burying Chan beneath his tombstone was the right thing. Even if his dying wasn't. "I have to go." She took a step toward the door.

"Wait," Miranda said. "One hug to hold you over."

The word "no" danced on Della's tongue, but stopping Miranda from hugging was like stopping a male dog from peeing on a fire hydrant. Impossible.

Della leaned in and pulled back extra quick, studying the witch and still seeing worry in her expression. "Later, we'll have a Diet Coke session and share our problems. But before then, you need to find whoever you promised that you wouldn't tell on and rescind that promise."

Miranda's bottom lip came out a bit. "I can't."

Della frowned. "Fine, then I won't tell you guys what's going on with me. And it's huge."

"That's not fair," Miranda said.

"Yeah, it sucks having friends who expect you to spill your guts, but that's what we do. So, get your guts prepared to fall out. Later." She shot out of Miranda's bedroom, and out of the cabin, hurrying to meet Burnett—hoping that burying Chan would at least bring some closure to this issue and free her up to work on the others.

Natasha and Liam were first on the issue list.

Then the whole Steve and Chase issue. Or maybe trying again to find her uncle. With all the issues Della had, she had choices.

The ghostlike clouds had passed, and the half moon, accompanied by the stars, spit out just enough light to turn the sky a dark navy. Burnett, dressed in black, waited by the front gate of Shadow Falls. His gaze fell over her as if trying to read her mood. Or maybe her ability not to emotionally crumble. Little did he know, that wall had come down months ago.

At times, she wasn't sure what she'd used to put herself back together, but she had a feeling it had everything to do with Shadow Falls. The people here. The friendships. Not necessarily the hugs— though she loved Miranda for it, she could do without those. But just knowing others cared had her pulling herself back together after each of life's disappointments.

She cared about them all. Even the stoic camp leader.

Face it, completely cratering meant letting people down. If her Asian father had instilled anything in her, it was loyalty. Which probably explained why even when her father seemed to have given up on her, she hadn't given up on him.

"Ready?" Burnett asked.

She nodded.

He started to run, his boots crashing against the dirt three or four times before he went straight into flight. Della didn't know if she could do that, but almost sensing it was a challenge, she gave it a shot. Her own boots hit the ground seven times before she sensed the strength. Forcing every muscle she had into action, she felt herself being lifted into the air. A sense of accomplishment whispered over her, and for one second, it dulled the pain of what she was about to face.

Burnett glanced back at her. The look in his eyes almost reminded her of the way her father looked at her when she'd made a good move at chess.

Warmth filled Della's chest as she sent Burnett a slight nod.

Yup, Della thought. The thing that kept her together had everything to do with the people she'd found at Shadow Falls. If she crumbled, they'd take it personally. And she wasn't about to let them take the blame for what was happening to her.

It took them twenty minutes, flying at speeds Della could only guess, before she spotted the graveyard. As soon as their destination came into view, Burnett slowed down to what might have been considered normal vampire speed.

As they circled the property, he started downward in the midst of some trees.

Della's feet weren't steady on the ground when she caught the scent.

She shot around and looked at Burnett. He had his nose up, too. Apparently he'd gotten the same scent.

"Someone you know?" she asked, hoping the agents bringing Chan's body were weres.

Burnett's eyes, already a bright green, told her the answer first.

Della didn't have time to think before three figures came bolting out of the trees, charging right at them.

Chapter Eight

"Stop!" Burnett's order rang out.

Damn it! Did he mean that for her, too? Prepared to fight, Della had to cut her nails into her palms to heed his order. Halting at Burnett's side, every muscle in her body screamed *danger*.

Drawing in a sharp breath of air that even tasted like menace, she stared at the foreheads of the three potential attackers to read their patterns. All supernaturals had patterns that identified their species, and these ones confirmed what her nose had picked up.

Weres.

She also noted the uniforms—security. What a joke.

"We don't mean any harm," Burnett announced. He pulled his dark shirt back to show his FRU badge hooked onto his belt.

Della had to give the man credit for going by the book. Not that she knew all the FRU rules, but she planned on learning them soon.

Her focus returned to Burnett, standing tall, his badge still on display. It came off so official-like, awe and admiration swept through her. Someday, she wanted one of those badges.

"We carry our own badges, too, you dirty vamp!" the were with shaggy red hair said. He pushed his chest out, which had a badge with some Celtic-looking cross in green and blue that was pinned to his dirty cotton shirt.

"I'll bet mine carries more weight," Burnett seethed, his eyes now gold in color.

The were's eyes grew a bright orange, but this time, he took a second to actually look at Burnett's badge.

The were in the middle, slightly bigger than the other two, spoke up next. "I've heard a lot of fake FRU badges have found their way into gangs."

"This one isn't fake," Burnett added, his tone getting deeper and more dangerous.

Della felt her gut tighten, prepared to face any threat they chose to throw at them. But they weren't really that big of a threat. There were only three of them. She and Burnett could take them with their hands tied behind their backs. Hell, with her new powers, she could probably take all three herself.

"You expect us to believe that's real?" mouthed off the redheaded were. "You show up in the middle of the night, at our graveyard, with your girl toy there and expect us to believe you're on official business?"

The girl toy comment just about did her in. Della growled, her vision brightening, telling her that her eyes had as well, and her canines came out to play.

"She's not a toy." Burnett's eyes now glowed a lime green, but his gaze shot back to the man standing in the middle as if he sensed he was the leader of the pack. "Show me your registration papers and tell your mouthy friend to back down or you all will be spending a night in FRU custody."

"Do as he says." The head of the pack pulled out his wallet. Della saw the redhead pull something out of his pocket. She spotted the tiny little problem immediately. It wasn't a wallet. It was a blade.

With a speed she didn't know possible, she bolted forward. Before he could say "uncle," or even *think* to say "uncle," she caught the were by his wrist, twisting his arm behind his back. In another fraction of a second, she'd knocked him down to his knees. Burnett suddenly appeared at her side, but he simply watched. Meaning he had faith in her. Her chest filled with the similar pride she'd felt earlier during flight. Making Burnett proud was almost like making her dad proud.

She snatched the knife from the were's hand, then pushed him facedown on the grass and put her knee in his back to keep him there. Amazingly, her breath still came evenly, her pulse didn't race. She hadn't even had to exert herself to do it.

"Do yourself a favor and stay down," Della said to the no-good dog beneath her. "Or don't. A good fight would suit me just fine."

The were raised his head back. Della saw the bright orange color of his eyes reflected on the ground. "I had to get my knife out to get to my card," he growled.

"Yeah, and Girl Toy had to take it away from you," Della snapped back.

Della could swear she heard Burnett chuckle.

"Just shut up, Evert," the lead were said. "I'm sorry for his behavior. He's new and obviously too hotheaded for this job." He held out an ID card, basically a driver's license but with a marking that meant he was registered, toward Burnett.

"I didn't know you were real FRU," the guy under Della's hold growled out.

The other were pulled out his wallet and produced his own card, too.

Burnett looked at the cards, then handed them back. He inched a step closer to Della and knelt down beside the guy facedown on the ground. "I'm going to try to talk my agent-in-training into releasing you, but you'll want to get up real slow. Then, you'll want to apologize, and I'll leave it up to her whether or not she thinks we should take you in."

Della moved off the lowlife's back. He stood up, keeping his still-orange glowing eyes on her the whole time. "Sorry," he muttered, but his tone made it clear he considered the apology below him. She wondered if it was because she was a vamp, or if it was because she was a girl. A girl toy. Guess he'd think twice before calling someone else that.

Burnett shook his head. "Surely you can do better than that."

He glanced at Burnett and then back to Della. "I'm sorry." Fury radiated from his tone.

For some reason, Della's mind went to the last guy who'd forced an apology out of someone who'd disrespected her. Chase. She pushed that thought away and the slight sense of longing it brought on.

Burnett looked at her. "Do you think we should take him in and let him spend a night regretting his behavior?"

Della glanced up at Burnett. He was really going to leave it up to her? She looked down at the pathetic excuse for a knife the were had pulled out of his pocket. "Nah, but I think he needs to know if he's going to pull a knife on a vampire, it should be more than a pocket knife." She handed the two-inch blade to Burnett.

Burnett nodded at the were. "Leave before I change my mind."

The redhead ran away, his limber gait reminiscent of all weres. Suddenly, silence fell like a soft rain, and that silence seemed to echo inside Della. Toeing her shoe into the green manicured lawn, she watched the were fade into nothing but a speck on the landscape.

For the first time, she became aware of her surroundings. Silver moonlight spilled over the flat terrain. Tombstones rose from the ground like arms of the dead reaching for the sky, needing escape from the cold earth.

Every few feet, an aging statuary of a saint or an angel stood above the stones, as if guarding the graves. But were they protecting the dead, or keeping them entombed?

The sad and haunted environment brought it all back—the reason she was here. To bury Chan. But the ghostlike chill and the thought of being underground also brought to mind Natasha and Liam.

Heavy grief accompanied with a sharp sense of urgency filled her lungs. Della swallowed a shaky breath and wondered how and when Chan's body would arrive.

A cold tingle ran down Della's spine. Was it a ghost? Feeling dazed, she forced herself to look back at the live people standing to her right. Burnett took a step forward toward the pack leader.

The were, a good three inches shorter than Burnett, didn't show fear, nor did his posture provoke aggressiveness. "Not to defend my ex-employee," the were said, "but I must say, you showing up at a graveyard that is managed by weres is rather strange."

Burnett stood a little straighter. Not to the point of defensiveness, but just enough to show he didn't appreciate the man's questions. "The FRU tried to contact the owner, Mr. Henderson, but was told by the receptionist he was out of the country."

"And I was left in charge," the were stated. "Why did you not contact me?" His words danced on the line of disrespect, but his tone held tight to caution, as did his posture.

"If you will look at your business phone, you'll see the FRU has left three messages. And I personally left one this afternoon."

The were brought his shoulders up a bit. "So you took it upon yourself to bypass legal procedures to obviously do something morally unethical. Is this the way the FRU regularly operates?"

Burnett's eyes increased in brightness. But Della could tell he held himself back. No doubt, he was prepared to verbally spar to avoid a physical confrontation. "I'm not here to do anything unethical."

The were's brows creased in disbelief. "But that would depend on who you ask. It's obvious you're here to exhume a body for some form of evidence. Probably to try to pin a murder on a were, being that you're vampire."

Della couldn't stop herself from speaking up. "And you make the mistake of assuming. No one is fairer than that man standing in front of you."

The were shot Della a quick look, then refocused on Burnett as if she didn't merit his attention. But damn, hadn't Girl Toy already proven herself? She let go of a warning growl. The desire to move in, demand respect, bit hard.

Burnett's gaze shifted to her ever so slightly. In that brief scrutiny, she could almost read his mind. *Back down.*

The pack leader adjusted his posture a little more defensively. "Do you know how much trouble this could bring down on my employer? Humans find desecration of the dead a big deal. It could cause a scandal."

Burnett stood, feet slightly apart, arms resting at ease at his sides, and took the man's verbal jabs without appearing insulted. He almost looked too confident—like a poker player who knew he held the ace.

"True," Burnett said. "However, that would cause less of a scandal than, say, a graveyard accepting payoffs from a funeral home to entomb empty caskets. The whole mystery of where the bodies have gone would not only make local news, but could go national. I can almost read the headlines: *Families of the deceased desperate to find the remains of their dearly departed.*" He let his gaze shift around the graveyard. "How many empty caskets have you accepted from Craig Anthony and his stepfather?"

The were's posture lost some confidence, as did the were standing at his side. Burnett obviously had the upper hand.

Though, the lead were didn't want to admit it right off. "Seeing you're vampire, you should know this practice is overlooked by FRU regulations."

Burnett crossed his arms over his wide chest. "Not when the fresh turns were being turned into slaves."

"We were not aware of that man's actions. Our contract was with his stepfather."

"Let's hope that's the way this shakes out once our investigation is complete. Yet, this brings me back to the reason I'm here," Burnett said, relaxing his posture, as if letting the were know compromise wasn't off the table. "I have the body of someone for whom you have the empty casket. I simply want to put the deceased to rest in his proper grave."

The were must not have been big on compromising. "That's not protocol. If we start that, we'll be burying and exhuming graves constantly. Besides, if the fresh turn died, his family will never know. They already think he's in the box. What they don't know can't hurt them. They're just humans."

Just humans! "I will know," Della said, her tone one shade lighter than black, and her eyes two shades brighter.

The were actually took a step back. "Fine. Dig up whoever you want. I'll even supply you with a backhoe. If the boss wants to murder someone over this, I'll tell him to go to the FRU."

Thirty minutes later, the grave dug, Della sat on green winter grass, running her hands over the manicured blades and watching the backhoe pull Chan's casket from the ground. Before the two security guards left, the other agents had shown up. The zipped tarp they brought with them now waited to the right of the gravestone carrying Chan's full name.

She knew Chan's body lay inside that plastic. Closing her eyes, she tried to decide if she wanted to see him. Should she hold on to the last memory she had of his face? The last time she'd seen him was when she was being Reborn and had fallen into the coma. They'd been in the clouds and he'd been happy, smiling his silly grin and teasing her about something. But about what?

She searched her mind, and the memory that had seemed so far away filled her head.

He'd been teasing her about her inability to bowl and one particularly memorable accident. She'd shifted her hand back to throw the ball, and it flew off her fingers, flying behind her in the opposite direction of the bowling lane. All five people waiting their turn had gone down trying to avoid being hit. Chan had insisted they count it as a strike because no one had been left standing.

A tear slipped out of her closed lids, remembering that moment in the clouds and how his smile had seemed so much like the old Chan. She wiped a few wayward tears away. Yup, that was how she wanted to remember him—not dead in a tarp.

She heard someone say something in a low voice, as if to purposely keep it from her. She opened her eyes. The agents, Burnett included, stood at the side of the grave, looking down at the opened casket as if something was inside.

Della's breath caught. Had someone taken up residence in Chan's casket?

"What is it?" She shot up. If it was a corpse, they'd better crawl their dead ass out of there, because they were about to get evicted. That was Chan's casket, and by God, he was going to be laid to rest there.

Chapter Nine

Della's heart did a double tumble before fixing her eyes on the open casket and possibly a decomposed body that she might have to remove.

Air, sounding a lot like relief, escaped her lungs and lips. Not a body. Just a box. A large shoe box.

She could admit it was strange, but the look of befuddlement on the faces of the three agents and Burnett seemed like overkill.

Then she saw it. The box vibrated. Like it held a heart.

Thump.

Thump.

Thump.

Right then, the moon's silver cast of light was blocked out by a large gray cloud slithering across the sky. The air she'd released in relief reversed and filled her lungs.

Just a rat, she told herself. But then, the oh-so-familiar sound of a heartbeat spilled out of the box.

"Someone needs to see what's in it," said the youngest agent, a warlock, but from his tone it was clear he wasn't volunteering.

"Who says we have to open it?" said another of the agents, a vampire.

As if the dang box heard him, it started moving faster, and then the top flew off. Della wanted to tell herself it was the wind, but the night air stood so still that even the leaves didn't stir.

With the moon's desertion, the contents of the box were unidentifiable. Della leaned down. Something metal lay on top, but she couldn't identify it. Then she spotted what looked like photographs.

Were these Chan's things? Della's heart yanked again. Was his ghost making the box tremble? Did he want her to look inside? Della looked over at the tarp where Chan's body lay extra cold. Extra dead. Right then, a coldness overtook her.

Is it you, Chan?

Giving in, she exhaled the stale air held in her lungs. "Raise the casket a little higher and I'll get it," Della finally said.

"No, I'll do it." Burnett sounded embarrassed she'd volunteered before him. He glanced over at the fae agent who'd been driving the backhoe and now stood with them. "Go pull it up higher."

The agent went back to the backhoe, almost eager to get away. Della watched and listened as the chains pulled the mud-caked open casket up another foot.

When Burnett started to reach in, Della stopped him. "It was Chan's. I think I should do it."

He nodded. She picked up the box and saw the wide-eyed stares from all the agents, as if fearing the thing would bite her.

It didn't. At least not physically. Emotionally, she was bitten as soon as she glanced down and identified the metal object on top. One of Chan's many bowling trophies. He'd told her once that he didn't care that being a bowling champion made him look like a dork. It was the only sport he was good at. Yet, he'd never really been a dork, just a skinny Asian kid, a bit of a nonconformist, but with a good heart.

Feeling her eyes sting, she walked away to a private spot. The cloud moved away from the moon, and silver light whispered down on her. As crazy as it sounded, the moon's glow almost warmed her skin like the sun.

She sat down between the rows of tombstones and put the open box and its lid in front of her. After seeing the box pulsate, fear should have been present, but oddly she didn't feel it. This was about Chan. And Chan would never hurt her.

In a matter of seconds—noting only the items on the top—she understood the meaning of the box. Chan had been burying his old life. All the boxed items stood for things that had meant something to him. All the things he'd lost the day he'd been turned. And damn it, she knew how that felt.

No, she hadn't faked her death, but she'd still lost so much.

She ran her finger over the bowling trophy sporting Chan's name. She spotted the pictures of his family and friends, and a letter from his one and only girlfriend. Sensing it might be personal, she didn't read it.

Instead, she picked up and studied a few of the photos: Chan with his little sister on their bikes; a family portrait of his mom, dad, and sister all together on a picnic blanket. Pictures of him at his eleventh-grade prom—his skinny frame decked out in a tux and his girlfriend, a slightly chubby Asian girl, dressed in a poufy pink dress. An unexpected smile pulled at Della's lips seeing her lanky cousin wearing a bow tie.

When she put the pictures back in the box, Della spotted the necklace. Her breath hitched. She'd given it to him on his last birthday—at the bowling party. It was a peace sign, and when she'd seen it shopping the week before his birthday, she'd thought of Chan, who had always been a bit of a hippie.

She grasped the necklace in her palm, half debating keeping it, but then she realized it didn't belong to her. It belonged to Chan. And now he'd be buried with all the things that had mattered to him. That felt right.

Della looked up and saw the agents had placed Chan's body in the casket and were waiting on her to make a decision to view him or not. Instantly, she knew the vision in the clouds was the memory she wanted to keep. She glanced at Burnett and shook her head. He started over.

"Do you want to keep the box?" he asked, obviously understanding that she'd decided not to look at Chan.

"No," Della said, and the one word sounded so heavy, like the weight in her heart. "It belongs with Chan." She reached for the lid and placed it on top. When she stood to pass it to him, the lid flew off.

Burnett and Della both let out a surprised gasp. "Just the wind," Della said, even when she didn't believe it.

"I wish." Burnett glanced around.

"Is he here?" Della asked, feeling the cold, but not sure if it was Chan.

"Someone is," Burnett said. "Do you think maybe he wants you to keep the box?"

She internalized the question, and found the answer quickly. "No, they're *his* things." She handed Burnett the box. Then realizing the agents waited on her, she reached down for the lid. Before she could fit the lid on top, a photo fluttered out, spiraled in the air for a second, and then landed on her shoe.

She picked it up and glanced at the photo. It was Chan, his mom, and . . . and another girl. She looked older than Chan by a year or so. Della looked closer at the image. The girl kind of looked like Della and her sister. A mix of Asian and American.

Again telling herself it was just the wind, she set the photo on top. But it flew out to land at her feet again.

Burnett's eyes rounded. "I think someone wants you to keep that."

Della nodded, swallowing a tickle of unease down her throat. She picked up the photo and slowly put the lid on the box. Both she and Burnett stood there under the silver moonlight waiting to see if the lid popped off. It didn't.

Burnett's gaze, filled with empathy, met hers and then he turned and walked back to the gravesite. With the picture in her hand, she watched him kneel down and put the box in the casket. Then he stood up and closed the lid.

The sound of the heavy top closing echoed in the night. Part of her wanted to scream for them to stop. Should she have forced herself to look at him, to say good-bye to his face?

But if she saw him, she'd have wanted to touch him, and she didn't want to feel him dead.

Holding back her tears, she watched as they lowered the casket. The motor of the backhoe and squeak of the chains sounded loud and sad.

She knew Chan wasn't really in that box. His spirit was in the clouds, in the happy place.

But it was still wrong. He should have lived.

A cold chill came again. Maybe Chan wasn't in the clouds; was he back here? Had he been the one who wanted her to keep the picture?

She looked at it again, but through her watery vision, all she could see was Chan. "I'm gonna miss you," Della whispered and dropped back to the ground, fighting the need to sob. As she watched the heavy piece of machinery shovel dirt over Chan's casket, she hugged her knees and swallowed back the tears.

Her chest felt hollow, yet heavy at the same time. The agents and Burnett stood only fifty feet away, yet loneliness crept in. Then the chill surrounded her like an invisible cloud, and she knew she wasn't alone. Someone was here with her. But who?

"Chan?" Della whispered, shifting her gaze left and then right. She saw nothing, but felt plenty.

But it didn't feel like Chan. She recalled Holiday saying there was probably a connection between her and the ghost who wanted her to find Natasha.

"Who are you?" she whispered.

Then the realization hit. She was in a freaking graveyard. She looked out at the hundreds of tombstones. If she really could feel ghosts as Holiday suspected, this cold could be anybody, or a bunch of somebodies.

There could be hundreds of souls standing beside her. The thought made even her bones shiver. If she didn't owe this to Chan, she'd be hightailing it out of here so fast, even the wind would be envious.

A few minutes later, Burnett came and sat beside her on the soft manicured grass. The cold had faded away. If he or she or the several someones had left, or just backed away, she didn't know. But she appreciated it.

Burnett dropped his palm on her shoulder. It wasn't warm, or tight, but the soft touch came with an emotional charge.

"You okay?" he asked.

Della had moved away from fear and back to grief. "I'm sure I will be sooner or later, but right now, I hurt like hell. He was . . . he was family."

Burnett's palm tightened, making the touch almost as emotionally stimulating as a hug, but not quite.

"I know you're hurting. Family is . . ." He paused, and then started talking. "A little over a year ago, I would have shunned the idea of having a family. And look at me now."

Della nodded, pushing her grief aside to think of little Hannah. "You three make a perfect family."

"Three?" Burnett chuckled. "Hell, when I fell in love with Holiday, I fell in love with Shadow Falls and all of you. We're not blood, Della, but you are part of our family, and don't you ever forget that."

Emotion tightened her lungs. And God help her, but she wanted to lean over and rest her head on his shoulder. Maybe even ask him to wrap his arms around her.

Perhaps she should have brought Miranda and Kylie with her after all. Hell, were hugs addicting? Was there a pill to help you get over needing them? An anti-hug pill?

Chapter Ten

"I'm going to go dismiss the other agents," Burnett said.

Della nodded and blinked away the threatening tears.

When he walked away, she studied the picture again. The girl. Who was she? She turned the picture over and saw nothing on the back.

Footsteps moved her way; she looked up. It was the warlock FRU agent. He didn't look much older than her. While he wore his hair short, he had a few unruly curls that probably made him look younger. He stopped a few feet away from her. Not liking having to look up, she stood and slipped the picture in her back pocket.

"Hey." He nodded.

She responded with a similar head bob.

"Uh, I was wondering if you would mind if I fixed the lawn so it wouldn't look . . . unearthed, just in case any other family comes, so there won't be questions."

"That's fine," she said.

He glanced back and waved a hand. Under the silver moonlight, and with the magic of one warlock, the uneven clumps of earth smoothed over. Perfect blades of grass grew to a manicured length, even a couple of yellow flowers popped up beside the tombstone. A breeze caught the flowers and they brushed against the marker with Chan's name.

"Thank you," Della managed to say, realizing she hadn't thought about bringing flowers.

"You're welcome." He looked a little shy, as if he wanted to ask her something. "Are you the same Della that helped arrest Craig Anthony?"

She nodded and remembered there had been a warlock agent there, but this guy was younger.

"So you know Miranda?" he asked.

"Yeah," Della said, surprised.

"I grew up in the same neighborhood with her. She was friends with my . . . little sister. Can you tell her Shawn Hanson said hello? And that . . . that I heard what she did that day, saving you guys with that amazing spell, and I just think . . . I think it's cool that she's finally coming into her own. I always suspected she was more talented than people gave her credit for."

"I'll tell her," Della said, getting a whiff of his pheromones. So, Agent Hanson had a crush on Miranda, did he? Della could bet Miranda would like to hear this. Not that she'd be ditching Perry, but what girl didn't want to know some guy had a thing for you? Especially an older guy.

He nodded and walked away. Right then, she heard Burnett's unhappy voice ring out. She looked up and saw he'd been on the phone and was now shoving it in his pocket. She'd been so tuned in to the warlock she'd missed the conversation.

Burnett came over, his posture telling her he came with bad news.

"What's wrong?" she asked.

He motioned for her to follow him. They moved within the

trees again. "Have you heard from Chase yet?" he asked, his voice still low.

"No, why?"

"I think he just broke into the FRU storage house."

Della frowned. "Why would he do that?"

"To get into Craig Anthony's files that we confiscated."

"How do you know it was him?" Della asked.

"The trespasser was described as young with dark hair, and he outran the best agents. Who does that sound like to you?"

Della couldn't explain why she was happy Chase had gotten away, but she was. "Did he take anything?"

"One stack of files that we'd set aside." He inhaled and met her gaze. "The ones that contained two fresh turns named Natasha."

Della's heart did a high five against her chest. "You found files on two girls named Natasha? Why didn't you tell me?"

"We just found them about eleven tonight. I was going to inform you of this as soon as . . . as this was over."

"Did you find any record of a Liam?"

"No."

All of a sudden, she felt a little panic seep in. "If it wasn't Chase who took those files, then we've lost them."

"I had someone scan them into our computers. So we're fine. But I think we both know who did this. And he can't be doing this kind of shit. You don't piss off the FRU!"

Della nodded, but didn't say anything. Hell, if Della had known the files were there, she might have broken in to get them, too. Then, suddenly, Della realized what this meant. Chase had been in the vision with her. Why else would he have gone and taken only those files?

"I'll go with you," she said, the urgency she'd felt at the falls about finding Natasha returning full force.

"No," he said. "I haven't gotten the clearance for you to work the case yet. I should have it tomorrow afternoon, then we'll set you up. I know this is hard, but for now . . . go back to Shadow Falls and try to get some rest. You haven't slept. Skip school today. We'll need you at your best tomorrow."

"What's hard is knowing I could be doing something instead of twiddling my thumbs. Why can't I just—?"

"No," he said firmly. "Go get some rest."

Della clenched her jaw to keep from arguing, then said, "I want to stay here for a bit and then . . . then I want to go see Steve. I'll go rest after that." She hadn't even given seeing Steve much thought, but the moment it came out, she knew it wasn't just what she wanted, but what she needed.

She needed Steve. Needed . . . his arms around her. More hugs? But crap, she really had to look into an anti-hug patch.

Maybe even an anti-Steve patch.

"Fine. I need to get to the agency. Do you want me to have an agent escort you—?"

"Will you stop babying me? I can take care of myself, or have you forgotten?"

Burnett frowned. "Fine, be safe. Keep the speed down and fly below the trees if it's daylight."

"I will."

"And if you hear from Chase, tell him I want to see him immediately, then call me."

She nodded, but it wasn't the most confident nod. What was Burnett going to do? He turned as if to go and she realized she needed answers.

"Wait," Della said. "Have you heard from the Vampire Council? Did Chase get in touch with them? Has the FRU made a definite decision about me and Chase working together?" If he hadn't told her about the files, there was a chance he hadn't told her about the other things.

From the look on his face, she was right. "The Vampire Council called and I asked about the possibility of Chase working for the FRU. Or at least you and Chase collaborating, and I was told they would consider it. I'm sure the FRU will accept it, but . . ."

"But what?" she asked.

He looked back through the woods to make sure the other agents were gone. "But if they discover he's the one who took those files, they aren't going to let him work with us. They'll arrest him the first chance they get. He can't be doing shit like that. The FRU doesn't tolerate disobedience. And if you care about him, make sure he understands that."

If she cared about him?

She did care. The thought hit that she'd just planned on going to see Steve—whom she also cared about. That's when she remembered her realization from earlier. She was hurting Steve. She had two choices. Give up working with Chase. Or give up Steve.

The mere thought of losing Steve sent every emotional nerve in her body rebelling and singing a tune of heartbreak. But the idea of pushing away Chase and lessening her chances of finding Natasha and Liam hurt, too.

Was there really no other way?

Find Natasha! Find Natasha!

Della's heart did a tumble when she heard the voice, but honestly, she wasn't sure if it was the ghost speaking or just her remembering.

"I have to go," Burnett said, bringing Della back to the present.

"What are you going to do?" she asked.

He looked down at her. "About what?"

"About Chase." Then suddenly, she couldn't let him answer,

afraid she wouldn't like it. "Look, you can't tell the FRU that it was him who broke in." She sensed Chase would help find Natasha. That somehow he was part of the plan and that was the reason they'd been called to the falls at the same time. "Don't do it for Chase, do it for Natasha and Liam."

Burnett ran a hand over the back of his neck and squeezed as if to relieve some tension. "I wasn't planning on turning him in, but let's hope he didn't leave any evidence behind that will lead them to him. I won't be able to stop them if they figure out it was him."

She nodded. "Are you sure I can't come? I could start going over the files you have on the two girls named Natasha."

Burnett scowled at her. "Della, I'm almost certain you're going to be working this case, and that Chase will be your partner, but you need to deal with losing your cousin for at least a day. You need rebound time."

"I've dealt with it for almost a month now," she said. "This . . ." She waved to the grave, "This was my closure."

His lips tightened in frustration like they always did when she argued with him. Yet, she knew he couldn't dispute her logic. The fact that her emotions had no logic was her own secret. She had a feeling she'd be rebounding over Chan's death for a long time to come.

"I can understand that, but you still can't go tonight. I don't have clearance to bring you on the case. Go see Steve, and then get some rest. Be ready to start on this tomorrow."

He took off. Della moved back to Chan's gravesite. She dropped back down on the cold earth and just sat there, curled up in a ball, trying to emotionally come to terms with her most pressing problems.

Chan's death.

Natasha and Liam.

Steve and Chase.

The stars and moon slowly faded. A tiny slice of sun chased the night away, but even with the promise of a new day, a sense of isolation filled her. She sat extra still, surrounded by gravestones. Alone.

The chill came back and she had to amend her last thought. Maybe she wasn't really alone. She looked around. She didn't see anyone. But she felt someone. Goose bumps spidered down her arms and spine.

"Do I know you?" Her words seemed to be swallowed by the predawn gray. She stared back at Chan's grave. The sun peeked a little higher above the eastern horizon, and stripes of bright pink and purple appeared.

She watched the ball of orange as it slowly inched up into the sky, drowning out the sunrise colors, but bringing dusty light and some white clouds that swayed in the blue sky. She tried to ignore the chill. A chill that felt haunted.

Her gaze locked on the sky as the cold around her increased and the clouds began to form shapes. Shapes that looked almost like three people posing for a . . .

Remembering the picture, she pulled it out and studied it again. When she looked up to compare the crazy cloud formation, it was gone. She stared again at the image, then turned it over. There, scribbled in light pencil, so light she'd missed it earlier, were three names. Chan, Miao—who was Chan's mother—and . . .

"Damn." Her voice seemed small in the big haunted place.

Natasha.

Chan knew Natasha? Was it the same Natasha? But what the hell was the connection?

Standing, she walked over to Chan's grave. She stared at the tombstone, the light breeze sending the yellow flowers dancing in front of the engraving.

"Who is Natasha? What's her last name?" She didn't know who she was talking to, Chan or the ghost from earlier—the one who spoke in a feminine voice. But somebody had better answer her. And fast.

"It's either Natasha Brian or Natasha Owen," a voice spoke behind her just as she heard the sound of someone's feet hitting the ground.

Chapter Eleven

It only took a flicker of a second for the male voice to become familiar and for his scent to find its way into Della's memory bank.

She turned and faced Chase.

In the silence of a day that hadn't fully woken up, they stared at each other. "Are you okay?" he finally asked, sounding and looking soulful, perhaps apologetic.

She guessed his expression and tone was about Chan. Like being hit with a switch, her resentment at him for not trying hard enough to save her cousin resurfaced. Then, as if the switch was suddenly reset, she found herself questioning the justice of those sentiments.

She recalled with clarity how much pain she'd endured at the second turn, and how Chase had endured it with her, just to offer her a better chance of survival. Then she recalled him telling her over and over again that he didn't believe Chan would have survived, even with his help. Would she have endured that for someone, someone she hardly knew, if she didn't think he would live? And knowingly let another innocent person die, someone she thought had a better chance?

She took in a sobering breath, pushed those feeling aside, and decided she would come back to think about that later.

"How did you know I was here?" she asked.

"I just got off the phone with Burnett." He dropped one hand into his jeans pocket.

It's either Natasha Brian or Natasha Owen. His earlier words tiptoed across her mind. Unfortunately, only first names were written on the back of her picture. "So, it was you that broke into the FRU storage unit?"

He nodded. "I didn't want to waste any more time."

"If they find out it was you, they won't work with you or the council, or let you work with me on this."

He frowned. "They won't find out. I covered my tracks. And don't think Burnett didn't already chew my ass out for it." He took a step closer.

In the golden hue of morning sunlight, his eyes looked crystal green. He kept his one hand in his pocket, making one shoulder lift slightly higher than the other.

Something about his posture looked less certain than before, slightly vulnerable. And the way he studied her made her wonder if it was because of her, perhaps because of what she'd said to him earlier.

I don't love you, period. I go back and forth on even liking you. It wasn't altogether a lie. Yet realizing how hard and hurtful her words had sounded, she regretted saying them.

Her shoulders tightened, feeling a crazy tension at his presence, and yet at the same time, his being here brought on some kind of inner peace. She recalled she'd felt it at the falls as well. Thoughts of the falls turned her mind to another subject.

"The vision . . . You saw it, or experienced it. Didn't you?"

He exhaled as if he didn't like admitting it. "Yeah, but I've never had anything like that happen. I wasn't sure what it meant. It wasn't until you said their names that I knew you'd been a part of it."

"You were Liam?" she asked.

He nodded. "Yeah, whoever he is. I couldn't find anything on him at all. And I went through all the files." There was a touch of desperation in his tone that mirrored what she felt.

She recalled knowing certain things about Natasha during the vision. "When it was happening, did you learn anything about him, or know things?"

"Just his first name and that he was scared. And . . . that he . . . he would give Natasha all his blood to save her. He's more concerned about her dying than worried about his own life. He's in love with her."

Hearing that sent an ache fluttering around Della's chest like a trapped bird. Tears stung her sinuses and she looked down, away from his scrutiny. She recalled Liam insisting Natasha drink more of his blood. Della had sensed he'd cared about Natasha. But what did Natasha feel for Liam? Della couldn't say for sure, but she had refused his blood.

Della's vision grew wet at the thought of two people, possibly in love, trapped, and feeling so damn desperate. Remembering what Holiday and Kylie believed about them. That option hurt more.

She blinked back her water weakness and looked at Chase. For one second, she debated not telling him, but then realized he had a right to know.

"Holiday, she's a ghost expert, and . . . she's afraid that Natasha and Liam are already dead."

"No," Chase said adamantly, his light green eyes brightening with emotion. "If we don't find them, they will be. I kept hearing this voice telling me to find Natasha."

"Me, too," Della said, finding it odd he'd heard the same voice, and for some reason it gave her more hope. But since Holiday was sort of the knowledgeable one in all things ghost, it didn't take all her concern away. "It still scares me because she thinks—"

"I don't care what she thinks. She's wrong," he insisted.

"I guess we have to believe that." And standing there—only a few feet from him, agreeing with him, she had some kind of a weird epiphany. They, her and Chase, were supposed to do this. They were supposed to work this case together. But who decided that? Fate? The death angels? The ghost? And who the hell was she? How was all this connected?

"Have you done this before?" Chase asked.

"Done what?" she questioned, having gone inside her head and lost track of the conversation.

"Visions? Voices?"

Like his earlier admission, hers came with a touch of hesitancy. "Yeah. Chan, and then . . . Lorraine. But the vision with Lorraine was different."

His brows tightened as if he was assessing what she said. "Lorraine? The female victim who was murdered in the case we worked?" His brow creased. "Why didn't you tell me that?"

Maybe because you don't tell me shit, either. She breathed in a mouthful of early morning air and it came with his scent: mint, some kind of herbs, and sunshine. "I . . . I kept hearing a voice, but I wasn't sure and . . ." The wind stirred her hair in front of her face and she pushed it away. "Hell, if I'd told you I was hearing ghosts, you would've thought I was crazy."

He dropped his hand from his pocket. "Probably. I didn't think we vampires did the ghost whispering thing." His gaze shifted and he glanced around at the tombstones.

Did he feel the same haunted feelings she did? As if something longed for her to walk the grounds and search for something—but what could be found here but the dead? Lost souls.

"Holiday thinks we have the ability because we're Reborns." Questions about when Chase had been Reborn started to percolate. Was he one of the few who survived on his own, or had someone helped him? Was he bonded to someone else? Now didn't seem the time to start littering him with questions. Besides, he wasn't known for handing over answers.

He ran a hand down his face as if fighting the edginess she felt. "Does Burnett deal with this shit, too?"

Oh, he was getting good at asking questions, wasn't he?

Was divulging information about Burnett wrong? Chase's eyes met hers and she decided he needed the truth. She didn't think Burnett would disagree. "He hasn't had visions, but he experiences a connection of some kind. Supposedly, anyone who can visit the falls without being repulsed has a little of the . . . gift. 'Gift' is Holiday's word, not mine."

He stood there as if considering something and then asked, "Can we communicate with anyone who's dead?"

She had the feeling he was thinking of his family who Della remembered had all been killed in a plane crash. Unexpectedly, her heartstrings tugged at all that he'd lost. "I don't know how it works. Holiday could tell you."

His gaze went back to Chan's tombstone. "I know this is tough." He paused and the silence of the graveyard seemed almost loud. Then his voice came again and it felt as if the wind pulled it away. "You actually spoke with Chan?" He looked back at her.

More questions. All she could do was nod.

His eyes tightened with some emotion she couldn't read. "Does he blame me, too? For his dying?"

She suddenly recognized that look. Guilt. She hadn't thought he cared. Had she been wrong?

"He didn't blame anyone," she answered around a tightness in her throat. "That wasn't Chan's style." Her heartstrings pulled again, this time for all *she'd* lost.

Another few beats of silence filled the haunted place. Her phone rang, the noise seeming to bounce against tombstone after tombstone. She looked at it, and saw Burnett's number.

"Did Burnett know you were coming here?"

"He forbid me to come here," he said matter-of-factly. "But he seems pretty smart, so he probably knew I'd come anyway."

"You seem to have a thing about breaking rules."

"I don't set out to break them. I just make my own."

She pretty much did the same, so she sure as hell couldn't judge him for it. She looked back at the phone and made a decision. Changing her phone to vibrate, she slipped it back into her pocket.

Chase's voice, deep and soulful, sounded again. "Do you want to go see the files?"

She'd told Burnett where she was going, and he would probably be pissed at her, both for not answering his call and for deviating from the plan. Emotions tied to the vision—desperation, hunger, fear—walked across her heart, leaving heavy footprints. Burnett would just have to be pissed.

"I'm ready when you are." But she looked back at Chan's grave one more time.

Chase took off, and much to his credit, he flew amongst the trees. They'd had to land twice to jog over urban areas where the early morning traffic moved and they could have been spotted. Della followed close behind him, vaguely recalling being unable to keep up with him earlier. Not that he was flying at full speed; he seemed to abide by Burnett's rules of not showing his true powers. But before, even at this speed, longer than ten minutes would have been pushing her stamina.

His route was a little different from Burnett's, but she recognized the terrain below. They were heading back toward Fallen, Texas . . . toward Shadow Falls. A couple of miles from camp, he followed a curvy dirt road and went down into a semi-clearing in the woods.

Her feet hit the ground with only a slight jolt. She looked behind her at a cabin. Not like the cabins at Shadow Falls, but like a fancy-schmancy cabin rented out to rich people to do yoga retreats or to get in touch with their inner spirit.

Whoever designed it did a good job. The logs formed an A-frame residence, constructed in such a way that it grew up and out of the natural landscape. Attached to the building was a large wraparound porch complete with wicker gliders and rockers. Only a few feet from the front porch seating were five bird feeders spaced out amongst the trees. The front part of the cabin held more glass than wood, so even those inside wouldn't feel closed up.

Chase walked to the front porch. She followed. As she made the steps, she spotted a car parked to the side of the house. A fancy, bright blue convertible. She was far from a car expert, but it looked fast—and expensive.

Was someone else here? She took in a big breath and didn't pick up anyone's scent. Except . . . a dog.

As she passed one of the wicker chairs, she noted a pair of binoculars on top of one cushion. She glanced back at the bird feeders and recalled Miranda's claims that birding was good for a person's soul and aura. Refocusing on Chase with disbelief, she asked, "You're a birder?"

"No," he denied it, a little too fast. She glanced inside through the large glass windows to the lodge-style decorations. Big leather furniture, wood floors, and colorful rugs.

"Who lives here?" she asked.

"I do," he said. "Well, me and Baxter."

"Baxter?" she asked.

He shifted a little and opened the door. "Meet Baxter."

A big black Lab with a gray muzzle came barreling out. Even though he ran right toward Chase, Della took a step back.

She wasn't afraid of dogs, just cautious.

Chase gave the dog a good scratch behind his ear and the animal's entire backside wagged with excitement. Della recalled Chase telling her that the only "someone" he hadn't lost in the plane accident had been his dog. Was this the same dog? She suspected it was.

"He won't bite," Chase said when she still stood a step back. "Will you, Baxter?" he asked the dog.

Baxter seemed to take that as an invitation and moved closer. While his gray snout put him in his older years, his toned body and movements didn't show signs of age. She held out her hand for him to sniff then she slowly turned her hand over and ran her palm over the top of his head.

The canine accepted her touch, but stared up at her with caution. Della pulled her hand back.

"Not a dog person?" Chase asked.

"No, I like dogs. My dad wasn't too big on them though, so we never had one. But my neighbor had several through the years, and I sort of got attached to a couple of them. My neighbor was a divorced man who was always late with the dog's supper; some nights he wouldn't even come home. I had my mom buy dog food, and I'd feed him when I saw he wasn't home after dark."

A slow smile appeared in Chase's eyes. "So Della Tsang actually has a soft spot?"

"It's not a very big spot." She shot him a frown. The truth was that soft spot was larger than she'd like.

She shifted and a bird swooped right past the porch. She glanced at the feathered creature as it landed on one of the feeders. It piped out part of a song, almost saying thank you, dug its beak into the wire mesh to snag a piece of food, and then flew off.

"I knew I heard a . . ." Chase said.

She looked back at him. He had the binoculars plastered to his eyes, and when he lowered them, his expression looked victorious. "That bird's not supposed to be here now," he said.

She almost grinned at his enthusiasm. "Not a birder, huh?"

He didn't really appear embarrassed, just caught. "Maybe a little. But it was forced on me. My mom was an avid birder. She dragged me to bird-watching events four or five times a year."

Della heard devotion in his voice when he talked about the woman who'd raised him the first fourteen years of his life, and it made her realize how little she knew about this guy. Not exactly her fault. He'd been secretive from the beginning.

And still was. Her gut said he knew more about who had sent him to check on her and Chan. And that someone could be the one person Della was searching for: her uncle. She'd recently learned her dad's brother was a vampire who'd faked his own death years ago, and she wondered if he'd made contact with Chase.

She wasn't going to forget that she didn't completely trust Chase. Hopefully, if they collaborated with the Vampire Council, she might get answers there. Hell, her uncle could even be one of the council members. That thought sent a wave of urgency to get this case started—to find Natasha and to find her own answers.

Chapter Twelve

Another bird swooped past, and awkwardness slipped into the moment. Della and Chase stood there on the huge front porch, gazes locked, each lost in their own thoughts.

She focused back on the trees and asked another question. "Did this place belong to your parents?" When he didn't answer right away, she looked at him.

"No," he said, watching the bird feeders. "Though my mom would have loved it."

And, just like that, in spite of just telling herself she didn't trust him, she felt herself wanting to know more. More about his past life, his present. That desire suddenly felt wrong and dangerous. Forbidden. An image of Steve flashed in her head as guilt sat on the edge of her heart.

She swallowed the uncomfortable feeling down her throat and remembered why she was here. "We should look at those files."

His right brow arched ever so slightly, as if he knew she was purposely pulling back, but he opened the glass door wider to let her in.

The aroma of wood and leather filled the room, along with light traces of Chase's smell and his beloved Baxter.

"Sit down," Chase said. "I'll grab the files."

She didn't feel comfortable enough to sit. Alone, she stood by the large coffee table and brown leather sofa and studied her surroundings. She gazed up, a little awed by the high ceiling and immaculate decorations. Against one wall was a huge pine cabinet holding a large television. She envisioned Chase there, Baxter curled up beside him watching TV. Next to that, she noted a few framed pictures decorating some of the shelves. She listened to make sure he wouldn't catch her snooping. Hearing him rummaging through a drawer, she edged closer and stared at the first image—two girls, their arms around each other, laughing like best friends. The second was a group picture. She picked up the image that appeared to be a family portrait.

She recognized a young Chase, probably thirteen, tall and a little lanky, but already showing signs of becoming a man. The girl, who looked like his sister, was one of the girls in the first photo. Della sighed, thinking about her own sister, and how little they were a part of each other's lives now.

Touching the glass, she passed her finger over the images of the other people.

Family. Family lost. Her chest suddenly felt empty remembering the pictures of her own family. Pictures now hidden in a drawer, not on public display. Did that mean losing someone to death was easier than watching them turn their backs on you?

She studied Chase's image in the photo. Happy. Surrounded by people he loved. Now they were gone. She supposed it hurt both ways.

Her sinuses began to sting. Swallowing, she put the picture back.

Baxter inched closer to her and sat next to her leg. The animal stared up with intensity. His gaze didn't come off threatening, just evaluating.

She dropped her hand and let him smell her again. He bumped her knuckles with his wet nose and breathed in her scent. Not just once, but twice. Slowly, his tail began to wag, and he moved in closer, lovingly leaning his head against her leg.

It was almost as if the dog could smell Chase's blood inside of her. Was that possible? Did she smell different now that she had his blood? She lifted her hand up and sniffed her own wrist near her vein. She didn't detect anything different.

She knelt down and stared into his large brown eyes.

She leaned close to the dog's ear. "I'm not out to hurt him, just work with him." She whispered the words so low Chase wouldn't hear. "Not that I haven't wanted to kick his ass a couple of times." She ran her hand over the dog's side.

Moving her hand up, she touched the collar and felt some engraving in soft, aged leather. Brushing the hair back, she turned the collar in a circle to read the inscription.

The tap of footsteps moved into the room. "Never turn your back on a challenge," she repeated what she'd read. "Is that for the dog or you?"

"Both," he said.

A flash of emotion touched his eyes. She had a feeling the saying meant something, but what? She batted back the curiosity. She was here to work the case, not get chummy.

"You two made friends?"

He held two files in his hands.

"Looks like it." Della stood and walked to the large table. The dog followed her and rubbed against Chase as he joined them in the center of the room.

She dropped into a chair. Chase sat in the one next to her. Not so close their shoulders touched, but close enough she thought about his nearness.

He nudged the files over to her, his brows tightened. "I've already gone over them. Dozens of times. I'm not sure they are going to help. Getting more information would require we pay either Craig Anthony or one of his hired goons a visit. I have a feeling the FRU won't allow it."

"Burnett will allow it," she said, certain Burnett would do everything in his power to save someone. She pulled the files closer.

"All we have are two possible names. There's nothing in there that can tell me which one is our Natasha. And while having a name seems important, I'm not even sure that will help us."

"It has to." Della flipped open the first file.

She scanned quickly, looking for . . . she found the name of Natasha Owen's mother. Jenny Owen. "It's not Natasha Owen." She closed it and reached for the other one.

Chase put his hand on top of the file. "How do you know?"

She decided not to lie. "Because her mother's name isn't Asian." There was a slight possibility that Natasha's mom might have taken on an American name. Lots of Asians did that, but usually it was the younger ones. Someone older than thirty or forty normally held tight to the culture of their parents.

"What? How? I don't understand," he said.

"Natasha's half Asian." She tried to pull the file from under his hand, but he flattened his palm on top of it.

"How do you know that? It was so dark in that vision that you . . . you couldn't have seen her."

"I didn't." She lifted up off the chair and pulled the picture from her back pocket. "But I've got this." She considered not

showing it to him until he released the file. But she was tired of
playing games. They had to trust each other.

Not on a personal level, she reminded herself, still believing he
held secrets, but enough to work on the case.

Enough to save two people . . . two people possibly in love, who
needed and deserved to be saved.

Save Natasha.

She handed him the picture and cut her eyes around the room.

He studied the photo.

"Turn it over," she said.

He did and then looked back up at her as if puzzled. "Turn it
over to see what?"

He handed her back the picture. Her breath caught.

"I don't . . . But it was . . . There were names here earlier. It had
the name 'Natasha,' along with my aunt's and Chan's." Glancing
up, hit hard by the doubt in his eyes, she frowned. "I'm telling the
truth!"

She stared again at the pristine white, unmarked back of the
picture. Oh, hell, was her mind playing tricks on her?

Or was it the ghost?

Della looked at Chase standing by his refrigerator. "It was there
earlier," she said for the tenth time in the last five minutes.

"So you think the ghost wrote it then erased it?" He held out a
canned drink for her.

"I . . . I don't know." She accepted the cold soda. It wasn't diet,
but she took it anyway. The icy cold against her palm reminded her
of what it felt like when a spirit came for a visit—when they felt too
close. She popped the top open. The fizzy sound triggered her need
to be with Kylie and Miranda at one of their round-table meet-

ings—to have them help her make sense of this, because it certainly wasn't making sense to her right now.

Then again, why should it? Nothing made sense. Ghosts, visions, being bonded—feeling emotionally tied to a practical stranger. It all sounded insane. And that became her arguing point.

"I know it doesn't sound logical, but does any of this shit sound logical to you? We're dealing with some dead woman, and having visions where we're different people. Tell me that makes any more sense than this, and I'll accept I'm imagining things and find some shrink's sofa to pass out on."

"I didn't say you were imagining it, I just think it sounds . . . messed up."

"All of this is a hot mess!"

"Yeah, it is." He opened his drink.

They both took a few carbonated sips, then she told him about the box vibrating in the empty casket and how the lid had fallen open and the picture had fluttered out.

Frowning, he stared at the picture as if half afraid. "Okay, so let's say that is Natasha. How is knowing her last name really going to help us find them?" He dropped back into the chair.

"I don't know. But it must be important. The ghost wanted me to see this."

He leaned in. His solid forearm pressed against hers. The zing of pleasure sent her heart racing and she scooted over.

He cut his eyes up as if he thought she was silly. But it didn't seem silly to her. No zings were allowed.

She reached for the second Natasha file again. She found the mom's name and let out a frustrated puff of air.

"And?" he asked.

She shook her head. "Kathy . . . not Asian. I mean, the mother could have changed her name, but . . . ."

"But it means we still don't know which Natasha is our Natasha."

"Right."

The room went silent. Baxter rubbed against his owner's leg seeking affection. Chase dropped his hand to pet the animal, but kept his focus on her. "And you really feel it's important to get this information?"

She considered his question. "Yeah, I do."

"Okay, then let's go find out Natasha's last name." He stood up.

She rose as well, ready and willing to get this show on the road. "What are we going to do? Go see both sets of parents and see if any of them are Asian?"

"No, we do it the easy way."

"Easy way?"

"We go talk to your aunt, Chan's mom."

She dropped back down in her chair. "Let's don't and say we did."

"We don't tell her the truth. Make up some story about how you ran across the photo and see what she knows."

"No," Della said again. "Let's go see if we can find Natasha's parents." She pulled the files over and checked. Both girls had lived outside of Houston, not that their families couldn't have moved since their daughters went missing. Who knew how long these girls had been enslaved?

When she looked up, Chase studied her. "Why are you afraid to see your aunt?"

"I'm not." Her phone gave off a short buzz, telling her she had a text, giving her the perfect reason not to answer.

Not to think about it.

She dug her cell out of her pocket.

Where are u? Don't pull this shit! Answer me. Burnett.

Suddenly, coming here behind the camp leader's back didn't seem like the best idea. Pissing Burnett off wasn't going to get her anywhere except smack-dab in the middle of an ass-chewing.

She and Chase needed to get this case approved by the FRU and the Vampire Council. While she liked to think they could do this alone, she wasn't stupid.

She looked up. "It's Burnett again." She exhaled. "We should go. We'll tell him we want to visit the parents of both the Natashas."

"Maybe I should just go by myself and get the answers now," he said. "You go back to Shadow Falls."

Was he dreading the ass-chewing he had coming for going to the graveyard? Probably. She didn't blame him. Burnett's ass-chewings weren't a walk in the park. Though she still thought it was funny that Chase, who didn't seem to fear much of anything, was afraid of the camp leader. Then again, she'd come here without letting Burnett know. Chase wasn't the only one in trouble.

And her chewing would be worse. When you cared about someone, it was always worse.

"No," Della said. "The ghost gave the picture to me. I think I should be there. Besides . . ." She studied the discomfort in his expression. ". . . you're going to have to face him sooner or later."

"Yeah, but I've always been a 'later' person."

"So, a coward, huh?" she asked, lifting one brow to add some sass to her comment.

He glared at her.

"You've got to learn to work with Burnett if we're going to team up on this case." And they were going to team up, because some dad-blasted higher power had apparently ordained it.

She'd like to kick that higher power's butt, but that was be-side the point. Point was, they had a job to do, and if they failed someone—two someones—would die.

"Burnett's bark is worse than his bite," she said.

"I don't like to be barked at." His tone deepened.

"Me, either, but I give Burnett some leeway. And so should you."

"Why?"

She considered downplaying her answer, but decided the truth would do just fine. "Because he never barks just to bark. He does it because he cares. And like it or not, we all need someone to care for us."

He exhaled. "Caring about someone doesn't give a person the right to micromanage their life."

"Yeah, he has a little problem with that, but he's working on it." Defending Burnett's hardheadedness felt strange, but oddly it also felt right.

Chase studied her as if mentally connecting the dots. But what kind of dots? Why did she get the feeling the puzzle he worked on this minute was about her?

Stay away from my dots, bucko.

He dropped back into the chair next to her, even closer this time. "Does your aunt not care? Is that why you don't want to see her?"

"Ya know, I'd love to spend a couple of hours telling you all about my family drama"—*not*—"but we don't have time." Honestly, she spilled her guts only to Kylie and Miranda. And by God, she needed some round-table Diet-Coke time with them right now. She jumped up. "You coming or not?"

Chapter Thirteen

Five minutes—down to the second. That's how long Burnett paced Holiday's office. She knew because she and Chase were facing the wall clock, and instead of getting dizzy watching him, she watched the clock hands tick away. It was almost nine in the morning, and she hadn't been to bed yet.

"Why?" Burnett finally spoke, walking from one side of the room to the other. Good thing he'd brought them to Holiday's office—his office offered no room to pace.

"Why what?" Della asked, trying not to sound like a smartass, but the question rolled off her tongue with sass.

He growled. "Why do I give orders if you guys don't listen? And why would I allow you to work with the FRU if you can't follow orders?"

"Because the death angels and some unnamed ghost have made it their job to make sure we do this." Della inhaled.

A second later, and in a calmer voice, she explained about seeing the names on the back of the picture, and how when Chase showed up it seemed like the ghost wanted her to go with him.

"You don't work for the ghost! You work for the FRU, and I tell you what to do!"

"I don't work for the FRU," Chase countered.

Della inwardly flinched, wishing he wouldn't push Burnett.

"So, you don't want to work with Della on this case?" Burnett snapped. "Because you can walk right out of here and I'll make sure you don't see her again."

"Say what?" Della let out a low, hot puff of air. "Since when—"

Chase barged ahead. "I'm just saying that as of right now, I'm not required to follow your orders."

Burnett countered. "I told you she had enough on her plate, to leave her alone. How difficult would it have been to do that?"

Chase's chin rose. "Difficult. We're bonded, and if she's in pain, I have to make sure she's okay. Would you not do it for Holiday?"

Say what? Della glared at the guy. "Just because you gave me blood doesn't mean I need you to babysit me!"

"I didn't say you needed me," Chase spit out. "I explained why I disobeyed the order—an order that I wasn't officially required to obey." He looked back at Burnett as if bringing home his point one more time.

Della let out a hiss of air. "Well, you made it sound as if—"

"Like what?" Chase faced her. "We're bonded, when are you going to accept that?"

"Maybe never! I didn't ask to be bonded with you."

"Stop!" Burnett fumed. "I'm the one who's mad here."

"No," Della snapped. "I'm mad, too. I don't like being used as leverage." She glared at Burnett then at Chase. "And I don't like our being lumped in the same category as Burnett and Holiday. We're working a case. That's all!"

"Show me the picture," Burnett snapped.

When Della and Chase sat there glaring at each other, Burnett repeated, "Show me the damn picture!"

Della drew in a deep, sobering breath and pulled the picture from the back of her jeans.

Burnett turned it over, looking for the names. Okay, so she'd neglected to mention the part about them disappearing.

"About that . . ." Della said. "The names, they . . . they sort of disappeared."

Burnett looked at her with puzzled eyes. "How did they disappear?"

"I'm assuming the ghost did it."

Burnett blinked. "You're telling me the ghost wrote the names on here and then erased them?"

"See?" Chase said. "I'm not the only one who found it hard to believe."

Della so wanted to give Chase a serious sharp jab with her elbow. She settled for a kick in his shin.

He muttered an ugly word, and feeling slightly vindicated, she ignored him and kept her focus on Burnett.

"I don't know how she did it," Della said. "But don't tell me it's impossible. You saw the box shaking, and how the lid flew off and the picture came out."

Burnett leaned his butt back on Holiday's desk and wiped a hand over his face.

Della plunged ahead. "I think we should visit both sets of Natasha's parents and find out which one is our Natasha. The ghost gave me this picture as a clue, I have to follow it."

Burnett glanced back at the picture. "Who is the older lady in the image?"

Della tensed. "My aunt."

"Couldn't you just ask—?"

"No," Della snapped.

Burnett studied her. "Why?"

"No." She met his eyes and begged him to concede.

He exhaled. "Problem is, both these sets of parents think their daughters are dead. Showing up and asking questions is wrong."

"We wouldn't ask questions. Just see if one of the parents is Asian. Since we know our Natasha is mixed."

Burnett didn't appear convinced. "The parents could have divorced, or one of them died."

"I know," Della said. "But the photo was a clue and I think . . ." She hated saying it, but it had to be said. "It's what the ghost expects us to do."

"What do you mean?" Burnett asked.

"I don't know. I just feel as if that's what she wants." And she did.

Burnett muttered, "Shit." He paused and then said, "I'll call and see if I can't get the case cleared immediately." He squeezed the back of his neck. "I've already called to see if either a Natasha Owen or Natasha Brian had a driver's license. Neither did."

Burnett looked at Della. "You go rest until I get clearance. You've been up since before three this morning and I doubt you even went to bed last night. You," he looked at Chase, "go . . . wherever it is you go, and be prepared to hear from me. Meanwhile, I'll see if Derek can find anything about either of these girls on the computer. The ghost might want you to go around asking questions, but I for one don't love the idea."

Della and Chase started out.

"One more thing," Burnett said, and they turned around. "We think we know who Liam is."

"How?" Chase asked. "There wasn't a file on him."

"I know," Burnett seethed, sounding as if he remembered Chase's breaking-and-entering oops. "But there was a missing person's report on file with the HPD—a Liam Jones went missing three weeks ago. The report says he'd come down with a serious flu then disappeared. He lived a few blocks from the Anthonys' funeral home."

"So he was turned and somehow one of Anthony's goons got ahold of him," Della said.

"That's the way it looks. I'd get another agent to look into it, but there were some problems in Dallas and several of our men are still cleaning up the mess there."

"I want to work the case," Della insisted. "The ghost wants me to work it."

"Wants both of us to," Chase said.

Burnett nodded. "I'll get Liam's information and pass it to you before you start."

They turned again, and almost got out the door, when Burnett spoke out again. "Della? Can I have a second?"

Chase looked back, and frowned as if he didn't like being left out of the loop.

"Go!" Burnett informed him.

Chase shot her a glance good-bye before leaving. Della, suddenly uneasy, stepped back into Holiday's office.

Burnett listened to Chase leave before talking.

"Two things. First, is there an issue about your aunt that I should be aware of?"

Della frowned. "No. If I go to her and start asking questions, she'll tell my dad and it . . . it could cause problems." Amazing how simple that sounded, and yet how badly it hurt. "My dad already has zero trust in me, so any suspicious behavior would only make me look like more of a drugged-out problem child."

Burnett nodded, not really happy, but apparently satisfied. "The other thing." He paused, as if choosing his words carefully.

"What?" she insisted, the pause killing her.

"When I called you earlier to inform you about the information we'd gotten on Liam and you didn't answer, I assumed you were with Steve. I called him and told him you had mentioned going to see him. I also told him that we had buried your cousin. He seemed upset that you hadn't told him. You might want to call him."

She nodded. Her stomach rolled over. How she was going to explain this to Steve? *Oh, I was coming to see you, but Chase showed up, so I went to his cabin instead.*

Oh, damn. It wouldn't matter that nothing had happened. She'd be hurting Steve again. What was her other option? Lie?

No, if he found out, it would only hurt him more. And he'd think she was hiding it because . . . because she was guilty. She wasn't guilty, so why was she drowning in the emotion right now?

Was it fair to keep doing this to him? The thought made breathing uncomfortable. But wasn't he doing it to her, too? He spent Monday through Thursday in the vet's office, working side by side with Jessie. Jessie, who wasn't bonded to Steve, but definitely had the hots for him.

Realizing Burnett stood staring at her while she indulged in her mini pity party, she took a backward step toward the door. "Thanks . . . I'll call him."

She took off, her last words repeating in her head. *I'll call him. I'll call him.* And she would, just as soon as she figured out how the heck to explain why she hadn't gone to see him.

Della got halfway to her cabin then shifted off the trail and hid behind a clump of trees. She pulled out her phone. She had to make this right. Staring at her cell, she suddenly found it odd that he hadn't called her. If he knew she'd buried Chan, he'd have called to check on her. Not calling wasn't like Steve.

Was he already mad? Mad because she hadn't called him and told him she was burying her cousin? Or did he guess she'd been with Chase? *I didn't do anything!* She started preparing her not-guilty speech.

Dread built up in her chest when she realized that even if she hadn't done anything, the simple fact that she'd relied on Chase instead of Steve was still going to hurt him.

Her head told her what she needed to do—to let him go—but her heart refused to accept it.

She swallowed a knot of pain and it fell like a lump of dough in her stomach.

Taking a deep breath, her mind still dithering, she dialed his number.

It rang once.

Twice.

Three times.

Then it went to voice mail.

"Hey . . . I'm at Shadow Falls . . . Burnett said he called you and . . . Call me, okay?"

She shut her phone and closed her eyes for a second. Steve always answered her calls.

Maybe he was busy with a client. An emergency of some sort. A dog who'd swallowed a sock, a werewolf with a thorn in his paw. That's what she wanted to believe. What she would believe until . . . until she knew differently. She simply had too many real issues to start imagining one.

"Crappers! What did Burnett say?" Kylie asked.

"What did he say before or after he gave us royal hell?" Della asked, appreciating that her two roomies and best friends had skipped lunch to chat with her. Their sympathy and understanding was the only thing keeping her together sometimes.

"Yikes," Miranda said. "Burnett's hell reminds me of my mother's pot roast, tough and hard to swallow."

Della picked up her empty Diet Coke can and squeezed it into a little ball. She'd tried to sleep as Burnett ordered but had failed. In spite of feeling like an emotional wreck, she'd told them almost everything—about the werewolves at the graveyard, the vibrating box, the picture incident. She'd told them about Chase showing up, against Burnett's orders, and about her going to see the files at his cabin.

The thing she hadn't mentioned yet was all the Reborn stuff—that would have to wait for another day—too much spilling at one time could cripple a vampire.

She saw her phone sitting on the table and remembered she hadn't told them about Steve, either. But that was because there was nothing to tell. And yet the fact that several hours had passed and he hadn't called now pressed hard and heavy on her heart.

"So the names just completely disappeared?" Kylie asked, stuck on that, and with good reason—ghosts were Kylie's thing.

"Yeah," Della said.

Kylie contemplated it. "I don't think they were ever really there."

"I saw them," Della insisted, thinking Kylie would be the last person to question this.

"I'm not saying you're lying, just that the ghost made you think you saw them. Like a vision of sorts. Were you feeling the ghost when you saw the names?"

Della remembered feeling the cold off and on while at the graveyard.

"Yeah." She chewed on that a moment. "Does that make what I saw . . . less true?"

"Nah," Kylie said. "Ghosts don't normally lie. Is Burnett going to let you go visit the parents?"

"As soon as he gets the okay from the FRU for us to work the case. He was supposed to call, but that was hours ago." She glanced at her phone again and her mind went to the other call she waited on. The one from Steve.

Feeling her own heartache reminded her of hearing Miranda crying in the predawn hours.

Glancing at the witch, she asked, "Did you rescind your promise so you could tell us what's up?"

"Rescind what promise?" Kylie asked.

Della, all too willing to get the topic off of her issues and onto someone else's, focused on Kylie. "Our little witch is holding back."

With them zeroing in on her, Miranda slunk down in her chair guiltily.

Della pointed at the witch. "She was up crying at three this morning, but said she couldn't spill what was wrong because she promised someone she wouldn't tell."

"What's wrong, Miranda?" Concern laced Kylie's three words.

"I still can't talk about it. Not until . . ."

"Until what?" Della asked.

"Until someone else says something." Miranda cut her eyes to Della.

And, just like that, Della got the crazy feeling that this was about her.

"You know we won't say anything," Kylie offered.

"I know that." After staring at her hands, Miranda glanced back up at Della.

"Is this about me?" Della asked, hoping she was wrong, because then she'd really be pissed.

Her focus on Miranda came to a quick halt when she heard footsteps heading up to the cabin. She tilted her head to the side to listen to the cadence, and immediately she knew who it was.

Chapter Fourteen

Steve's knock on the door sounded too loud. Della considered hiding and telling her two roommates to lie.

"Come in," Kylie called out before Della could initiate her plan.

Steve opened the door. Della planted her eyes on him. Then Miranda let go of an awkward sigh. Shifting her focus back to Miranda, Della saw guilt flash in the girl's eyes. Well, crap! Whatever the little witch was hiding didn't just involve Della, it had something to do with Steve, too.

"What's going on?" Della muttered to the witch.

Miranda sank deeper into her chair as if guilt had her weighed down.

"Can I talk to you?" Steve asked, and his tone set Della's pulse to racing.

She looked at Steve, really looked, and the hurt in his eyes smacked Della in the heart so hard, she had no doubt it left a bruise.

Drawing in air, her lungs only accepted a tiny bit, making her breath shudder. She had no idea what this was about, but somehow, one thing was extra clear. Steve knew she'd been with Chase.

I didn't do anything wrong. I'm not guilty. But freaking hell if she didn't feel as if she'd been dipped, rolled, and deep-fried in the ugly emotion.

"I won't keep you long," he said, the somber sound of his tone echoing in Della's head.

"Sure." She picked up her phone so she wouldn't miss Burnett's call—a call that would once again put her with Chase.

Two choices, her mind chanted. *Let Steve go or refuse to work with Chase.*

She stood up, knowing what she had to do. Dread and nerve-splitting pain spilled out of her heart, into her chest, flowed into her limbs, and traveled all the way up to her scalp and down to her feet. Even her pinkie toe hurt.

She was five-foot-three of nothing but raw pain. But the only thing that would hurt worse than losing Steve was knowing she was hurting him.

Decision made. Ready to crash and burn, she started toward Steve.

Steve led the way through the woods. He seemed to know where he was going. She didn't even note his direction, she just followed, her heart and mind on what she had to do.

He never spoke; neither did she. Their footsteps seemed to be swallowed by the trees, as if they breathed in sound and not air.

He stopped at a spot right next to the swimming hole, abandoned by most of the campers due to the fall cold. The vampires, more resistant to the temperature than the others, still came here, but not nearly as much. It just seemed much more fun when all the campers participated.

Today, however, there were no sounds of laughter or splashing, the water lying so still, it became a mirror to the fall-dressed trees. Yellow and orange and an occasional patch of red leaves reflected on the quiet stillness of the lake. Della tried to pull some calm from the vision that some saw as beautiful. She failed. Fall meant death to the leaves, and Della sensed some part of her would die here today as well.

The sound of Steve's breathing had Della looking away from the water and to him.

His brown eyes reflected regret, sorrow, pain. And was that guilt?

"I can't do this anymore." They had spoken in unison, and the same words.

She saw the surprise on Steve's face that she knew she wore on hers. Her throat tightened.

"I didn't do anything wrong." She wasn't sure why she had to say it, but it felt important. Steve didn't deserve to feel betrayed. And maybe she didn't want to be thought of as a betrayer, either.

He took a step closer. So close, he could touch her if he chose to. He didn't choose to. And that almost brought her to tears. "Nothing's happened between—"

"I know." He stuffed his hands into his pockets. He shuffled his feet and stared down at the ground, but not before she saw that hint of what looked like guilt again. An ugly thought hit . . . had Steve betrayed her? Had he and Jessie hooked up? Had she been wrong to trust him?

"You?" she asked, and she didn't have to say more. When he looked up, she knew he understood her question.

"No. God, no." There was honesty in his tone and she believed him.

He exhaled and ran a hand over his face. "You were dying, Della," he stated as if he had a speech planned but forgot the beginning.

"That day, when Chase called me . . . he told me that you two would be bonded. I'd never heard of anything like that, but I also knew it didn't matter. If saving you meant losing you, I'd do it. But now . . ."

His eyes grew darker, and Della's grew moist. "You haven't lost me," she said. Suddenly wanting to take it all back. She couldn't lose him.

"Not completely, but . . ."

When he didn't continue, she said, "You told me you wouldn't let the bond thing change things," she reminded him, even though she knew letting go was right—even when she accepted this had to happen—but for some reason it still felt wrong.

"I know, and I thought I could do it. But when I think about you and him—"

"I haven't done anything. We haven't—"

He pulled a hand out of his pocket and pressed a finger over her lips. "I know." His warm touch brought more tears to her eyes and she felt a few slip from her lashes onto her cheek. "What we have"—he waved a hand between them—"it's real and I want it more than you know. But there's something—something between you and Chase, too. I saw it in the way you two looked at each other today."

He'd seen it? Seen it today? "What . . . ? How . . . ?"

"When Burnett called and you didn't show up, I went to Chase's cabin. I'd followed him there a while back."

Della remembered the bird, the one Chase had pointed out to her, and now she knew it had been Steve. "You have so little faith in me that . . ."

"It isn't you I don't trust. It's Chase. It's this whole bond thing. I've waited for weeks for you to assure me that it isn't real, that it means nothing, but you never have."

He swiped a hand over his forehead. "Not that I can blame you for that, either. You didn't want to lie to me, and when I saw the way you two looked at each other, I knew I couldn't do this anymore."

She felt the need to say something, but what? So she didn't speak, she just stood there and listened as he told her good-bye.

"All I've thought about these last few weeks is you and him. Holding my breath, waiting for the other shoe to drop. I've resorted to following him around. I'm so eaten up with jealously that I can't think straight. This isn't me. I hate feeling this way." He ran another hand over his face. "All my life, I've felt as if I took second place to my parents' careers. To their dreams, and their goals. I don't want to be someone's second anymore."

Damn that hurt. "You think you're second? How could—?"

He ignored her and continued, "Do you realize how long it took me to get you to even give me the time of day? And that low . . ." He paused as if admitting the truth cost him something—like pride. "Chase comes here, and in no time, he's got you wrapped up in him. I don't want to compete for your affection."

She wiped the tears from her face. "It's not a competition."

"It feels like it." He dropped his hands back in his pockets. "Besides, you just told me you couldn't do this, either. You know I'm right."

"Yeah." *But for different reasons.* She wasn't letting him go because she couldn't trust him, but because she thought she was hurting him.

He let out a big heartfelt puff of air. "We need to take some time."

Time? Another few tears slipped from her lashes. It looked as if he noticed because he started to reach for her.

"No." Confused, she held out her hand to stop his touch. He wasn't breaking up with her? Just wanting a reprieve. That felt . . . wrong.

He tried to reach for her again.

"I'm fine." Her voice trembled along with her heart with that bold-faced lie, but she reined in what little strength she had. No matter how much this hurt, she had to accept it was for the best.

He nodded, and again looked away as if struggling to find the right way to say something. But hadn't he already said it?

"I'm leaving," he finally blurted out.

She hadn't thought she could feel more pain, but his words did it. Steve was leaving. She wouldn't see him anymore. Her heart did a complete tumble in her chest.

The questions left her mouth before she could stop them. "Leaving Shadow Falls? Why? Where?"

"To France. There's a school in Paris. It's especially for shapeshifters. It's very elite, they only invite two or three a year, and both Perry and I were asked to attend for some special classes."

She heard it—the tiniest bit of pride in his voice. He was excited. He had a right to be, she told herself. Yet, all that pain twisted inside her until she felt anger. "Excuse me if I don't congratulate you." A voice inside her head said her rage was unjustified. Or was it? "How long have you known about the invitation?" The question came out like an accusation.

He stared at her, confused—or was that guilt again?

"How long?"

When he didn't answer, she blurted out her thoughts. "Are you just using this whole 'Chase' thing as a way to justify your leaving?"

He shook his head. "I found out a month ago, but I hadn't made up my mind about going."

He'd known about this for a month? A month that he'd been working his way into her heart, stealing kisses, making her care, and the whole time he'd been considering leaving?

She closed her eyes for a second, dealing with the swarm of emotions. His earlier words finally sank in. She snapped her eyes open. "Wait, did you say Perry's going?"

He nodded. "It's such an honor to be invited. He can't turn it down." She thought of her roommate/best friend losing her beloved Perry. The witch was going to be miserable, inconsolable. And Della would be right there with her. Hell, Della was even going to miss Perry.

Steve just stood there staring. Della blinked away a few more tears, knowing this was what her roommate had been holding back from her. Thankfully, she was so emotionally bombarded over Steve, over what Miranda was feeling, that she didn't have any angst to aim at the girl for keeping secrets.

Nope. All her angst went in one direction. Right at the sexy shape-shifter standing in front of her. "Enjoy France." She turned to walk away, but heard him say her name. For some unknown reason—just call her a masochist—she turned around.

"This isn't all about the school, Della! Did I want to go to the school? Hell, yes. Did I feel torn about going and leaving you? Yes. But then it occurred to me that it wasn't just about missing you that made me not want to go. It was about losing you. Losing you to Chase. And that's when I started questioning everything. And then I saw you two staring at each other and I knew . . . I knew that even if I passed up the school opportunity, there was a good chance I'd still lose you. There is something between you two and you need to figure it out. And I can't stick around and watch it without going crazy."

She nodded, giving him that much. But if he wanted her to say it was okay—okay that he'd pushed his way through her guard, gotten her to care about him, all the while knowing he was going to leave—well, that wasn't okay!

A month ago, she could have let him go and not hurt so much, if only he'd let her be. If only he hadn't pushed his way into her nightly runs. Into her life. Into her heart.

He started talking and she had to concentrate to hear his words, because on the inside all she could hear was her heart breaking. "The classes could last from three weeks to six months," he said, "depending on how things go. There is a chance that I could be accepted full-time, and that would mean four years, but that's a very small chance." His eyes grew wet with emotion and the knot in her throat doubled.

No matter why he was leaving, or if he was right or wrong, it was still hurting him. But was that her fault? He'd been the one initiating the kisses on all those late-night runs.

But now she saw the raw pain in his eyes. And damn it, she still cared. Cared because he was hurting.

A bolt of achiness shot right to her chest. How could his pain hurt her more than her own?

She wanted to fall right there on the ground and sob. No, not just sob, but beg him not to go. Beg him to understand the whole bond thing when she didn't understand it herself. How unfair was that?

"I imagine I'll be back in a few months," he said. "Maybe . . . maybe while I'm away you can . . ." He stared down at his feet for a second. "You need to figure out exactly what this bond thing is, and what it isn't. Maybe then we can . . . see how things stand."

She didn't know what to say. But those damn "maybes" hurt. Hurt too much to think, much less to try to form words.

Her phone rang and she knew it was Burnett telling her it was time to leave.

She didn't even answer it. "I have to go," she said, and she did.

In one leap, she was at the top of the trees. She left the stillness of the lake. She left Steve.

Would he even come and say good-bye? Or was this good-bye?

She heard him call her name, but this time, she didn't look back.

Chapter Fifteen

Kylie and Miranda sat ready, waiting and worried on the cabin porch. As she moved up the stairs, Della saw leftover tears in Miranda's eyes. A watery mist, much like the one Della would've had if she hadn't taken a few seconds to wipe away the evidence.

Della studied the pain in Miranda's eyes. Had she spilled to Kylie about Perry leaving? Probably.

Della would have loved to grab another Diet Coke and commiserate with the witch, or maybe even find some anger at her for keeping secrets, but she didn't have that luxury. And her emotional bank account was already overdrawn.

The call had been from Burnett, and he'd told her to be at his office in fifteen minutes. She had exactly ten minutes now to clean her face a little more and to bury her emotional havoc.

Stopping in front of her two friends, she said, "Burnett called and I have no time to chat. Sorry."

"But you're upset. You need to talk," Miranda spouted out as new tears pooled in her large green eyes. Eyes that showed just as much concern for Della as they did for her own pain.

"I'm fine," Della insisted. She started to stomp off, then stopped and looked back at Miranda, who'd stood up to stare at Della with a frown. "And you'll be okay, too."

Miranda nodded. "We'll get through this together, right?"

"Right," Della said, and because she didn't have a choice, she let the witch hug her—for a second. Then she ran inside and shut her bedroom door and let herself have a mini pity party.

Three minutes to spare, she lit out of her cabin door—waving at her two best friends, but not giving them time to say anything. Guilt for leaving Miranda in her crisis made her ascent slow, but Kylie was with Miranda, she told herself. And Kylie excelled at consoling. The chameleon always knew what to say, while Della always said the wrong thing.

Besides, burying all that raw pain had been hard, keeping it buried was going to be a bitch. Talking about it to her best friends would only make it harder. Heck, being around Chase would be tougher yet. But she would give it all she had. She had to. Her full-blown breakdown could come later. Commiserating with Miranda could come later. Natasha's problem—facing death—made Della's and her roommate's issues look small. And that's what Della needed to focus on, before it was too late.

Burnett informed them that Derek hadn't found any pictures of either of the girls on any of the social media sites. Which seemed odd. And after a rule-spouting, one-sided conversation from Burnett about safety and making their eight o'clock curfew, Della followed Chase into the parking lot to a bright blue car. Burnett had insisted they travel in cars during the light of day. He must have told Chase when he called him, because this was the same car that had been parked at his cabin.

Chase hit the clicker to unlock the vehicle. Della noted the model of the car this time. Camaro. She slid into the soft leather front passenger seat that screamed "expensive" right along with the car's name.

She almost stepped on a large bag on the floorboard.

"Sorry," he said. "I brought my camera. I can put it in the back."

"It's fine. I've got plenty of foot room."

When Chase settled behind the wheel, she stared straight ahead. Those words had been the first she'd spoken to him.

She hadn't had a chance . . . the moment she'd walked into the office where Burnett and Chase were, Burnett had started talking. During the camp leader's litany, she'd felt Chase studying her. She'd swallowed hard and tried to keep her face passive, hiding any remnants of pain.

She could still feel his gaze. He started the car. The engine came to life. She heard another soft vibrating noise and the car's top started pulling back. A cool breeze tossed a few strands of hair in her face.

She cut her eyes to the driver's side and reached deep for a subject as far removed from the pain pulsating just under her chest bone as she could find.

"Nice camera bag. Probably a nice camera inside," she said, glancing to the floorboard. "Nice ride." She looked up at the blue sky, filled with a few puffy white clouds. "Nice cabin earlier, too. Does the Vampire Council pay this well, or are you just independently wealthy?"

It appeared as if he wasn't going to answer, but then he slid his hand down the steering wheel with male pride. "I paid for this car myself. The cabin, I'm just renting, but I'm considering buying it. The council doesn't pay all that well."

"So, independently wealthy, huh?"

He shrugged. "Not independently. My parents. Since, to the

human world, I was dead, too, Jimmy, who found me, was able to finagle my father's will. All his money and life insurance funds went to a clinical study my father was helping with. But when I turned eighteen, Jimmy handed it over to me."

"Is Jimmy the one who took you in and raised you?" she asked. "The supernatural who isn't registered with FRU?"

He nodded and she could swear he flinched as if he regretted having told her about Jimmy. And that just made her want to know more. What all was Chase hiding? And why?

"Did this Jimmy know your father?" she asked, determined to unearth all Chase's secrets.

He drove out of the parking lot. His shoulders tightened. Was he not going to answer? Was he trying to come up with a lie?

"Yeah. They knew each other," he finally said, his voice mingled with the sound of the engine.

The car picked up speed. Della's hair whipped around her face. So she could see, and study his expression, she pulled it over her shoulder and held it bunched in her hand. If he lied, she might be able to detect it.

He looked at the road, but continued talking. She kept her eyes on his face and twisted her legs so she wouldn't step on his camera.

"They knew each other for almost a year." He didn't blink and appeared not to flinch.

Did she believe him? Yes, for some reason, she did. "Did your dad know Jimmy was a vampire?" she asked, sensing if he answered one question, he might be inclined to answer more.

She saw his Adam's apple shift as he swallowed. Was answering hard? If so, why?

"Jimmy worked part-time with my dad at a free clinic. He'd figured out that my dad was a carrier of the virus. He'd come clean to my dad."

"And your dad believed him? I mean, Jimmy just says, 'Hey, I'm a vampire and you're a carrier of a virus that can turn you into a vampire.' That's doesn't sound realistic." How many times had she considered how she might tell her parents about herself?

Chase glanced at her and he almost smiled, before looking back to the road. "Jimmy said he could prove it. He had my dad drive them out on some dirt road. He took off flying, and when that didn't work, he picked up my dad's Porsche. That got my dad's attention. Nobody messed with my dad's car."

The chuckle in Chase's voice spoke of his admiration for his dad, and Della couldn't help but wonder if that was why Chase had bought this car—because his dad would have liked it.

Chase focused on the street, making the turns and changing gears with ease. The engine purred. Della wasn't into cars, but she had to admit she liked how this one moved. The power. How Chase looked driving it. His hair in the wind, his confidence in the way he sat in the driver's seat and shifted gears.

"I'd love to have seen my dad's expression," Chase said, apparently still with his dad in his head. "It still took months before my dad agreed to have us tested."

"Who got tested?" Della asked.

"My sister and I." He stared at the road and his hands tightened on the wheel. "That's where we had been coming from when the plane crashed."

He'd never talked this much about himself, and she almost felt thirsty for the information, wanting more. "Is Jimmy a Reborn?"

Chase rolled his shoulders as if he was suddenly uncomfortable with the conversation. "Yeah." He cut his eyes to her. "In the glove compartment there's some hair-band thingies for your hair."

So you've had other girls in this car? She pushed that thought aside and went back to their conversation.

"Is he, the one who . . . are you bonded with Jimmy?"

"Yeah," he said.

She let that thought run through her head. "How does that feel?"

"What?" he asked.

"Being bonded to two . . ." She glanced at the glove compartment and thought about one of those hair-band thingies. "How many people are you bonded to?"

He glanced at her, his smile different this time, almost as if he had read her mind. "Careful, you almost sound jealous."

It wasn't jealousy, she wanted to insist, but couldn't think of how to explain what it was. Hell. She couldn't explain because she didn't understand it.

"I'm just curious how this works," she spit out. The wind snatched a few strands of hair loose and slapped them against her cheek. She should be used to the hair in her face—but obviously, sitting still in the wind and flying in wind felt different.

Leaning forward, she opened the glove compartment. A brand new pack of three elastic hair bands sat at her fingertips.

"I picked them up on the way here when Burnett said we had to use the car. My sister hated it when my dad put his top down. And the day was too pretty to drive with it up."

So, no girl? "Thanks," she said, and then for some reason, wished she hadn't. Being grateful to him felt wrong when she was hurting over . . . *Not now!* She needed to be thinking about Natasha.

Snatching one hair band from the pack, she shut the others back up and pulled back her hair. A new spray of fall sun peeked out from behind a white cloud and warmed Della's face.

He glanced at her, his smile gone. "I'm only bonded to Jimmy and you."

So many questions sat on the tip of her tongue. And not just to understand Chase, to unearth his secrets, but to understand what was happening to her. "How many can a vampire bond with? How many Reborns can we save?"

"It hasn't really been proven," he said, focusing solely on the road again.

"How many has this Jimmy bonded with?"

His hands tightened on the steering wheel, her question no doubt making him uneasy. She realized he was more comfortable talking about himself than Jimmy. Was he afraid she'd pass the info of an unregistered vampire to Burnett?

For a second, she wanted to tell him about her uncle, and how she hadn't told Burnett because she, too, feared he might be unregistered, but she wasn't ready to open up that much.

Face it, trust was earned. And Chase had yet to earn hers. But he was getting close, a voice inside her said. He was answering her questions.

"I wouldn't . . . I don't care if Jimmy is registered or not. I need to know all of this for me," she assured him.

You need to figure out exactly what this bond thing is, and what it isn't. Steve's words echoed inside her.

"I need to know," she repeated, again pushing back the pain.

He didn't look at her, but his shoulders loosened. "Jimmy has bonded with three, but the last time he almost died. And . . ."

"And what?" she asked when Chase paused.

He inhaled. "Each time a Reborn bonds, you give away some of your power. Jimmy is almost back to being a regular vampire now. He can't afford to do it again."

Della digested that. "Did you . . . lose power when you bonded with me?"

"Some." He leaned forward to see the freeway sign in the distance, then sped up and zipped past a car to enter the ramp.

So Chase had not only suffered, he'd given up power? And seeing him drive this car, she had a feeling power meant a lot to him.

He'd barely known her. Why had he done it?

"You shouldn't have . . ." She dropped back in her seat. "I still think I might have made it on my own."

"We all want to think that." He cut his gaze to her again and she spotted emotion in his gaze. "I don't regret it," he said in a tender voice.

She didn't want tender.

He shifted gears and she watched as he did it with ease.

"You know how to drive?" he asked, probably having seen her watching him.

"Of course."

"Stick shift?"

"No."

"I'll teach you."

"That's okay," she said, but she couldn't deny it looked more fun that driving an automatic. "I wouldn't want to wreck your car."

"If you wrecked it, I'd just buy another one."

"Stop," she said.

"Stop what?"

"Being nice."

He laughed.

She lowered her attention away from Chase and his niceness to the files tucked tightly between the seats—the files with the addresses of both Natashas.

At least they'd have a last name soon. Would that help find her? For some reason the ghost seemed to think so. And Della could only hope.

Find Natasha.

Della flinched at the sound of the voice. This time she didn't question if she'd really heard it or just conjured up the memory of the voice.

She'd heard it. Goose bumps tickled the back of her neck, as if the words brought on a chill.

The ghost was here.

Della cut her eyes to the tiny backseat. Empty. Maybe the ghost wasn't actually in the car, just buried in her head.

The car's engine roared louder. She glanced again at Chase. His hands gripped the wheel so tightly his knuckles were white.

"You heard it, too, didn't you?"

"Shit, yeah," he said, completely understanding what she meant. Then the car shot forward.

As if trying to outrun the ghost.

But if what Holiday and Kylie said about ghosts and their perseverance was true, Chase's Camaro didn't stand a chance.

Chapter Sixteen

"That's it." Less than an hour later, Chase inched his car in front of a one-story, redbrick house with lots of windows. Located in a small town outside of Houston, it was off a dirt road, not in a sub-division. Larger than the house Della grew up in, it had a wrap-around porch with a wicker swing that swayed ever so slightly in the afternoon breeze. A big live oak tree, twice as tall as the house, stood to the right of the property, and a tire swing dangled from a rope. It looked aged, as if it had been someone's play toy and they'd outgrown it.

But something about the home spoke of family, a place where on lazy Sunday afternoons, people who loved each other gathered out front to eat homemade ice cream. Della remembered doing that on her parents' back patio when she'd been part of a loving family. Or at her Aunt Miao's when they'd go for dinners.

Pushing past that thought, she noted the untended gardens lining the front of the house. The sign of neglect hinted that all those loving times had somehow become lost.

Was this where Natasha had lived? Where her parents still lived and grieved for their daughter who they thought was dead? Who would be dead if Della and Chase couldn't find her?

Tension filled Della chest. Was the sadness she felt from this place imagined, or was this somehow a clue?

She almost asked Chase if he felt it, but worried it sounded crazy.

The tires of Chase's car slowly crunched over the gravel as he came to a complete stop. He cut off the engine and turned his head to the side just as she did, to see if they could catch any sounds inside the house.

"No one seems to be home," she said.

"Maybe they're at work," Chase said. "Or maybe they're just resting and not moving around. The car could be in the garage." He dipped down a little and studied the attached garage.

Today had been one of those days that she'd lost track of time, so she pulled out her phone to see the hour. "It's almost five." Dropping the phone in her lap, she pulled out the files. "Is this the Owen or the Brian house?"

"The Owens," Chase answered.

Della looked at the information they had on the file—basically names and the address of the parents, the name of the graveyard where a casket was placed in the ground to make her parents believe Natasha Owen was dead. It was the same graveyard Chan and other fresh turns held their fake funerals. The one where Chan's body really was buried now. She looked up through the windshield at the lowering sun. The day was on its way out. The sky already had a dusky look to it.

"You want to knock on the door just in case?" he asked.

She glanced back at him. They hadn't come up with a sure bet plan. She just wanted to check and see if one of the parents was Asian.

"I guess," she said, her mind churning, still feeling the unexplainable sadness and loneliness. Was it because of this house, or were her emotions over Steve leaving finally sneaking out?

Chase's gaze stayed on her eyes for a second longer than needed. He leaned in, bringing his face closer to hers . . . his mouth closer to hers. She jerked back, hitting her shoulder on the car door.

"I wasn't . . ." Frowning, he turned to snatch something from the backseat. When he pulled back, he dropped some papers in her lap. "I was just getting this. I thought we could say we were selling magazines to help pay for a trip to Mexico to help build houses for the poor."

Annoyed at her overreaction, she muttered, "Then maybe you should drive a few blocks up and hide the car."

"Why?" he asked.

"Because people who drive souped-up Camaros don't sell magazines to help the poor." Della inwardly flinched. Why was she being a bitch?

"Fine." His frown deepened. He drove down the dirt road and around a curve so the car was hidden from the home's view. When he parked, he looked back at her. "But you're wrong. My sister and I did this twice a year. And you probably could have papered the whole state of Texas with the amount of magazines my mom bought. Of course, she'd turn around and donate them to shelters. Most of them before she even opened them."

"Sorry." Now even more embarrassed, she got out of the car with the paperwork on selling magazines in her hand.

He did the same, and in the blink of an eye, he stood at her side. "I didn't take you for the prejudiced type. What do you have against people with money?"

"I'm not . . . prejudiced. I apologized." She shut his car door, and the sound seemed to echo through the semi-wooded area that surrounded them. Feeling almost watched, she looked around at the Lots for Sale sign staked in the ground. A few large and beautiful trees had already been cut down and lay dead in the thick brush.

"So, it's just me?" He stepped closer, and she took a tiny step back. Her backside came against the car.

"Yeah. It's you." She said the truth. "And all this. I'm on edge."

"But you blame me, huh?" His closeness seemed to be a challenge. She didn't move, not wanting him to know it disturbed her so much.

"Blame you for what?" She tilted up her chin and met his eyes.

"Steve leaving."

She frowned. "How did you know?"

"Today, after I left Burnett's office, I heard someone say Steve was leaving."

Emotion—anger, hurt, and maybe even some guilt—worked its way from that place she'd buried it earlier. The realization that Steve had told everyone he was leaving before he'd told her did a real number on her heart. She hated that number. She swallowed a knot that appeared in her throat. But the damn thing wouldn't go down. It just grew bigger.

"I'm sorry," Chase said, so close his breath tickled her temple.

That's all it took. His breath and two words to gather all the emotion rising inside her and target it right at him. "Don't lie. You're not sorry." She hit his chest with the palm of her hand.

He didn't budge. He kept staring at her, into her eyes, as if he could read her heart, her mind, and her pain. And for that one second, she didn't think there were any secrets between them. He knew everything. More than he pretended to know. He knew all her failings, all her regrets.

She didn't like anyone knowing her that well.

"You're right," he said, his voice deep and sincere. "I'm not sorry Steve is leaving. I'm not sorry that I get a chance to prove to you that you and I belong together. But don't you dare doubt that I'm sorry you're hurting. The pain in your eyes when you walked into that office, the pain you're working so hard to hide, I saw it. I feel it. And for that, damn it, I'm sorry."

She didn't know when she'd started crying. She wasn't an easy crier. But she'd lost Steve. And yet here she was less than a few hours later with Chase. Feeling guilty, telling herself that the only reason she was here was about the case, but down deep she knew it was more. She leaned her head forward, resting it on Chase's chest, and let a few more tears fall. His arms came around her and he held her.

And as crazy as it seemed, it felt right. So right. And yet, still wrong. So damn wrong.

She stepped to the side, out of his embrace, and swatted at the tears on her face. "We should go see if anyone is home," she said, working to keep her voice from shaking.

He nodded, stepping closer, and with one finger, he wiped away a tear she must have missed. "It's going to be okay. Believe me."

She turned and started walking. Then a realization hit.

Hit hard.

Hit fast.

She did believe him. But she didn't know what "okay" was, or what it meant. Because everything in her life was changing. Again. And she hated change.

No one answered at the Owen house, so they left to go to the Brian's place, which was about twenty miles away. Della didn't talk for the first fifteen minutes. Neither did Chase.

All she'd done was rest her head on his chest. Let him put his arms around her. Why did it seem like more?

The answer came. Came with clarity. Because she'd leaned on him. Physically. Emotionally.

Della Tsang didn't lean on people. At least not many people. Definitely not someone she barely knew. Especially not someone who had basically caused the problem plaguing her.

Fracking hell. She was so damn confused.

She glanced up at the cars moving willy-nilly on the four-lane freeway, her emotions experiencing the same kind of traffic.

A green Saturn jumped lanes two cars ahead. Houston drivers drove like werewolves trying to reach a fresh kill before another wolf got all the good parts. She suddenly recognized the stretch of freeway. They were only a few miles from the turnoff to her neighborhood. And just like that, mentally she was back in the car with her dad when he taught her to drive.

It's the same as playing chess. You have to be on the offensive and the defensive. You have to guess what the man in the car beside you is going to do.

Funny thing was, he never lost his temper with her, not even when she accidentally pulled into the side of the garage and ran over his golf clubs. Her chest grew heavier remembering what Derek had told her about the calm and gentle man who'd raised and loved . . . used to love her. The police suspected he had been the one who murdered his sister, Bao Yu. It just couldn't be.

He never hit her or her sister. He didn't need to. The look of disappointment in his eyes was punishment enough for both her and Marla. Right then, a new pain wiggled its way into her heart. She missed them. Missed them so badly it hurt.

She pushed a finger against her temple, wondering why she was suddenly thinking about all that.

"Damn!" Chase seethed.

Della jerked her gaze up as a red van shot into Chase's lane. He swerved, tires screeching, into the left lane between two speeding cars. Then the car in front of them slammed on its brakes. Chase did the same, and then to prevent rear-ending that car, he jumped back into the other lane. Horns blew all around them.

Della saw the accident in her mind: cars piling up, people hurt, blood, lots of blood. But Chase somehow, God only knew how, managed to keep from being hit.

Chase, hands still grasping the wheel, muttered another curse. Della, adrenaline shooting into her veins, let go of a deep breath. Then she glanced out the side window to see a gold Honda pulling up beside her.

In slow motion, she saw the driver start to turn his head.

"Shit!" With super vampire speed, she unlocked her seat belt. Her gaze darted to the floorboard, already occupied by the huge, expensive camera bag. She did the only thing she could to hide from the other driver—she threw herself over the console, between the gearshift and the seats, and plopped her face in Chase's lap.

"Frack!" he muttered, as his butt shot up from the seat at least two inches. He groaned.

Perhaps her chin had come in contact with his boys. She did have a pretty hard chin. But she didn't care. Oh, she cared. Being here was the last place she wanted to be. But she wasn't moving. Couldn't.

If it was a choice between burying her face in Chase's crotch or letting her father see her driving around Houston in a zippy-looking Camaro with a good-looking guy, she'd go with Chase's crotch. Her father would have a shit fit.

He'd probably pull her out of Shadow Falls and stick her butt in some reform school. She couldn't lose Shadow Falls. Couldn't lose Kylie, Miranda, Holiday, Burnett, and even little Hannah Rose. Chase's crotch was a better choice. And she was going to stay there, nose-deep, until he got off the freeway. But if he farted, she would have to kill him!

Chapter Seventeen

"Della?" Chase hissed.

"Get off the freeway," she snapped, then she remembered her dad's exit was next. "No, don't get off the freeway." She turned her head to the side a little and the tip of her nose shifted across his zipper.

"Della?" he said, firmer. "What the hell are you doing?"

You mean other than trying not to think about where my face is? "What do you think I'm doing?" Then, realizing what his answer might be, she added, "Forget I asked that. I'm hiding. My dad's in the gold Honda in the lane to the right."

"Shit," he said.

"I already said that," Della spit out. And then another wave of panic set in. "Did he see me? Is he staring at the car?"

"No," he said.

"Then why did you say 'shit'?"

"Because . . ."

"Did I hurt you?" she asked, remembering how hard she'd slammed into his lap, and feeling her face getting warm with embarrassment.

"A little."

"Sorry," she said, patting the side of his leg before she realized how awkward that would feel. Her hands on his leg. Then again, why should patting his leg be awkward when she had her nose in his private parts?

The next noise he made was a chuckle. Deep, honest, and almost musical. It still pissed her off.

"Don't laugh," she said between tightened lips.

"Sorry, it's funny."

"No, it's not," she snapped back.

"Oh, yes it is." She felt his hand gently brush some of her hair from her cheek. The car's emergency brake handle bit into her ribs.

She closed her eyes, the heat of humiliation burning all the way inside her chest. "Has he turned off the freeway yet?"

"Not yet," he said. "Just stay there." His finger brushed over her ear, as if tracing the outer edges.

"Are you watching the road?" she blurted out.

"Yes."

"Then quit playing with my ear."

He laughed again. "You're worried about your ear?"

She moaned.

He chuckled again. "Try not to move too much."

Could someone die of embarrassment? Della wondered. And after a couple of seconds, she asked, "You're not lying, are you?"

"About what?"

"About my dad still being on the freeway."

"No. I'm not lying. He's about to pull off. I'll tell you when it's clear." He paused one second. "Clear."

She raised up. And with no other option, she looked at him. He burst out laughing.

"Your face is so red," he said between gulps of laughter.

She growled at him, and then for reasons she couldn't explain, it all of a sudden seemed funny to her, too. The chuckle leaked out and she couldn't stop it.

They laughed practically all the way to the second address.

They made it back at 7:59. One minute before curfew. Burnett sat outside on the office porch, his phone in his hand, when they walked up. Della hadn't reached the office yet when it hit her. The whole Steve leaving issue.

"I was just about to call you," Burnett said, and stood up to open the cabin door. Chase and Della followed him into Holiday's office.

"Anything?" he asked as he moved toward the desk.

Della suddenly wished she'd told Chase not to mention the near disaster of almost running into her dad. Knowing Burnett, the least little thing would put him back into protective mode where she was concerned.

"The Owen family wasn't home," Chase said.

Della held her breath, hoping and praying he didn't bring it up, and ready to intervene with some other subject if he did.

"We did drop in on the Brian family," Della added.

"Did you get anything there?" Burnett leaned against Holiday's desk.

"Yeah. Both the parents are white." Della filled Burnett in about knocking on their door trying to sell magazines.

"I knew that," Burnett added. "Right after you left, the DMV finally sent me over copies of their driver's licenses. I also got both Mr. and Mrs. Owen's. White as well."

Della nodded. "But as you said . . ."

"It could just mean they aren't her biological parents," Burnett finished her sentence for her.

"I still believe it's one of them," Della said. "Actually, I think she's Natasha Owen." The moment she said it, she felt certain. "If we'd had time, we would have gone back by their house." She'd almost called Burnett and asked for an extended curfew, but being her first night to work the case, she knew he'd balk. "But if we left now—"

"No, it's late. You need rest. You can go tomorrow evening." Burnett ran a hand through his hair and looked over at the door. Della could hear someone coming up the office steps outside. Then she heard a baby's coo.

"Why do you think her name is Owen?" Burnett asked, cutting his eyes to the door, obviously waiting for his wife and child to walk in.

Della looked at Chase. She hadn't asked him earlier. Probably because she hadn't wanted to think about it. "I felt something at her house. A sadness. I think the ghost was there. I didn't feel that at the Brians' house."

Chase's brow tightened.

"Did you feel it, too?" she asked him.

"Yeah," he said. "But I was hoping I imagined it."

Me, too, Della thought, but didn't say it.

"Fine," Burnett said. "You can go back tomorrow. Maybe you'll find something out."

"Not so fast," Holiday said, standing in the door with a baby on her hip. "I'm a little worried about this."

Hannah Rose started flapping her hands at the sight of her father. Burnett reached for her, pulling the little bundle close to his chest. "I've checked with the local authorities on both the Brian family and the Owens. Neither have any criminal history. I don't think they pose any danger."

Holiday frowned. "It's not them I'm worried about." The red-haired fae's gaze went from Della to Chase.

"Then who?" Della asked, almost certain the woman was going to say something about Chase. Chase's shoulders tightened as if he had the same thought.

"The ghost," Holiday said.

"Why would the ghost hurt us?" Della asked. "All she wants is for us to find Natasha."

"I agree," Chase said.

"Maybe." Holiday reached for a strand of hair and twirled it. "But she managed to bring both of you into a vision, and if she did what Burnett told me, with those names on the back of the picture, then she's pretty powerful. A ghost with that kind of power, and that desperate, can be dangerous. Even if their intentions aren't evil. Spirits have been known to cause mud slides, tornados. The last twenty-car pileup that happened in L.A. was because of a spirit."

Della thought of the near accident on the freeway. That wasn't the ghost, was it? Why would she attempt to hurt them if they were trying to help her?

"I'm not going to stop looking for Natasha," Della insisted, and shot Chase a glance hoping to communicate to him not to mention the near accident. If Holiday or Burnett thought the ghost was dangerous, they'd be even more out to put a stop to this.

Chase's eyes widened as if he recalled the accident. Della shook her head so slightly.

Holiday spoke up again. "I'm not suggesting you stop. Just make her give you a little more information before she sends you off on more wild-goose chases."

Della appreciated Holiday's concern but . . . "You said ghosts do what they want, when they want. It's not like I can text her to send me some info."

"But if you stop following her leads, she'll be forced to give you something else. The more she gives you, the more able you'll be to figure this out."

"I don't want to stop," Della said, and the ghost didn't want her to stop, either. She felt it, didn't like feeling it, but she did. "Natasha and Liam are going to die if we don't find them. And fast."

Della saw it in Holiday's eyes again. She didn't think they were alive. "Don't say it," Della said, tilting up her chin in defiance.

"Don't say what?" Chase asked.

Della glanced at him. "I told you, she thinks they're already dead."

"They're not dead," Chase said, with the same conviction as Della.

Find Natasha!

The voice came so loud in her head, Della flinched. When she looked at Chase, he had his eyes closed. He'd heard it, too.

"I know it's hard to accept, but we don't know that they're alive," Holiday said.

Instantly, the temperature in the room dropped so fast that steam billowed out of everyone's lips as they breathed. A glass vase of flowers sitting on the edge of Holiday's desk burst. The glass fell to one side, the water another. The water turned to beads of ice like that fancy dot-like ice cream, and all those tiny ice beads rolled around the desk until they formed letters.

A
L
I
V
E

Right after the E formed, the door to Holiday's office slammed shut with such a loud crack it sent an echo through the frosty air. All the little balls of ice ran off the desk and bounced around the floor, making tapping sounds until they melted.

Della held her next breath, too scared to breathe. She saw the same raw panic on Chase's face. Burnett clutched his daughter closer.

Holiday simply lifted her right brow. "So, okay," she said, sounding completely calm. "Maybe they're alive."

Thirty minutes later, Della and Chase were dismissed after more words of caution, but a commitment from both Holiday and Burnett, and even a coo of approval from Hannah, to move forward on the investigation.

Burnett had agreed they could go tomorrow afternoon to see if the Owen family might be home. They were also going to hang around the neighborhood where Liam lived to see if they could get anything there.

Burnett was going to go back and interview the men arrested with the Craig Anthony case and see if he could "persuade" them to give up any info on the last missing vampires. By the look of worry in the stern vampire's eyes, Della wasn't sure she wanted to know what type of persuasion he'd use.

As they walked out onto the porch, Chase stayed close to her side. Under the almost full moon, she moved off the cabin's porch and turned toward the trail back to her cabin.

"Walk me to the car," he said under his breath.

"Why?" An image of Steve from earlier with so much pain in his eyes filled Della's head and heart, and the guilt from earlier tap-danced its way into her conscience.

Frowning, Chase cut his eyes back to the cabin, as if saying he wanted to make sure no one was listening.

Oh, hell, she'd walk him to the car. She'd spent the day with him, she could handle a few more minutes. Besides, a little guilty voice whispered, Steve's leaving.

When they passed through the gate into the parking lot, Chase's shoulder brushed against hers and she did a quick sidestep. He looked at her and frowned, and then spoke. "That was scary."

"Don't worry, I'll protect you," she said with sass.

He glared at her. "Do you always have to be a smartass?"

"Only with special people," she said.

"So, you admit I'm special." He smiled. But the smiled vanished quickly. He ran a finger under her eye. "You do look tired."

She moved his finger away. "I'm fine." But in truth, he was right. She was tired. Borderline exhausted. And she hadn't even started to digest everything that had happened today.

He nodded. "Do you think it was the ghost who almost caused the accident on the highway?"

A tickle of fear stirred in her gut thinking the ghost had that much control. "I don't see why she would do it."

"I know, but it was weird. I don't know if you saw it, but all the cars started going a little crazy right before it happened. And for a second there, it almost felt like the car was driving itself."

"You think she possessed your car? Possessed a bunch of cars on the freeway?" Della asked, not wanting to believe it. Nope. Didn't want to!

"After what she did in there, I think it's possible. Besides, Holiday said—"

"No." Della shook her head. "She did the freaky ice thing in there to prove to a point. She didn't need to prove anything on the highway."

He exhaled as if he only halfway believed her. To be honest, she only halfway believed herself.

"All I know is I don't like it." Chase lowered his voice as if afraid the ghost might be listening. "And I want you to tell her to stop this crap. Let her know we'll do our best to find Natasha and Liam, but stop messing with my car and my head."

"Wait," Della said. "Let me see if I understand . . . you want *me* to tell her this?" Sarcasm spilled out with her words.

"Yeah," he said as if he didn't understand her issue.

"Why don't you tell her?" Della slipped a hand to her hip.

He made a face. "She's your ghost."

"My ghost? Why the hell is she *my* ghost?"

"Because she's closer to you."

"Says who?"

He opened his mouth and nothing came out right away. Then words spurted out of his lips. "Because . . . Because she . . ." His eyes widened as if he'd figured something out. "Because she gave you the picture of Natasha. And Natasha has some connection to your family."

His reasoning made sense, perfect sense, but Della didn't want to see it that way. Refused to see it that way. She didn't want to be alone in this with some dead person. Sharing it with *him* wasn't the ideal situation, but she hadn't come up with this plan.

"That doesn't make her mine," Della insisted. "She talks to both of us. We've got joint custody here, buddy. You should have thought about this before you bonded with me. And don't you try to skip out of your responsibility."

"It's a ghost," he said. "Not a baby."

"Same thing!" she muttered and turned to walk away.

"There's a big difference." His words still reached her ears. "Bye," he said when she didn't stop walking. "See you tomorrow."

"Bye," she offered, but didn't look back.

She started down the dark trail. An achiness swelled in her chest. Each step toward her cabin hurt just a bit more. Hurt as if she was walking away from something that felt like home, instead of going to it. The sensation of being alone consumed her.

Or maybe not so alone.

A strange, repetitive whooshing noise came behind her. A kind of scary, repetitive whooshing noise. Her heart did a small tumble.

Did ghosts whoosh? And smell like . . . fowl?

Chapter Eighteen

Refusing to give in to the urge to run like hell, Della swung around, her canines already out and her eyes feeling tight as if glowing.

The damn huge bird cocked its head and looked at her. "It's just me." Perry's voice came out of the bird's beak as sparkly bubbles started popping off, signaling that the shape-shifter was changing form.

"You realize I could have ripped your head off," she seethed, watching the bird fade and Perry appear.

"Because I scared you, or because you're mad at me?" he asked, his words a little slurred due to his beak being in the process of turning into lips. Della looked away—it was too creepy to watch.

Staring at the woods, it took only the tiniest fraction of a second to remember why she would be mad. Perry was leaving. And forget the fact that she would miss the twerp. One of her best friends was going to be devastated.

Della didn't like people devastating someone she cared about. Even when the person doing the disappointing was also a friend.

She swung back around. "Definitely because I'm mad. And I

wasn't scared!" Her heart thumped to the tune of a lie, but shape-shifters couldn't hear that, so her little white fib didn't count. "Do you know what your leaving is going to do to Miranda?"

He frowned and kicked at the dirt. "It's going to hurt me, too. But what am I supposed to do? Turn it down? It's my one chance to maybe . . ."

"Maybe what?" Della asked.

"Nothing," he said.

"Don't 'nothing' me! What were you going to say?"

He kicked at another rock on the ground. "To change things."

"Change what?"

"Me," he said.

Della shook her head. "There's nothing wrong with you."

"Right," he said as if he thought she was making shit up. Couldn't he see she was too tired to make shit up right now?

"What's wrong with you?" she asked, suddenly realizing she didn't understand why Perry was going to the fancy school. She got why Steve would go. They were going to give him a crash course in supernatural medicine. But Perry wasn't into medicine.

"Spill it, bird boy!" Della snapped. "I'm dead tired and don't want to dance around this conversation."

"Haven't you noticed I have to hide on parents' day? And if Burnett uses me in a case, I have to go in already shifted?"

"Why?"

"Because I can't control things."

"What things?" Della asked.

"My eye color. And when I get mad I . . . shift without meaning to."

Della thought back. "So you turned into a dragon and a super-sized lion once or twice. That's not the end of the world."

"Not here, it's not, but if it's in the human world, it could stir up a lot of shit."

Della couldn't deny it. It would make national news. She could see CNN covering it now. They'd probably blame it on one of the political parties. That, or stem cell research. "And you really can't control it?"

"I wish."

Her heart, already broken in a hundred different ways, still hurt for the guy. "Then go and learn how to control yourself and come back. Miranda is bonkers about you, I'm sure she'll wait."

"She shouldn't."

"What?" Della asked. "Oh, crap! Please tell me you aren't breaking up with her."

"Not breaking up, just taking a break."

"It still has the word 'break' in it, idiot. You can't do that to her!"

"You and Steve did it."

Della's mouth dropped open. "No. Steve and I weren't together. You can't break up when you're not made up." It was another lie, emotionally—they had made up and made out, but she ignored that point, ignored the sting of pain connected to the lie. Right now, she just felt for Miranda.

"Why the hell are you doing this?" Della seethed.

His blue eyes tightened. "She needs to figure out what she wants."

"Duh, she already has! She wants you." And that's when a thought hit. And that thought shot to her gut, burned, and completely pissed her off. Being pissed off took the edge off her exhaustion.

"Is this about sex?" she asked. "Because if this is about sex, I'm gonna open up a huge can of whoop ass on your butt."

Her question seemed to shock him. "It's not . . . I mean . . ."

"Boys!" she seethed. She moved in and poked the shape-shifter in his chest. "Listen to me, you little horny twerp! Nobody should be forced to do something they're not comfortable doing. Especially when it involves getting naked."

"It's not . . . You don't understand."

"Oh, I understand all right." She gave Perry another poke. "Guys are jerkoffs who think if they can't get what they want from a girl, they'll just move on and get it from someone else."

"Stop," he ordered, his tone deep and vibrating with frustration. "You don't understand."

His eyes grew a bright red. He was about to shift into something big and mean, but in the mood Della was in, she'd be happy to take him on. That can of whoop ass was begging to be opened. But before he started shifting, the coward turned and walked away.

"That's right," she called after him. "You'd better tuck your tail and run." Then it hit her. "By the way, you were able to control yourself right then! You don't need to go to Paris. Stay with Miranda."

He didn't answer. Just kept walking. Angry, she started running back to her cabin, ready to find a crying Miranda. Much to her surprise, only silence met her when she entered the door.

Silence and a cold chill.

She stopped and looked around, waiting for ice pebbles to start dropping. But then the cold evaporated. Telling herself she'd imagined it, she started toward her bedroom, but spotted the note waiting on the kitchen table. Edging closer, almost afraid it was left by the ghost, she relaxed when she saw it was written in Kylie's handwriting.

Della, we didn't know when you'd be back. Miranda went to a witch meeting and I'm with Lucas. But if you need us, call, and we'll both be back in a snap. I'll listen to both you and Miranda whine.

Best buds forever!

Della sighed. "You two are the best." She almost pulled her phone out, but she didn't want to come off as needy. She'd see them when they got home. Walking into her bedroom, her gaze zeroed in on the bed.

Instantly, all she wanted to do was crawl in and lose herself to slumber. She didn't want to think. Didn't want to cry. Sleep and forget. An hour, maybe two. Since she'd been Reborn, that was all she really needed to refresh her.

She fell back on the bed, her eyes shut by the time her body hit and bounced on the mattress. Sleep lingered seconds away, so close she could touch it, but her phone, still tucked in her pocket, dinged with a text.

Don't look at it, a voice whispered inside her head. She moaned, then, unable to stop herself, she yanked her cell from her pocket and rolled over onto her stomach. She had to concentrate to get her eyes open.

The second she saw the number, she dropped her head, face-down, on the pillow. And the pain she'd been pushing back rose up in her chest.

Lifting up again, she read the message.

Hey . . . I think it would be easier to just say good-bye this way. I'll miss you. Bye, Steve.

He'd inserted an unhappy face. As if the unhappy face would make her feel better. She dropped her face back into the pillow and cried herself to sleep.

Two hours later, Della awakened to someone walking up the cabin steps. She lifted her heavy lids and took in a noseful of air to see if she could identify the visitor. The door to the cabin opened and

Della recognized the fresh, herby smell that belonged to a certain witch. Remembering her brief encounter with Perry, Della's heart instantly went to aching for the girl.

Miranda inched open her door and stuck her head in. "You awake?"

Della sat up. "Yeah. But no hugs, okay?" The words were out of her mouth before she saw the look in the girl's puffy eyes.

Della hadn't been the only one crying tonight. Right then, she wished she'd kicked Perry's ass.

Miranda didn't deserve this.

And Miranda deserved better than Della. The witch deserved Kylie. Kylie knew how to deal with heartbreaks. Della always said the wrong thing. Even when she tried really hard.

"Are you okay?" Miranda asked her.

The witch was hurting, breaking inside, Della could almost hear it, and yet the sincerity in Miranda's voice said the girl was worried about her.

"You know me, nothing fazes me." Her heart did tumbles at that huge lie.

"What did Steve want?" Miranda asked.

"To end it," Della said, biting back any sound of weakness.

"I wish I was more like you," Miranda said.

No you don't. "How are you?" Della asked, because it seemed the right thing to say, but she really didn't have to ask. Miranda's pain hung in the air like a cloud.

"Hur . . . ting." Miranda's breath shook as she drew in air.

Damn it, Miranda was her friend. "Okay, one hug," Della conceded. She could suffer through one, then hopefully Miranda would go to bed.

The witch barreled into the room, dropped down on the bed, and wrapped her arms around Della. And it wasn't the just-one-

and-go-to-bed kind of hug. It was the kind that said she didn't want to let go.

And as crazy as it felt, neither did Della. She wanted to hang on to the way things had been. *It's going to be okay.* She heard Chase's words, but Della knew "okay" meant Steve wouldn't be around. And neither would Perry.

Chapter Nineteen

"I just . . . don't get this whole . . . take time off crap," Miranda cried into Della's shoulder. "People don't do that."

Yeah, they do. The witch's hot tears seeped into Della's shirt and she thought of all the people lately who'd walked out of her life. Then, finally uncomfortable with the clinging, she managed to pull out of Miranda's arms. Hugs should never last more than fifteen seconds.

"It's going to be okay." Della repeated Chase's words, but without the same conviction as when he'd said it. What she wanted to say was all this sucked. And at the top of the sucky list was the fact that Della sucked at consoling people.

"No, it won't!" Miranda snapped. "I told him I would wait on him. Three weeks, months, years. I don't care. But he said no, that it wasn't fair to ask me to wait. Then he said that if I still loved him when he came back, that we'd walk off into the sunset and be happy."

"The sunset? Who even says shit like that?" Della bellowed, saying the first thing that came to her mind, and from the expression in Miranda's eyes, perhaps it was the wrong thing.

Miranda took some hiccupy breaths, sobbed into her hands for a good minute, then looked up with mascara-induced raccoon eyes.

"Do you want me to walk you to bed?" Della asked, hoping the witch would say yes before Della said something that made it worse.

Miranda either didn't hear her, or couldn't in her mental state. "I asked him about him still loving me. Do you know what he said?"

"Something terrible, I'm sure," Della answered.

"He said that he couldn't imagine not loving me."

"Bastard," Della said, still giving it her best shot, but cringing at her lack of consoling ability.

"Then he said we needed to look at this rationally." Miranda let out a high-pitched moan. "He's acting like such a . . . an adult!" She spit the last word out like it tasted bad on her tongue.

"Yeah, who wants that?" Della said.

"I know. I don't want to be adult about this," Miranda continued. "I know a long-distance relationship would be hard, but does he care so little about me that he doesn't want to try? He's just going to give up. I guess I'm not worth at least trying to make us work."

A lump formed in Della's chest. Wasn't that exactly how she felt about Steve? He was giving up on her, on them, and even with her confused feelings for Chase, she hadn't been ready to give up on Steve.

Oh, she knew it wasn't fair to want to hang on to him, but dad-blast it, it hurt.

"I'm so sorry," Della said, this time with complete honestly and she gave the witch another hug, her heart aching right along with Miranda's.

. . .

An hour later, Della lay in silence. Miranda, taking up half of Della's pillow, had cried herself to sleep.

Della heard Kylie walk into the cabin. The chameleon stopped in the living room and listened. Probably turned vampire to tune in to her super hearing to see who all was home.

She moved to Della's door and cracked it open. It only creaked once.

"Shh," Della said in a voice lower than a whisper. "If you wake her up, you're in charge of getting her to sleep next time. It took five hugs."

Della crept out of the bed with the slowness of an inchworm.

Kylie stepped back into the living room and Della cautiously and silently shut the door. They moved all the way outside to the front porch. They each sat down at the edge and let their feet hang down a few inches from the grass.

"I'm sorry." Kylie looked at her and nipped at her bottom lip. "I should've come home hours ago. Holiday asked if Lucas and I would go to Walmart. They ran out of eggs and asked if we'd make an emergency run. I called Miranda and she said she was fine. I didn't think you'd gotten home yet. And I didn't know it would take that long."

"It's okay," Della said.

Kylie looked back toward the door. "Was she an emotional wreck?"

"She's just Miranda," Della said.

"So she was an emotional wreck." Kylie smiled sadly. "And you dealt with her while you're hurting, too. Damn."

"I'm fine," Della said.

"Liar." Kylie, obviously still in vamp mode, titled her head slightly to the side as if hearing Della's heart stumble.

"Okay, I'm hurting, but I'm tougher."

"No," Kylie said. "You're just better at pretending." She gave Della the look that said "spill." "What did Steve want?"

Della sighed. "As if Miranda didn't tell you."

"She did," Kylie said, "but I was afraid it was more."

"It was more," Della said, her heart replaying the pain. "He said he can't take seeing Chase and me working together."

"Isn't it the same thing as seeing him work with that smiley chick at the vet's office who has the hots for him?"

"He doesn't think so."

"What do you think?" Kylie asked.

"I think . . . Oh, I don't know what I think. I feel a million different things right now, none of them good."

Kylie let go of a deep breath, filled with empathy. "So, he's for sure leaving?"

Della nodded and felt the lump in her throat, then her thoughts went back to Miranda asleep in her bed. "I kind of understand why Steve is doing it, but Perry . . . that just pisses me off. Do you think it's because Miranda hasn't put out? I came right out and asked him, but he denied it, and his heart didn't actually call him a liar, but I'm not sure I believe him."

Kylie pulled one of her legs up and hugged it. "I could be wrong, but I just don't see it being that. Not Perry. He's so in love with Miranda."

"Yeah, but you know what guys love more than anything."

Kylie shrugged. "As sad as it sounds, I really think Perry is trying to do Miranda a favor. I ran into him this afternoon, and he looked so depressed that it hurt me to look at him."

"Duh. Then he shouldn't go to frigging Paris! How hard is that?"

"Pretty hard," Kylie said. "Put yourself in his shoes. He's basically ostracized from the human world. You and I, we think about college, and what we're going to do with our lives. He can't do that. If he can't learn to control himself, he's basically in hiding the rest of his life. And I'm sure Miranda talks about what she wants to do. He has to feel as if he's going to hold her back."

"Damn it! It sucks being a supernatural teen."

Kylie sighed. "I pretty much thought it sucked being a human teen, too."

"I didn't," Della said. "I had it great."

Kylie looked at her. "Didn't you tell me that your parents wanted you to be a doctor?"

"Yeah," Della said.

"And were you going to do that just to make them happy?"

"No," Della said.

"Then sooner or later you would've had to stand up to them, and then things wouldn't have been so great. I'm just saying that both humans and supernaturals have it tough when it comes to being a teen."

"Maybe," Della said with sass. "But being turned vampire added a little fuel to the fire. And not being able to stop yourself from shifting into a fire-breathing dragon sucks even more."

"True," Kylie conceded. "Seeing your dead father hanging out when you didn't know he was even your father wasn't a piece of cake, either. But I know human kids who have it almost that bad." Kylie bit down on her lip. "Look at my friend, Sara. She got cancer."

Della shook her head. "You know, you kind of sound like Holiday. Logical, upbeat."

"Am I that bad?" Kylie frowned. "I hate it when she takes something completely batty and turns it around to make perfect sense."

Della chuckled. "You are going to make a perfect counselor." Then she added, "Come to think of it, maybe you can help me make sense of something else."

"Counselor Galen at your service," Kylie teased. "What do you have? Wait. Let me guess. A certain vamp tried to kiss you today and you don't know how you feel about it?"

Della frowned. "That's not it." He hadn't kissed her, but Kylie hit the nail on the dad-blasted head about her not knowing how she felt.

"So, he didn't try to kiss you?" Kylie asked, tilting her head to listen to Della's heart.

"No. I thought he was, but he wasn't."

"So he wasn't too touchy-feely?"

Della's mind took her back to leaning on him, to him holding her in his arms. Then it went to him touching her ear. And that took her back to the whole nose-in-his-crotch incident. An unexpected giggle spilled out of her lips.

"What?" Kylie asked.

Della debated not telling, but realized this was exactly the kind of thing they shared. The crazy things, the stupid things, the embarrassing things. That's what being a friend was about. Telling each other everything.

In spite of the cool temperature, Della's face felt warm. Then she bit the bullet and told Kylie about seeing her dad on the freeway.

"Did he see you?" Kylie asked with complete concern.

"No. I . . . hid. The floorboard was full of Chase's camera stuff, so I . . . I had to go facedown on his lap. And I think my chin might have bruised his boys."

Kylie burst out laughing and Della joined in. They were laughing so hard they didn't hear the person move behind them.

"What's so funny?" Miranda asked, sounding sleepy. She sat down beside them, dangling her feet off the side of the porch. Della repeated the story about putting her nose in the Panty Perv's crotch.

And they all three sat there in the dark, the insects singing in the distance, laughing like girls. When they sobered, Kylie looked at Della. "So, what was the thing you needed me to help you make sense of?"

Della looked at Miranda, and knew the girl wouldn't like this subject. Hell, Della didn't like the subject, but she needed advice, and Kylie was the go-to person for these issues. Especially if it was something you didn't want Holiday or Burnett to get wind of. "Ghosts."

Kylie made a funny face, then looked at Della all serious-like. "Ghosts seldom make sense."

Miranda let out a moan. "I'd rather talk about you putting your nose where it didn't belong."

Della grimaced. "Then maybe you want to go back inside."

"I don't think so. I'd rather be with you two talking about ghosts than by myself knowing you're talking about ghosts. My imagination can be scarier than the truth."

Della didn't agree. What she had to talk about was pretty damn scary.

Chapter Twenty

Della told Kylie about the near accident on the freeway and what Holiday said about ghosts being able to cause crap like that.

"Did you see the ghost when it happened?" Kylie asked.

"No, I've never seen her. I hear her. I feel a cold presence."

"And you still don't think you know who she is?"

Della remembered that both Holiday and Kylie had said she probably had a connection to the ghost. "No. But we already know what the connection is. It's that Chan knew Natasha."

Kylie looked doubtful. "Most of the time it's more than that."

"Well, this time it isn't," Della said.

"Did you feel her when the accident was about to happen?" Kylie asked.

"I don't know," Della answered honestly. "It happened so quickly and then I saw my dad and—"

"That's when you saw your dad?" Kylie asked.

"Yeah," Della said and realized she hadn't put those two things together. "Do you think he has anything to do with it?"

"Duh," Miranda added her two cents' worth.

Della shot a frown the witch's way. "If you can't say something constructive, just keep your mouth zipped."

The witch scowled back. "I could say something constructive, but you don't want to hear it."

"What do I not want to hear?" Della asked, annoyed.

Miranda looked at Kylie as if asking permission to speak.

"You don't need her approval. Just say it already," Della snapped.

"Fine. You act as if you don't know who the ghost is, but I think it's pretty evident."

"It's not Natasha," Della snapped.

"I'm not saying that it's Natasha."

"Then who?" Della and Kylie asked at the same time.

Miranda looked at both of them and then appeared almost scared to say it. "Your aunt."

"My aunt Miao is alive."

"No, the other one."

Della's breath caught. "You mean Bao Yu?"

"Is she the one who was murdered?"

Della nodded.

"Then yes, that one. It makes sense. She spotted your father, she freaked out, and made all the cars go crazy—"

"No!" Della felt her chest burn and her eyes burned with it. "My dad did not kill his sister!"

Miranda did a quick shift away from Della.

Kylie reached out and gently held Della's arm. The calm emotion radiating from the touch told Della the chameleon had turned fae.

"I didn't say he killed her," Miranda said, sounding sympathetic. "There could be all kinds of reasons that she could be mad at your dad."

"What reasons?" Della asked, Kylie's calm touch easing her

fury, but not her fear. Like it or not, what Miranda said made sense. And Della really, really didn't want to believe it.

Miranda's brows puckered. "I can't think of any off the top of my head, but I'm sure there are some. Aren't there, Kylie?"

"Yeah," Kylie said, not sounding extremely confident. "But first, we don't know if the ghost is your aunt. Second, let's say the ghost is her. We still don't know if she made the cars go crazy because she's angry."

"Right," Miranda said. "Maybe she wanted you and your father to see each other so you'd make up and stop fighting." Miranda pulled her arms into her shirt to hide from the cold.

"If he'd caught me riding around with a hot guy in a fancy convertible, we wouldn't have been making up."

Kylie brought her other foot up and hugged both her knees. "Maybe she was warning you that he was there and didn't want you to get busted." Miranda cut a look at Kylie. "Did you miss the fact that she called him hot?"

Della growled. "It can't be my aunt. What would my aunt, a teenager who was murdered almost twenty years ago, have to do with Natasha?"

Right then, a breeze so cold it came with tiny bits of ice, moved over them. Little BB-sized bits of hail started clicking against the porch.

Chills prickled Della's neck and she remembered what happened earlier in the office with the water and the ice. She glanced at Kylie and found the girl staring back, her eyes wide as if trying to tell her something.

Miranda's teeth started chattering, clicking almost at the same tempo as the ice pinging against the wood porch. "Tell me . . ." Click, click. "That . . . this is just a normal storm."

"This *is* just a normal storm," Kylie said, and stood up. Della didn't even have to try to hear Kylie's heart registering the words as a lie. The truth, along with fear, reflected in her light blue eyes.

Miranda huddled up in a tight ball and looked up at the chameleon. "You're just saying that, aren't you?"

"Yup." Kylie looked around. Della followed her gaze and didn't see anything, but that didn't mean it wasn't there.

"We should go inside," Kylie spouted, sounding leery. And right then, a bolt of lightning hit the ground a foot in front of the porch. The electrical current vibrated the air. The hair on Della's arms stood up.

Wasting no time, Miranda bolted to her feet and shot through the cabin door. Della waited for Kylie to follow the witch. With her friends safe inside, Della took a step to do the same. Before she crossed the threshold, the door slammed shut with a loud crack that was followed by another ground-shaking bolt of lightning.

"Shit!" Kylie screamed from the other side of the door. "Della, are you okay?"

Della, feeling the icy fingers of cold fear, but too stubborn to admit it, turned back around and faced the storm and the ghost. "Who are you? Tell me, damn it!"

And just like that, darkness swallowed her. Her arms and legs went numb. Her heart stopped beating. She felt frozen.

The blackness faded and the back of her eyelids turned red. She forced her eyes open and saw it.

Saw her father when he was young, standing over her. Gripped in his right fist, he held a knife. Blood, thick and red, dripped from the blade and splattered on the wooden floor right beside where she lay.

Where she lay . . . not breathing.

Where she lay . . . dead.

Sensing a floating sensation, she left the body. She saw the bloody scene again from above. The person on the floor, resting in a pool of blood, wasn't her. The Asian girl's long, silky black hair lay fanned around her body; her eyes stood open, staring at nothing, but there was so much blood on her face it hid most of her features. Della saw only her eyes.

So still.

So sad.

But her dad was there.

He stood over the body, knife in hand, murder in his eyes.

No!

No!

No!

"Della? Della?"

She heard Kylie's voice. Deep and dark, as if she was in protective mode. The sound of a door being forced open echoed in the distance. Then Della felt Kylie's hands on her shoulders.

Della's vision faded and the blonde chameleon, a shimmer of brightness surrounding her, appeared standing in front of her. Behind Kylie stood Miranda, tears and fear pooled in her green eyes.

"Are you okay?" Kylie asked.

Okay?

Hell no!

He had given her life. Loved her. Read *Charlotte's Web* to her when she was a child. He taught her to play chess. Helped her with algebra.

He had killed his sister.

Her dad was a murderer.

No!

Everything in her wanted to deny it. But she'd seen it. How could she *not* believe?

No, she hadn't seen it. There had been so much blood on the

girl's face, she didn't know if it was really her aunt or someone else.

"I'm fine," Della lied. She pulled away from Kylie and ran past Miranda.

Della entered her bedroom, turned, grabbed the doorknob, and glanced back at her best friends. Concern and worry filled their eyes, but Della couldn't deal with it now.

"We need to talk," Kylie said.

"No." Not this time. She couldn't say it. Didn't want to think about it. "I just want to be left alone!" She slammed the door.

When she turned, she saw the book on the bed. The yearbook she'd gotten to help find her dad's twin. It hadn't been there when she walked out. How had . . . ?

The ghost? Could she have . . . ?

And just like that, her mind started connecting the dots.

One dot.

Two dots.

Three.

"I'm sorry." Kylie's voice came from behind her with the click of the door being opened. "I don't care what you say, you don't need to be alone. You had a vision, didn't you? I know how they can make you feel."

"We're best friends." Miranda's voice echoed behind her. "We don't slam doors on each other."

Della swung around, hearing what they said, but lost in her own thoughts. "They're twins. It might not have been him."

"What?" Kylie and Miranda asked at the same time.

"My uncle wasn't dead then. He was just vampire. So it could have been him, my father's twin, who I saw standing over her."

"What could have been your uncle?" Kylie came closer. Her blue eyes filled with compassion.

"I was dead. I don't know who I was. I could have been my aunt. And my uncle could have killed her."

"Your aunt?" Kylie said. "So Miranda was right, and your aunt is the ghost?"

Della shook her head. "I don't know. She had so much blood on her face."

"I'm sure I was right," Miranda said. "Who else could it be?"

"I said I don't know for sure!" Della snapped.

Kylie stood there as if thinking. "Did she tell you how she and Natasha are connected?"

"No." Della fought the sting in her sinuses. "I saw her dead. I saw a man who looked just like my father standing over her with bloody knife."

"And you think it was your uncle?"

"It has to be," Della said. "It has to be."

Della spent the rest of the night doing more tossing and turning than sleeping. Not that it surprised her. The vision had been just as mind reeling as her first FRU visit, when she'd seen two dead bodies. She'd get to sleep and be jarred awake by the image of her father—no, her uncle—holding the bloody knife.

It had to be her uncle. Believing that made it almost acceptable. Forget that she'd had grand hopes of finding said uncle. She'd give up having a family member who was vampire, who understood her and loved her. She'd toss all that away before she would believe her father could kill.

Della rolled over again. From her window she could see a sliver of sky slowly growing pink with the rising sun. A new day. A better day, she hoped. By the time that light had gotten one shade brighter, she heard the footfalls.

Footfalls walking toward her cabin . . . her window. Only one person visited her window on a regular basis. One person who said he didn't want to say good-bye in person and who'd texted a sad face.

Since the vision last night, she'd put all the hurt of Steve leaving in a tight pocket and buried it in her heart. But that sound. Those familiar footsteps—both the pain and pleasure of everything Steve was in her life danced on her heart.

Before Della could decide whether to run and hide or let him come inside and give him an ass whooping, his sad face appeared at her window. She stood up and gripped her hands at her sides. She wanted to scream, to laugh, and to cry all at once.

He pushed open the window and leapt in as if he belonged here. Belonged in her bedroom and in her life.

And damn it, no damn him, because she wasn't sure that he didn't.

Chapter Twenty-one

Steve took a step toward her. Della took one step back. Behind him, the rising sun had turned the sky purple. "You said—"

"I couldn't do it."

"Couldn't leave?" She held her breath, didn't blink, even her heart stopped beating as she waited and hoped he'd say she was right. *But then what?* a voice inside her said. *What about Chase?*

"No, I couldn't go without saying good-bye. But leaving is going to be hell."

He moved forward and slipped his warm hands around her waist. Slowly, he pulled her against him and she didn't resist. Couldn't. The thought of kicking his ass was yesterday's news.

He didn't kiss her, just held her. Her head came to rest on that special spot on his chest. The one she claimed belonged to her. His smell, a tangy, earthy scent mixed with the aroma of fresh wind, filled her senses.

She breathed it in greedily. Tears formed in her eyes.

When he pulled back, even his eyes were misty. "I want you to know that no matter what happens, I will never regret what we were. What we had. And if I lose you, you will always be the one who got away that I'll never forget."

He stopped and looked up at the ceiling for one second. Two. Three.

He inhaled and his breath sounded shaky. Or was that hers?

"Promise me," he said, looking back at her. "Promise me that you won't do something stupid and get yourself killed. Promise me that you'll stop letting your parents' ignorance hurt you so much. You don't deserve that. Promise me that before you fall in love with Chase, you'll remember that I loved you first."

That's when the need to whip his ass came back!

She hit his chest with her palm. He stumbled back, but remained standing. "Why did you make me care about you when you knew you were leaving? You could have just left me alone! I wouldn't be hurting now! Why?"

He grabbed her and kissed her then. His lips tasted warm, tasted like Steve—so sweet, but oddly salty. Perhaps from her tears, and maybe even his. Before she knew it, way before she wanted it, the kiss ended. She opened her eyes. He was gone. She saw several tiny bubbles floating in the air. Then she spotted the bird, a peregrine falcon perched on her windowsill.

Looking almost regal, the bird bowed his head at her then leapt up and flew away. With him, he took a part of her heart. And she wasn't sure she'd ever get that part back.

Della heard Miranda and Kylie leave in time for the morning meal. Della skipped breakfast and the campmate hour. She managed to pull herself together enough to go to her first-period class. Math. From there she went to science. The class was halfway over, and

Haden Yates, Jenny's brother, was up discussing sound waves. It might have been interesting if she gave a shit.

She didn't.

Not while she was still reeling over last night's vision. Reeling over the mere possibility that her father, and if not him, her uncle, was a killer. Over the fact that another day had passed and she wasn't any closer to finding Natasha. Add that a part of her heart was halfway over the ocean heading to France, and was it any wonder that she didn't give a rat's ass about sound waves?

Someone in the back of the room chuckled. Della looked back and right then she realized something wasn't right. She turned her head around to make sure she wasn't mistaken.

Nope. No mistake. She'd been so busy wallowing in self-pity that she hadn't realized Kylie and Miranda were missing. Damn.

What kind of friend was she? Especially considering Miranda was in the same sinking boat as Della. Well, she didn't have her dead aunt haunting her ass, but at least romantically the girl's heart had been yanked out of her chest.

Della shot up out of her seat to leave, only to remember that one didn't just leave class and discussions on sound waves.

"Della?" Mr. Yates said.

She looked at him. She started to explain she needed to go find her friends, but that didn't sound like a good enough excuse to leave class. And lately, Mr. Yates had been complaining about absences— even when they were approved by Burnett.

"Uh . . . I need to be excused."

"Because . . . ?"

"Personal reasons," she said, hoping he wouldn't argue, and if he did, he wasn't going to like her alternative get-out-of-class answer. But she wasn't above using it—even if it was a lie.

"What kind of personal reasons?" he asked, sounding slightly annoyed.

Well, damn, she'd tried to spare him. She put her hand on her hip and met his unhappy gaze.

"I just started my period and it's about to get messy. Of course, you wouldn't understand that."

Mr. Yates's mouth dropped open, but he didn't excuse her from class so she continued.

"I mean, I know guys don't understand the whole period thing."

Red color climbed up his neck to his face and almost looked cartoonish, but he still didn't excuse her.

"But seriously, if your penises bled once a month—"

"Go!" he almost yelled, and she barely heard it over the laughter from the other students.

"Thank you." She shot out of the classroom and didn't slow down until she stopped at her cabin.

She could hear Miranda and Kylie inside. Miranda's broken voice echoed the loudest.

Feeling terrible about abandoning them when they'd been there so much for her these last few months, she stormed inside. They sat at the kitchen table. Miranda had a pint-size carton of Chunky Monkey ice cream in her hands, and three empty cartons sat on the table. And they looked licked clean.

Kylie stared at Della as if she didn't know what to do with the witch. Not that Della had any great ideas.

"I'm sorry. I didn't know we were having an ice cream party." Della stopped at the table.

Miranda let go of another sob and shoveled another big scoop of banana ice cream into her mouth. "He haaaasn't even called," she whimpered around the sweet goo in her mouth.

Della exhaled and reached deep for patience. "He's only halfway there. Once you get up to around twenty thousand feet, it's kind of hard to find a cell tower."

"I gave him a special phone." She hiccupped. "It doesn't need a cell tower."

"All cell phones need . . . Oh, you mean a magic one?"

Miranda nodded and let out another sob.

"Cool," Della said.

"Not cool when he's not calling . . . me. Why hasn't he . . . called me?"

Kylie frowned at Della as if saying she didn't know what to say.

"I'm sure he'll call," Kylie said and the chameleon's heart raced to the lie.

Della dropped down in a chair and couldn't help but wonder if lying was the best option. She tried to envision Perry flying and suddenly a question arose.

"How is Perry flying with humans if he can't be trusted to be around them?"

Miranda dove back into her pint of ice cream. "Burnett gave him a Benadryl. It slows down a shape-shifter's ability to shift."

Della gave that some thought. "Then why doesn't he just take Benadryl daily? Then he wouldn't have to go to some school to teach him to stop shifting."

"He had to take a dozen pills," Miranda said.

"A dozen?" Kylie asked.

"Well, duh," Della said. "Maybe he passed out on the plane and that's why he's not calling."

"I think he's purposely not calling me," Miranda moaned.

"I don't think that's it," Kylie said, and her heart did somersaults in her chest, telling Della that was exactly what Kylie thought. Hell, Perry had probably already confided in Kylie and told her he wouldn't be calling Miranda.

Damn Perry! It didn't even matter if the reason he was breaking up with Miranda was because of his own insecurities. He was still breaking her heart and her spirit. Miranda's spirit was fragile. And that royally pissed Della off to the nth degree. She took a deep breath and tried to calm the fury from brightening her eyes.

Miranda shoved another heaping spoonful of Chunky Monkey into her mouth as tears rolled down her cheeks. She looked pathetic and gross because her nose was running down to her upper lip and she was still eating.

And just like that, Della lost it. She couldn't stand by and see Miranda like this. "Stop!" she screamed and yanked the ice cream from Miranda's clutches.

"Give that back!" Miranda demanded and jumped up and tried to dig her spoon into the carton.

"Let's not fight," Kylie said. "Give her back her ice cream."

"No!" Della jerked the pint back from Miranda's spoon. But the witch went for it again.

Della stuck her finger into the ice cream. "My fingers are filthy!" She glared at her teary-eyed roommate. "I had some nose problems earlier." She kept poking her finger in the ice cream, hoping to discourage the girl.

"I don't care! I want my ice cream," Miranda screamed and went to grab the carton.

"Stop this," Kylie said.

Della ignored Kylie, lurched back, and yanked her finger out of the cold substance. She pretended to hand the carton to Miranda, but instead she threw it on the floor, and doing a vampire-speed polka dance, she stomped her boot heels in the Chunky Monkey until the witch would need a straw to slurp it up off the floor.

Miranda stood there, staring at the mess with fury in her large green eyes. "I skipped school to get that ice cream."

Looking completely wacko, she held up her pinkie and it started to twitch.

"Stop this!" Kylie screamed.

"No. Let her do it!" Della put her face in Miranda's. So close, her nose touched the witch's. And that was kind of gross, because she had ice cream on it. At least she hoped it was ice cream and not . . .

"Don't do it!" Kylie pulled Miranda back a step. "This could end so badly."

Della held up her hand. "Stay out of it!" she told Kylie. "Let the witch turn me into a kangaroo, or give me pimples, I don't care."

Della glared back at Miranda. "You are my friend, damn it! And I'm not going to stand by and watch you eat yourself sick and get fat."

"I don't care if I get fat," Miranda said.

"Well, I do!" Della snapped.

"You don't understand," Miranda sobbed.

"The hell I don't!" Della said and suddenly tears filled her eyes. "Look, they left us! We didn't want this. We didn't ask for this. They should be the ones hurting, not us!"

"But I love—"

"I know you love him, but you don't deserve this. I don't deserve this! Steve and Perry basically told us the same thing—to figure out what we want. Well, damn it, that's what you should do. You aren't going to wallow around in this self-pity shit and get fat eating ice cream. You're going to go on with your life and figure out what you want! And guess what? You just might figure out that you want better than Perry."

"The vamp has a point," Kylie said.

Miranda sniffled. "But I don't want—"

"Look, I'm not saying go fall in love with someone else, but maybe flirt a little, open yourself up to the possibilities. You might even have fun."

"Who am I going to flirt with? Everyone here knows that—"

"Well, flirt with someone who's not here."

"There's no one I want to flirt with."

And bam, Della remembered something she hadn't told Miranda. About the warlock FRU agent who'd helped bury Chan. She had to search her brain for his name, but she found it. "How about Shawn Hanson?"

Miranda's mouth dropped open. Then she slammed it shut. "You dirty little, blood-sucking vamp. You've been reading my diary?" The pinkie came back up. "I should, I should . . ."

"I haven't read shit." Della made a face. "But I would've if I'd known you had one. Where's your diary? I'll bet it's got some good stuff in it."

"Don't lie to me," Miranda snapped. "How else would you know about Shawn?"

"I know about him because I met him."

"Liar!" she said, and looked at Kylie. "Turn vampire and check her heartbeat."

Kylie shrugged. "I am vampire and she isn't lying."

Della smiled in victory. "Listen to the chameleon, she has a point."

When Miranda didn't say anything, Della continued. "Not only that, but when he said your name, he started polluting the air with all kinds of pheromones. The guy's got a hard-on for you."

"Now I know you're lying."

"I swear," Della said.

Miranda made a face. "How would he even know you knew me? Where did you meet—?"

"He was helping out with Chan's funeral. And he knew I knew you because everyone's talking about the arrest and how you turned those five goons into kangaroos. He told me you were friends with his sister and that he'd always known you have more talent than you let people believe."

Miranda's eyes sparkled just a bit. "Everyone's talking? Seriously, he really said that stuff about me being talented?"

Della made a gesture over her heart. "Cross my heart and hope to die."

"And stick a needle in your eye if you're lying?" Miranda asked.

"Yes, the needle, too," Della said.

"And the pheromones . . . He really . . . ?"

"I swear!"

Miranda dropped back into her chair. She sat there thinking for several seconds. Then her eyes lost the twinkle. "I still don't want Shawn. I want Perry."

"I know. But you can't make yourself sick because Perry called it off until he comes back. Look at this time as a chance to make sure this is what you want. It's hard. But darn it, go kiss a few toads and see if they turn into princes."

Miranda folded her hands in her lap and then looked up at Della. "Are you going to do it?"

"I don't know any toads," Della said.

"No, I mean are you going to open yourself up and see if maybe Chase isn't really a toad, but a prince?"

"I don't think the Panty Perv is—"

"Stop right there!" Miranda stood back up and sent Della what some would call the stink eye—an evil glare. "You can't destroy someone's break-up ice cream, dish out advice, and then not follow it yourself."

"The witch has a point," Kylie said.

"Here's another point," Miranda added. "You haven't called him the Panty Perv in a long time. Why is that?"

Because she'd stopped distrusting him so much, Della thought. And because he hadn't said anything else about her panties, which was how he got the nickname in the first place. "Fine. I'll follow my own advice." In a way, she'd already been doing it. And maybe she should remember how much she'd distrusted Chase in the beginning, too.

"Pinkie promise." Miranda held out her little finger.

Della locked pinkies with the witch, but she couldn't help but wonder what the penalty was for breaking a pinkie promise. Yesterday, she'd let herself lean on the guy, today there'd be no leaning. Not until her doubts about the Panty Perv completely vanished.

"Say you promise," Miranda repeated.

"Promise," Della said, realizing the promise hadn't entailed any leaning. All she'd promised was to attempt to decipher if Chase was more toad or prince. And so what if he was a prince? That didn't make him *her* prince.

Chapter Twenty-two

Della went to her last class, and right after it was over, she went straight to her cabin, where she called Derek and asked him to meet her. As much as she'd been thinking about Steve and Perry and Miranda, she hadn't forgotten the vision. And if there was anyone who could help her find answers, it was Derek. He was Kylie's ex and he'd once worked in a private investigator's office, so he'd helped Della dig up information about her family in the past. He'd been the one to discover about Bao Yu's murder.

"What's up?" he asked.

"Just some questions . . . about my aunt's case."

He paused for a minute. "I don't really know a lot."

"I'd like to know all you know," she said.

"Okay. I'm with Jenny, can she come?"

"Sure," Della said, realizing she'd been neglectful about initiating any more friendship with Jenny, the new chameleon at camp. But Della had been kind of busy, right? A thread of guilt whispered through her.

Della sat on the porch waiting after they hung up. The fall air felt good, the sky was a perfect blue, and the sun was warm on her face. It seemed too pretty of a day to be thinking about murder. A murder that happened years ago, but the ghost had given her the image, and she could only assume it was important. Or maybe she just needed to prove to herself that it hadn't been her dad committing the murder.

When she heard two sets of footsteps walking down the path, she glanced up and watched as Derek and Jenny came around the corner. They held hands and chatted quietly, smiles on both their faces.

Della's heart did a dip, feeling the emotional tug of seeing two people who were so right for each other. She'd always gotten that feeling when she saw Kylie and Lucas together. And maybe even a little with Miranda and Perry—the little twerp.

Jenny saw her, let go of Derek's hand, and ran up and hugged her. Della allowed it. "I know you've been working a case for the FRU, but I've missed you. And I've been worried about you . . . with Steve leaving."

"I'm . . . okay and I'm sorry," Della said, her mind still stuck on people being right for each other, and she wondered if others saw her and Steve as "right."

"Sorry about what?" Jenny asked.

"Being too busy. Let's do lunch tomorrow."

"Am I invited?" Derek asked.

"No," Jenny said. "We wouldn't be able to talk about you if you were there." The girl laughed, sounding almost giddy. Was it because of love?

Derek frowned. "What are you going to say about me?"

"You'll never know," Jenny said. "But I'm sure it'll be good."

Della rolled her eyes. Her heart might have tugged earlier, but this was getting too mushy.

"You want to come inside?" Della offered before the two of them started kissing or something.

"It's so pretty, why don't we just sit outside?" Jenny answered.

They all sat down, leaning against the front of the cabin. Derek pulled one knee up, and when he looked at Della, she knew he was thinking about the reason she'd asked to see him. "I think I told you just about everything I found out."

"You never said how she died," Della corrected. "Did you actually get a copy of the report?"

"No, my PI friend just told me what the detective told him." He paused as if thinking, then he frowned. "I'm pretty sure he said she was bludgeoned to death. He said the report noted there was a lot of blood."

"So, she wasn't stabbed?" she asked. "If she'd been stabbed, it would've said that, right?"

Derek considered it a minute. "I think so. Why?"

"Nothing important," she lied, now even more unsure if the ghost haunting her was really her aunt. Just because she was Asian didn't mean she was related. So okay, it might be wishful thinking, but Della deserved to wish a little.

Then, all of a sudden, she realized that she hadn't seen the ghost actually get stabbed. She'd only assumed that the victim had been killed by the knife. Oh, hell, now she was more confused than ever.

"Can you find anything else out? Maybe you forgot something. Or didn't think it was important. Can you ask him to tell you everything again?"

Derek looked as if he was going to say no, but then sighed. "I'll ask him, but . . ."

"But what?" she asked.

"It's just . . . you didn't like what I found out the first time—about your father being the only suspect—and I don't think it's going to be any different."

"I need to know," Della said. "Me liking it is beside the point."

A couple of hours later, Della spotted the Panty Perv as soon as she took the first curve in the path leading to the office. He'd texted her and said he needed to see her early.

He walked with a sense of purpose . . . no, more like confidence. He wore jeans, a bright yellow shirt, and a brown hoody mostly zipped. His boots matched his hoody, a worn yet warm color. The yellow of his shirt made his light green eyes appear lighter. Almost a gold green.

She felt her pulse pick up speed as if she'd been anticipating seeing him. She hadn't, she told herself, but it felt like a lie.

"What's wrong?" he asked as soon as he got within five feet of her.

"What do you mean?" She answered his question with a question to avoid having to lie.

His expression said he was on to her. She didn't care. It simply wasn't fair that Chase could control his heartbeat and therefore lie. Sure, she could almost tell from his facial expressions, but it wasn't 100 percent accurate.

"What do you need to talk about?" This afternoon she'd started worrying that Chase had seen the same vision she'd had last night.

If so, would he suspect that the victim was related to Della? Would he know that either her dad or her uncle was responsible for a murder? Chase could have easily put two and two together if what she suspected was true—that her uncle had been the one behind the Vampire Council sending him to check on her and Chan. For that matter, her uncle could even be on the council.

Or, Chase could be telling the truth when he said that he'd just been following orders.

Either way it brought her to the issue she needed to tackle. When was she going to get to meet the council and get a chance to see if her uncle was connected?

"You answer me and I'll tell you."

"Answer what?" She continued walking. Chase reached out and took her by the elbow. Not a tight grip, but softly. As if the touch should mean something. That annoyed her.

"Stop playing games, Della. Tell me what's wrong."

Did that mean he knew? Or that he just knew she was avoiding lying? Her heart did a few somersaults.

"Why do you think something's wrong?" She pulled away from his hold and continued moving toward the office.

"You look upset." He fell into step beside her.

"Bad day." That wasn't a lie. She'd been within an inch of being turned into a kangaroo by one of her best friends. And her conversation with Derek about her aunt Bao Yu had her second-guessing everything she thought was true.

She didn't look at Chase as she moved, but at her feet. Her black boots still had Chunky Monkey sludge on them. The scent of banana ice cream floated up from the soles of her shoes. She probably should have wiped them off.

Her next breath, she caught the scent of spicy male soap, and found herself wondering why she hadn't bothered to change clothes. Then she remembered that she shouldn't care how she looked. They were on a mission, not a damn date.

"I think it's more than just a bad day," he said.

Della stopped walking and faced him. "Why do you think it's more?"

"Cut the crap of answering a question with a question. Just talk to me."

More suspicious than ever, she lifted one hand to her hip. "Did the ghost tell you something?" The moment she posed the question, she wanted to suck the words back into her mouth.

He stared at her. "No. I just . . . I can read you . . . it's part of the bonding, I guess."

"What do you mean by 'read'?" Surely he couldn't know what she was thinking. That would be disastrous.

"I can tell you're upset by looking at you."

"How?" she asked.

"I notice little things. Things that I don't think I'd notice otherwise."

"What things?"

"First, you're a tad more of a smartass." He almost grinned. "And second, your right eyebrow lifts about an eighth of an inch when you're tense."

She purposely dropped both her eyebrows.

He chuckled. "Do you find yourself noticing things about me?"

She so wanted to say no, but it would have been a lie and he'd know it. Hadn't she already noted what the color of his shirt did to his eyes? And the confidence in his gait. And . . .

"I've always been the observant type." There was some truth in that, too.

The twinkle in his eyes faded. "Seriously," he said. "What's wrong?"

"It's personal." He couldn't argue with that one. She commenced to walking.

"Wait." He caught her arm again.

So maybe he could argue.

"Did the ghost give you something? Is that what this is about?"

See, she'd been right about that being a mistake. She pulled away. "Burnett's waiting on us."

"We're early, remember? Damn it, talk to me. If the ghost—"

"I told you, it's personal."

"Is it about Steve leaving?" Disappointment rang in his voice, and his eyes grew a bit brighter as if the thought disturbed him.

Her first impulse was to tell him that Steve was none of his business, but perhaps she could use this to get Chase off her back. She tilted up her chin. "And that's personal."

He nodded as if satisfied that was all she'd been worried about. "Fine, but if you need to talk, I'll listen."

She could tell he didn't really want to hear her whine about Steve, but his offer came off sincere.

"Yeah, like that'll happen," she said.

"There goes the smartass attitude again."

"But I'm so good at it," she countered, half teasing.

"That you are." He smiled.

His smile, genuine and sexy, caught her off guard and she stared at it a fraction of a second longer than she should have. He noticed, too. She could tell by the way his gaze—soft and alluring—shifted slowly to her eyes.

Pushing the thought away, she tightened her spine. "What did you need to see me about before we talk to Burnett?"

He stopped walking and pulled a twig off a tree that lined the path. "I want to ask for a later curfew. If we're going to hang out by the funeral home and see if we can run into anyone who knows anything about Liam, we might need to be there a while. But if you think Burnett will say no, then maybe we should follow the theory that it's better to say you're sorry than to ask for permission."

She made a face. "Burnett doesn't like that theory."

"Fine, we'll ask."

"Is that how you work with the Vampire Council?" She grabbed the opportunity to move the conversation toward the council.

He made a get-real face. "The Vampire Council doesn't micromanage like Burnett. You'd think you were his daughter."

"So they don't care about you."

"They care, they just trust me to get the job done without overseeing every little detail."

She started walking again. "I imagine when I'm a full-fledge agent, instead of just a junior part-timer, it will be the same." She couldn't stop herself from defending Burnett, but then added, "But I'm looking forward to meeting them."

When he didn't respond, she looked at him. "When do you suppose that will be?"

"When what will be?" he asked, and she recognized her own tactic of answering a question with a question.

"Now who's doing it?" she asked. He feigned innocence. "Meeting the Vampire Council," she answered directly. "When is it going to happen?"

"I wasn't aware that was set in motion."

"Oh, I just assumed since they had a hand in our work, I'd meet them just like you've met with Burnett."

"I could look into it," he said. "But I have a feeling Burnett wouldn't approve."

"What Burnett doesn't know won't kill him," she answered.

"But you want to ask him about moving your curfew. How does that make sense?"

"He'd know I stayed out late," she said, pointing out the difference. "He doesn't have to know—"

"I still think he'll have a shit fit about me keeping you out late and he's going to say no."

"A shit fit never killed anyone. And we won't know until we ask."

"Which brings me back to my point," he said. "Let's ask him about you meeting the Vampire Council."

"No," she said.

Chase's brows tightened, and a thin line—a worry line, perhaps—appeared between his eyes. She got the distinct feeling that it wasn't just Burnett who didn't approve of her meeting the Vampire Council. Was there a reason Chase didn't want her meeting them?

Could it be because she was right? Her uncle was part of the organization? Her uncle, whom she believed murdered her aunt? And Chase knew it.

She recalled her pinkie promise to Miranda. To discover if Chase was more of a toad or a prince. Right now, the Panty Perv was looking more and more like he ate grasshoppers for supper.

Burnett handed them a picture of Liam Jones. "He's a good kid. No criminal history. Was going to college to be an engineer. He's part African-American and part white. He lived with his mother."

Della looked at the image, and while it had been too dark to see his face in the vision she'd had, she somehow knew this was the right Liam.

Chase stared at the image, and Della could tell he felt it, too. This was their Liam. He looked up at Burnett. "By the way, we'll need a later curfew tonight."

Burnett's expression hardened. "How late?"

"As late as it takes," Chase said, looking back at the image. She could tell he almost felt a bond with Liam. Not that she could blame him, she sort of felt one toward Natasha as well. Feeling as if you were in their skin, in their head, sort of did that to you.

"We'll be fine," Della added. "You know we can take care of ourselves."

"Being stronger and faster doesn't make you invincible." Oh, boy, Della had heard that one about a hundred times since she'd been Reborn.

"It almost does," Chase argued.

Della inwardly cringed. That wasn't the right thing to say. She cut Chase a look of warning.

"And that tells me why I can't trust you."

"Do you want us to look for Liam or not?" Chase asked.

Burnett contemplated it for a few long, silent seconds. But he wasn't going to stay silent long. He never did.

"Yes," he said, firmly, "but I'll assign another agent to accompany you for that portion of the evening."

Chase leaned forward. "I hate to argue with you, but I did some checking. There's a couple of supernatural gangs that hang out around there. Young, teen gangs. We don't need some old fart hanging out with us. They'll blow our cover right off the bat."

Burnett's eyes got brighter. "I'll go myself."

"And my point remains the same." Chase crossed his arms over his chest.

Holy shit! Had Chase just called Burnett an old fart?

Della held her breath, afraid Burnett would call off the whole mission.

Burnett's eyes brightened and she saw him clamp his jaw shut as if to keep from going bonkers on Chase's ass. "I'll send a younger agent."

Chase exhaled. "We really don't—"

"I. Will. Send. A. Younger. Agent." Burnett's dark and very loud voice left it clear that it wasn't up for debate.

When Chase settled back in his chair, Burnett continued, in a more normal voice. "I'll call with details when I have them."

"Fine." Chase rose and started out. Della got just out of the office and looked back at the still-pissed Burnett. She let Chase get out of the front door and then she stuck her head back in the door. "I don't think you look like an old fart. He hasn't ever seen you without your shirt."

"Thank you," he said. "I think." He stood up. "Be careful. And watch him, he might be even more of a wild card than you."

"I will."

A radio was on inside the Owen house. But again, it appeared as if no one was home. Or someone inside was sleeping with such low breathing they couldn't pick it up. Della took in a noseful of air. She had to bypass Chase's clean scent to see if she could pick up any traces of human.

It was there. "I smell . . ."

"I know, but I smelled it yesterday, too," Chase said. "They probably have a workout room and it's filled with sweat. Haven't you ever been to a human gym? The smell is almost overpowering."

Della hadn't been in a gym since she'd become vampire. Cutting him a look, she wondered why he would go to the gym. The machinery wasn't strong enough to offer a vampire a real workout. Then she remembered why most guys go to gyms: to meet hot girls.

She gave the door a good hard knock again. They stood another couple of minutes at the kelly green front door with no answer. Della reached back and twisted her ponytail, the hair band from the Camaro's glove compartment again.

On the drive here, Chase had tried to start a conversation, but she'd avoided it. She was still stuck on the possibility that Chase might actually know her uncle.

"We have choices," Chase said and took a few steps back to look up.

"What kind of choices?" Della asked, fighting off the wave of disappointment as well as the overwhelming sadness—the same one she'd felt when they'd been here yesterday. Was it the home? Or was it the ghost?

"We could go inside and see if we find any pictures that might tell us for sure if Natasha Owens is our girl."

"I think that's called breaking and entering," Della said.

"Just entering," he said. "I saw an upstairs window that's open. And we'd hear if a car pulled up."

She considered Burnett's parting words about Chase being a wild card. But the temptation lingered.

"It's not as if we're going to steal anything," he added.

She backed up and looked up at the second-story window, raised a good four inches. Oh, hell, what was the worst that could happen?

You could get caught, arrested, and then for sure your dad will pull you from Shadow Falls.

Her mind flashed an image of Natasha and Liam. Okay, was that the ghost? Or was it just her accepting that sometimes you just had to take risks? "Let's do it."

Chapter Twenty-three

"Or maybe we shouldn't do it," Della added a second later, when she realized what they were about to do was really a crime. And at seventeen she could be tried as an adult.

Chase cut his eyes to her. "Do you want to wait outside?"

"No," she snapped, feeling as if he was calling her a coward.

He looked around and tilted his head to the side as if to confirm no cars were coming.

"Then let's do it." He leapt up, caught the windowsill, let go with one hand, and then lifted the window up. Only after he'd climbed in did she jump up.

She caught the windowsill and Chase offered a hand. She ignored it and pulled herself into the room. A game room. A large brown leather sofa cornered the room and a large television sat in the other. A treadmill and a set of weights were set to the side, which she hoped explained why the scent of human was so strong.

Music, a Dido song, piped into the room from two speakers in the ceiling. Della looked around at the nice interior, feeling the sense of sadness even stronger in here than outside. She glanced around for any personal photos, but other than a few prints of wildlife, nothing hung on the wall.

Chase walked to the door, slowly opened it, and started moving down the hall. Della, feeling like a criminal, crept behind him. He appeared to be heading down the stairs, but her gaze shifted to the hall wall that was lined with what looked like family photos.

"Look," Della whispered, still feeling edgy. Her gaze shifted from the two parents—one American and the father looked at least part Asian—to a young girl. Natasha. Her heart sang a little victory song.

"It's her," Della said. "I knew it."

"Okay," Chase said. "Now we know her name is Natasha Owen. Let's see if we can find her bedroom and see if there are any clues in there that might help us."

He moved to the first door on the right and opened it. A bedroom. Decorated in soft cream colors, the room looked devoid of personality. The bed appeared freshly made or perhaps never slept in. Guest bedroom, Della surmised, and both she and Chase stepped back at the same time. The door made a slight clink when he shut it.

The next room he opened sent a warm wash of emotion over Della. Painted and decorated in bright purple with whitewashed furniture, it had teen written all over it. Even the bedspread, a brighter purple, screamed that this room had been lived in by a young person. Someone who loved life and lived it with gusto.

This was it. Natasha's room. Della knew it.

Three pairs of shoes were scattered around the room, jeans and some blouses were piled in one corner as if the last time Natasha was here, she hadn't been sure what to wear and had changed clothes several times.

Had she been going on a date? Or going out for pizza with her friends? Oddly, standing in the room, Della felt bits and pieces of Natasha's personality seep into her pores. A few CDs were on the dresser. She loved music. Maybe even to dance.

Pushing the crazy thoughts away, she started doing what they'd come in here to do: to see if they could find any clues.

The bed wasn't made, as if the world had stopped the day she had gone missing—or as her parents saw it, the day she died.

For one second, Della remembered how her mom hadn't touched her room after she left for Shadow Falls. Was that a sign of love?

On the bedside table was an eight-by-ten photo of Natasha and two other girls, all laughing and capturing a moment of happiness, of friendship.

Della moved closer to the picture and thought of her two friends Miranda and Kylie. Were these Natasha's best friends? Had they too been devastated at what they thought was her death?

Picking up the frame, Della recalled the few friends she'd left behind in her old life. Oddly, they hadn't been nearly as important to her as Miranda and Kylie.

Pulling herself out of her past, she noted another picture of the three girls with graduation caps sitting on all of the girls' heads. Natasha was older than Della had originally thought. That, or she'd finished school early.

She put one picture down to pick up the other. Natasha's face drew her attention. There was something . . . almost familiar about it. And it was more than just having seen it in the photo with Chan and her aunt.

The sound of Chase opening drawers and rummaging through things behind her called her attention. She got a big sensation that they were intruding on the parents' personal shrine to their daughter, and she put the picture back down, almost wishing she hadn't even touched them.

She glanced back at Chase. "Don't move things around too much," she said, sensing the mom or dad came in here often and had memorized the placement of all their daughter's things. Things that told of her life.

"I'm just looking for anything that might give us something to help find her."

Della didn't know what that something would be, but being here felt right, almost as if the ghost had led them here. On top of a dresser was a picture of a man. Dark hair, slanted eyes. Della was almost certain it was the same man in the family photo that hung in the hall.

Funny how Natasha looked more Asian than her own father. Luck of the draw, Della thought, remembering how she hardly looked Asian.

All of a sudden, behind the soft music and lyrics, came the sound of a car moving down the road. "Someone's coming," she said.

"I know," Chase said.

By the time they got to the window, the car was pulling into the drive. "Shit," Della muttered.

"No problem," Chase said. "We'll wait until he unlocks the door, then we'll jump out this window. It's going to be okay," he said, as if sensed her near panic.

Sensed it correctly. Della's adrenaline pumped like crazy. The thought of being caught sent bolts of fear coursing through her veins. And then she heard it. Not the driver in the car outside who had cut the engine off. The car was the least of their problems. What Della heard were footsteps. Footsteps moving up the steps from inside the house.

Someone *was* already inside the home. Had been there the entire time. Had they heard them? Were they coming to check?

Chase, obviously hearing it as well, looked back out the window.

"He's not out of the car yet." His voice barely reached her ears.

"So what do we do?" she replied in the same low voice.

"Plan B," he said.

"What is it?"

He paused one second. "I don't have a friggin' clue."

"Shit," Della whispered again.

The footsteps thudded closer, down the hall, almost in front of the bedroom door. Nothing but a thin piece of wood stood between them and being caught as intruders.

Never had Della been this envious of Kylie's gift of turning invisible. But wishing was going to get her nowhere—she needed a plan. She needed one fast.

"The closet." She latched her hand around his arm and pulled him inside.

They had barely gotten the door closed and sunk down amongst a few shoes and clothes that had fallen on the floor, when the footsteps stopped. Stopped right outside the bedroom door.

Della pulled her knees to her chest. Darkness filled the small space. Her shoulder pressed against Chase's. Needing more air to attempt to deal with the panic gripping her lungs, she took fast, and hopefully silent, breaths. The smell of perfume and shampoo, obviously Natasha's, filled the air. Then Chase's scent, spicy male soap and outdoors, filled Della's senses. While she could barely see anything, she still shut her eyes. Tight. And prayed.

Don't let them come in here. Don't let them come in here.

The door clicked open and the footsteps entered into the room. Soft footsteps sounding like a woman. What came next? If the person belonging to the footsteps had actually heard them, wouldn't she check the closet? Oh no. Why had Della chosen the closet?

Della's insides knotted with the thought of having to explain to her parents why she'd broken into someone's home.

Damn! Damn! She and Chase were going to get caught and this was going to be bad. Really, really bad.

The footsteps came farther into the room. Eyes still forced shut, she heard the person inhale, deeply. Chase's lips came against her ear.

"If they open the door, we fly right through the window. Just keep your head down and watch out for glass. If we go fast, they won't be able to describe us to the cops."

Della opened her eyes. Light snuck through the small space where the door didn't meet the wood floor. That, or her vision had adjusted to the dark and she could make out things—the clothes on the floor, the pair of worn tennis shoes in the corner. She shifted her gaze back to the door, preparing herself to run like hell if it opened.

She counted to three, thinking that was about the time a person would need to decide to check the closet.

One.

Two.

Three.

The door didn't open.

The sound of the bed's mattress sighing with weight added another layer of sadness to the song playing in the background.

Then came the heartfelt sob. A feminine sob. Not part of the music, but so much more emotional. It sounded like pain. Pure. Raw.

"Why do I keep hearing you?" the woman said. "Are you here, baby? Why can't I accept that you are gone? Can you hear me? I love you. I miss you. Miss you so much."

She's not gone, Della wanted to say. Tears filled her eyes. While she ached for Natasha and her mom, Della couldn't help but wonder if her own mother missed her.

Did her own mom ever walk into her room and cry?

Della didn't realize she still held Chase's hand until his fingers, laced with hers, gave her a light squeeze. Was he hurting for the woman, too? It felt as if he was trying to communicate to her that it would be okay.

But how could it be? The woman's grief grew thicker, the air, even in the tiny closet, felt heavier. The feeling of injustice, of grief, wiggled its way into Della's chest and made her insides feel crowded.

The music suddenly stopped and the sound of a phone ringing piped over the intercom.

The ringing became replaced with an electronic voice announcing: *Call from Miao Hon.*

Della's breath caught. Surely she'd heard it wrong. But the message repeated. *Call from Miao Hon.*

Why was her aunt, Chan's mother, calling Natasha's mom?

Della let out a shuttered breath. She cut her eyes toward Chase, but he hadn't seemed to put Chan's last name together with the person who was calling.

The slight sound of the mattress rising filtered through the door. Then footsteps left the bedroom. The click of the bedroom door shutting reached Della's ears, but it somehow sounded different. Distant. Too distant. Immediately, the closet seemed to grow darker. Instead of a hiding place, it felt like a prison.

Della turned to tell Chase she wanted to leave—she wanted out of there, away from the pain—but it wasn't Chase sitting next to her.

Chapter Twenty-four

Fear was her go-to emotion, but when she went there, the fear faded into a whole different kind of feeling. Something that gave her butterflies in her stomach. Good butterflies.

With her shoulder against his, she stared at the guy, trying to understand. He had dark brown, almost black, almond-shaped eyes, smooth skin the color of coffee with lots of cream. His short hair was black and hung in loose curls over his brow. His features were . . . perfect, except for a scar that was still red over his left brow. Something about him tickled her memory bank, but she couldn't quite grasp it. Yet she had the oddest desire to run her finger over the healing wound.

All of a sudden, another recollection whispered across what little brain power she had. She didn't see everything, but had vague flashes of a fight, and she knew he had gotten that wound trying to protect her.

He stared at her with warmth and passion. She wanted to close the distance between them, but then she didn't have to. He leaned closer, his mouth a whisper from hers. His light breath touched her lips.

He was going to kiss her.

Correction. He was kissing her.

No, not her. He was kissing Natasha.

He was Liam. And Natasha was kissing him back.

"You are so beautiful," he whispered, pulling back from her mouth, running his finger over her lips, moist from his kiss.

"I am not. My hair's caked in mud, I need a shower." She chuckled.

"That's not what I see," he said.

"Then good thing it's dark in here," she countered.

He kissed her again, and this time the kiss went from soft to hot. His mouth tasted so good. Sweet and tangy like blood. Her blood. His blood.

They must have just fed off each other again. But this time she wasn't repulsed. She was too into the kiss, too into Liam, to care.

She may be facing death, but right then she wanted to feel alive. To feel passion. To touch. To be touched.

The next thing she knew, they were lying on their sides. The hard dirt beneath her didn't even feel bad. All she cared about was Liam. He rested beside her. His shirt was off. She traced a tattoo of an odd-looking cross symbol on his shoulder.

His hand slipped under her shirt and the kisses grew hotter, sweeter.

Natasha moved her hand down his abs and around his waist.

They should stop before it went too far, but then logic intervened. All they had right now was each other. How could it be wrong to cling to that?

His fingers slipped beneath her bra and brushed over her nipple. It felt heavenly and so real. Even more real than before.

She turned her head, let her eyes drift open and saw a tennis shoe. Natasha's shoe. Natasha's closet. The she felt a hand again, on her breast.

"Shit!" Della muttered, snapping out of it. "Get your hand off my—"

"Shh." Chase's other hand, the one that wasn't fondling her boob, pressed over her mouth.

Della instantly remembered why they had to be quiet. But his hand, still gently cupping her breast, stayed where it was. And while she hated admitting it, it felt heavenly. But also wrong. Crazy wrong.

"Move your other hand, now," she whispered through his palm in a voice low enough he couldn't complain, but he must have heard her deadly intent, because his eyes widened.

"I'm sorry, I didn't . . . I wasn't." His voice came lower than a whisper, for her ears only. "Oh, hell, I'll move my hand if you move yours."

My hand? Still struggling to connect with her own body and to leave the vision, her breath caught with the startling realization. Chase wasn't the only one getting touchy-feely. Her hand was down the back of his jeans, under his soft cotton underwear, and gently caressing his butt. Blood rushed to her face instantly.

She yanked her hand out of his pants.

"Easy," he said again, slipping his hand out from under her shirt and pulling her against him. She started to struggle and he whispered, "You're going to hit the wall and we're going to get caught."

Caught making out in Natasha's closet while her parents were downstairs, a voice inside her said. She listened, not to the voice, but to what was happening in the house. Sure enough, she heard voices, a male and female.

She took a deep, sobering breath and slowly shifted away, getting a few inches from Chase. But it didn't make her feel better. How could it?

She'd just gone to second base with the Panty Perv. Unintentionally. But it still counted, didn't it?

She tried to remember anything about it—him touching her, her touching him—but all she could remember was being Natasha and being high on Liam's kisses.

That's when she knew Chase had been inside Liam, just as she'd been inside Natasha. Did that mean she couldn't get mad at Chase? Probably. Somehow, she got the feeling he hadn't been the one to slip *her* hand in *his* pants. She'd done that all by herself. Or with Natasha's help.

Oh, but she still wanted to be mad at Chase.

And when he looked at her, she glared at him. It might have been wrong, but it still felt good.

He frowned. "I think we can leave . . . quietly. They both seem to be downstairs. We should be able to open the window and jump without them seeing us."

She gulped tension down her throat. Two kinds of tension. The one she felt low in her belly from Chase touching her, and the other kind. The kind that said they weren't out of the woods yet—they could still get arrested for breaking and entering. It didn't matter if the window had been open.

On her hands and knees, she followed him out of the closet. As she rose up, her gaze shifted up to his butt, his cute muscular butt, and she blushed again.

He carefully and quietly lifted the window then looked back at her. "Jump to the right, out of view of the front window. Stay behind the trees, and head to the car. I'll be right behind you." His words came so low she barely heard them.

She did as he said, and landed to the far right of the window. She made it to the line of trees. The sun had already started to rest in the west. The golden light caught on the red and yellow leaves and made them look even brighter.

Adrenaline took her another few steps, then she stopped. She hadn't heard him land. She looked back. Chase wasn't there. Where the hell was he?

One. Two. Three. She was giving him to ten, then she was going in after him.

She got all the way to nine when he finally appeared at the window and leapt out, landing on his feet a good ten feet away from the view of the window.

Together, they made their way through the small patch of trees to the road. When Della spotted the blue Camaro, she could almost breathe.

"What took you so long?" she asked.

"Get in, and I'll tell you."

And that's when Della noticed the bulge under his shirt. "You took something!" she seethed. "They'll know, damn it. They probably have everything in that room memorized."

"It was in the closet, behind some shoe boxes. I don't think they even knew it was there." He pulled out a small book. "I think it's a diary."

Della instantly thought of Miranda and her diary. Sure, Della had teased her about wanting to read it, but she wouldn't have. Those were private.

"That wasn't yours to take," Della said.

"If it helps us find Natasha and Liam, I'll gladly take any hell you want to give me for stealing."

Della fought with her conscience, debating if he'd been right or wrong, then decided she probably would've done the same thing.

But for some reason that didn't stop her from feeling as if Chase had done something wrong.

Maybe she was just still angry at him about other things. Things that involved them on a closet floor. Oh, yeah, that had been so wrong.

They got in the car and Chase raised the top to make them less noticeable, and took off. As they passed the house, a man and woman were outside the house looking up at the open window. They zipped past, but Della did notice the man standing beside Natasha's mom wasn't the man in the family picture. Nevertheless, seeing them outside told Della just how close they'd come to being caught.

Too close.

"You getting anything helpful?" Chase asked fifteen minutes later, She hadn't spoken since they'd left Natasha's neighborhood as she read through the diary.

"No," Della said. "It's normal stuff, and it dates back almost two years." She looked down at the handwritten notes from Natasha's diary.

Another two minutes passed when he asked, "Do you want to talk about it?"

"The diary?" she asked, but she honestly knew what "it" was. Or at least, she feared she did.

"You're giving me the silent treatment. So let's just talk about it."

She hadn't purposely not spoken to him. She'd been busy reading Natasha's diary, and feeling guilty for doing it. And then, trying to figure out why her aunt had been calling Natasha's mom.

There was a connection. One she'd assumed had just been Chan. But if Chan's mom was calling Natasha's mom, it had to be more. Della was going to have to figure out what that was. But how, without going to see her aunt? Without making her father furious at her?

"Did you hear me?" he asked.

"Yes and no."

"What?" he asked, confused.

"Yes, I heard you, and no, I don't want to talk about . . . 'it.'"

"You can't be pissed at me about that."

"Sure I can," she seethed in a low voice.

"You're not being fair."

"Where did you get the idea I was fair?"

He chuckled. "Hey, you had your hand on my ass and I'm not mad at you."

"Well, that just says which of us has a better handle on this. Because you should be pissed. Fondling strangers isn't—"

"We aren't strangers." He glanced back at the road, but not before she saw the laughter in his eyes. A few seconds later, with his humor gone, he added, "We're bonded. Sooner or later, you're going to have to accept that."

She started to tell him she'd never accept it, but she didn't even know if it was a lie. So she just kept her mouth shut. Oddly enough, that seemed to bother him more than anything. She tucked that info away for another day.

"Look," he said. "It happened because of the vision. And instead of being worried about it, we should be trying to figure out if maybe we got anything from the vision to help us."

"You're right," she said.

"Wow, can I have that in writing?" he asked with sarcasm.

She frowned and closed the dairy. The entries were about a boy she liked and what her girlfriends did. And it sort of broke Della's heart because the relationship between Natasha and Amy and Jennifer seemed so special. Special like her relationship with Miranda and Kylie.

What had happened to these girls? Were they still missing Natasha?

"I don't remember much of the vision," Della said.

"I could see better this time," Chase said. "I don't know if that means there was more light in there, or if the ghost let us see."

"I could see better, too. And I guess it could be either." Della tried to remember details. "Liam had a cut over his brow." She let her mind go back to the vision, trying to put the pieces back together. "He got it defending Natasha."

"From who?" Chase asked, as if Della might hold a key to finding them.

And damn it, she wished she did. "I don't know, I just . . . Natasha thought about the fight, and I saw him being hit, and her trying to stop it and her feeling guilty. What was Liam thinking about?" she asked.

He cut his eyes at her, looking almost guilty.

"Oh, hell! Why did I even ask? All you were thinking about was getting her naked, right?" She let out a low growl.

"Hey, it was him. Not me." He looked back at the road. "And I don't think he was the only one into it."

Della couldn't deny it. Natasha had wanted Liam, too. She just wished Natasha's wanting hadn't led to her groping Chase's ass.

"She had a tattoo," Chase said, shifting gears.

"She doesn't seem the type to get a tattoo," Della said.

"Well, she had one. On her shoulder." Della suddenly remembered seeing one on Liam's shoulder as well. Oddly, she recalled Natasha tracing it with her finger, knowing it was there, when Della could hardly see it.

"That's strange," Della said.

"What's strange?"

A ring sounded in the car. She put their conversation on hold and pulled her cell out of her pocket. Her heart took a nosedive.

Don't let it be Steve.

When she saw it wasn't Steve, her heart rose back up. Then went right back down. He hadn't called her. Probably wasn't going to call her. Just like Perry. But damn, that hurt.

Staring at the phone, she forced herself to speak. "It's Burnett."

Chase readjusted in his seat, making the leather crinkle. "Making sure we haven't done something stupid, no doubt."

"We did do something stupid," she said.

"That wasn't stupid." He looked at her with a sexy hooded-eye grin. "Hate me if you want, but I enjoyed it."

She growled at him. "See, you are like every other guy. All you think about is sex. I was talking about going inside their house."

"Oh, then that was definitely not stupid. We found out what we needed to know."

She agreed with him, but couldn't stop from making a point. "It would have been stupid if we'd gotten caught."

"But we didn't," he said. He looked at the road and then back. "And that's not all I think about. Not with you."

"Right." She looked back at the ringing phone.

"You'd better answer or he'll have an aneurism."

She cut him a disapproving look. "You need to get over your animosity toward Burnett."

"He's way overprotective."

"Because he cares." She answered the call. "Hey," she said into the phone.

"Where are you at?" Burnett's voice boomed out of her phone into the car.

Della picked up a shitload of tension, but decided to ignore it and hope it was just the vampire's normal I'm-worried-therefore-I-roar voice.

"Just left the Owens' house about fifteen minutes ago."

"And?"

"It's her," Della said, feeling Chase looking at her. And unable to stop herself, she shifted her eye to him. He looked concerned and held out his hand as if saying he was willing to do the talking. She shook her head.

"And the parents? You didn't rock the boat?" The question came off almost defensive.

Maybe a little. "We didn't turn the boat over," she answered, hoping to talk around a lie.

"Then friggin' explain to me why the cops are on their way there now?"

Chapter Twenty-five

Della reluctantly explained everything to Burnett. Yeah, he'd been pissed that they'd gone into the house, but not as pissed as she thought he'd be. It seemed he had obviously done a little breaking and entering of his own in the past. Why else hadn't he gone ballistic?

She wondered if the reason Burnett and Chase butted heads so much was because they were just too much alike. She recalled how Kylie had told her the reason she and Burnett were so confrontational was because they had similar traits. That had been Kylie's way of saying they were both hardheaded punks who didn't think before they spoke.

Was that the same reason she and Chase butted heads? No, they were not at all alike. He was a pain in the ass.

And that ass was really firm, too. Della gave that thought a good goal-winning kick from her mind. Leaving an empty spot in her brain. And wouldn't you know what slipped in to fill it?

A certain shape-shifter, whose butt was equally cute. Whose butt had left her. Whose butt was now in Paris, probably flirting with all the French beauties. And in a culture where the television and books made it appear sex was as common a practice as brushing one's teeth. There had been a time when that culture might have intrigued her, but not when the guy she cared about, a hot guy, was visiting said culture.

Damn! Damn! Damn!

Trying to move from that thought, she landed back on the phone call Natasha's mom had received. As much as Della hated the idea, if they didn't find another lead soon, she was going to have to go see her aunt.

And her aunt would probably tell her dad. And then her dad would probably pull her from Shadow Falls. Yeah, she remembered overhearing her dad telling her mom about taking Della over to see her aunt: *We don't hang out our dirty laundry.*

Dirty laundry.

Della's dad considered her to be his dirty laundry.

Her breath shuddered in her chest. *Sorry, Dad!*

The thought of her dad led her back to the vision, to seeing either him or her uncle standing over her aunt's body with a bloody knife. Correction, seeing her uncle. She'd already mentally established that her dad wouldn't do that. He couldn't. She knew him better than that. She did!

"We going to get out, or just sit here?" Chase's voice brought her out of her little pity party.

Looking up, she realized he'd parked and they were sitting at the fast-food restaurant where they were supposed to meet the other agent—a backup, in case they ran into trouble.

"Nah, I think I'll just stay here," she smarted off and got out of the car.

He met her as she rounded the back of the car and started walking into the restaurant. "What's wrong?" he asked.

Just the question, or maybe his caring tone, brought a knot to her throat. She swallowed the damn thing down whole, too. She wasn't about to start unraveling right now.

"Let's just do our job," she said, trying not to be so snappy. She looked up at the neon sign hanging over the small building. Buck's Burgers, but the B was out, so it read: UCK'S BURGERS. Not a very appetizing name.

She opened the door to the restaurant and took a noseful of air to catch the scent of any supernatural. The smell of old ground beef and outdated French fry grease filled the air so thick, she couldn't be sure.

Uck's Burgers suddenly seemed like an appropriate name. At one time, she used to love the smell of cheap greasy food, but since she'd been turned, not so much.

A chorus of voices echoed around the space, along with the sound of meat sizzling on open grills. The place wasn't what she would call first class. The floors looked like they needed a good mopping, and the booth tops looked sticky. This was for sure a hangout for the rough and tough.

Della took in another breath, trying to catch the scent of company. She could swear she picked out a vampire, but wasn't 100 percent sure. Chase stopped beside her and spoke in a whisper. "Didn't you say you knew this guy?"

"I met him once." Della shifted her gaze from booth to booth.

"Where?" Chase asked.

"There he is." Della walked toward Shawn Hanson, the warlock who'd been so kind as to fix Chan's gravesite, and the one who had a thing for Miranda.

Chase had insisted to Burnett that they needed someone who looked young. Burnett had come through. Shawn couldn't be more than twenty, maybe even nineteen, but he looked sixteen, wearing a hoody and a pair of worn jeans. Add the earring, and he not only looked young, but kind of tough, and even cute.

His blond hair, curls and all, looked a little messy—not like those guys who got their hair styled. She had a feeling this was the Shawn who Miranda had crushed over, too. In a way, his non-fussy look, kind demeanor, and basic blue-eyed-boy good looks reminded Della of Perry.

"Hey," she said.

"What took you guys so long? I've been waiting for almost half an hour." His eyes tightened as if in warning.

Not that she needed it. Shawn's immediate slip into undercover told Della something was up. She fought the need to stick her nose up and take another deep sniff.

"Sorry," Chase said, slipping into the role as well. "Della's dad had to show me his gun again. I guess I shouldn't have kissed her in front of him." He nudged her into the empty side of a booth and then climbed in beside her.

"He's gonna use it on your ass if you don't start respecting him," Della said.

Shawn laughed. "Y'all wanna get something to drink, or go to the park and hang and sip on what I got?" He leaned in closer.

At first, Della thought he meant to tell them something real. "I got what you asked for." Obviously, this was still part of the cover.

He picked up the backpack that sat beside him. "Two pints of O. And it's fresh."

That told Della that whoever Shawn was putting on this show for was probably vampire. Her next intake of air, she caught their scents. There were two, no, three.

Then Della got a whiff of something tangy and sweet. Damn,

Shawn had actually brought blood, and it even smelled like O. Her mouth watered . . . it had been a while since she'd had any of the good stuff.

"Hell, I'm ready." Chase stood up and offered her a hand.

Della eased out of the booth on her own. Lifting her butt up, she saw three guys sitting in the corner. Vamps. Young but rough looking. Possibly gang members. Chase put a hand on her waist as they walked to the door. She stepped out of his reach, and right then caught another scent. A were. One hung close by.

His scent filtered up her nose and tugged on her memory bank. She wished she could turn around and find him. The trace didn't bring an out-and-out negative vibe, but with the exception of the Shadow Falls wolves, were memories were seldom good.

They got out the door and a good distance away before Shawn spoke again, and this time in a whisper. "I'm assuming they'll follow us."

"They aren't yet," Chase said.

"Did you see the were?" Della asked Shawn, who was to her right, while Chase walked at her left. "His trace is familiar."

"I never saw a were," Shawn said. "But about six guys in there were wearing hats and there were a couple of guys working in the back. It could have been one of them."

"I smelled him, too." Chase glanced at Della. "Do you know where you would have run into him before?"

"No, and it wasn't completely a bad trace. Just made me leery."

"From Shadow Falls?" Chase asked.

"No. I'm not leery of any of the weres at Shadow Falls."

They continued down the sidewalk. Shawn's light blue eyes cut to Chase. "I'm Shawn Hanson, by the way. It's good to meet you."

Chase nodded. "Same here."

Shawn looked at Della and something about his expression changed. "You doing okay?"

She knew he meant about Chan's death. "Yeah," she said and almost felt guilty how little she'd let the grief consume her. "Thanks again for . . . fixing the gravesite."

"It was nothing."

Della felt Chase's shoulder brush against hers and she looked at him. "Shawn was one of the agents who helped bury Chan."

"I see." Chase tilted his head slightly to the side. "They're following now."

Della focused and could hear the slightest sound of footsteps, but they were still some distance back. No doubt, they thought they were out of hearing range. But along with the additional strength, a Reborn also had extra-sensitive hearing.

"Should we turn around and face them?" she asked.

"No," Shawn said, lowering his voice. "Let's get to the park. There's a spot in the back where hardly anyone hangs out. We'll have more privacy to ask them some questions."

They continued down the sidewalk, their footsteps echoing in the night. Shawn made it sound so simple—find a quiet spot and ask the guys a few questions.

Call her a pessimist, but she didn't see it being that easy. Some feeling, a premonition of sorts, told Della this night wasn't going to end without trouble.

That was okay, she told herself. She could handle three vampires. It was matters of the heart that were her downfall, and her thoughts went back to Chan.

They arrived at the park and continued down a path that led behind one of the ponds. Only the stars and the moon gave them light. Della listened to the distant footsteps blending with the night sounds, and even caught the shuffling sound of some unhappy wildlife going for cover.

After a few minutes, the footsteps following them changed course. Della got the feeling the three vamps thought they knew where they were going and wanted to take a different path to try to ambush them.

She cut her eyes to Chase, and he nodded at her as if he was aware of it as well. Della reached out and touched Shawn on his arm and sent a warning look. He nodded as if he understood exactly what she meant.

They arrived at the pond, the moon and stars reflected off the too-still water. They kept walking around to an area toward the back.

A few steps later, she caught the strong smell of skunk. Both Chase and Shawn groaned from the stench. Not that she minded. She was one of those weird people who actually liked the smell. She took a deep noseful. Mixed in the musky scent, she picked up another odor. Oh, hell, she smelled a rat. Three of them. No, a lot more than three.

She cut her gaze, already brightening from the sense of a threat, to Chase. He had a hand covering his nose, and didn't seem to notice. Which was exactly what the rogue vamps had hoped. They'd obviously gotten skunked on purpose in hopes of going undetected. Not even a bad idea. "We've got company."

She barely got the sentence out when eight vamps landed in a circle around them.

With the threat now visible, her fangs lowered.

"You don't want to do this," Shawn said.

"Looks like they do," Chase seethed, his eyes now glowing and his own fangs clearly extended.

"Hey . . . that guy's pretty smart," said one smartass vamp pointing to Chase.

"Slow and easy," Della whispered, warning Chase, hoping he understood that he should let Shawn, the agent Burnett put in charge, do his thing before attacking.

"But I like fast and hard," said one of the dirty vamps, grinding his hips in a vulgar motion.

Chase growled.

"Calm down," Della whispered.

"Hand over the backpack, Witchboy," said the dark-haired vamp to Della's right.

"I think we can work this out. I've got a plan," Shawn said, sounding cool and collected. Della admired his calm approach. Not that she thought it was going to work, but she had to give him credit for trying.

"Here's what we'll do," Shawn continued. "I'll give it to you and tell you where another few pints are buried close by. All you guys have to do is answer a few questions."

"You got more O?" asked the vamp who liked it fast and hard.

"That's right. And all you need to do is answer a few questions."

The dark-haired vamp, obviously the leader, and even more obviously a rogue, pulled a knife from a holder strapped to his calf. It was an impressive knife—four- or five-inch blade. Big enough to do some damage.

She remembered the knife she'd taken in the chest on her first mission, which was about that same size. Not that it could happen again. Being a Reborn, this guy didn't stand a chance. Or at least, she hoped that to be true.

"Yeah," the rogue said, "but you see, I don't like questions. But I do like O blood. So why don't you just tell me where the blood is, and that might convince me not to kill you. Or at least to kill you fast."

The threat made the blood in Della's veins fizz. The knife-wielding vamp smiled and it came off so evil, Della shivered. Not from fear, but from anticipation. Wiping that smile off his face was gonna be fun!

She glanced at Chase. "Okay, so maybe slow and easy wasn't a good idea."

"Not yet," Shawn said, holding a hand toward them, then he spoke to the leader of the pack. "You don't want to mess with us." He raised his shirt and exposed his badge and a flash of his tight abdomen.

Yup, Della could see why Miranda had a thing for the guy.

Things went dead silent. Even the leaves didn't move. No doubt, the rogue leader was weighing his options: cooperate, run like hell, or go forward with his threat.

"We ain't scared of you," said the mouthy, fast-and-hard vamp. "Are we, Marco?" he asked the leader.

Marco didn't say anything at first. Apparently, he wasn't quite as stupid as his friend.

"There's just three of them," said another of the vamps.

Marco, the caller of the shots, shifted his stance. His shoulders tensed in a defensive posture. Maybe she'd overestimated his intelligence.

His eyes glowed a bit brighter, telling her he wasn't planning on backing down. She almost wanted to clap her hands.

Marco held out his knife. "I think we get extra points for taking out an FRU agent, don't we, boys?"

Della saw all the vamps reach down for their own knives, and in a flash, they charged. All eight.

Chapter Twenty-six

Della went after Marco first. She snagged his knife and tossed the weapon at a tree trunk, where it sank all the way in, handle and all. Swinging up and around, she gave him a good kick in the stomach. That didn't take him out. So she went for his balls. He landed on the ground moaning.

From the corner of her eye, she saw the fast-and-hard vamp lying facedown on the ground. Chase was now taking on one of the other vamps and looking good while doing it. She twisted her head to check on Shawn. He had two swords in his hands, and the friggin' things glowed. They reminded Della of Kylie's magical sword. He had some moves down, but with three of them swiping blades at him, he probably could use some help.

Della calmly walked up, tapped one on the shoulder. When he turned around, knife held out, she kicked him in the crotch. Hey . . . if it worked the first time, why not go for it a second?

He fell to the ground and curled up in a fetal position, moaning like his leader. She started to step in and assist Shawn with the other two, but spotted one of the other vamps making a run for it with the backpack and O-negative blood.

And that just wasn't acceptable.

"Come back here, you coward!" Della bolted after him.

The escapee had a good stride. Probably would do well in the Olympics if he wasn't racing with Reborns. She caught him by the scuff of his neck in less than thirty seconds.

He turned, his knife aimed forward. She dodged it. Catching his wrist, she turned it, almost to the point of breaking it, before he dropped the weapon.

He also dropped the backpack and took a swing at her with his left hand. She hadn't expected it and he clipped her chin. It hurt like hell, but pissed her off even more.

"You're going down!" she heard Chase scream from behind them, and the bushes rustled with his fast approach.

"No. He's mine!" And wanting to change her tactics a bit, she fisted her hand and coldcocked the vamp. He fell to the ground in an unconscious lump.

She hadn't finished shaking off the pain in her knuckles when Shawn's yelp filled the darkness. From pain or anger, Della didn't know. Didn't take the time to consider. Both she and Chase flew back to the warlock.

The blond agent had blood oozing from his shoulder and he'd lost one of his swords. But his determined look said he hadn't thrown in the towel yet. He moved in even, liquid steps, holding off the tallest and the last of the vamps.

Della caught Shawn's eye. "Can I help you?"

"No," he seethed as he came down hard and blocked the vamp from moving in to use his knife again. "I got it!" he muttered. And he did. As the vamp cut his eyes to Della and Chase, Shawn knocked the weapon from the vamp's hand. He started to turn and run, but suddenly he froze. Not froze as in just stood extra still. But literally *froze*.

A few tiny icicles hung from his nose.

Della looked back at the warlock and he still had his pinkie out.

"Why didn't you just do that to start with?" Della rubbed her chin where she'd taken the blow. It wasn't broken, but felt swollen.

"It takes a second of calm to do it. They came on fast. I can pull up swords faster than I can curses."

"Ahh," Della said, not getting the whole magic thing.

"Nasty," Chase said, moving close to see the guy's face.

"You okay?" Della said, motioning to Shawn's arm.

"Just a flesh wound." He held himself proud, but having been stabbed once, she knew it had to sting like hell.

"I have some electric cuffs in the backpack if you want to start containing those guys." He looked around for the backpack.

"Oh, one of the guys took off with it. I'll get it," Della said, but when she turned, Chase was already returning with the backpack in one hand, and dragging the rogue she'd coldcocked with the other.

"That was easy," Shawn said a few minutes later as he watched her and Chase cuff all but the frozen vamp. "You two are good."

Shawn nodded at Della and then his gaze shifted to Chase. "Burnett's right. We need to steal you away from the Vampire Council."

"Thanks, but no thanks," Chase said.

"You do know we pay twice as much as them?"

"Not happening," Chase said with sureness.

Why not? Della wondered, but then pushed it away to consider at a later time.

Exhaling, feeling the adrenaline lessening, she fisted her hand that felt slightly swollen from the knock-out punch, and right then her jaw started to throb. A slight noise came from the frozen guy, who must have been defrosting because saliva dripped from his mouth. She glanced at Shawn.

She tossed him the last pair of cuffs. He caught them and locked up the frosty vamp. "You didn't do too bad, yourself," Della told him.

"Actually . . ." Shawn forced the cuffed vamp onto the ground next to the others, and then stepped back and pulled out his phone. "My orders were to get info without trouble. Burnett's not going to be happy."

"Is he ever?" Chase mouthed off, then moved next to Della and took her chin in his hand.

"That idiot left a bruise." He looked back at the unconscious culprit.

"It's nothing." Della stepped away from his touch.

"It's over." Shawn's voice echoed behind them. "Yeah, she's fine."

Della rolled her eyes knowing Burnett asked about her first as if she couldn't handle herself. How embarrassing!

"Told you he's overprotective," Chase whispered as he lifted her chin again.

"And what are you?" She slapped his hand.

"We're all fine," Shawn said, a little louder as if to caution them that Burnett could hear.

She and Chase faced him and Della tilted her head to the side to hear the voice on the line.

"Is everyone else okay?" Burnett's voice came from the phone.

"Yeah." Shawn looked down at his bleeding shoulder.

"What's wrong?" Burnett asked, hearing his lie.

"I got cut, but it's not bad."

Burnett moaned. "Did we get anything?"

"Well, it didn't go down like we wanted. We're going to need a paddy wagon."

Burnett moaned again. "How many?"

"Eight." Shawn walked off and Della couldn't hear Burnett anymore.

"You really okay?" Chase asked her and reached for her hand that she'd used to knock out the rogue.

"Stop," Della snapped.

"Hey?" Shawn looked back over his shoulder. "They are all alive, right?"

Chase glanced at the eight vamps lined up like downed dominos. "Yeah, but I could fix that." He glared daggers at the vamp who'd hit her.

Della and Chase followed the car with the rogues to the FRU offices. Burnett met them in the entrance. He walked right up to her and lifted her chin.

"It's just a bruise!" she fumed.

"Which one did it?" he asked in quiet fury.

"What does it matter?"

"The one in the brown T-shirt," Chase volunteered.

Della scowled at Chase and then back to Burnett. "Why is it that Shawn, who took a knife to his shoulder, just walked past and you never went mother hen on his ass?"

Burnett frowned. "Because my daughter isn't named after him. Besides, I have a doctor meeting him right now. Now, were you hurt anywhere else?"

"No, I'm fine."

"The fist," Chase answered. "She knocked one out. Did a good job of it."

"I am fine!" Della growled.

Only then did Burnett glance toward Chase. "You okay?"

"Not a bruise."

"Bragger!" Della mouthed off.

Burnett looked at the door. "Can you see that Della gets back to Shadow Falls? We'll take over from here."

"No!" Della and Chase said at the same time.

Della tilted her bruised chin back. "I . . . we want to know if they have anything on Liam."

Burnett's expression hardened, but the look in his eyes said he wasn't going to give them a fight. He turned and looked at another agent standing by a front desk. "Take them into room six to watch the interviews."

Chase moved beside Burnett. Della noticed that Burnett only had about an inch of height on Chase.

"I should do the interviews," Chase said.

"Sorry." Determination tightened Burnett's expression. "Hire on with us, and you'll get full privileges. Until then, you do only what I say you do."

Chase's eyes grew a bit brighter, but he didn't respond. Remembering his negative response to Shawn earlier about signing on with the FRU, her curiosity about his employment with the Vampire Council piqued again. Why was he working for them? How had he come to work for them? Was there a reason for his loyalty to his employer?

The other agent, a were, walked up and motioned for her and Chase to follow. While Della did as requested, she recalled smelling the were at the restaurant.

The agent pushed open a door at the end of a drab, gray hallway. "They'll bring them in one at a time . . . in about three minutes. You can see and hear them, but they can't hear you." The were motioned to the glass wall. Not that he needed to explain. Both Chase and she had been here once before. "Burnett will be doing the interviews."

Once alone in the room, Della looked at Chase and her curiosity bit. "Why the loyalty to the Vampire Council?"

"What do you mean?" he asked.

"You seem really loyal to them."

His shoulders tightened. "They aren't the rogue group as you've been led to believe. We might not agree with all the FRU politics but—"

"I didn't say that. I'm simply asking why you're so loyal to them?"

He looked cornered by her inquiry.

"That's a strange question coming from you, who defends Burnett even when you hate it that he's coddling you."

His counterattack, rather than giving her a straight answer, made her even more curious. Was he hiding something?

"Not so strange," Della answered. "That's exactly why I'm curious. I'm loyal to Burnett because . . ." She paused, finding it just a bit hard to admit out loud. "He's more than just a route into my career, he's family. What's your excuse?"

He didn't answer right away. Was he thinking of a lie, or . . . "I like my job. I like the freedom the council allows me. It's no secret I find Burnett's micromanaging to be ridiculous."

"Yeah, but that's Burnett—with me. We're talking about working for the FRU, not working for Burnett."

"True, but I get the feeling he carries a lot of weight in the unit. And the rest of them are just like him."

Della could have argued the point. No one cared as much as Burnett, and while she hated his coddling, she wasn't above caring for him right back. That said, she couldn't deny seeing reason in Chase's answer.

"How did you hire on with the Vampire Council?"

He looked at the glass wall into the empty interrogation room. "They became aware of me being a Reborn. They sought me out."

Out of habit, she listened to his heart. It hadn't skipped, but she hadn't forgotten his ability to control that organ. Her suspicions grew. Had he turned away so she wouldn't note the telltale signs of him lying?

She was just about to call him on that fact, when she heard them: An agent, one of the vampires who'd come to help transport them here, brought one of the rogues into the room and forced him down in a chair.

A few seconds later, Burnett came in and sat across the table from the unhappy cuffed vamp. Burnett carried a file and opened it on the table. His gaze stayed on the paperwork. He didn't come across as violent, but being Burnett, just his presence carried a certain amount of intimidation.

He sat there without speaking. Never even looking up. Even hidden behind the one-way glass, Della could feel the tension building.

The vamp couldn't handle the silence any longer. "We weren't going to hurt them. We just wanted the blood."

"Funny, it didn't seem that way, did it?" Chase asked Della.

"No," Della admitted.

Slowly, Burnett looked up. "Tell that to the agent who got knifed and the one who got clipped in the jaw."

"Hey, that chick kneed me in the balls."

"You're lucky she didn't remove them to play badminton with."

Chase chuckled lightly. "Burnett knows you well."

Della shrugged, but didn't answer, too busy studying what was happening in the other room in hopes of learning a thing or two.

Burnett leaned back in his chair, squaring his shoulders, making the guy sitting across from him appear smaller. Did he do that on purpose?

Finally, Burnett spoke, but looked back at the file. "She doesn't normally go so easy on lowlifes who threaten her life."

"I told you we weren't—"

"Jason Von, right?"

When the kid didn't answer, Burnett leaned forward, his eyes glowing. "Is that your name?"

"Yes," Jason said.

Burnett nodded. "Look, Jason, I'm not going to beat around the bush. All eight of you are going down for attempted robbery, two of you get the added bonus of assault. Our facilities are almost filled. We have two spots left at Burton. It's not a walk in the park, but Parkrow, our other facility, it's rough. Only about fifty percent who go in, come out. And twenty-five of those will end up killing themselves. And the first two of the five of you with the lesser counts who tell us what we need to know will get to go to Burton."

He pulled a photograph out of the file and pushed it in front of the rogue. The rogue, who suddenly seemed too young to be up to his yin yang in this kind of trouble.

"Are you going to be one of the lucky Burton attendees?" Burnett tapped the picture with his index finger. "I need info on this kid." He looked the guy straight in the eyes. "Do you know him? Have you ever seen him before? I know he was hanging out in your gang's territory."

The vamp, probably no older than Della, glanced down at the image, and his eyes widened with recognition. In his round brown eyes, Della saw something else. Fear.

"He's afraid," Della said.

"He should be," Chase answered. "I've seen Parkrow, you might as well go to hell."

"No," Della said. "When he looked at the picture he was afraid. He knows something and is scared to tell."

The kid looked back up at Burnett. "I . . ."

"Burton or Parkrow?" Burnett said.

"I . . . uh," the vamp stuttered.

"Fine," Burnett said. "Parkrow it is." He stood to leave.

"No," Della muttered. "He knows something."

Yes, he knows something. Find Natasha.

The voice echoed in Della's mind. She looked at Chase to see if he'd heard it, but he didn't appear to have.

Still reeling from the voice, Della got a fresh scent of werewolf again. She looked behind her to see if a were had somehow snuck in the room, but nope.

She inhaled again to see if she'd been mistaken. The scent hung on. And the familiarity of it tickled her senses. This was the same scent she'd gotten back at the restaurant.

"Do you smell that?" she questioned Chase.

He looked confused, but lifted his face and inhaled. "Smell what?"

Damn! The ghost was trying to tell her something. But what?

Her gaze shot back to the kid, to the fear in his eyes. "I don't know shit," he said.

Della saw his left eyebrow wiggle. Just like Chase's wiggled when he lied.

Burnett stopped at the door. "You're going to regret this."

He's lying. The ghost spoke again.

Burnett turned the doorknob. "No!" Unable to stop herself, she took two steps to the wall and raised her fist.

"Don't!" Chase shot forward as if to stop her.

Too late, she pounded on the glass.

Both Burnett and the rogue vamp's gaze whipped toward the wall. The kid looked kind of shocked, but Burnett looked pissed, and not just kind of, but full-blown, over-the-top pissed.

He shot out of the door. No doubt coming to have a powwow with the person who'd dared to knock. But that was okay. She needed to see him, too. She started toward the door when it flung open and banged against the wall so hard that tiny white pieces of Sheetrock fell like snow from the ceiling.

"What the hell are you doing?" Burnett roared. "You never interrupt an interrogation."

Chapter Twenty-seven

Chase moved closer to her, almost as if fearing Burnett would strike her. Della knew better. Not that she didn't fear Burnett. She feared disappointing him, feared he would see her weaknesses. But she never feared he would physically hurt her.

"I'm sorry, but he knows something," Della snapped.

Burnett's scowl deepened. "I know he knows something!" He tossed up his hands in frustration. "And he was about to tell me what he knows!"

"No he wasn't. He was going to vague up the truth because he's afraid."

"No, he's going to tell me the truth because he's afraid!" Burnett demanded.

She shook her head. "You need to ask about the werewolf."

"What werewolf?"

"I . . . don't know. But if you ask . . . Wait, just let me ask him, I'll act like I know more and I'll get the truth out of him."

"What?" Burnett seethed, and when she didn't answer instantly, he shifted his glare to Chase. "What the hell is she talking about?"

Chase appeared confused, but then his light green eyes met hers and he almost smiled. "I'm clueless, but I'd bet my right arm that she's onto something. If you're smart, you'll trust her."

Burnett looked back at Della. "I do trust her. But I still need an explanation."

Della gave one. One word. "Ghost."

Della stood outside the door gathering her courage and pulling the elastic band of her big-girl panties up. She'd asked for this, now she had to come through.

Even with the core temperature of a vampire, she felt little pin-sized drops of sweat appear on her brow. Nerves. Nothing but nerves.

What if she was wrong? What if she'd only imagined the smell of were? What if the kid didn't know crap? What if she failed? Both Burnett and Chase were watching back in the room with the glass wall.

Lordy! What had inspired her to do this?

Find Natasha.

Oh, yeah, that was what. The voice. The ghost.

Stiffening her spine, remembering Natasha and Liam's lives were on the line, then cramming any sign of insecurity deep inside, she opened the door.

Remembering how Burnett's presence had filled the room, she stepped inside. She didn't immediately look at the vamp.

"They sent *you* in?" he asked in a condescending voice.

She crossed her arms and finally looked at him. "It's because of what I know."

"What do you know?" he asked, his brown eyes not showing the same fear as they did with Burnett.

She swallowed a lump of doubt. She considered picking him up and slamming him against a wall. But she suspected Burnett wouldn't respect that.

"Cat got your tongue?" he asked, almost smiling.

Failure loomed right ahead, but she wasn't going down without a fight.

She pulled out the chair across from him, letting it screech across the tile floor, and dropped down into the seat. "I know that you were about to vague up the truth when answering the agent."

"You know that, huh?" He smirked.

She wanted to smack him. "Yeah, you weren't planning on telling him about the weres."

The look in his brown eyes told Della she was going to be able to walk out of here with her head held high.

"You don't understand . . ." He paused, then added, "Shit!"

"Give me the names now and you'll be placed in the best facility."

He actually seemed to cringe. "I think I'd rather take my chances at the bad prison."

"Really?" She leaned in, purposely getting into his space, hoping to push him to talk. " 'Cause I'm imagining about half the convicts in Parkrow are werewolves. And from gangs," she added, hoping like hell the weres he feared were wrapped up in a gang. "And you know we're going to find answers and they'll assume you were the snitch."

He jumped up, grabbed the chair with his chained hands, and tossed it against the wall. It clattered against the floor a few inches from where she stood. It wasn't so much an attack on her, as an expression of fury.

Della held out one hand to the wall where she knew Burnett and Chase watched, hoping they'd realize she was asking them not to come in. Getting the rogue angry was part of her plan.

She went over, carefully picked up his chair, and dropped it back down by the table. "Sit down!" she ordered, and when she stared him in the eyes, she was reminded how young he was. Being young didn't excuse his behavior, but she again felt fortunate that she'd had her cousin to help her through the turn, then Shadow Falls to keep her grounded. Had this guy had anyone?

When he didn't immediately respond, she tried another tactic. "Look, I know you're pissed. And you're probably scared. But tell us what we need to know, and I'm thinking the FRU will make sure you stay alive long enough to make something out of your life."

He practically flung himself into the chair. His pride looked chipped, he looked . . . desperate. She knew that feeling too well.

"I . . . don't know much. I saw a group of weres with that kid. I think his name was Liam. Marco was going to try to recruit him when we spotted the weres with him. He backed away really quick like. He said the weres were bad ass, said they collected fresh turns and it wasn't worth fighting for him."

"What's the name of the gang?" Della asked.

When he didn't answer, Della banged her hand on the table.

"I don't know. He didn't say the name of the gang. I'm not even sure they are a gang." He paused a minute. "He said the name of one of the weres though. A Damian Baker, or maybe Bryan, a B name. That's all I know."

Della believed him. She started to leave, but then remembered getting the familiar trace of a were at the restaurant.

"Does Damian or one of his friends hang out at Buck's Burgers?" she asked.

"I don't know. I guess they could."

"What did the weres look like?"

"Like all weres—dirty dogs."

Without warning, she got this empty-pit feeling in her stomach. Hunger to the point of pain, and she knew it came from Natasha.

"I'm going to need more than that!" she said, and her hollow-feeling gut said she was going to need it quick if she was going to find Natasha and Liam alive.

Burnett interrogated the other rogues using the info Della had gotten from Jason Von. He ended up getting more info. The name of the were seen kidnapping Liam was Damian Bond. Burnett was going to run the name through the FRU's computer database to see if they came up with anything.

Before they left the FRU office, Burnett called her aside and told her how well she'd done in the interrogation. Yet even now, still whirling in the feeling that Natasha and Liam were running out of time, Della couldn't bask in the compliment.

In spite of Burnett's orders to go straight home, she and Chase had gone by Uck's Burgers. At almost one in the morning, it was closed, most of the businesses were, and they sat in the parking lot, top down. No weres were in the area that they could smell. It was quiet, and they shifted their seats back just bit, comfortable in the night and the silence, and just watched the stars.

"I see the little dipper," Chase said.

"Yeah. I just spotted it."

"My mom was a stargazer," Chase said. "Sometimes, at night, she'd bring our sleeping bags out, and we'd just lay out there and stare up at the sky."

"That sounds nice," Della said, and glanced at him. "Do you still miss them?"

"Yeah, but it's not as bad as it was."

After another ten minutes, with thoughts of pissing off Burnett, she told him they should go.

When Chase pulled into the Shadow Falls parking lot, she

snagged the diary, offered a quick "later," and leapt out of his car without even opening the door. She had the craziest feeling that if she didn't get away he might try to kiss her.

As she moved from his car, she felt him looking at her.

"See you tomorrow," he said and got out.

She didn't look back, but damn it if a part of her didn't feel as if she was walking away from something important. A part of her wanted to turn around and fall against him, to ask him to reassure her that they would find Natasha and Liam.

"I'll miss you," he called out just as she passed through the gate.

Me, too. The thought ran through her mind, but she refused to say it. Then she remembered something and turned around. Before she spoke, she turned her head slightly to hear if anyone was around. No one.

"Make sure you look into me meeting the council."

She watched him wave and get into his car. She stayed there and watched his taillights disappear down the street. Funny how her request sent him driving off, when before he'd seemed happy to linger. Was there something to that?

Chapter Twenty-eight

It was almost two in the morning when she walked into her bedroom. The cabin was silent. Only the soft sounds of Miranda and Kylie sleeping in their beds filled the space. Della stripped off her clothes, donned PJs, crawled into bed, and hugged her pillow. Her mind spun, too hyped up to sleep.

Now, in bed, feeling a slight unnatural chill, thoughts of Chase faded and became replaced with thoughts of . . .

She looked around the room for any sign of a ghost. She didn't see shit, but it didn't mean shit wasn't there. "Are you my aunt?" Her words seemed to rise up and hang above her in a small cloud of mist.

Della pulled the covers up to her neck, then spotted the diary beside her and picked it up to read. She found the spot she'd stopped reading earlier. Some of the dates didn't have the year, but Della could tell the inscriptions were written several years back when Natasha was still in high school.

Wanting to know if there was anything about being turned, she flipped to the back of the book to see the date. Written on the last page were the words: *Good-bye, diary*. But the date on top was October thirteenth of last year.

Which would mean that reading her diary wasn't going to offer any help, it was just an invasion of privacy. Boring privacy, but an invasion all the same. She closed the book and went to put it away, but it suddenly flipped open.

Looking around, still feeling the chill, she closed the book again. This time, when it popped open, Della got the feeling she was supposed to read. Just like she'd been supposed to find the picture in Chan's casket.

"Fine. But how is this going to help find her? It's normal everyday stuff." Which Della had just referred to as boring, but truthfully, normal sounded nice. What would it feel like if your biggest problem was that the guy you liked didn't know you existed? She used to have that life, Della thought. And so did Natasha, she realized. Her life had gone to hell, too.

Della looked down at the page dated January 10. She started to read.

Mom called me into her room today. I knew what she was going to tell me. I felt it coming. She's going to marry Tom.

Della let go of a sigh. So Natasha's life wasn't so perfect. Della recalled the picture of the part-Asian man on Natasha's bedside table. That must have been her real dad. Had he died, or had her parents divorced? Then she recalled the man standing outside looking up at the window. That must have been Tom.

She went back to reading.

I did the right thing. I told her I was happy for her. But it was hard. It's also hard to realize how selfish I am. I want her to myself. I don't want to share her. But I don't plan to live at home forever. I'll graduate in less than a year. And then she'll be alone. She doesn't deserve that.

It's not as if I don't like Tom. Well, maybe I don't like him, but I don't dislike him. And I don't think he's bad. I can tell he loves my mom. And he's nice to me. But he's not my dad. And I feel as if he's trying to fill his shoes. I don't want Tom as a dad.

And having him around reminds me that I lost the one I did have. It's insane how you can miss someone after all these years. Miss them like crazy, but time also makes you forget. Like his voice. I used to think I would always remember it. The way he would call me honeybun—but it's faded away. But it has been seven years since he died. I still look at his picture almost every night and try to see me in him. And I do a little, but not enough. I wish I had his nose.

Della stared at the page and realized how much she had in common with Natasha. How many times had she looked in the mirror and wondered why she didn't look more like her dad, more like his family and the culture he was so proud of? Maybe being of mixed race just sent you down that path—a path where you felt as if you didn't belong to one group or the other.

Della read on, but the diary went back to mundane stuff. An argument she had with Tom, picking out her prom dress. She read them all, and was a few pages from the end. This entry was longer than the others.

One week until I turn eighteen. Today, Mom asked me what I wanted for my birthday. I knew she'd ask, she always does. She's good like that, wants to get you what you want and not just something she likes. But this year, I looked her right in the eye and decided not to lie. I want the truth, I told her. Her expression almost made me cry. It reminded me of how she looked when the police showed up at our door and told her that my father had died in the plant explosion. I think she's afraid she'll lose me. She won't lose me, but I am going to be angry if what I believe is true. She should have told me years ago.

Curious, Della turned the page to read on, but there wasn't

more. What was Natasha talking about? What lie had her mother told her? Della closed the book, her feelings toward her father's lies stinging while she felt Natasha's pain.

Della put the diary down on her bedside table and watched it fly off and hit the wall. And the cold in the room grew more intense.

"Why are you unhappy?" Della looked up and saw white crystals of ice cascading from the ceiling. It was freaking snowing in her bedroom.

"Enough of the cold crap," she said and sat up. "Why can't we just talk? Tell me where Natasha is and I'll save her. Tell me how you two are connected."

Her words caused more wisps of steam to billow up. It hung a few inches from her lips. "Tell me . . . tell me who killed you. And I swear to God, if you say my father, I'll know you're a liar."

Della held her breath. Her heart took her back to the father-daughter time she'd spent with her dad in his office. The laughter they'd shared. The love they'd shared. Her father might not have died like Natasha's, but she missed him just the same.

"Talk to me," she said again. No answer came. And that pissed Della off. "Fine! If you're not going to talk, then get your icy ass out of here." She dropped back onto her pillow.

Footsteps sounded in the cabin. Her door swung open. Kylie stood there. "You okay?"

"I have no patience for ghosts," Della said with a tight voice and batted a snowflake from her lashes.

"Want me to sleep with you?"

"I'm not scared, just pissed." Her heart did an abnormal jolt. If Kylie was in vamp mode she would have heard it. Della didn't check. She was too tired to lift her head.

Kylie crawled into bed with her. Even tired, Della found the strength to tell Kylie about her day. From the vision in the closet,

Chase taking the diary, to the fight at the park behind the pond. Her frustration that time was running out for Natasha and Liam.

"You can only do so much," Kylie said, but in her voice Della heard it. She, like Holiday, still held doubts that Natasha and Liam were really alive. Della refused to believe it.

Eventually, the room's temperature went back to normal. With a protector at her side, Della pulled her covers up to her chin—not to hide from the cold, but to keep away thoughts of murder, ghosts, and two people trapped somewhere and running out of time.

Della was almost asleep when Kylie asked one last question. "Did you do what Miranda told you to?"

"What?" Della murmured.

"Did you open your heart enough to Chase to know if he was a prince or a toad?"

"I think he's both," Della said, and she recalled how his hands had felt on her breasts when she'd come out of the vision. How it felt to touch him. She suddenly felt too warm and wished the ghost would come back and make it snow again.

Wednesday morning, the ring of her phone jarred Della awake. She sat up and recalled hearing Kylie getting out of her bed and listening to her and Miranda getting dressed for school. Glancing at the window, she saw the sun pouring in.

"Crap!" She must have fallen back to sleep. If she started sleeping in and missing school, Burnett would probably start curtailing her time working.

She grabbed her phone. Her heart did a jolt when she considered it might be Steve. Looking at the number, she closed her eyes, dropped back on the bed, and berated herself for even wanting it to be Steve.

Then she begrudgingly answered the call. "What do you want?"

"Good morning, sunshine."

"Go to hell."

Chase laughed.

His laugh went through her like warm syrup. Damn him! That's when she remembered what she'd told Kylie. *Both prince and toad.*

She heard him shift, almost as if he was still in bed himself. "You know, the only thing better than hearing your raspy morning voice, would be waking up beside you. Your hair kind of messy, the sunshine streaming into the window shining off your soft skin. I'll bet you're sexy as hell."

She ran a hand through her hair and looked down and realized she was wearing her Smurf PJs.

"You'd lose that bet."

"Don't tell me. You're wearing the Smurf pajamas, aren't you?"

She bit her lip to keep from giving him directions to hell. She refrained, not because she wasn't aggravated, but because he'd know he was right.

"Do you have matching underwear?" he asked, no doubt baiting her.

"You really are a panty perv!" she said.

"A what?"

"A panty pervert!"

He laughed. "Nah, I'm just a Della perv," he said and sounded sincere. "You okay?"

"Of course I am. Why?"

"You're sleeping late. Did you stay awake thinking about me?"

She started to say a big hell no, but it would have come off as a lie. "The ghost came to see me," she said the truth, instead of answering his question. "What's your excuse?" Had he been thinking about her? No wait, she didn't want to know.

"My excuse for what?" he asked.

She couldn't find a way to blow off the question, so she just put it out there. "It sounds like you're still in bed, too. Or wasn't that the mattress I heard sigh?"

"I am. Do you want to know what I'm wearing?"

"No!" But an image formed in her mind. Her face heated and she remembered being in that closet and fondling his butt.

"I was up working on the case until almost four." He paused. "And maybe thinking about you." She heard him roll over again.

She closed her eyes and didn't know what to say to that. So she didn't say anything.

"What did she say?" he asked.

"What did who say?" she countered, her mind racing, her face still warm.

"The ghost?" he asked.

Good, she needed a change of subject. "That's the problem, she didn't say anything. Just made it snow."

"Snow?"

"Yes and in my bedroom!"

He paused. "Do you know who she is?"

"I'm not completely sure," she answered.

"Who do you think she is?" he asked.

Maybe this subject wasn't any better than the last. "What time is it?" she asked, hoping to derail the conversation.

"Eight thirty."

"If I hurry, I can still make my first class. I should go."

"So you don't want to know what I found out about our guy Damian Bond?"

Oh, hell, she was slipping. Of course she wanted to know. "What did you find?" She sat up.

Chapter Twenty-nine

"Who do you think the ghost is?" Chase asked, as if only willing to share if she would.

"I'm not a hundred percent sure." Della spoke the truth.

"So, who do you think it is?" he asked for the second time.

"Aren't you the one who said she was my ghost?" she countered and sat up on the side of her bed.

"Aren't *you* the one who said we had joint custody?" he shot back as if frustrated. "If it will help us find—"

"If it would help us, I'd tell you, but right now I'm just confused. So cut the crap and tell me what you have on Damian Bond."

He let her suffer for a few seconds before he started talking. "The most important thing is that he's in California right now, and has been for the last three days. So it wasn't him you got a trace of last night."

"How . . . how do you know this?"

"The FRU aren't the only ones who have databases. I had the Vampire Council do a rundown on him. When I was heading home last night, they got back with me. We've got him on a watch list. At one time, he belonged to a gang that targeted vampires. Supposedly, he's dropped out, but we have an address on him. I paid a visit to his home. His girlfriend told me he was in L.A. He does some stunt work for a few movies. But he's flying home on Friday night. I think we should meet him at baggage claim, don't you?"

Della's mind spun. "Yeah." But she couldn't deny feeling disappointed that Damian wasn't the one at Uck's Burgers whose trace she'd picked up. Especially when that was the trace the ghost had given her when she'd been watching the interview. How did this all fit together?

Exhaling, she stared down at her bare toes. "Have you told Burnett this yet?"

"Not yet. I thought I'd tell my partner first."

Something in how he said "partner" made her stomach flutter. And it was a good flutter—as if she was part of something . . . or someone . . . that mattered.

She brushed her hair from her face and looked back at her bedroom door when she heard footsteps running up her cabin's front porch. One deep breath and she recognized the witch's scent.

"Here comes Miranda," Della said into the phone. "I gotta go. Call Burnett and fill him in. If you don't, he's going to be pissed."

"Isn't that his regular state of being?"

"Just do it." She hung up as her bedroom door swung open and Miranda rushed in.

"What's wrong?" Della asked.

The witch took a deep breath as if she'd been running. "Kylie told me Shawn was stabbed," she said, sounding a bit panicked. "Is he okay?" She still had her fork in her hand as if she'd gotten the news during breakfast and forgot to leave it behind.

Della made a rash and quick decision to manipulate the truth a little. Hey . . . if Kylie could play matchmaker, maybe Della could pull it off. "I don't know. He was hurt pretty badly. I have his number. You should call and check on him."

Shawn had actually been fine. A few stitches and he was as good as ever. He'd given his number to her and Chase when they left, just in case they got anything else on the werewolf. Supposedly, he was going to continue helping them with the case.

Miranda frowned. "Why would I call him?"

"Hmm, let's see. Maybe because you're worried enough about him that you ran all the way from the dining hall, with a fork in your hand, to ask me about him," Della said.

"But . . . I'm not . . . we're not . . . friends."

"You could be."

Miranda rolled her eyes. "I remember what you said about him putting out pheromones and all, but he's older than I am."

"By what? Two years? Call him."

"But I'm not . . . I just . . ."

Della could read the witch's mind. "Has Perry called you?"

A sad and pathetic look filled the witch's eyes. "No."

"Let me see if I understand. Perry tells you he wants to take a break from your so-called relationship. He leaves. You give him a magical phone that can call you anytime, anywhere, and he hasn't bothered to use it. Right?"

Miranda's bottom lip trembled a bit, but she nodded.

"Then damn it to hell and back! Call Shawn!"

Della pulled out her phone and texted Miranda the warlock's number. "Call him!" she snapped when the witch's phone dinged. "We had a deal, remember?"

Miranda pouted and stared daggers at Della and it was hard to do both, but she managed. "Did you keep up your end of the bargain . . . with Chase? Because if you didn't, I'm not—"

"He had his hand in my bra, and I had mine on his bare ass. Does that constitute my end of the bargain?"

An hour later, on the way to math class, Della's phone dinged with a call. She glanced at the screen; it was one of those junk calls trying to sell her insurance. But right before she went to stick her phone back in her pocket, she realized she hadn't spoken with her mom in . . . forever. Her mom didn't call every day, but at least twice a week Della would get the "just checking in" call.

The realization swirled around her head, then dropped like a dead bird in her heart. Was her mother trying to forget she existed along with her dad now?

Or maybe her mom was just busy. Before she could chicken out, she hit her mom's name in her contact list and listened for the ring.

Once.

Twice.

Three times.

It went to voice mail. "Hey, Mom, it's me, Della." *In case you forgot who I am.* "I just realized we haven't talked, and I wanted to make sure everything is okay." *I love you. Miss you.* "Call me."

Della had just tucked her phone back into her pocket when Holiday came walking up.

"Hey, I was looking for you."

"Why, did my mom call you?" Della asked, thinking maybe she'd just somehow missed her mom's call earlier.

"Uh, no. Is something wrong?"

"No, I just . . . I haven't heard from her in a while. Has she called you lately to check on me?"

Holiday pondered a second. "Not in the last week. You worried about something?" the camp leader asked, picking up on Della's emotion.

"Normal crap," Della said, and then asked, "What did you need?"

"Oh, well, I needed to stretch my legs and thought you'd join me."

Della studied the camp leader. "What did I do?"

Holiday laughed. "Nothing."

"So what do you need to talk to me about?" Della asked. "And don't tell me nothing because that would be a lie and good faes don't lie."

Holiday made a face. "We do sometimes. White lies." She grinned. "So, okay, I want to talk with you, but you're not in trouble."

"If you're pregnant and want me to deliver your second child, the answer is no," Della teased. "I'm not over the first one yet."

Holiday chuckled. "Well, if you need therapy, I'll pay for it. Come on, let's walk to the lake."

They entered the path in the woods and it got quiet. The sounds of the other campers faded, and only an occasional insect made a noise.

"You sure I'm not in trouble?" Della asked.

"I'm just a little worried," Holiday said.

"About what?"

"You . . . and the whole bonding thing with Chase. You're spending a lot of time with him. I just wanted to make sure that you're . . . okay."

"We're not bumping uglies," Della told her.

Holiday laughed. "You do have a way with words, young lady. And yes, that was one of my concerns, but only part of it." Holiday looked serious again. "So you aren't interested in him that way, at all?"

Della kicked at an innocent rock that happened to be at her feet.

"I wouldn't say 'at all.'"

"So what *would* you say?"

"I would prefer nothing." She shrugged.

Holiday sighed.

They arrived at the lake and Holiday motioned ahead. "Let's go sit out on the pier." They walked all the way to the end of the wood planks.

Holiday plopped down, took off her shoes, and rolled up the bottom of her jeans. Her toes barely met the water. "It's a nice day," she said.

"Yeah," Della agreed, and it was. Not cold, not hot. The sky was a bright blue, the clouds puffy white and the sun felt warm on her shoulders. Della dropped down beside her and removed her boots and socks. The water held just enough of a chill to be refreshing on her feet.

"Where's Hannah?" Della asked.

"I've hired a nanny to come in and help take care of her for part of the day. I feel as if I've been ignoring my job."

After a few minutes, Holiday spoke again. "Burnett's checked into the whole bonding thing, and there's a little information that backs up the fact that it's real, but what it says is vague. Very vague."

"What did it say?" Della asked, wondering if she knew more than Chase had told her.

"That the two vampires are emotionally connected. There is some proof that it can be between family members, so it's not necessarily a romantic type of bond."

A fish jumped up a few feet from the pier and both Holiday and Della looked over at it. "What do you think the bond means? Is it a romantic connection?"

"Did you know fish pee and poop in the water?" Della said as Holiday stretched her legs down to submerge her whole foot.

Holiday rolled her eyes. "I do. And that was probably the worst attempt to change a subject I've ever heard."

"Yeah, but I couldn't come up with anything else," Della said.

Holiday grinned and then her expression got serious again. "I guess what I'm saying is that what Chase did for you was a wonderful thing, but I don't want you to feel you have to offer part of yourself that you don't want to offer."

"He's not pressuring me to have to sex," Della said, knowing it was true. The whole closet thing had been about the vision, not about them. Even if he did enjoy it. And she did, too, she admitted to herself.

"That makes me feel better," Holiday said, and ran her foot along the top of the water. "But you feel something for him. I can tell. And I can also tell that you aren't altogether comfortable with it. And that worries me."

Della kicked at the water. "I hate when you do that, you know."

"Do what?" Holiday pulled her hair over one shoulder.

"Read me." Della frowned. "Because while you're right about me being uncomfortable, it's not what you think. If I'm uncomfortable, it's because of what I feel, not because he's trying to push me into something."

Holiday looked at her. "And what do you feel?"

"Crazy," Della said.

"That makes sense." She reached over and touched Della's arm. "I just want to help. And I know you are a very private person, but sometimes it does help to talk about things."

"What things?" Della asked.

"About what you feel?"

Della swallowed her frustration. "I told you: crazy." She sighed.

"Look, if I knew the truth of exactly what I felt, I'd tell you, but I don't. Do I like him? Yes. Am I attracted to him? Yes. Do I think the bonding thing is real?" She almost said no, but the truth came out. "Yes. But I don't know to what extent, or where it will lead. Part of me trusts him. Part of me doesn't. So there, did you get anything out of that except I'm completely confused and feeling pretty much bonkers?"

Holiday smiled. "Love's confusing and can make you bonkers."

"I didn't say anything about love," Della said.

Holiday smiled. "I don't mean 'love' as in the-rest-of-your-life love. Just romance." She leaned back and looked up at the sky. "However, I wouldn't be doing my job as a camp leader if I didn't share Burnett's concerns with you."

"Oh, hell! He sent you to talk to me about Chase?"

"No, it was my idea, and when I mentioned it, he . . . well, he sort of shared how he felt about it."

"He doesn't like Chase," Della said.

"He doesn't completely trust Chase. He *really* doesn't trust the Vampire Council."

"And I think he's being a tad overprotective."

Holiday grinned. "It would be out of his character if he wasn't. But he does have good instincts. So I just want you to be careful."

"I'm always careful." *At least most of the time.*

Chapter Thirty

Della had lunch with Jenny, Kylie, and Miranda. They got their food and took it behind the office and sat under the trees to eat.

They spent half the time laughing due to Miranda recounting some of her goofed spells. Like the day she wanted to remove a stain from her dad's shirt and ended up removing all his clothes.

Seeing as they had their elderly "human" neighbor over, it caused quite a stir. Especially because the clothes disappeared when he was bent over pulling a roast from the oven. Moments later, her dad had used two pot holders to cover the important parts.

Della needed a laugh. Once or twice, she saw the temptation in Miranda's eyes to bring up what Della had told her about Chase and the whole his-hand-her-hand thing, but the girl must have read Della's "I'll-kill-you" glare and bypassed that conversation. Della had no need to talk about that.

Especially after Holiday's little talk. Not that Holiday made her feel any different, but she didn't want Burnett to get wind of anything and really start flipping out.

Miranda didn't mention if she'd called Shawn. Della decided

that she wouldn't push any more. It had to be Miranda's decision. But if she started back into the ice cream and tears mode, Della might change her mind.

She couldn't, wouldn't, stand by and watch her friend suffer and punish herself for a boy's stupidity. And yes, she considered Perry stupid. Miranda cared about him, and for him to ask for a break, when in fact he cared about her, too, was stupid.

After such a fun lunch, the day seemed lighter. After school, Della waited for Chase at the front gate. Burnett had to leave on another case so they weren't going to get their regular rule-checking meeting first. The plan was to go back to Uck's Burgers and see if she picked up any more traces of weres.

When Chase's blue Camaro pulled up, she moved to the car. She hadn't driven in a car this much in months, and while she loved flying, all the car time made her feel a little more human. Like a real teenager. And that was kind of nice.

He came to a stop right beside her. His hair was windblown, he wore sunglasses, and his smile held the warmth of the sun. She felt the familiar thrill she got every time she saw him. The bonding? Or was it like Holiday said, just normal romance stuff? But for right now, she didn't want to think or judge. When she jumped over the door, landing in the passenger seat, he held out a bag.

"What's this?" she asked.

"I bought you some new hair bands. You keep taking them and not bringing them back."

She took the bag, and when she turned it over in her lap, more than just hair bands came out. A small stuffed Smurf—Smurfette— fell into her lap. She looked at him.

His grin widened. "I'm sorry, I saw it and I had to buy it. Seriously, I tried to walk away and couldn't. It called my name and wouldn't let me leave. And you should have seen the look I got from the big bald tattooed guy at the register."

Before she realized it, she was smiling back. "Thank you," she said.

"You're welcome." Their eyes met and held for a second too long.

She pulled one of the hair bands loose and put it in her hair. He watched her and she saw his gaze slip to her breasts for a couple beats, and she sensed he was remembering their time in the closet. And, for one tiny second, she almost envied Natasha, who had lived it all while she'd only gotten to live a few seconds of it. How odd was it that a girl facing death was experiencing and letting herself live more than Della was?

"We should go," she said, remembering her conversation with Holiday.

"Yeah." He started the car, and as he backed up, he put his hand on the back of the passenger seat, twisting around to look over his shoulder. The move came off as something he always did when he was backing up. But while his hand was there, his fingers brushed against her bare neck. The touch, accidental or intentional, sent a sweet shiver down her spine.

She watched as he drove out of the parking lot, shifting gears. Something about the process just seemed cool. She recalled how when she was younger and her dad would watch the car races, she'd been sort of captivated by the drivers in the cars. When she looked up, Chase was watching her again.

After a few minutes, enjoying the wind in her hair, she noted he'd turned onto a back road.

"Where are you going?"

"You'll see," he said.

He drove a few more miles and then pulled into what looked like a country road that ended in an undeveloped subdivision. There were roads, but no houses. He parked the car and then got out and came around to her side.

"What're you doing?" she asked, still in the passenger seat, looking up at him and seeing herself in his sunglasses. For one second, the vision reminded her of the old Della, one who could have enjoyed just taking a drive with a good-looking boy.

"Scoot over."

"What?"

"Get behind the wheel. I want you to drive."

"No." She shook her head, her ponytail swinging back and forth and tickling the back of her neck. "I told you I don't know how to drive a stick shift."

"You don't know how to drive a stick shift . . . yet. I'm going to teach you."

"I . . . I don't—"

Before she knew what he intended to do, he slipped into the seat beside her, scooped her up and over the console and gearshift, setting her in the driver's seat. The quick touch against her butt sent another wave of tingles through her.

She frowned at him, but he just smiled. He was having fun. And God help her, so was she. Maybe it was the lunch of just laughing with friends. Maybe it was the fact that this felt different because she could try something new without having to listen to Burnett ramble on about danger and rules. Or maybe she was tired of the pressure of everything, and, for just a little while, she wanted to forget and have fun.

"Now," he said. "See the pedals? It's just like an automatic or a regular car. But it has another pedal. The first one to your left is the clutch, the second is the brake, and the third is the gas. When you start the car and put it in gear, you are going to push the clutch in, then slowly let it out as you push on the gas. It's that easy. Clutch releases as gas increases. Then you take your foot off the clutch."

Della had her head turned sideways looking at the pedals. "It's not that easy, you have to change the gears."

"Yeah, but that's simple. When the car needs another gear, you'll hear and feel it. You let off the gas and do the same thing, clutch in, change gears, then gas again."

He caught her hand in his and put it on the gearshift. His palm stayed on top of hers to show her how to shift. "Here's first. Do you feel that?"

She felt his hand. Felt the tingles. "Yeah," she said, hoping her voice didn't sound as wispy as she felt on the inside.

"Here's second." He moved the shift down. His thumb inched up and down beside her pinkie, sending all kinds of warm wonderful zings to her heart.

He went through all the different gears. Della tried hard to think about the placement of the gears and not the placement of his hand.

"Now you do it." He moved his hand from on top of hers. Only pride kept her from pretending she couldn't do it and having him show her again.

She did as he showed her. The only one she couldn't find was sixth gear.

"Right here." His shifted a little closer, his hand pressed on top of hers again as he showed her the slight move of down and slightly to the right side. "Do you feel it?"

"Yeah." She felt everything. How he'd slipped his left arm over the back of her seat and how his forearm now brushed against her shoulders. How when he spoke this close, his breath tickled her cheek.

"You ready to try?" he asked.

She looked at him. His question echoed inside her. Was she ready? Ready to stop fighting what she felt? Fighting the so-called "bond" that made something inside her feel complete?

The answer whispered across her mind. Maybe.

"Yeah," she answered him, while the "maybe" was all she could give her own question. And she knew what held her back. She still wasn't completely sure he didn't know more about who'd sent him to make sure she got through the rebirth.

"Okay," he said. "Let's do it."

She had to adjust the seat to make sure she could reach the pedals. Taking a deep breath, wanting to master this, she put the car in neutral, put her foot on the clutch, and turned the ignition. She felt him watching her and cut him a smile. "Piece of cake."

The way he'd parked meant she didn't have to put the car in reverse, so she put it in first. She did as he said, put her foot on the gas, and slowly released the clutch. The car moved forward. A sense of victory waved over her, but jolted to a stop at the same time the car sputtered and died.

"What happened?" she asked, looking at him. His grin made her moan.

"You let the clutch out too fast. You need to let it out slower. But you almost had it. Try again."

Determined to do it, she repeated her steps. And this time, the car moved about twenty feet before it sputtered and died.

She growled, thumped the steering wheel, and shot him an unhappy look. "Something's wrong."

"It's not wrong. It just takes a little finesse." He chuckled.

"Stop laughing," she said.

"Hey, I'm not laughing at you. I'm laughing because . . . because I remember Jimmy trying to teach me. And because I love . . . being here. With you. With you not fighting me, but fighting my car." He leaned in. "Try again."

His lips were so close. Then they lightly brushed against hers.

Chapter Thirty-one

"For luck," Chase said, then he pulled back as if frightened Della was going to be pissed off.

She wasn't. Or maybe a part of her was, but she didn't want to let that part matter right now.

When she didn't say anything, didn't complain, he did it again. This time, the kiss lasted a few seconds.

She put her hand on his chest and gave him a slight push. "You're supposed to be teaching me to drive your car."

His tongue came out and passed over his bottom lip. "Okay," he said, his smile so bright that damn it if it didn't make her want to kiss him again. Then he gave her ponytail a yank. "Remember, slow and easy."

Yeah, she thought. That's how she wanted to take this thing. Slow and easy.

After about three more tries, she finally got it. "See," he said. "I told you you'd get it."

She started driving a little faster. The wind felt good; the rumble of the engine felt good. She felt powerful.

"It's almost as good as flying, isn't it?" he asked, watching her drive down one paved street to another.

"It might even be better," she said, changing gears and loving how smooth she was able to make the shift. "How fast can it go?" she asked and glanced at him.

"It's fast," he said. "Push it a little."

She looked around and there wasn't another car in sight. So she did it. She pushed her foot on the gas and felt the roar. Glancing at the speedometer, she saw she'd hit ninety miles an hour.

She was just about to let off the gas when she heard the sirens.

"Shit! My father's gonna kill me," she muttered. Before she could say anything else, before she could even look into the rearview mirror, Chase had grabbed the wheel with one hand, lifted her ass with the other, and swapped places.

Then he quickly slowed the car down and pulled over.

"What are you doing?" she asked, snapping her head around to watch the police car come to a stop behind them.

"Making sure your father doesn't kill you," he said. "Because if he hurt you, I'd have to teach him a lesson, and that's not a way to start our relationship."

She started to tell him they didn't have a relationship, but then she bit down on her lip. "It's a convertible; he probably saw I was driving."

"You were going so fast, he couldn't tell who was driving."

Della looked at him. "Right. *I* was going fast. I was the one—"

"It's okay," he said. "Just let me handle this."

"But, it's my fault. You shouldn't—"

"I'm the one who forced you to drive."

She could hear the litany, the one her dad gave each and every time she took the car out. The one about the danger of texting and driving. About . . . "Your insurance will go up and—"

"Money isn't a problem."

"Won't your dad . . . I mean, Jimmy, be upset? I don't want you taking the blame for something I—"

Chase reached into his back pocket and pulled out a wallet, getting ready to take the blame for this. "I'm eighteen, Jimmy doesn't parent me anymore."

Della looked back at the police car again, feeling almost sick. "What's he doing? Why isn't he coming over here?"

"Don't worry. He's just checking to see if the car is listed as stolen."

She cut Chase a panicked look. "Crap! It's not, is it?"

He shot her a frown. "I'm not a thief."

"I know . . . I'm sorry, it's just . . . I've never been pulled over before."

"Just calm down. We're not going to be arrested."

"Oh, God, I didn't even think about that. My dad would really kill me then. And Burnett . . . he'd kill me again. What was I thinking? I shouldn't have been speeding. Oh, Lordy, I got us in this mess!"

Chase reached over and touched her shoulder. "Chill. It's going to be fine. If speeding is the worst thing you do, you're good." Then he grinned. "You're cute when you're scared."

She slapped his hand. "I'm not scared. I'm . . . worried."

"I know, but it's going to be fine. I promise. Trust me. And no one will ever find out. Not your dad or Burnett. This is our secret."

She stared at his light green eyes. And a part of her did trust him. But only part.

All of a sudden, she felt guilty. Guilty for taking the time to have fun when they should have been looking for Natasha and Liam.

She shot another look at the police car and started tapping her feet on the floorboard. "Seriously, what's taking him so long?"

Chase touched her shoulder again. "Calm down or he's going to think I kidnapped you or something."

"Okay. I'm calming down. I am." She stared straight ahead. Then, taking a couple of deep breaths, she leaned her head back and closed her eyes.

"You know it's going to be okay. We'll get out of this."

Chase had just told her that, but when she reheard his words, the voice in her head wasn't Chase's. She opened her eyes. The sun, the blue sky, the Camaro, the police car, it had all disappeared.

Gone.

All gone.

Darkness, all she saw was darkness. She blinked again.

"You okay?" This time she recognized the voice.

Liam.

"Can I ask you something?" she said. Oh, hell yes, Della had questions, too. *Where are we?*

"Yeah," he answered.

She turned her head and could barely see him. He was handsome, even though one of his eyes looked a little swollen.

Tell me where you are, so I can get you and Natasha out. She tried to say the words, but they wouldn't come out. She might be inside Natasha's body, but she didn't have control.

Instead, Natasha asked, "Is there someone else?"

"What do you mean?" Liam asked.

"Do you have a girlfriend?"

He reached up and touched her face. "I think after what we did, three times, that means we're . . . an item." He laughed.

Natasha smiled, but in reality she wasn't in the mood for humor. "I mean before now."

He hesitated. "I used to. A year ago, she graduated and went off to USC."

"Did you love her?" Natasha brushed some dirt off her knee and Della felt how badly she wanted Liam to say no.

"I thought I did. I wanted to go with her, but even with the scholarship they offered me, my mom couldn't afford it. She was already working a second job to pay for here."

"So, you're smart. I figured that," she said.

"Yeah," he said. "But I'll bet you didn't do too bad in school, either."

"I'm not USC smart," she said. She paused, then asked, "So you two just broke up when she left?"

"No, we were going to try to make it work. You know, wait on each other. Fly out to see each other when we could. But just a few weeks in, she met someone else."

"I'm sorry."

"I'm not," he said. "Getting turned would have ended it anyway."

"Yeah, it kind of puts a damper on things, doesn't it?" Emotion rose up in Natasha's chest and Della realized Natasha's feelings were much like the ones she felt about being turned. Her life had been ripped away from her.

"Please don't tell me you've got someone," Liam said. "Because I'm not going to like that."

"I don't," she said. "Like you, there was someone, but I had to walk away when . . . when I got turned."

"Did you fake your own death?" he asked.

"They guy at the funeral home told me I had to. He said that I'd end up killing my parents or something."

"That's a lie, you know." He pressed a kiss on Natasha's brow.

"I don't know, it was pretty crazy at first."

"I know, but I'm not a killer, and I don't think you are, either." He put his arm around her. She buried her face in his shoulder.

"That's what they want us to be. Or wanted. Why do you think they didn't come back?"

"I don't know."

Della tried to figure out what they meant, but didn't have enough information.

A sound rumbled above, like some kind of big equipment digging. Natasha looked up. "Did you fake your death?" she asked Liam.

"No, I never had a chance. That group of weres found me like the second day. I was wandering the streets, hurting like hell. They caught me and put me with the others." He paused and then reached down and tilted up her chin and looked at her. "I didn't care if I lived or died. I was about to end it, then I saw you. You were so scared, and all I could think about was making you feel better. You saved my life."

"No, you saved mine. And nearly got yourself killed doing it." She lifted her hand and touched his brow and eye.

"Nah, I just got beat up a little. It was worth it."

A few minutes of silence passed. Natasha's stomach rumbled from hunger and her thoughts took her back. "I miss them," she said.

"Not that boyfriend, I hope," he replied.

"No, he was just . . . we weren't serious. I miss my parents. My friends, Amy and Jennifer. I had two of the best friends in the world. And I know they're all hurting. Especially my mom. She loved me so much." She started to cry.

Liam picked her up and sat her on his lap. "We'll get out of here, then you can go see them."

"How? They think I'm dead." She pressed her face to his chest.

"We'll make up a story. Say that you were kidnapped or something. We'll say that they got the wrong body. Hey . . . I'll make it
happen. Somehow, Natasha, I'll fix it."

Della felt despair swell inside Natasha's chest. "Who are we kidding?" She grabbed a handful of Liam's shirt. "We're not getting
out of here, Liam. We're going to die."

"Damn it! Don't say that. We're getting out of here, then we'll
find out how others like us live. There has to be a way."

Natasha cried a few more minutes, then finally exhausted, she
just leaned against him. He knew just how to hold her to make her
feel . . . loved.

And she loved him, she realized. She hadn't felt this way toward
anyone before. Almost as if he sensed her thoughts, he leaned down
and kissed her brow again. "Oh, and if you get some scholarship to
some school, I'm coming with you. I'm not losing you. Okay?"

"You won't," she said. And while she wanted to believe him,
that they would get out of this alive, that they would actually get a
chance to make a life together, she didn't. She didn't believe.

But at least they had now. She lifted her face and kissed him.
Kissed him with desire and passion. "Wanna make that four
times?"

"I asked you a question!" the voice came from somewhere else.
And now it wasn't Liam's voice, or Chase's.

Della snapped open her eyes and the sun nearly blinded her.

"I'm sorry," Chase said.

Della turned and looked at Chase, he wore the same stunned
expression on his face that she must have. Then she saw the officer
standing outside the driver's door, and she met his brown-eyed gaze.
Unhappy gaze. Unhappy man. He looked like a bulldog—one that
needed a little less time at his food bowl. He even had flabby cheeks
like a bulldog, one of those kinds that drooled.

"We're nervous," she spit out. "I mean, I'm nervous. I've never been pulled over before."

"That's probably because you haven't been hanging out with Speedy Gonzales here for that long."

Chase lost his usual look of superiority and his expression was one of apology. "I was trying to show off for my new girlfriend," Chase said to the officer. "I know I was wrong. Ticket me if you have to. But at least I brought her out here so I wouldn't risk an accident."

"You mean so you wouldn't risk getting caught." The cop frowned, his jowls jiggled. "Let me see your license, son," he barked.

Chase handed it to him.

He walked off, or rather wobbled off. He even walked like a bulldog. He got into his car again, where his blue lights still flashed.

Chase looked at her. She didn't say anything, but he must have read the pain in her eyes.

"We'll find them."

"We have to," Della said.

Her phone chimed. She yanked it out of her pocket and looked at it. Probably her mom. She still hadn't returned Della's call.

She glanced at the number. "It's Burnett. You don't think he already knows we've been—?"

"If he does, then he has an informant in every cop shop in Texas."

Della prepared herself for an ass chewing. "I wouldn't find that too hard to believe."

Chapter Thirty-two

Burnett didn't know they were being pulled over and ticketed. He'd called to inform them that Shawn wouldn't be meeting them at Uck's Burgers. The agent supposedly was working on another case. The fact that Burnett was vague about the details almost made Della suspicious.

Burnett's voice came across the line. "I was thinking you should probably just go back to Shadow Falls."

"No, we're going to Buck's."

"Why? Our main suspect isn't going to be in town until Friday. You'll be wasting your time."

"No, remember, I got a familiar trace of a were at the restaurant that night. I think it means something."

"I know but . . . Shawn can't make it and—"

"And we'll be fine," she said in a determined tone. "Trust me."

Burnett got quiet. "Fine, but remember the rules. Don't initiate any trouble. If you get a lead, call me ASAP. And . . ." He went on for another two minutes and ended with, "But I really think you are wasting your time."

Thankfully, he hung up before the officer came back to give Chase *her* ticket.

Unfortunately, thirty minutes after sitting in Uck's Burgers, Della was afraid Burnett was right. Neither she nor Chase had gotten any scent of a were. There had been a few vamps, and they certainly had checked Della and Chase out, but obviously decided not to cause waves.

Chase ordered them two sodas. He remembered she drank diet, and for some reason, the thought made her feel good. They chatted about mundane things, knowing others were listening.

But when the vamps left, the conversation got a little less mundane.

"Did you get anything from the vision that might help us?" Chase asked.

Della let herself be pulled back into the memory that could easily break her heart. "They said something about someone wanting to make them murderers."

"I know."

"Do you think someone's making assassins out of fresh turns?"

Chase shook his head. "They could, but you'd need to trust anyone you sent out to do something like that."

"The noise?" Della said. "It was like some construction equipment above them."

He nodded. "But it could have been anything."

She trailed her finger down her cup. "We need to tell Burnett about it. We never even told him about the other one."

"If you think it will help, go for it. I just don't see what good it'll do." He grabbed a napkin and wadded it up in frustration. "What I don't understand is why the ghost is doing this. Putting us there for no reason. We're not getting anything that will help us find them."

Della felt the same way, but then suddenly, she knew the answer. "But we care."

"What?"

"We care. She wants us to care about them."

Chase exhaled and looked down at his drink. "Then she's succeeding." He stabbed his straw into his cup.

They both grew quiet, as if trying to come to terms with caring. Then Chase looked up at her and she could tell he'd moved his thoughts away from the vision. "Why didn't you fake your death like most everyone else?" he asked.

She shrugged. "I had Chan, and when my parents took me to the hospital because I was sick, I ran into some other supernaturals and they gave me the number for Shadow Falls. Holiday's not big on vamps faking their death."

He nodded and stared at his soda for a while. "But it obviously hasn't been all that easy for you. I've heard you complain about your dad . . . and your aunt. And the one parents' day I was there, you . . . looked pretty miserable sitting with them."

She exhaled. "There were times I thought it might be easier the other way, but after hearing Natasha, I don't know. Holiday may be on to something."

He nodded. "Did you lose other people, too?"

Remembering the conversation they had both been privy to between Natasha and Liam, Della suspected he meant a boyfriend. "Yeah. I had someone."

"Were you close?"

"I thought we were. I was wrong."

"He hurt you?" he asked, and his eyes grew a tad brighter with obvious anger.

"Yeah." She turned her drink in her hands, tracing a drop of condensation down the glass, finding the courage to ask the same question. "What about you?"

"I was only fourteen." He paused as if that was the answer, then he added. "But yeah, there was someone."

"Did you love her?" Della asked.

"Young love," Chase said. "She was a friend of my sister. I'd had a crush on her for a long time. She'd finally stopped looking at me like the younger brother."

"Do you ever go see her? I mean, I know she thinks you're dead, but have you ever just watched her from afar to see how she's doing?"

"No." He cut his eyes down at his own glass. "She died."

"How?" Della asked, her chest feeling full.

"She was on the plane with us when it went down."

Della's heart really crunched with pain then. "I'm sorry."

"Me, too. But I saw her, sort of."

Della picked up her straw and stirred the ice around. "You mean as a ghost?"

He made a face. "I guess that's what you would call her. I was in pretty bad shape from the crash, and I was sort of there . . . with them. Or halfway there, if you know what I mean?"

She nodded. "I do. The same thing happened to me when I was . . . being Reborn."

"I'm glad you decided not to stay there," Chase said.

"You, too," Della admitted.

He smiled. "You know, I think she knew about you."

Della made a face. "Your girlfriend? How could she have known about me?"

"She said they could peek into the future and that I'd meet someone who was a real challenge."

"That doesn't mean it was me," Della insisted.

He chuckled. "I don't think I've met anyone who is more of a challenge."

She lifted her third finger up off her glass just a bit.

He saw it and laughed. "I had fun today."

She bit down on her lip. "I'm paying you back for the ticket. Who knew they could charge four hundred dollars?"

"Yeah, but I was going fifty miles over the speed limit."

Della frowned. "*I* was going fifty miles over the speed limit."

"And you enjoyed every second of it," he said. "I'd pay twice that much to see you having fun again."

"Yeah, but you're not going to pay it. I'm getting some compensation for working this case and I'll reimburse you."

"See, you're a challenge," he said. "I've got plenty of money, Della."

"And you're just a rich pain in the ass," she said, but she couldn't help but smile at him. Damn if her partner wasn't coming off as more of a prince than a toad right now.

That night, Della laid in bed with the Smurfette doll sitting on the bedside table staring at her.

Why did the stupid thing mean something?

Because he'd bought it for her. Because he'd been embarrassed and still bought it for her. Because it was apparent that he'd been thinking about her when he saw it.

She recalled Holiday's words of warning. *Just be careful.*

She would, she told herself.

Before she let any of this get carried away she wanted . . .

What did she want?

The answer came to her. She wanted to know for sure that she trusted Chase. Wanted to make sure that he wasn't keeping more secrets.

While she was listing off wants, she grabbed her phone just to make sure she hadn't missed a call from her mom.

No call.

She half-ass debated calling again, but then it just hurt too much.

If her mom didn't care enough to call back, Della wasn't calling her.

Thursday, right after classes, Della's phone rang. Expecting it to be her mom, she hurried and caught the call without even looking at the number. It wasn't her mom. Burnett again—needing to see her. She took off, and swore not to think about her mom again. The camp leader was waiting on his cabin's front porch. Not a good sign.

She followed him into his back office because Holiday had someone in hers. He leaned against the desk and motioned for her to sit down in the chair. One glance around, and Della knew Holiday had done a room makeover—a crystal paperweight sat on the desk, along with more colorful pictures of Hannah, Burnett's little pride and joy. In the corner of the room hung a plant, a live plant. The room no longer looked so stark.

Or it didn't until Della noted Burnett's expression.

Something was wrong.

"What is it?" Della asked.

"We tried to run down Damian Bond in California. He's not staying where he told the girlfriend he was, and he was let go from his stunt job two days ago. But I checked, and so far, he's still scheduled to fly back on Friday afternoon. So I was thinking, why don't you take tonight off, stay here, and get some rest."

"It's because I slept late yesterday, isn't it? I was fine today."

"It's not that," he said. "Well, maybe a little bit. You've been going nonstop. I know you were out running last night until almost two. You can't keep pushing yourself like this. I know, I'm an agent. You need to calm down, breathe."

Della held her temper in check. "I'm fine. I don't need that much sleep anymore. You should know that, too. And I'm still breathing. Can't you hear me?" She inhaled.

He frowned. "I can see it in your eyes. This case is all you think about. You have to learn to let go. It can eat you up inside if you don't learn to set it aside."

"I'll let go and relax when we find Natasha and Liam. You told me yourself, they don't have much time."

He exhaled in frustration and Della sensed that he knew something more. What was he not telling her? "There's something else, isn't there?"

When he didn't answer immediately, she wanted to scream, but she forced herself to stay seated and ask again in a calm voice. Hey . . . if he wanted her calm to work on the case, she'd give him calm . . . even if it killed her.

"What are you not telling me, Burnett?"

He moved around the desk and sat down in his chair. "One of the other weres who was arrested finally decided to talk yesterday. He validated what Jason Von told you. And what the Vampire Council dug up in their files. But . . ." He paused. "He also said it was four weeks ago when they took Liam. He knows exactly because it was his brother's birthday." Burnett shook his head. "Della, there's no way they could have survived this long."

Still holding her emotions in check, she said, "You were there when the ghost did her thing. She spelled out 'alive.' You saw it. How can you still question it?"

"Even Holiday said that ghosts sometimes . . . get confused. It could be Natasha is the ghost and she doesn't want to accept—"

"No." She shook her head. "We don't know that they put them in that tunnel, or whatever it is, four weeks ago. They could have just locked them away recently."

Burnett's expression stayed firm, and Della saw it in his eyes. He had proof, or he thought he did.

"What else? Just tell me what you know," she said and her heart gripped from what she knew she didn't want to hear. What she knew she didn't want to believe.

He let out a deep breath. "I wanted Holiday to be here. She's supposed to be done in just a few minutes."

"I don't need Holiday, Burnett. I just need to hear what's going on."

He nodded. "They were kidnapping fresh turns and using them to host underground fight matches."

Della remembered the vision she'd had yesterday . . . now it made sense.

Burnett settled deeper into his chair. "We discovered the same thing happening in Dallas and were able to stop it. We arrested those involved there, and even freed several of the fresh turns that were being held. They were actually bringing them in from other countries."

Della kept listening, but so far, he hadn't said anything that proved to her that Natasha and Liam were dead.

"Until the other rogue spoke up today, we didn't know it was happening here. He gave us the names of those responsible. At five this morning, we arrested three of them. We think this Damian Bond could be one of them as well."

"So this is good news," Della said. "We're getting closer to finding them. Why are you—?"

"There's more." Burnett folded his hands on the desk. "We're told that when the first arrests went down in Dallas, they sent word to their Houston partners and were told to eliminate the evidence."

"Eliminate?" Della repeated. "They killed them?"

He nodded. "We've been informed of a mass grave. It's in a junkyard where they destroy and bury cars."

Just like that, Della remembered the noises she'd heard in the vision, the sounds of large equipment. Doubt started pulling at the threads of hope she held so tight to her heart.

"The FRU is still collecting the bodies, and we'll take them in to be identified. I know you don't want to believe this, but there's a good chance Natasha and Liam are among the victims."

Tears filled her eyes, but she didn't care.

Find Natasha.

The voice whispered in Della's head. Was the voice wrong? But what about the vision—the vision of the woman murdered by someone so like her father and uncle? Questions started bouncing off her sore, unraveling heart.

She wiped the tears from her eyes. "How long . . . before we know for sure?"

"It could take up to a week to confirm identities of all the dead."

Della stood up. "Fine, but until you find Natasha's and Liam's bodies, I'm going to keep looking. And I won't believe they're dead until I see them on the morgue table myself."

"Della, you need—"

"No!" Della said. "I'm going to keep looking."

"Where? You've run out of leads."

Call from Miao Hon. The words suddenly echoed inside her head. Not from memory, but obviously sent by the ghost.

But why? The answer came to her with clarity. The same reason she'd sent her the picture. Her aunt knew something that Della needed to know. And just maybe it would be the information she needed to find Natasha.

"No, I haven't," Della said. There was still the one she'd been avoiding.

She left Burnett, not looking back when he called her name. She flew off the office porch and headed to her cabin. She found the photograph in her nightstand drawer, and then she left. She took off and jumped the gate. She knew it would sound the alarm and Burnett would know it was her.

She didn't care.

She needed to get to the one person she thought would understand how she felt. The person who could help her do what she had to do.

Chase.

Chapter Thirty-three

Chase was on his front porch when she cleared the top of the trees. He had his phone in his hand, his gaze focused upward, as if watching for her.

"She's here," she heard him say as she moved in.

Probably Burnett, more than likely pissed she'd left without permission. Who was she kidding? He was definitely angry.

She didn't care.

Chase ended the call and dropped the phone on one of his wicker patio chairs.

She landed on his front porch with a not-so-graceful thump.

She didn't care.

He launched forward as if to catch her, but she'd already caught herself on the front porch rail.

He didn't have a shirt on. He obviously hadn't been expecting company.

She didn't care.

The dampness on her face told her she was crying.

She didn't care.

He looked at her with concern, tenderness.

And damn it, she cared. She cared about Chase. She knew he cared about her, too. How she'd come to this point, she didn't know, but it wasn't important right now.

"That was Burnett," he said.

"He told you?" she asked, her emotions swirling inside her, almost making her dizzy.

"Only that you were upset about some news and had taken off. He started to explain, but I saw you and hung up. What's wrong?"

"They think they're dead." Her sinuses stung and she had to swallow to keep more tears from falling.

"But we know they're not," he said and came closer. She could smell him, the outdoorsy scent of wind and some natural herbs.

When he reached for her, she took a step back. She had to tell him. Then she wanted him to chase off all her doubts, to convince her that her fears held no merit. "But some of what they said makes sense."

"What makes sense?"

"Burnett said there was a rogue were gang setting up fights between them for entertainment. Remember they said they wanted them to become murderers?"

"I remember, but how does that—?"

She told him about the organization in Dallas, how the FRU wasn't aware others were doing it, about how those doing the same thing in Houston were told to eliminate the evidence.

His eyes widened with her news. "But they could still be alive. That doesn't mean they killed everyone."

Her vision blurred a little more from the watery weakness. "They found a mass grave. It's beneath a junkyard." She swallowed again. "Remember the sound of equipment we heard? What if that's what it was? What if . . . ?"

Doubt filled his eyes, but then he blinked and it was gone. "No.

What I remember was them talking, kissing, laughing, crying. I remember them being alive. So, no," he said with the assuredness she wanted . . . she needed . . . to hear. "I don't believe it. We've been them. We've felt what they feel. They aren't dead. They're alive."

"But what if we're wrong?" Della's stomach knotted. "What if they just want us to know?"

"Know what?"

"I don't know . . . maybe that they loved each other."

He shook his head and then moved to her and put a hand on each of her shoulders. "They are alive. I believe that."

"I want to believe it." A tear slipped from her lashes.

He pulled her against him. She rested her head on his bare shoulder, gathering comfort and strength in his embrace, by his nearness. But she hadn't come for this. She knew what she needed to do. What she felt almost certain the ghost wanted her to do.

She pulled back. "I need you to loan me your car."

"To go where?"

"I'm going to see my aunt."

"Because of the picture?" he asked.

"Because the ghost wants me to."

He reached back to the wicker chair and snagged his phone and then grabbed a T-shirt that hung off the back. "Did she tell you this . . . that she wanted you to go to your aunt?"

"Sort of."

"Sort of how?" he asked.

She held out her hand. "Are you going to loan me your car, or not?"

"No. I'm going to come with you," he said. "But I want to know what's really going on first." At her small nod, he looked back to the door. "Let me grab my keys and shoes. You can tell me on the drive."

. . .

She gave Chase the address and he punched it into his GPS. He asked her if she wanted the top up or down. She said up, just because she was afraid of being this close to her old neighborhood and being spotted by someone else who knew her.

She sat in the front seat, her mind spinning with different ways to ask her aunt questions. Questions about Natasha. Questions about her uncle and aunt who her father never told her about. Then she had to figure out a way to ask her aunt not to tell her dad that she'd been there.

"Explain 'sort of,'" Chase said, interrupting her thoughts.

"Huh?"

"How did the ghost 'sort of' tell you to go see your aunt?"

When she didn't answer right away, he spoke again. "Talk to me, Della."

"She called. The day we were in Natasha's closet, she called."

"Your aunt called you?"

"No, she called Natasha's mom. Don't you remember the music stopped and the loudspeaker announced a call from Miao Hon?"

His eyes grew a little wider. "That was Chan's last name. I didn't put it together. Miao's your aunt?"

She nodded.

"Why didn't you tell me?"

"I forgot," she lied, not caring that her heart echoed the mistruth.

He stared at her with a frown. "What did your aunt want with Natasha's mom?"

"I don't know. That's what I think I'm supposed to find out."

"And why do you think that? Did something else happen?"

She told him about rehearing the message that had played on the Owens' sound speakers when she'd been talking to Burnett.

"Then it must be important," Chase said as he cut his eyes back to the road. After a few seconds, he stopped at a red light and looked back at her. "Why are you afraid of your aunt?"

"I'm not afraid of my aunt," she said.

"Why didn't you want to go ask her about Natasha's picture in the beginning?"

She hesitated to answer, but then she just said it. "She'll tell my dad."

"Tell him what?" he asked.

"That I went to see her."

"And that's a bad thing, why?"

She shook her head and stared straight ahead. "He's Asian," she said before she could stop herself.

"What does that have to do with it?"

Feeling uncomfortable, she exhaled and reached down to bring the back of the seat forward. "You wouldn't understand."

"I might, if you explained it," he said.

She got the back of the seat up, then searched beside the door to find the lever to move the entire seat forward. She found it and it squeaked when she shifted it forward.

"What does your father being Asian have to do with you not seeing your aunt?" he prodded.

With the seat adjusted, it still didn't feel right. That's when she had to accept it might be the conversation making her so uncomfortable.

In her head, she heard her father's voice. *We don't expose our dirty laundry.*

"He's embarrassed," she blurted out, admitting it cost her a big chunk of pride. And instantly she wanted that chunk back.

"Embarrassed about what?"

"Me," she said, knowing she couldn't take the comment back and wanting to get this conversation over with.

"What? Why . . . I don't get it."

She swallowed the hurt. "I'm . . . different now. Or . . . he thinks I am. Hell, I am different. Just not in the ways he thinks. Can we not talk about this anymore?"

He frowned. "Not until you start making sense."

She exhaled. "I'm different since I was turned. He thinks I'm into drugs, or pregnant. And that I steal from them."

"But you aren't, and I don't see you stealing from them, either. So that doesn't make sense."

She stared out the side window, suddenly not wanting to look at him. "I told you that you wouldn't understand." She closed her eyes a second, but for some stupid reason, she still wanted to explain it—wanted him to understand. "I was his pride and joy. And then . . ."

"Then what?"

She blinked, and when she opened her eyes she watched the trees zip past. Was he speeding? She glanced at the speedometer. He wasn't breaking any laws.

No, only she did that.

Her father would have a fit if he knew. And thanks to Chase, he wouldn't. She owed him for that. Not just the four hundred dollars, but for the trouble it would have caused.

When she looked up, his expression told her he still waited for an answer.

"It was like some law in their family that they shouldn't marry out of their own race. So we had to show his family that we were just as good as regular Asians. I did better in school than all my other cousins and I never got in any trouble. But when I was turned, everything changed. My grades slipped a bit, I was . . . grumpy, and . . . he didn't want his family to see me."

"Just because he broke his family's law doesn't mean you should have to pay for it. And so what if your grades slipped?"

She shook her head and realized how big of a mistake it had been to try to explain. "Asians are very private people. They don't want anyone to see their screwups. And I was . . ."

"His screwup?" Chase asked and hit the steering wheel.

"In a sense, yes, but not like—"

"Oh, now I understand. You're father's an asshole!"

"He's not," she snapped and looked at him. His eyes were brighter, as if he was angry. And she could feel hers tingling and lightening in defense of her father.

"And the fact that you still care about him makes him an even bigger asshole."

Della shook her head. "Chase, it looked like I was a screwup. When I got turned, and before I came here, I got caught leaving at night to get blood. I wasn't eating my mom's cooking. I was tired during the day. I was hurting because I lost my boyfriend, I wouldn't let anyone touch me because I was cold, and I wasn't very pleasant."

"Most teens are like that all the time," he said. "I was, and my sister could be a real pain in the ass. My parents would just shake their heads and say, 'You'll have to excuse them, they're having a teentude.'"

"My father was raised in a different culture."

"I know all about the Asian culture. They're not pricks."

"My dad's not a prick!" she said. "I could have tried harder to hide things, to pretend—"

"You were friggin' turned vampire, it wasn't your fault."

"But he didn't understand that. And I couldn't tell him."

Chase ran a hand over his face and took in a deep breath. When he cut a glance at her, she saw his eyes were back to their normal light green. "I'm sorry. It just makes me so mad that . . ." He sighed. "Don't worry. I'll be nice when I meet him."

Della's mouth fell open a bit. "What do you mean, when you meet him? We're going to my aunt's, not my dad's. And you're not even coming in."

He pulled the car over and Della realized they were there. Her heart started to race with nerves and her stomach knotted. She stared at the small rusty-colored brick home that had been etched in her memory. She and her sister, Marla, had spent a lot of weekends here, running around with Chan and Meiling, his younger sister. Hiding Easter eggs in those bushes, eating popsicles on that front porch, raking leaves into a pile and then diving into them.

Chase reached over and put his hand on her shoulder as if he understood her emotions were on overdrive. "I didn't expect you to ask me to come inside." His voice sounded super calm, as if trying to offer her the emotion. "And I meant when I meet your dad later. It's going to be okay."

She ignored the "okay" comment, because nothing felt okay, and she faced him. "Why would you meet my dad?"

He looked at her as if she was the one who was confused. "Because we're bonded." His hand still rested on her shoulder. And as much as she wanted to deny it, it offered her some comfort. But realizing that added to her emotional havoc.

She rolled her eyes at him in an over-the-top Miranda fashion. "You are bat-shit crazy. And I do not do well with bat-shit crazy!" She pointed a finger at him. "After I get out, pull the car down the street and don't even think about snooping around."

Then, pushing the car door shut, and without a plan of how to approach any of this—not Chase, or the questions about the picture of Natasha—she walked to her aunt's door.

She recalled a piece of advice someone had given her once. *Fake it until you make it.*

She waited until Chase's blue Camaro pulled down the street to knock. And when she heard someone walking toward the door, she wanted to run like a scared puppy. It appeared even faking it took some amount of confidence. No doubt, her confidence account was empty.

Just when she'd decided how bad of an idea this was, the door swung open.

"Della? Oh, my God, Della Rose! You've come home." Her aunt stepped out and embraced her before she could find a way out of it. "Oh, my. You're freezing. Where's the rest of the family?" she asked and looked over Della's shoulder as if expecting to see her father, mother, and sister.

"It's just me." Della forced herself to speak. And those words echoed inside her. It had been "just her" for a long time.

"So, you're still at that school?"

That school. Della nodded and wondered what her aunt had been told. If, like Della's father, she thought Shadow Falls was a camp for troubled teens, or if he'd told her something else.

"Well, come in out of the cold."

Della stepped inside. She hadn't even realized that the day had turned cold until the heat in the house surrounded her. The air felt thick.

The gold-and-red décor of the home was exactly as it had been a year ago. It had always reminded Della of a Chinese restaurant, but a nice one. There was even a huge aquarium of saltwater fish in the entryway.

Della watched a big yellow fish swim the length of his tank, and then inhaled hoping to calm her nerves. The breath smelled, and almost tasted, like soy sauce. Like her own home, when her dad took over the kitchen or when her mom cooked to please him.

"Look at you," her aunt Miao said, her gaze shifting up and down Della. "All grown up. What's it been, a year, since I saw you?"

"I think so," Della said.

Her aunt grinned, even though it didn't show in her eyes. Della remembered when her smiles always made it to her dark eyes and they regularly came with a light laugh. That was before Chan's death—the one he faked.

For some strange reason, Della recalled her aunt at the funeral saying she couldn't believe it, that Chan didn't feel dead, and a mother would know.

Did she feel it now? Did she sense that Chan was really gone? Della felt the air shutter in her lungs.

Just like that, Della felt guilty again. She'd lived and Chan had died. And the guy who made that choice was waiting in the car. She'd stopped blaming Chase, but perhaps she hadn't completely gotten over the guilt.

"You finally got some boobs, young lady," her aunt said.

"It's a padded bra." Della tried to tease back, but the humor fell short when she realized how much she'd missed her aunt. How much she missed her old life.

"It can't all be padding," her aunt said. And then her smile faded. "Is something wrong? Everyone is okay, right?"

"Yes. I just . . ." She had to think fast. "I was . . . my class went to the Funeral Museum. You know, that crazy museum about caskets, embalming people, and all that crap."

"Oh, my, that would make for a cheery afternoon," she said. "For what class?"

"Science." She really should have come up with a better lie, but it was the only museum Della could remember around here.

"I wish Meiling was here to see you. She's at the library studying with her friends."

"I'm sorry, too," Della said, but she wasn't. She needed to talk to her aunt alone. "I realized how close we were to your house and I had one of my friends, who was driving, stop off so I could say hi."

"Well, bring her in."

Him. Then Della decided it was best to let her assume. "Uh, nah. She's totally attached at the hip to her phone. Facebook and stuff."

"Kids are like that nowadays. I refuse to allow Meiling to bring hers to the dinner table. Families need to talk." A touch of sadness filled her expression. Della knew she was thinking about Chan.

"Yes," Della agreed, but talking about things had been hard in this family—especially if it had anything to do with the past. She tried to figure out how to bring up the subject of Natasha.

"Let me fix you some tea," her aunt said.

I don't have time for tea. "I can't stay but for a few minutes." They moved deeper into the house.

"Just one cup." All of a sudden, her aunt looked up at the heating vent in the ceiling. "I swear my heater is on its last leg. Let me turn it up."

Della felt it then. The balminess in the room had vanished, an iciness filled the air, but it wasn't a normal kind of cold.

A dead cold. *Don't make it snow. Don't make it snow!*

Miao left to go adjust the heat. Della muttered under her breath, "So, you *are* my aunt, Bao Yu?" Saying her name made it somehow feel real.

No answer came. And that's when she saw it. Like a smear on a glass, something flickered a few feet in front of her. Slowly, the shimmer became visible and the ghost appeared. While she stood with her back to Della, staring in the direction Miao had gone, Della stared at her.

There was something familiar about the way the spirit's black hair rested on the shoulder. The shape of her head. The curve of her neck.

An emotional current shot through Della's veins.

"Natasha?" Della said. Tears formed in her eyes and her knees weakened. Holiday was right. Natasha was dead.

Chapter Thirty-four

"Did you say something?" her aunt said, walking back, never glancing at the spirit, and with good reason. She obviously couldn't see her.

The spirit turned and looked at Della. The sharp edge of Della's panic faded when she saw her face. Della grabbed the edge of an overstuffed chair to steady herself. It wasn't Natasha.

It was her aunt. The face was the same one she's seen in her father's yearbook. The same face she'd seen in the vision covered in blood. But the similarities between her and Natasha were too strong to be a coincidence.

Right then, Della knew the lie Natasha had mentioned in her diary. She'd been adopted. And she also knew the tie between the ghost and Natasha. They were mother and daughter.

Natasha was her cousin.

But how could that be? Her aunt would have barely been a teen when the child would have been born. Della quickly did the math, guessing ages, and realized her aunt could have been fifteen or sixteen.

Show her. The ghost's words seemed to echo in the house, but Della figured only she could hear them.

Show her what? Then Della suddenly knew. She reached into her pocket for the photo. "I . . . Chan gave this to me." It was a lie, but what else could she say? The truth certainly wouldn't suffice.

Her aunt's hand shook as she took the picture. Her breathing came quicker. When she looked up, her eyes shimmered with tears. "I have searched for this picture." She blinked several times and then swallowed.

"She's my cousin, isn't she?" Della asked.

Her aunt nodded then looked back down at the photo. Slowly, she ran her finger over the image of Chan and then Natasha. "Yes. I . . ." She blinked and a few tears slipped from her short black lashes. "She showed up on my doorstep, and I knew before she even spoke to me that she was my niece. She is so much like her mother." Her voice shook a little. "I had to tell her. Tell her the truth. She cried and I cried with her."

Bao Yu moved closer. *What truth? Ask her for the truth.*

"What did you tell her, Aunt Miao? What is the truth?"

"That her mother . . . is gone. But Bao Yu loved her. She only gave her away because our parents couldn't accept it. They were old-school. And the father's parents would not even accept it was his child. She didn't have a choice. She had to give her away. She was told that the child would go to a family with some Asian heritage. That they would love her."

I wanted to keep her. The ghost's voice rang out in desperation. *I cried so hard when they took her away from me. She was my baby. Mine!*

Another question sat on the tip of Della's tongue. She needed to ask, needed to know. "How? How did Bao Yu die?"

Her aunt closed her eyes. "She was killed. And now Natasha is gone, too. Like Chan. Why does life give us something so precious and then take it away?"

Natasha's not dead, Della told herself, and fought to believe it. "How? How did she die?"

"I'm told it was a car accident. It was only a month ago."

"No, not Natasha. How did Bao Yu die?" The temperature in the room grew colder. Even Della's skin prickled with goose bumps. Her aunt Miao folded her arms from the chill and, if her expression was any indication, from the memory.

Looking over her aunt's shoulder, Della saw Bao Yu standing so close and listening. Almost as if she needed the answer as much as Della.

"I don't know," Miao said.

But Della heard her heart reveal the words as a lie.

"I think you do," Della said. "Tell me. Please."

"No. It doesn't need to be repeated. There are some things that are just best forgotten." She looked at Della as if pleading for her to accept it.

Della recalled the pregnancy tests her parents had insisted she take. Had her father been thinking of his sister then? "That sounds like my dad, and I think he's wrong. Because you haven't really forgotten, and neither has he."

"Oh, my!" Her aunt pressed her fingers to her trembling lips. "Your father will be so angry at me for telling you any of this."

Della wanted to insist she hadn't told her nearly enough, but her gut said it would only upset her aunt and wouldn't lead to any information. "My father doesn't need to know," she said. "I won't even tell him I came here. It will be our secret."

Her aunt looked suspicious of Della's proposal, but she nodded.

"Tell me what happened?"

"No, I can't. I have told you too much already." She held up her hands. "No more talk about the past. No!"

Della felt the heat spewing out of the vent above. She glanced over Miao's shoulder and the ghost's image had evaporated, as did her chill.

"Let me get that tea," her aunt said, swatting at the tears still on her face. "We can still visit."

"I'm sorry, I don't have the time, I . . . I should probably go."

Her aunt looked at the photograph in her hands. "Can I keep this?"

Della almost said no, but she got the distinct feeling that Chan would have wanted her to have it.

"Sure." Della started walking to the door, and her aunt moved with her. Certain her aunt would try to hug her again, Della quickly reached for the knob and almost got out when a hand caught her arm.

"I miss you, Della."

A lump appeared in her throat. "I miss you, too."

"Then fix whatever is wrong with your life and hurry back home to your parents. You belong with them, not at that school. You are a good girl. I know this in my heart. So fix it."

It can't be fixed. Della stiffened her backbone and told one more lie. "I'm working on it."

"What did you get?" Chase asked as Della jumped in the car.

"Let's go," she said, her heart racing, and looking back to make sure her aunt hadn't followed her out. Which she would have heard, but she still had to check. Then she felt sweat pop up on her forehead. She couldn't remember the last time she'd sweated.

He started the car and pulled down the street. Then he glanced at her again as he revved the engine and put it in second gear. "What happened?"

The gears in her mind spun with what to tell him. Or how

much to tell him. Didn't she trust him? "I know how Natasha is connected to me now."

"How?" He cut his green gaze toward her.

"She's my cousin."

His brow creased and he looked puzzled. "That's impossible. There's only four of you. You and Marla and Chan and Meiling."

There was something about how he named them off so easily. No, it wasn't how he named them, it was that he knew the names. How did he know Chan's sister's name?

It occurred to her that Chan could have told him. But had she told him her sister's name? She didn't think so.

She just stared at him. "How do you know that?"

"Know what?" he asked.

"Their names?"

His eyes widened as if the question put him in the hot seat. He looked back at the road. "It was in the file," he said. "So your aunt had another child?"

She ignored his inquiry to ask her own. "What file?"

He changed gears again. The car's engine purred. "The file I got on you and Chan. Just like the file I showed you on Natasha and Liam."

"That was the FRU's file," she said.

"Yeah, but the Vampire Council's files are practically the same."

There it was again, the feeling that he knew more than he'd told her. "Do you still have that file?"

"No," he said without looking at her. "Once a case is over, you turn it back in."

"What else did it say?"

"Just normal stuff. Where you lived, your parents' names."

Something wasn't adding up, but she couldn't put her finger on it. "So, if you knew their names, why didn't you get that it was my aunt that called when we were in the closet?"

He lifted up one eyebrow and half smiled. "When we were in the closet, I had my mind on something else."

She frowned at him. Then bam, her brain found that thing that bothered her. "So, in this file you had, it listed that I was at Shadow Falls?"

"Yes."

She tightened her eyes. "Then why did you join the Blades? You told me you'd joined them looking for me and that's where we met."

He stared straight ahead and his hands tightened on the steering wheel.

"Answer me, damn it! And look at me when you do it!"

He turned and met her gaze. "The Vampire Council knew you were being sent on that mission. They didn't want me going into Shadow Falls at first because they were afraid Burnett would be on to me."

"How?" she asked.

"How what?" he came back.

"How did you know I was going on that mission?"

His jaw muscles tightened. "Why are we talking about this instead of talking about how this visit is going to help us find Natasha and Liam?"

"Because I need to trust you to work with you."

He jerked the car over into a parking lot, cut off the engine, and then slammed his hand on the steering wheel. "You don't trust me? I gave you my blood, went through the turn with you—which was damn painful, in case you don't remember—and I gave you some of my power. And you still think I'm out to hurt you?"

Fueled by his anger, she squared off. "I didn't say you would hurt me. I think you're hiding things. Or not telling me things. And just for the record, I didn't ask you to bond with me. I seem to remember telling you I didn't want you to do it!"

He growled, tightened his grip on the steering wheel, pressed his head back, and closed his eyes. "You are the most stubborn—"

"Not any more than you!" she seethed. "Just answer my questions. How did you know I was going on that mission?"

He turned his head, loosening his grip on the wheel. "And you'll report it right back to Burnett, correct?"

She didn't see any reason to lie. "Probably."

He exhaled loudly. "So, to win your trust, I have to betray the council?"

"Yes," she said.

He looked appalled that she'd made it that clear.

He stared at her for a second as if debating, and then answered. "There's a leak in the FRU. And before you ask, I don't know who it is. And from what I hear, they don't even give away anything that would really be detrimental to the organization."

She believed him, not so much about the detrimental part, but about him not knowing who it was. But since he was finally answering questions, she had a few more. "What was the mission with me and Chan?"

"What do you mean?" he asked.

"What exactly was your mission?" she repeated, her patience thinning.

"I was to check on you, attempt to help you both through the rebirth."

"So, you were sent to bond with one of us?"

"No, that was totally at my discretion. I was there to try to make sure you kept up your strength. I told you that it's been proven that those who are in better physical condition have a higher survival rate. Remember me making you run?"

She nodded. "Now all I need to know is why and who?"

"Why and who what?"

"Why were you sent and who initiated it?"

"I just told you that I was sent to help you through the rebirth."

"So they have a list of every possible Reborn?"

His expression tightened with more frustration. "I don't know what all they have . . . but I do know they know that there are only a few bloodlines that lead to rebirths, so maybe they do." He passed a hand over his face and then glared at her. "Do you know what all the FRU has?"

No, she didn't. But she wasn't satisfied. "There has to be a reason they sent you, Chase. In a perfect world, maybe they just care about people. But this isn't a perfect world. And I don't think the Vampire Council gives a shit about a few people dying unless it's in their benefit to make sure they don't."

"They aren't the monsters you make them out to be. The problems between the council and the FRU are political. Not because one of them is evil and the other isn't."

She heard what he said, but she was too busy trying to answer her own questions. All of a sudden, an answer came to her. "Did they send you so that I would come to work for them? Or maybe that I would be one of their spies in the FRU? Is that what they really wanted? What they want?"

"I already told you they want you to come and work for them."

"But was that their plan all along? Save me, then use you to try to convince me to become a traitor?"

Chapter Thirty-five

"A traitor?" Chase asked. "So the Vampire Council is terrible to ask you to work for them? What the hell do you think Burnett has been doing since he discovered that I'm a Reborn? Is the man you hold the utmost respect for evil for trying to get me to work for the FRU? For that matter, why the hell do you think he's working with Shadow Falls? Or haven't you noticed how many of the students are working for the FRU? He's handpicking the cream of the crop."

His point gave Della pause, but only for a second. "Burnett cares. He'd die for any of the students at Shadow Falls. And he didn't get involved with the camp just so he would have access to the students."

"Oh, I'm sure that never crossed his mind," Chase said with sarcasm.

She leaned closer to him. "I happen to know that he's gone against the FRU and their rules to protect someone. He's put his job on the line for the school. And even you made the point that he coddles his agents. Why do you think that is?" She poked him in the chest with her finger. "Could it be because he cares?"

"Could it be that he's not the only one?" Chase snapped back.

"The Vampire Council doesn't care."

She went to poke him again and he caught her finger, his eyes bright. He leaned in, she thought to give her more hell, but she was wrong.

"I wasn't talking about the council. I'm talking about me."

His lips met hers in a kiss that tasted like anger, passion . . . he tasted good.

So good.

He let go of her finger and one hand came to the back of her neck, the other cradled the back of her head. Della's hand dropped to press against his chest.

The kiss deepened and so did Della's confusion.

His tongue slipped between her lips. She allowed it. Welcomed it.

Finally, seeing reason, she pulled back. "You can't just kiss me to avoid answering."

"Really?" He drew her closer and kissed her again.

And damn it, she let him.

She finally pushed back. "Answer me," she said, but without a lot of conviction.

He smiled at her. "I forgot the question."

She wanted to smack that smile off his face, especially when she realized she'd forgotten the question, too.

He passed a finger over her lips, and the sexy way he looked at her told her he was about to kiss her again. She caught his finger this time. "Why haven't you arranged a meeting with me and the Vampire Council?"

"I have. We're going there before we go to the airport to pick up Damian Bond."

"Why didn't you tell me?"

"I was going to, but ever since you showed up at my place earlier, all I've focused on was coming to see your aunt." He pulled his finger free and touched her chin. "Now, will you answer my questions?"

"What questions?"

"Natasha is Chan's sister?"

"No," Della said and decided to tell him the truth. "The ghost is Natasha's mom. She gave Natasha up for adoption."

"So you had another aunt?"

"I guess the council missed that in their report, huh?"

"I guess so," he said and looked concerned. She almost asked if he knew about her uncle. The question sat on the tip of her tongue.

"How did Natasha's mom die?"

"She was murdered," Della said, but she couldn't bring herself to tell him more.

Questions and concerns quickly started forming in Della's head. "Because Chan and I were both Reborns, does that mean Natasha will be, too?"

"It's not a given, but her odds are fifty/fifty."

Della started thinking about other odds. "I've heard that in families that carry the virus, the odds of them actually getting turned are like one in a hundred. And only then when they're young." This was why Della hadn't really worried about her sister. "Do those odds of being turned go up if you belong to one of the bloodlines that are more likely to be Reborn?" When he didn't answer immediately, she asked, "Are my sister and Meiling at a higher risk of being turned?"

He nodded. "The statistics are that one in ten of the stronger bloodlines are actually susceptible to being turned."

"So, me being around my sister or my cousin can expose them?"

"It's exposed only through blood. Like the HIV virus. So just being with them isn't going to get them turned."

Della sat back in her seat and tried to digest what she knew.

"Hey," he said and touched her shoulder. "Don't worry about things that haven't happened. Let's worry about saving Natasha and Liam right now."

She looked at him, and knowing he was right, she nodded.

He spoke again. "You said you felt as if the ghost wanted you to come here. Did you learn anything that would help?"

She tried to consider everything she'd learned. "I don't think so." She looked at Chase and offered him more of the truth. "I think this is about something else."

"Like what?"

"She wants me to find out who killed her."

"Okay," he said, sounding leery. "Do you think you know who did it?"

She looked at Chase and debated telling him everything again. She almost did, then stopped. Oddly, it wasn't because she didn't trust him, but because he already held a prejudice against her father. She didn't need him assuming the worst right now.

"Can we just try to find Natasha and Liam?"

"Okay," he said, but his expression said he didn't like it. "What do you want to do? Where do you want to go?"

"Back to Uck's," she said.

"You still think the were you got a trace of at the restaurant has something to do with Natasha?"

"I do," she said. "And so does the ghost. She's the reason I knew it was werewolves that the rogue was scared of last night."

"Then to Uck's we go." He reached over again and brushed a strand of hair behind her ear. "We are going to work this out."

"Work what out?"

"Everything," he said. "Natasha and Liam. You and me."

Her heart gave a big tug, and all she could do was nod.

He started the car, and for some crazy reason, she heard Steve's voice in her head.

Promise me that before you fall in love with Chase, you'll remember that I loved you first.

Then she heard Holiday's voice. *Just be careful.*

Oh, hell. Was she really falling in love with Chase?

She called Burnett and told him she'd be home in a couple of hours to give him a full report. He started to interrogate her over the phone and she insisted they'd talk later. He wasn't happy, but he accepted it after she told him exactly where they were heading. He obviously felt there was nothing to worry about at Uck's, and didn't mind them going.

What pissed Della off was that he was right.

They got nothing at Uck's. But because there were a few vampires there, they ordered Cokes and talked about mundane stuff. Stories about his parents and his sister. But for some reason, it didn't feel mundane. She wanted to know all those things.

Then he asked her about her past. Wanting him to know the good side of her father, she told him about how they played chess and even entered a few competitions. She told him about her father taking her fishing. About Scrabble night, and how the family would get together and play.

It was sometime during that conversation that she understood why the ghost wanted her to read the diary. When you cared about someone, you wanted to know the little things. Details of their life. Her aunt, Bao Yu, wanted to know the little things of her daughter's life.

. . .

At almost nine o'clock, Chase pulled up at Shadow Falls. "Do you want me to come with you to talk to Burnett?" he asked.

"No," she said. "I got it."

He stared at her. "Are you going to tell him about the leak in the FRU?"

"I have to," she said. "Are you going to tell the council that I know about it and for him to get the hell out of there?"

"I already have—when you went to the bathroom right after we got to the restaurant."

She inhaled. "At least we're being honest."

"Working for adversaries doesn't change what's between us, Della."

It would, Della sensed it. It just hadn't risen to a head. And when it did, she didn't have a clue how she was going to handle it.

But that was only part of her problem. "I'm not a hundred percent sure what is happening between us," she said.

He leaned over and kissed her again. She only let it happen for a second. She put her hand on his chest and pushed him back an inch.

"I can clear that up for you," he said. "It's called being bonded. And it's a powerful thing. We belong together now."

"I have to go." She walked away from him sitting in his car. And she listened to him drive away, feeling the emptiness she felt each and every time.

She went in and gave Burnett a full report. And when she told him about the leak in the FRU, a part of her almost felt disloyal to Chase. *Working for adversaries doesn't change what's between us, Della.* She reheard Chase's words, and again, she knew he was wrong.

No sooner had Della told Burnett about the leak, he picked up the phone to call someone at the FRU.

He was promptly informed that one of their agents had already cleaned out his office and left a letter of resignation.

"Do you see, I told you the Vampire Council was up to no good?"

Della leaned back in her chair. "Do you not have agents trying to get their information?"

"Whose side are you on?" Burnett asked.

"The FRU's," she told him, "but I'm not sure there should be sides."

"Tell that to the Vampire Council," he snapped back. "They're the ones who refuse to work with us."

After a moment of him fuming, Della asked, "Did you get anything else on the bodies?"

"They've found a total of twenty now."

"No identifications yet?" she asked, almost scared of his answer.

"None."

She almost told him about Natasha being her cousin. She didn't because she knew he'd discover that her aunt had been murdered. Then he'd discover the connection to her uncle. Maybe she wanted him to discover it? If her uncle killed her aunt, didn't he deserve to be discovered? Yes, he did, but she wanted a little more time to find her own answers before Burnett started stirring up the pot.

And it had nothing to do with her thinking her father was guilty.

It didn't, she told herself as she walked back to her cabin. When she looked up and saw the stars, instead of appreciating the night, she realized another day had passed and Natasha and Liam were still trapped.

Or dead. The thought whispered through her mind, and as much as she wanted to deny it, a part of her feared that she believed what Bao Yu wanted to believe. What if her aunt just refused to believe Natasha was dead?

. . .

Call it growth, or weakness . . . she didn't know which, but Della finally accepted she needed to reach out for help and support. Instead of locking herself away in her room, she went to the fridge, got out three diet sodas, and waited for her two best friends to come home.

About fifteen minutes later, they came in, smelling like smoke. They'd obviously been at a bonfire.

When they stepped in and saw her, then the diet sodas, their laughter halted.

"What's wrong?" Kylie asked, and they both took up their places at the table.

"Everything," Della said. Her problems spun in her head and she wasn't sure she could fix any of them. Powerless. That's how she felt. Even though she had more now than she'd ever had.

So she started with that truth, the one she should have told them weeks ago. She wasn't just a normal vampire anymore. She didn't tell them that Burnett was a Reborn, but she refused to keep secrets from them anymore.

They sat there and looked at her, then at each other, and then Miranda said, "Tell us something we don't know."

"You knew? How?"

"We saw you flying way faster than you should have," Kylie said.

"And once, you flew off the porch and didn't even run," Miranda added. "We were wondering when you were going to 'fess up. I told Kylie I was giving you about another week and then we were going to have to call you out."

Della made a face. "I hate getting called out."

"Why didn't you tell us?" Kylie asked, almost sounding hurt.

"Burnett suggested I not tell you. So you can't mention it."

"What happens at the kitchen table stays at the kitchen table," Miranda said and turned a fake key on her lips. Kylie nodded.

"Now tell us what's really wrong," Kylie said.

Della explained the whole bond thing—how she didn't like thinking it was real, but feared it was.

They listened. Commiserated. But didn't offer any real advice. How could they? They didn't understand it any more than she did.

"Did you get anything more from the ghost?" Of course, Kylie would guess her issues had to do with the ghost.

Della told them what Burnett had found, and then how she'd gone to see her aunt Miao. Her voice shook a little when she told them how hard it was to see her—someone she'd been cut off from because her parents thought she was doing terrible things. It shook a little harder when she told them what Burnett had found and now believed.

Kylie just sat there and didn't say anything, but Della could tell she agreed with Burnett.

So then she told them about knowing for certain the ghost was her aunt Bao Yu, and about Natasha being her cousin.

"The crazy thing is," Della said, "when I asked my aunt about Bao Yu's death, it was almost as if Bao Yu was waiting to hear. As if she didn't know what happened."

"That's not that unusual," Kylie said. "Especially if it was a violent death. They block it out to protect themselves."

"So the vision she gave me could mean nothing?" Della asked.

Kylie hesitated. "It has to mean something. Maybe it's what she thinks happened."

"Does this ever get any easier?" Della muttered.

"Not even a little bit," Kylie answered. "Every ghost brings a new challenge."

Miranda squirmed in her chair. "Not to change the subject. Well, that's a lie, I really don't like talking about ghosts. But you told us about the bond thing, but . . . did anything happen with Chase tonight? Did any hands or noses go places they shouldn't?"

Della exhaled, and growled. She hadn't really planned on dishing about that, but why the hell not? "He kissed me. Three or four, maybe five, times."

"So bond or not bond . . . is he still a toad?" Miranda asked.

"He's losing his warts," Della admitted.

Miranda looked down at her hands and then back up. "I called Shawn this afternoon."

"You did?" Kylie asked and looked shocked, if not even a little disappointed.

"All we did was talk. I told him you'd mentioned he'd been stabbed, and we just talked." She looked at Kylie and got tears in her eyes. "I feel like I cheated on Perry."

"You didn't cheat," Della snapped. "He broke up with you. Has he even called you yet?"

"No," Miranda said. "But why do I feel guilty?"

"Because you're a nice person." Della shook her head. "No, I take that back. It can't be that. Because I felt guilty, and I'm not a nice person."

"Yes, you are," Miranda said and wiped a tear that rolled down her cheek. "You're just grumpy sometimes. And blunt." She sniffled. "And you stomp people's breakup ice cream into the floor."

Kylie giggled.

Della just smirked at Miranda. "And I'll do it again if you get all mopey and start gorging on ice cream when your nose is running."

"My nose was not running," Miranda said.

"Yeah, it was," Kylie said. "But we love you anyway."

Socks, apparently jealous that she wasn't in the conversation, jumped up on the table. Della ran her hand down the cat and listened to her purr. The cat turned around and started butting noses with Della, giving her kitty kisses.

"I wouldn't let her kiss you," Miranda said.

"You're just jealous that she's loving on me," Della said and pouted her lips at the kitty.

"Nope, that's not it. It's because I watched her eat a mouse today."

"Eww." Della set the cat on the floor and they all started laughing.

She went to bed feeling better, even if she had been kissed by a mouse-eating cat. At least, she felt better until her phone dinged with a text at three in the morning. She rolled over, ready to find out who she was going to kill for robbing her of her first good night's sleep in weeks.

Her thoughts went to Steve. She reached for her phone, and when she did, she saw Smurfette on the nightstand staring at her. And bam, just like that, she missed Chase, and all those little details about his family that she'd learned last night played across her mind. Confused at thinking of Chase and Steve in the same heartbeat, she grabbed her cell.

The number was anonymous, but the message gave the caller's identity away. She wasn't going to kill anyone.

The caller was already dead.

The message, written in all caps and in red, simply read: *FIND NATASHA!!!*

"I'm trying," Della said, and sat up the rest of the night in a very cold bedroom, trying to figure out what she needed to do next.

At 5 a.m., her phone dinged again. This one wasn't from the ghost. The message was simple. *I miss you. Steve.*

Chapter Thirty-six

"Della?" Mr. Yates, her science teacher, motioned Della to come up to his desk the next morning.

Oh double damn! Was he going to call her on spacing out and not paying attention? Probably. But Della could hardly think about school. Her thoughts went from picking up the rogue were, to Damian Bond, to missing Chase, after only being away from him for a few hours, and realizing there was a part of her that still missed Steve.

Then there was the issue of meeting the Vampire Council. Would she learn anything? Was she completely wrong that her uncle was behind Chase being sent to check on her and Chan?

And if so, did that completely exonerate Chase from her lack of trust? And if so, would that change things between them?

"Della?" Mr. Yates said again.

Della stood up to do as Mr. Yates requested, and he added, "Go ahead and grab your books."

Her books? This reminded her of being sent to the principal's office. She'd only gone once, and it totally hadn't been her fault.

Scooping up her books, she walked to Mr. Yates's desk. "Yes?"

"Burnett wants to see you."

Okay, she was sort of being sent to the office. But hopefully not for something she'd done wrong. As she walked out, Miranda and Kylie gave her a wave.

All sorts of thoughts shot through Della's mind as she left the classroom. And the worst one had Della almost hyperventilating. Had one of the bodies been identified as Natasha or Liam?

In less than a minute, Della arrived. Burnett's voice echoed from Holiday's office. Since the door was open, Della walked right in.

"What is it?" she asked.

"It's not anything terrible," Holiday said, instantly picking up on Della's emotions and standing as if to come give her one of her touches.

Della held her hand out, wanting to deal with this alone.

Burnett, having been half-sitting on Holiday's desk, stood up. "I just wanted to go over what will happen tonight at the airport."

Della let out the breath she'd been holding. "Okay." She moved the rest of the way in, plopped down on the sofa, and placed her books beside her. This was a piece of cake.

"I'll be going with you. We'll meet Chase at the airport."

Okay, the cake wasn't as sweet as Della thought. She and Chase had pre-airport plans that involved a trip to meet the Vampire Council, and she knew Burnett would balk at that.

Oh, hell, who was she kidding, he'd do more than balk, he'd be livid.

"Uh . . . why can't Chase and I take care of this on our own?"

Burnett stared down at her and his brows tightened the way they did right before he started arguing. The fact that she knew his pre-arguing expressions said a lot about their relationship.

"He's a known criminal with a three-page rap sheet. I wouldn't send two of my best agents out alone to pick him up. I'll be there, as well as another agent, as backup."

His tone told her he wouldn't compromise on that. "Fine, but I'll ride with Chase. He's picking me up around four this afternoon."

"The plane doesn't land until nine."

"I know," she said, not offering anything else.

"So . . . ?" he asked.

She knew he meant "so" as in "so, what the hell are you planning on doing until then," but she didn't plan to play. If he wanted to know, he would have to ask. Not that she would tell him. She couldn't.

"So I guess we'll see you at the airport around eight, or earlier. Just tell me where you want to meet."

He frowned. "I don't know exactly how to put this, but I don't approve of Chase."

Della knew this was where it was going, but she hadn't planned what to do about it. "I know you don't approve of him. But . . . I do."

Burnett leaned back against Holiday's desk again. Holiday rose and came around to stand almost between them. No doubt, the fae could feel a pending argument brewing. She probably knew it before Della ever arrived. And that look in her eyes, almost an apology, told Della to get prepared—this conversation wasn't going to be easy.

"I don't trust him," Burnett said. "And if I remember correctly, you weren't too keen on him in the beginning, either."

"I know, but I've worked with him all this time and I've seen another side of him. Plus, I remember when Holiday wasn't so keen on you."

Burnett grimaced. "So now are you comparing you and Chase to me and Holiday?" He turned to his wife. "I thought you said there wasn't anything romantic going on?"

Holiday shook her head. "No, I told you she said they weren't having sex."

Della huffed. "I'm glad you two get off on talking about my sex life."

Burnett glared back at Della. "So, you're emotionally involved with Chase?"

She almost denied it, but then couldn't. "Sort of." And then feeling defensive, she added, "You're the one who assigned me to work with him."

"That was before I knew he worked for the council and had info about the FRU leak."

"In his defense, he told me about it."

"He should have told us about it a long time ago."

He grew quiet, and having seen his interrogation techniques, she knew he used it to put a person on edge. And whether he meant it that way or not, it worked. She was all edge. But she wasn't backing down. She needed to meet the council.

"You assigned me to work this case with him and I plan to finish this case with him."

"And then?" he asked.

And then? The question bounced around her head and heart. "I don't know."

Burnett ran a hand over his face. "Fine. But there are some things you need to know up-front."

She nodded. And she saw Holiday grimace as if she knew what was coming.

"After this case, if you continue to see Chase, your career with the FRU is over."

Della felt the blow to her gut. The pain shot up to her throat and it tightened. She had expected to have a fight on her hands with Burnett about Chase, but she never expected this.

All her hopes, her dreams she'd worked so hard for since coming to Shadow Falls, were sitting on the chopping block.

"You would do that?" she asked, and it took everything she had not to cry.

"No." Complete honesty deepened his voice and he shook his head. "The FRU will do it."

She titled her head up and didn't bat an eyelash for fear a tear would fall. "Then I guess, after this case is over, I have a choice to make."

Making it clear she planned on meeting Chase, she stood to leave. Burnett caught her arm. "It's not me doing this, Della."

Hate the message, not the messenger, her heart said. Never mind that the messenger knew how badly she wanted this. That since working her first case with the FRU, she knew it was what she wanted to do for the rest of her life.

"I believe you," she said, but couldn't deny it hurt like hell. She pulled away and tore off to her cabin. She had a lot to think about.

Della's phone dinged with a text fifteen minutes before three. Chase had arrived early. His message read he'd wait for her in his car. Did he sense he was unwelcome in Shadow Falls? Had Burnett confronted him?

She wouldn't put it past the camp leader.

She walked out the gate, noting Burnett looking out the window. Her breath caught at the sight of him. Then she saw Holiday appear at his side. Probably to touch him so he'd calm down. Maybe she should have let Holiday touch her, too.

Della tried not to feel guilty about disappointing Burnett, but she pretty much failed. She tried not to be angry, but she flunked out on that as well. How would Burnett feel if someone tried to blackmail him into turning his back on someone?

Someone he cared about.

Someone who very well could turn out to be a part of his life forever.

And yes, that's how she felt about Chase. Part of her believed the ties between them couldn't be cut. Another wanted to bring out a pair of scissors.

The sight of Chase standing beside his car, watching for her, melted her regret about disappointing Burnett, but not much of her anger.

Chase wore his sunglasses, looking cool and collected in jeans and a long-sleeved, light green shirt. Even with his glasses on, she felt his gaze touch hers. Felt it pulling her to him, reading her, needing her.

He needed her.

She hadn't really sensed that before, but she did now. He needed her. The feeling made the ache in the center of her chest spread.

"What's wrong?" He walked toward her.

So Burnett hadn't given him the lowdown.

She stepped away when he reached out for her and headed for the car.

"Della?" he asked.

She looked at him. "What isn't wrong?" she asked, prolonging having to tell him. Or trying to decide if she needed to tell him.

"I could name a few things," he said and moved closer. "The sky's blue. It's not raining. We're going to ride with the top down, and I got you some more hair-band things. Later, we're going to pick up one bad-ass were who I'm thinking is going to lead us to

Liam and Natasha. Top off that with . . . you, other than appearing upset, look sexy as hell."

His gaze lowered. "I love those jeans on you, by the way. You were wearing those the first time I saw you at Shadow Falls." He paused a second and raised his eyes. "And I get to spend the whole afternoon with you."

He moved a little closer and ran a finger down her cheek. "And that, Miss Tsang, is what isn't wrong."

She caught his finger. "Why are you always touching my face?"

He grinned. "Because other parts are still off-limits to me."

Chapter Thirty-seven

Della growled and hopped in the car. But her face tingled where he'd touch it.

Chase moved around the car, opened the door, and with ease and style, lowered himself into the driver's seat. "Hey, I've got an idea. Why don't you drive?"

"No," she said.

"Scared?"

"Scared I can't do it? No. Scared I'll get another ticket? Yes."

He studied her then leaned back in his seat, lowering his glasses to look right at her. "What's wrong?"

"You already asked that once."

"Yeah, I did, didn't I?" he said sarcastically, pushing his glasses back up and folding his arms. "But I don't seem to recall you answering."

Della looked back at the gate and envisioned Burnett stepping out. "Let's go," she said.

"Not until you tell me what's wrong."

"Let's go and I'll tell you." *Or maybe she would.*

He started the car and the motor purred, loud but smooth and powerful. He drove into the street.

"Start talking," he said, his voice only slightly raised over the sound of the engine and rush of wind. Thanks to their super hearing, conversation with the top down wasn't impossible.

"Burnett and another agent are going to meet us at the airport."

"That doesn't surprise me. The council is actually sending another agent as well. Supposedly, this Damian is a bad ass." He glanced at her. "You worried about meeting the council?"

"A little," she admitted, letting herself off the hook from explaining anything more. And it was true. She didn't have a clue how she was going to get information from them. If her uncle wasn't on that council, she didn't know how just walking up to them and asking if they knew him would work. No, she realized, what she needed to ask them was why? Why had they sent Chase to help her and Chan? Someone was behind it, weren't they?

"If you can handle Burnett, you can handle the council, no problem."

And that was the problem. She couldn't handle Burnett. Not if the meeting today was any indication. It wasn't Burnett, she reminded herself, but the FRU. She didn't have a clue how to handle them.

"Our meeting isn't until five and it's close. You want to go back to my place for a while?"

"What for?" she blurted out before she realized that made her sound like a scared little girl. But she was, wasn't she? She wasn't ready for what he might have in mind. Or maybe it hadn't been in his mind, but now he probably thought it was in hers.

"We could sit out on the front porch and bird-watch," he said and smiled ever so slightly.

Was he making fun of her, or trying to let her know he didn't have anything else in mind? With his glasses covering his eyes, she couldn't tell for sure. But other than a few kisses, some sexy banter, oh, and the closet—which she couldn't blame him for—he hadn't tried to do anything.

He's not trying to pressure me into having sex. She recalled telling Holiday that, and she still believed it.

"Fine," she said. "Birding it is."

It was fine. They went to his place and sat out on the front porch. He brought her a glass of O-negative. It was fresh and tangy. It could have been the best she'd ever had.

They sat out there for a while without talking. It wasn't an uncomfortable kind of silence, but peaceful. Baxter joined them. Every few minutes, he'd nudge her leg with his nose for her to pet him. And for right now, Della let herself forget about meeting the council, forget about her powwow with Burnett.

Several birds fluttered back and forth. He told her the names of the birds. She almost chuckled when she realized he really was a birder. Then, damn it, she realized she kind of liked it, too. Miranda would have a field day with this.

Then Della's mind took her back to when she was here before. When a certain bird, named Steve, had shown up.

Not that she feared he was one of the birds now. He was in Paris. And for some reason, that made getting close to Chase easier. Out of sight, out of mind.

Not really, her heart spoke up. She had thought about him. And damn if she wasn't even more confused about how she felt, too.

No, that wasn't exactly true. She knew how she felt about Steve.

In spite of being angry at him for getting close to her when he knew he was about to leave, she still cared about him. Liked him. Liked him too much. Was attracted to him.

What confused her was that she felt all that for Chase, too.

And more.

It was the "and more" part that scared her. Before, she could compare what she felt for Lee to what she felt for Steve. The same emotional draw. The same kind of desire. This, what she felt for Chase, couldn't be compared to that. It seemed bigger. More intense. More powerful. And she felt more vulnerable to those feelings. Much more than she was with Steve.

Was it the bond? She didn't like thinking it was, because she didn't want anything to have control over her. Even if at times, giving in sounded rather delightful.

Chase stood up from his chair and came to stand in front of her. He set his sunglasses on top of his head, and then pulled her up. He slid his hands around her waist, and his fingers went slightly under her shirt. He leaned forward. His forehead came against hers.

"What you said earlier?" His thumbs touched her bare skin and she wondered how just a simple touch could feel so good.

"About what?" she asked and pulled back just a bit. She knew where this was going. She just didn't want to go there.

"I wouldn't have brought it up, but after what you said—"

"Then let's just forget I said anything."

"Look, Della, I'm not going to deny that as much as I like those jeans on you, I would love to take them off, but—"

"Now there's a come-on line I haven't heard. What country-western song did you steal that one from?" She glared up at him.

He frowned. "Let me finish. *But* . . . when the time comes, you will be the person to say when. I would never pressure you into doing anything you didn't want to do. Got that?" he asked. "You say when, not me."

His words whispered around her head and made her dizzy from want. Or was her dizziness due to his thumbs making little circles on the tender skin of her waist?

He exhaled. "For the record, if it was up to me, I would've said 'when' a long time ago." He grinned, and while flattered, she was equally flabbergasted.

She opened her mouth to talk, but nothing came out for a second, and then she finally said, "I'm . . . I'm not much on saying 'when.'"

But his touch, his breath against her temple sent shivers to parts of her body that didn't normally shiver. And she knew "when" would feel nice on her tongue, just like his hands felt around her waist.

He arched one eyebrow. "Have you said 'when' before?"

That was it. The feeling of being flattered crashed at her feet and flabbergasted took over in first gear. Had he actually asked her that? She punched him in the gut.

"Ouch." He grabbed his abs and stared at her. "That was not nice."

She glared at him. "I know. A guy's not supposed to ask that. You're lucky I didn't go for your balls."

He took a step back, and now he looked befuddled. "Guys *are* supposed to ask that. A guy who cares needs to know. You don't have to tell me now, but before we . . . go there, we should talk."

Embarrassment started making her feel uncomfortable in her own skin. "First, who said we're going to go there?"

"I . . . well, you kind of hinted that you thought I was going to take it there. And we're bonded, so odds are we're going there eventually."

She stared at him, not believing his nerve. Then she felt her face flush like when she'd had her nose buried in his crotch.

He studied her. "If you haven't gone there yet, there's nothing to be embarrassed about."

"I'm not embarrassed," she lied, and then she felt pissed that he made her feel that way. "You're the one who's dancing around the word 'sex.' I'm not a virgin, I just don't think it's any of your business."

"Okay," he said, now looking uncomfortable. "I was trying to be polite."

She cut her eyes up to him. "Are you a virgin?"

He laughed.

She wanted to punch him again. Really hard.

"No . . . I'm not."

"Then why are you laughing? Is it because you've got a ton of notches on your belt and you're proud of them?"

"No," he said seriously. And he seemed to grasp for words before he finally said, "I guess I'm a little embarrassed, too. I was trying to deal with this like an adult. But I guess I screwed it up. Give a guy a break."

"You've asked that once. And you never told me what you wanted broken. But I have a few ideas."

He chuckled. "You aren't going to make anything easy, are you?"

"If you want easy, you're climbing down the wrong foxhole."

"No, you're the right one, even if you're difficult." He took a step closer.

She took a step back, remembering her meeting with Burnett. "I wouldn't count on it." Then, realizing how much time had passed, she said, "We should probably get going."

"I just have to ask one other thing," he said.

"What?"

"This." And then she was in his arms. And he was kissing her again. And it felt good. Too good. His palms moved up under her shirt to her back. The sweet touch brought back the memory of his hand on her breast and made her want to say "when."

Instead, she pulled back and looked up at him. With some effort, she repeated herself. "We should go."

"Yeah," he said and then he touched her nose. "Let's go introduce you to the council. They are in for a treat."

Ten minutes later—ten minutes that she'd worked feverishly to come up with different scenarios of how to approach the subject of her uncle—Chase pulled into a Benny's parking lot.

She stared at the family diner, which was almost like the one her father took them to most Sunday mornings. Or had taken them to . . . that treat had been dropped since she went to Shadow Falls.

"Are you kidding me?" Della asked.

"What?"

She'd envisioned several different types of meeting places with the Vampire Council, but never a family diner that was mostly a hangout of the over-sixty crowd. "Benny's? I'm meeting the Vampire Council at a family diner where you can get eggs and raisin toast for a buck ninety-nine?"

"I personally like their pancakes," Chase said.

She continued to stare. "Really?"

"They're good pancakes."

She tightened her eyes at him, knowing he was toying with her.

Chase pushed his glasses up on top of his head. "There's a room in the back that the restaurant rents out."

"And they rented it to meet me?" she asked.

He nodded as if he didn't see her problem. And maybe it was nerves making her see it as a problem, but she couldn't seem to let it go. "But this isn't like their office?"

"No," he said.

"But they have an office?" she asked.

"Yeah."

"So, they don't trust me enough to bring me there."

His brow crinkled. "You work for the FRU. Just meeting you is a big step."

"Burnett took you to the FRU office."

"That's different," he said.

"How?"

"The FRU is listed in the phone book under federal businesses."

"I see," she said. "Because the FRU is a legit, aboveboard type of organization, but the Vampire Council isn't."

He frowned. "Oh, so the FRU has more merit because they hide themselves as a human organization behind the guise of a government identity?"

"They're only hiding from the humans. Supernaturals know who they are."

"But if the Vampire Council hung up a shingle, the FRU would be there to take it down and put them all in prison."

"Only if they committed crimes," Della said.

"Right. And being unregistered is a crime."

Della had debated this in her mind. It wasn't unlike the debate between socialists and libertarians. One believed in organized government and the other didn't want government anywhere near their door.

"I'll admit, I don't see being unregistered as a crime, but the problem is the majority of criminals and evildoers come from that side. They don't want to be registered because they know they're up to no good. And because there aren't any records, their chances of getting away with it are great."

"Or they just don't want someone else poking their noses into their lives. Not everyone who is unregistered is a criminal."

"I know," Della said, "but wasn't it less than thirty years ago that the Vampire Council farmed humans and used them for food?"

"Wasn't it just a little more than thirty years ago that the FRU allowed the hunting of werewolves?"

"So both organizations have mud on their faces," Della said, admitting it. "You can't deny that most all the crimes out there against humans are from those who refuse to be registered. And if any justice is going to be done, we need a way to hold people accountable."

"Which is why the Vampire Council has their own unit to attempt to deal with rogues."

"The FRU is trying to get the different species to work together."

"We aren't promoting prejudice. We just think that each species should be held accountable for their own."

"The Vampire Council was actively trying to shut down Shadow Falls," she accused.

"Yes, at the time, they saw it as a brainwashing camp to get teen vampires registered."

"That 'brainwashing camp' saved my life and it's saved the lives of many others."

"I don't disagree. The council was wrong. And in the last few years, they've stopped their attempts to shut it down."

"You're registered?" she asked, knowing the answer because Burnett had mentioned it before.

"The council felt it would allow me more cover."

"Have you felt it has been an invasion of your privacy?"

He hesitated.

"Be honest," she said.

"I guess not. But that could change."

She frowned. "We aren't going to agree on this, are we?"

"Probably not," he said. "And I'm *not* taking you in there if all you plan to do is argue politics."

"I can't ask questions?"

"Questions about the case? Yes."

"How about questions about mine and Chan's case?"

"I've answered all those," he said, his jaw set firmly.

"Maybe they know something you don't." *Or maybe you're still keeping secrets.*

He ran a hand down his face as if frustrated. "If you came to work for them, you could ask all kinds of questions."

"What does that mean?"

His expression hardened and his hesitation said he was trying to find an answer—so probably something a little off from the truth. "I just meant that as long as you work for the FRU, they aren't going to completely open up to you."

"So what will they hide from me?"

"I didn't say they would hide anything," he said.

"You implied it," she countered.

"I didn't imply shit," he said. "Look, go talk to them, but don't start interrogating them. They won't like that. And the last thing I want to have to do is . . ."

"Is what?" she said.

He looked at her. Honesty filled his eyes. "Take on the council to defend you. They aren't Reborns, but they're bad asses."

"You would do that?" she asked before she could stop herself.

"If I had to. But I don't want to. So behave."

"I'm gonna ask questions," she said.

His frown tightened. "Fine, ask. But don't get your back up if you don't get answers."

They got out of the car and walked into Benny's. The smell of burnt bacon and eggs filled the air. The hostess was a vampire, and after checking their patterns and offering Chase a flirty smile, she motioned for them to go ahead to the back room.

Della followed him, her stomach a knot of nerves. She almost wished she hadn't drank the blood at Chase's place. The door to the back was shut. While he'd been motioned to go on back, he still knocked.

"Come in," she heard a low and deep voice say on the other side.

Chase looked over his shoulder at her and mouthed the word, "Behave."

Chapter Thirty-eight

Unlike the front of the diner, the back room held heavy curtains. And they were closed. The only light came from a chandelier that held a couple of sixty-watt bulbs.

Six men sat behind a long table. Della's gaze shifted fast, taking in each of their faces, searching for one face. The face of her father. Or rather, her father's identical twin.

He wasn't there.

Disappointment stirred in her already nervous gut. Though, why she thought it would be that easy was beyond her. But that didn't mean her uncle wasn't behind this.

Chase introduced her. He didn't give the names of the men individually, just calling them the Vampire Council. And she supposed that was all she was going to get.

They didn't stand up, but nodded their heads appropriately. Each of them had a brown mug set in front of them. She'd bet it wasn't coffee in those mugs.

She studied them each briefly. Not one of them was Asian. Two looked Hispanic, one Native American, one African-American, and the other two were Caucasian. Their ages ranged from early thirties to early hundreds. Or at least, that one Hispanic dude appeared older than dirt.

For some reason, she remembered finding herself in the courtroom with the FRU judge and jurors.

In front of the long Benny's table were two chairs.

"Miss Tsang, Mr. Tallman," the oldest of the group spoke. "Please sit. Would you like something to drink?"

Della found her mouth a little dry, but didn't think her stomach would take anything. She forced herself to move to the chair and to speak. "No, thank you."

"We have heard wonderful reports from Mr. Tallman about you," another of the men said.

"I'm sure he exaggerates," Della answered.

"I doubt that," said another of the six, one of the blond guys who looked around her father's age.

"She is everything I told you," Chase spoke up.

The older dude added, "We were delighted to hear you wanted to meet with us. And we shall not pretend that our hope isn't that you intend to join us as one of our agents."

Okay, this was going to be very tricky. "I can't say that is my intention at this time. However, I've always been one to like options."

"Disappointing, but well delivered, young lady," said another of the six.

"So, what is your intent in meeting us?" asked the eldest.

"I guess you might say curiosity."

"About us?" the eldest questioned.

"Yes. And more."

"The 'more' being?" asked the youngest of the council.

She stiffened her spine and heard Chase shift in his chair beside her. She hadn't gotten this far to be too afraid to ask. "I'm curious as to why you would send an agent to ensure my cousin and I would get though the rebirth?"

"We offer sympathies for your cousin's death," said the talk dark man on the council.

Sympathies? She realized she might not be able to be angry at Chase for being unable to save both her and Chan, but . . . "Could you not have sent two Reborns to help us and saved him as well?" She glanced back to the youngest of the group, who seemed more opt to answer.

"Unfortunately, we do not have the staff to do that," he said.

"Then how do you have the staff to check on every possible Reborn?"

When he didn't answer right away, she said, "Is there a reason you sent someone to check on my cousin and me?"

"It's apparent that someone with your talents and abilities would be an asset to our team of agents," answered the youngest of the council again.

"So, you *do* have a list of all potential Reborns?" she asked. "And you send someone out to all of them?"

"We make it our business to stay informed," said the eldest again.

Della got the sense he wasn't answering her questions as much as placating her.

He waved his aged hand and continued. "We strive to offer help to all those possible."

But they hadn't strived that hard to save Chan. If they were that concerned, they could have sent two agents, couldn't they?

She heard Chase say something under his breath, but she ignored him. "So who informed you about me and my cousin?"

"You are indeed filled with curiosity, Miss Tsang," the eldest spoke again. "And if you were working for us, you would have access to a colossal amount of information."

Della stiffened. Why did that almost sound like a bribe, the same one Chase had offered earlier? *Go work for them and she'd get her answers.*

"Considering that I *am* in a sense working for you, I thought you might respect me enough to answer my inquiries now."

"And we did," said the eldest.

Bullshit!

"Is there another question you would like to pose?" the man continued. "Perhaps one that might encourage you to join us in our struggles to help provide justice to our kind? If not, I think we shall call this meeting over."

Something about his tone came off as condescending. "I don't think you've really answered—"

"Enough," Chase whispered, and reached over and squeezed her hand. Then he stood up. "I appreciate you taking the time for us."

Della sat there debating the wisdom of speaking out one more time. They hadn't actually done anything to prove her right, nor had they done anything to prove her wrong.

"Good luck finding the missing vampires, Chase. And you, Miss Tsang," said one of the blond men.

Chase nodded, then looked at her and motioned for her to stand. When she didn't move, he reached down. She stared daggers at his hand, which was literally pulling her up and out.

"Miss Tsang?" one of the council spoke. She looked back over her shoulder, not caring that her eyes were probably bright from fury.

"If you change your mind about working for us, you will find there is a place for you here."

She swallowed the retort she wanted to give, something about a cold day in hell. Then, without another word, she left the room and restaurant so fast, she probably appeared as a blur to the patrons eating in the front.

It wasn't even five-thirty, but the sun had already set and it was almost dark. She leapt into the passenger seat of the car and waited for Chase to open his door and slide in with a calmness that downright irritated her.

"That was bullshit!" she told him.

"They answered you, Della."

"They did more talking around my questions than answering them."

"And you think the FRU is better? You think if I went in there asking questions to the bigwigs of the FRU that I'd get straight answers?"

She remembered her little encounter with those FRU bigwigs. "Maybe not, but why couldn't your council just have told me instead of . . . ?"

"I seem to recall one telling you that you had talent and abilities that we could use. That seemed pretty straightforward to me."

"Then why didn't it feel like the truth?"

"Maybe you just don't want it to be." He paused and looked out the front of the car as someone passed by. "What is it you're hoping to learn?"

When she didn't answer, he asked, "Do you want to put blame on them for Chan's death?"

"No. I want . . ." She almost told him then about her uncle, about the murder of her aunt, then she heard his words from earlier in the car: *If you came to work for them you could ask all kinds of questions.*

He swore he hadn't been implying anything, but . . . she still had a tiny whisper of doubt.

"Maybe I don't know what I want," she said, and there was

some truth in that. Did she really want to find her uncle now that she suspected he'd killed her aunt?

Chase pulled out of the parking lot. "We should probably just head to the airport. Do you know where we're supposed to meet Burnett?"

"He said he'd call."

Her phone rang. She pulled it out of her pocket. "Speak of the devil."

"So you're admitting he's the devil," Chase said with a touch of humor.

She cut him a smartass look and answered the phone. "Hey, I was wondering when—"

"Where exactly are you?" Burnett barked.

"About fifteen miles outside of Fallen, we were just heading toward Houston."

"Where?"

Della recalled the street signs she'd just seen. "We're in the twenty-nine-hundred block of Howell Street."

"Hold on," he said, then she heard him say to someone else, "They're close." And then, "Della, do you know where Cooper Airport is?"

She looked at Chase and he nodded.

"Yeah. Chase knows. What's wrong?"

"We put a man on the plane with Damian Bond. Ten minutes ago, he realized the guy sitting in that seat is only a lookalike. He confessed to our agent that Damian took an earlier flight, a smaller plane that should be arriving at Cooper airport in fifteen minutes. We're pretty sure it's flight ten-twenty-six on Token Airlines. We're already in Houston. Even flying it's going to take us twenty to get there. You might make it in ten if you ditch the car and fly. Both of you should have just gotten his mug shot on your phones."

Della heard both of their phones ding. Chase looked around for a place to park.

"Stay away from any major streets," Burnett continued. "It's not quite dark enough, and I don't want you getting spotted."

"We won't," Della said.

"And don't . . . do *not* . . . confront Damian. Just follow him. He carries a Glock and he likes using it. You got that?"

"Yeah," she said.

"Do you understand, Chase?" Burnett barked.

"Yeah," Chase answered, and he grimaced as he pulled over in a drugstore parking lot beside a patch of trees.

Perfect for taking off.

The line went dead. Della pushed a button and stared at Damian Bond's face. *Ready or not, here we come.*

Nine minutes and thirty seconds later, they landed in a wooded lot a half block from the airport. It was the first time since being Reborn that Della had flown that fast. If she wasn't so worried about what they were about to do, she would have really enjoyed it.

The sun had completely faded, only the corner of the western sky held a touch of color to bid the day good-bye.

They didn't speak. No time. If the plane came in early, their last lead to finding Natasha and Liam could be gone. Her blood zinged through her body, preparing to do whatever it took to keep Damian in their sights.

She ran her hand through her winded hair as they headed out of the woods toward the one-story airport.

"Look." She spotted the lights of a plane already on the ground and rolling in to the airport.

"That's probably him," Chase said. They hurried their steps, trying not to call attention to themselves as a couple of cars pulled into the airport parking lot. Walking into the building, which was mostly glass, there were about two dozen people standing around waiting for passengers.

Della noted a mom and her two red-haired kids. Burnett's idea of just following Damian seemed like a good one, the last thing she wanted was someone innocent to get hurt.

Following Chase through the crowd, she could see the plane through the glass doors. Passengers were disembarking and waiting at the foot of the steps for their luggage. But so far, she hadn't seen Damian.

She pulled out her phone again to study his face and then slipped it back in her pocket.

"There's Daddy," said the woman with two kids who'd moved up to the glass. "Wave at Daddy."

Della glanced at Chase. "We just follow him," she whispered. "I don't want trouble here."

"I know." He glanced at the woman, obviously knowing exactly what Della was thinking.

"There," he said and her gaze shot to the were walking out of the plane. The light on the outside of the building pointed toward the plane, giving Della a good view. Early thirties maybe, Damian wore jeans and a black jacket, probably to cover his gun. His dark hair was slicked back, reminding her of some mobster. His eyes were too far apart. His mouth too thin. A woman walked out of the plane at the same time, and their suspect, not exactly a gentleman, cut her off to make the steps first. No doubt, he was as ugly as he was mean.

"Let's pull back," Della said, afraid he would spot two vampires and know they were onto him. Sure he'd smell them, but if they weren't too close he might not suspect they were here for him.

They moved behind the crowd, but Chase stayed between two groups of people so he could keep an eye on their suspect. Della shifted a little to the right behind an older lady so she too had a line of vision. The passengers started moving inside. The noise level in the mostly glass room grew as people greeted each other.

"Shit!" muttered Chase.

"What?" she asked, looking at him and realizing that he wasn't even looking at Damian, but behind them.

Della twisted and saw exactly what had him panicking. Two police cars screeched to a halt in front of the airport. Their lights whirled around giving everything and everyone a blue cast.

"Did Burnett call the police?" Chase seethed.

"I don't think so," Della said as she watched four officers rush inside the building.

Della grabbed her phone to call Burnett, but before she could dial, a woman screamed. A child cried out.

Then a gunshot.

Chapter Thirty-nine

The bullet ricocheted off something metal and binged around the room.

"Police," screamed one of the four officers behind them. "Get down!"

"Drop your weapon," ordered another.

Everyone plummeted to the floor. Della and Chase went down on their haunches, both prepared to launch off if needed. Then he put his arm around her, holding her down, and preventing her from seeing. Refusing to be blocked, she knocked his arm away.

Damian and one other man stood in front of the glass wall. Both of them had guns. But Damian had something the other didn't. He held the red-haired baby girl dressed in pink, about the same age as Hannah. He pressed his gun to the screaming child's head as the mother on the floor sobbed.

"You don't want to do this," called one officer.

Della again noticed the other guy with the gun. He wasn't supernatural. Did Damian have a human accomplice? Then she noted how the two guys shot each other puzzled looks.

Crap. What were the chances they had two criminals on one plane?

Damian looked back at the officers. "Drop your guns or I'll blow this kid's head off."

The mother's sobs rang out with others' screams. Della's heart clutched and she felt her canines extend and her eyes stung from the oncoming brightness.

The other guy just stood there, gun out, but appearing stunned. Della glanced back at the officers, wondering which of these guys they were after. Had Damian's crimes become a human problem, or were they after criminal number two?

"Keep your head down," she heard Chase whisper, but she could barely hear him over the screams of the crowd.

She lowered her head, but cut her eyes up, still able to see what was happening in front.

"There's four of us," said one of the officers. "And it's not going to end well."

Damian gave the baby girl a cold look. "Yeah, and we know who it's going to end badly for," Damian said and lifted his head as if to sniff the air, no doubt picking up on their scents.

"He knows we're here," she muttered in an almost silent whisper.

"Yeah, but he doesn't know who we are yet," Chase whispered back. "So keep your head down. We'll have a better chance of overtaking him."

Feeling her blood fizz in her veins, she could hear her heartbeat hitting her ribs as if it wanted to escape. The child's screams had her wanting to attack.

"Drop your guns or the kid dies!" yelled Damian, but he was busy looking around the crowd for them instead of focusing on the cops.

The mother screamed again and Della saw someone holding the woman back. But no one was holding Della back.

She tightened her calf muscles, ready to lunge, but Chase must have felt her slight movements. His arm came back down on her.

"Not yet," he said in her ear.

But Della didn't see any choice. She saw Damian's finger go for the trigger. Bolting up, she dove for him, praying she got there in time.

Still airborne, she saw Criminal Number Two turn his gun toward her.

Chase dove in front of her.

The gun exploded.

Chase! Her heart stopped, but she couldn't. She had to save the baby first.

Seconds felt like minutes. She grabbed Damian's right arm and twisted until she heard it break. He dropped the baby, but the mother bolted over and caught it. Damian's gun clanked to the floor and Della kicked it and heard it skid across the tile. Then with force propelled by fury, she shoved him to the ground. His head hit the hard floor with a thud.

Another gun went off.

More screams exploded. People started scrambling.

The police rushed forward. Della stepped away as they reached Damian.

Her heart stopped midbeat as she turned to look for Chase.

People were everywhere, falling over each other to try to get out. The cops had the other guy on the ground. Another two were standing over Damian.

She shifted her gaze from left to right.

Right to left.

She couldn't find Chase.

Tears stung her eyes. Where was he, damn it?

She felt someone step behind her, but her nose said it wasn't Chase, so she ignored the presence and continued to look for him.

But then the scent hit. Not Chase, but another were.

"Are you here to help? Or part of the problem?" a voice asked behind her.

Turning her head, she saw one of the officers. She'd been so tense earlier she hadn't picked up on his scent.

But a quick glance at his forehead confirmed what her nose had already told her. He was half were, half human.

"To help. I'm . . . we're with the FRU." Della turned back to look for Chase, feeling her panic climb at frightening speeds.

The officer grabbed Della by the arm. "Then you need to show me your badge."

Before Della could cut him a sharp look, a growl sounded behind her. "Release her."

She swung around, pulling out of the were officer's grip. Her eyes landed on Chase, and only then did air get to her lungs.

"You okay?" she asked. Then she cut her eyes down and saw blood high up on the arm of his shirt. "You're hit!"

"Just grazed," he said, still glaring at the officer.

"I still haven't seen a badge," the were in the uniform said.

The officer could strip naked and howl for all she cared. All she cared about was Chase. And not trusting his assessment of his injury, she reached up, found the hole in his shirt, and ripped it open to see for herself. He hadn't been lying. The bullet had just grazed his forearm.

He'd dove in front of her. He'd taken a bullet for her—put his life at risk. Her heart started pulling in about a dozen different directions, as did her emotions. She wanted to slap him for doing something so stupid, she wanted to kiss him because he was okay.

"Happy?" he asked, looking down at her.

"Yeah," she said. Only then did she look back to the were wearing the uniform and waiting for answers. "I'm a junior agent, working under Burnett James. He and several other agents should be here in less than ten minutes. We'll be taking Damian Bond."

He must have recognized Burnett's name, because his eyes that had started to brighten faded back to their hazel green. "Well, they'd better hurry. And have the proper paperwork. They," he nodded to the other officers, "aren't going to just let him go. And if you two don't want to be dragged into this, you'd better disappear."

Chase looked at Della. "I think that might be best."

Della frowned. "Not until Burnett has Damian." He was their last link to Natasha and Liam, and Della wasn't going to risk losing him.

Chase looked back at the officer. "I guess we'll be staying a while."

An hour later, they were all at the FRU headquarters. Burnett had arrived at Cooper Airport less than five minutes after everything went down. He was followed by two official cars, and three other agents, who showed off their badges, and their authority, managing to piss off the Oak, Texas, police department.

Face it, this was probably the first time their tiny police department had caught a bad guy, especially two at once, and they hadn't wanted to lose any of the credit.

However, Burnett, with paperwork in order, wasn't about to walk away empty-handed.

He also got Della and Chase out of having to go down and give their statements—insisting the local police leave them out of the paperwork and media hype because they worked undercover. But before they left, the mother of the child who Damian had held hostage came up to her and offered a tearful thank you.

A sense of rightness filled Della right then. This was what she wanted to do. But was she willing to lose Chase for it?

Burnett had a doctor waiting at headquarters to look at Chase's arm as soon as they walked into the building. Of course, Chase tried to get out of it, but Burnett wasn't taking no for an answer. He told Chase to see the doctor . . . or leave.

Chase glanced at Della, huffed, and then went into the room to see the doctor.

After the door closed, Burnett approached her, concern etched in his frown. The airport had been crazy, and this was really the first chance she'd had to speak—not that she hadn't seen him visually checking on her—since he'd threatened her career. She felt an achy sensation, a mixture of hurt and love, right in the middle of her chest.

She looked at Burnett and her throat grew thick.

"You okay?" he asked.

"Yeah."

"You saved that baby's life. Seems you're good at doing that," he said, referring to her delivering Hannah.

"Just lucky," she said.

She looked back at the door where Chase had disappeared. "He took that bullet for me."

"I heard. Which is the only reason I care enough to make sure he sees the doctor."

Della nodded, but she didn't buy it. She knew he had some major problems with Chase, but somehow she also sensed a level of respect. She could only hope that came in handy when the case was over and Burnett put pressure on her to end things.

Because honestly, she wasn't sure she could.

If push came to shove, would she choose him over her career? She prayed she didn't have to make that choice.

"Go on into waiting room six, I'll be interviewing Damian in about five minutes and you can watch."

She looked back up at Burnett and thought of Natasha again. "Make him tell us where they are."

"That's my plan," he said.

Damian Bond didn't want to talk. Burnett slammed down photos of Liam and Natasha on the table. The were refused to look at them. Della's blood pressure rose and her canines extended just watching him.

Someone had given the were a sling, and he sat there with his broken arm held as tight as his lips. Burnett, looking pissed, turned to the wall where they watched. "Do you know who's in there?" he asked.

Damian didn't respond, but Burnett answered anyway. "An agent with the Vampire Council."

The were's eyes widened just a bit, but then he went back to pretending he didn't hear. But Della did see him glance at the photos on the table.

Did he know them?

Burnett continued. "Have you heard what they do to weres in the Vampire Council prison? It makes going to one of our facilities seem like a day at the spa."

Della looked at Chase. "Is that true?"

"We don't believe in segregation," he said. "And since most of our prisoners are vampire, the were will have it rough."

Della shuttered, wondering what "rough" included.

"And if you don't talk," Burnett continued, "we've agreed to pass you over to them."

The were looked up at Burnett and snarled. "Good try. But since when do the FRU and Vampire Council work together?"

Burnett dropped in the chair across from him. "Since over thirty fresh turns came up missing, and were being sold into slavery. You've got three seconds to start talking, or I'm turning you over to them."

"If Burnett's serious, we'll get the answer out of him," Chase said.

Della swallowed and told herself it was the right thing. But the thought didn't settle well in her stomach.

Burnett looked back at the wall. "I guess you can come and get him." He started out.

"Wait," Damian spouted. "Okay, I'll talk. It wasn't me, though. It was my boss. Tyler Myers. He used them to hold fight matches. People paid big bucks to see them fight, and then he got a cut of the profits. But Tyler got word that you guys were aware of the operation and had closed down the Dallas branches, so he shut down. He got rid of them."

Della's chest gripped. She felt Chase move beside her as if afraid of what Damian might say.

"You mean he had them murdered?" Burnett asked.

The air in Della's lungs turned to syrup and it took everything she had to not to let her knees buckle.

"Yeah. But I was just following orders."

Burnett gripped his fist. "How many? And where are the bodies?" His eyes turned orange with fury and Della felt her own brighten even more.

"I don't know. The boss and the others got together and got rid of all of them. I heard something about a junkyard."

Chase's arm came around Della.

"But I swear I don't know where it is." Damian looked down at the photos. "But these weren't ours. They might have been with the others, but they weren't ours. I'd remember her."

Chase took Della's hand in his and she heard him breathe for the first time. "It's still not over," he said.

"Then why does it feel like it?" she asked and felt the knot in her throat expand.

He turned and pulled her against him. She rested her forehead on his chest. She closed her eyes and smelled blood. But it wasn't Chase's blood.

She pulled back and looked up at him. Liam, not Chase, looked down at her.

Chapter Forty

Della had done this numerous times—slipped into a vision, or whatever it was—but that didn't make it any easier. Especially now, when her faith that Natasha and Liam were still alive had shrunken to nothing but a tiny seed of hope.

Natasha was reclined on a dirt floor, halfway on top of Liam's naked body.

Della focused really hard and tried to force Natasha to ask Liam where they were, but all the effort was wasted because she didn't speak. She rested her chin on Liam's chest and she felt her bare breasts press against the solid feel of his abdomen.

Liam pushed her hair out of her eyes. "What is the first thing you want to do when we get out of here?"

Natasha frowned, and Della knew why. She didn't think they were getting out. But she was willing to placate him. She looked back at his chest, shifted her hand up to just below his right shoulder and traced the emblem that appeared to be part tattoo and part scar.

"What do you say we go get our tattoos removed?" She ran her fingers over his tattoo again.

Della studied the cross-like symbol. Could that mean something?

Liam chuckled. "I like that idea. How about we go listen to a band play? Do you like to dance?"

"Love to. Sometimes my friends Amy and Jennifer and I go."

That loud noise came again. The sound of heavy machinery.

Liam put his arm on her back, as if he knew the noise bothered her. "Then we'll go dancing first thing."

What's the noise? Della screamed in Natasha's mind, hoping she would hear her, but her question went unanswered.

"Maybe we should take a shower first," Natasha teased. She rested her head back down and looked around the dark room.

Della took it all in. The walls were like blocks, but the floor was dirt, and there was what looked like an open passageway into another area that appeared just as dark.

What was this place?

"Together?" Liam asked, his hand running across her naked back. "Let's take a shower together."

"Yeah, together." She giggled and spread her hand flat on his chest and glanced at it. Natasha was a shade or two lighter than Liam.

"Is your mom or dad black?" Natasha asked.

"My dad was half black."

"Was? Is he dead?"

"Not that I know of."

"Did you ever know him?"

"Yeah, he came around some when I was younger. Mom didn't like it." He got quiet for a minute. "They would always fight. The last time he was there, I was like thirteen. They got into a real big fight. He accused my mom of trying to raise me to be white. Mom told him all she wanted to do was raise me to be a good man, and that had nothing to do with color, and everything to do with character, and that if he was going to see me, he'd have to get himself sober and set an example."

"What did he say?" Natasha asked.

"He hit her." Liam's body under Natasha tightened. "It wasn't the first time, but it was the first time I decided to stop him," he said.

Natasha pushed herself up and looked at Liam's face. "Oh, my God. What happened?"

"I came out with a baseball bat. I hit him in the arm. I don't think I broke it or anything, but I could tell I hurt him. I told him to leave and never come back."

"Did he ever come back?"

"I don't think so. Mom got married to Hank a few years later. He was a good guy. Black, too. But Hank was twenty years older than my mom. He died of a heart attack less than a year after they got married." Liam ran his hand over her back. "Didn't you tell me your dad died?"

Natasha paused. "Yeah, my adoptive dad died when I was eleven and when I went to look for my real parents I discovered my real dad was dead, too."

"How old were you when you found out you were adopted?"

"Almost eighteen." She inhaled. "Mom said they were going to tell me when I was thirteen but when my adoptive dad died, she just thought it'd make me feel worse." Natasha grew silent and just breathed for several seconds. "I think part of me always knew. My adoptive dad was half Chinese. Even as child I would stare at his face and wonder why I didn't look more like him."

"Didn't you say your real mom was dead, too?"

"Yeah," Natasha said. "Someone killed her. But they never found out who did it."

He ran his hand alongside her hip. Not sexily, just tenderly, but there was something totally intimate about being naked against another person. "That must have been tough, looking for your real parents and then finding out they were both dead."

"It was for a while. But I did find an aunt. She was nice. And she had a son about my age."

They lapsed into silence and then Liam asked, "How did your adoptive dad die?"

"A work accident. One day he was there, and the next he was gone. But Mom remarried a few years ago."

"Do you get along with your stepdad?"

"Yeah, he's all right. Well, a lot better than all right . . . compared to your real father. He loves my mom, but I always got the feeling he was just waiting for me leave so he could have her all to himself."

"Well, that's okay," Liam said. "Because when we get out of here, we'll get our own place. I've only got two more years before I graduate. We'll find a cheap apartment. Both of us will go to school and work part-time. We'll make it. Since we don't need food that much anymore, we won't have to worry about who's going to cook. We'll share the housework. I'll take out the garbage. And I promise not to leave my dirty underwear around."

She laughed. "I'm not the best housekeeper."

"Good, we can live kind of messy, then."

She lifted her chin and rested it on his chest. "Will you put the toilet seat down?"

"I'll try." He laughed.

Della felt Natasha's sinuses sting. "I want that," she said, her voice cracking. "I want that apartment. I want to give you a hard time about leaving your dirty underwear out and leaving the toilet seat up. But I'm so scared it's not going to happen. I'm so afraid this is all we'll have."

Saturday, at ten fifteen, Della sat in the dining hall watching everyone visit on parents' day. The voices of all the campers and their parents bounced around the huge room and echoed down from the rafters. Della tried not to let her emotions leak out into the crowd—too many faes around—but honestly, she really wanted to go find someplace quiet and cry.

Damian Bond had nothing. They were back to square one.

She'd come home last night and stared at the ceiling for half the night, feeling useless and angry. Feeling alone. She missed Chase. She wanted to help Natasha and Liam. Save them. Give them a chance at life.

She wanted her mom to call her.

No, she wanted her parents to show up. Where were they?

The doors to the dining hall swished open. Della looked up, expecting it to be them. Wrong. It was Derek's mom. Della watched as she smiled at Derek who sat at a table toward the back of the dining hall with Jenny.

Della looked around. Kylie and Lucas and her mom sat chatting about selling her house. Lucas must be getting used to Kylie's mom, because he actually looked comfortable instead of miserable, like he usually did when Kylie forced him to spend time with her mom.

Miranda was playing the part of the good witch, sitting and listening to her mom talk about the upcoming competitions.

Della pulled out her phone to check the time. Her parents were fifteen minutes late. Strange. Her dad didn't do late.

Then again, maybe he wasn't coming today. He'd missed one out of three parent visits lately. But her mom and her sister, Marla, were usually on time, too. The sooner they got here, the quicker they could leave. Or at least it felt that way.

Glancing at her phone, she debated calling her mom then decided against it. Looking back up, she saw Holiday and Burnett studying her with empathy.

Oh, friggin' hell, the last thing she wanted was for everyone to start feeling sorry for her. She was fine. Her family would show up. Her mom never missed parents' day.

All of a sudden, Burnett's phone rang. This far away, Della couldn't hear the person on the line, but Burnett didn't look happy.

Probably FRU business. Was it about Natasha and Liam? She tilted her head to the side and heard him whisper to Holiday, "I need to take this in the office."

Della watched him walk out. Her need to know bit deep, but she accepted there wasn't a dang thing she could do. If it was news on Natasha and Liam, he would tell her. And if it was about them, it was probably bad news.

Ten minutes later, Della's phone rang. Glancing at the number, Della's breath caught. Her sister, Marla, never called her.

"What's up?" She shot up, and dodged tables in the dining hall to move away to have a private conversation.

"Hey." Marla's voice sounded small. "Uh, Mom asked me to call you and tell you we weren't going to make it today."

"Okay," Della said, fighting the pinch in her heart and walking outside. "Is something wrong?" *Or have you guys just decided to give up on me?*

"Hold on a second," Marla said quietly.

Della continued toward the woods, a spot she knew where sev-

eral large trees created a little alcove. She heard her sister on the
move, too. Then she heard the door close.

"Sorry. I just wanted to go in my bedroom in case Dad was
listening."

Yeah, you wouldn't want Dad to know you were talking to me.
Della's mood stood on the verge of sliding down the slippery slope
of self-pity when Marla spoke again. "Something's going on, Della.
I don't know what it is, but it's bad. Can you come home?"

Home? Uh, no! "What? What's happening?"

"That's just it. I don't know. They won't tell me anything."

"Are they fighting?" Della asked. Her parents weren't perpetual
fighters, they actually loved each other, but they'd had a couple of
fights. And Della had hated that tension she'd felt during those
times.

"Not really. Mom's just so upset. Every time I see her, she's got
tears in her eyes. And Dad is acting strange. He didn't come home
until after ten last night. And when he did get home, he took Mom
in his office and they stayed in there forever talking." She paused.
"You don't think Dad's got a girlfriend, do you?"

Della's mouth dropped open. "No."

Then it hit her. The reason her parents were upset. "Has dad
talked to Aunt Miao?"

"I don't know," Marla said. "Why?"

"Nothing," Della said, and closed her eyes. Shit! She'd done it
again. Disappointed her dad, caused her mom more heartache.

"I want you to come home. I need you. I don't like this 'only kid'
shit."

Since when did her sister say shit? "I can't, Marla." She bit down
on her lip, but her throat felt tight hearing her sister's request. While
it felt so good knowing she was finally being missed, it felt equally
bad knowing she could never go home. Never. Ever.

"Where is Mom?" Della swallowed a lump of pain down her throat.

"She left. Said she was going to the grocery store. Mom never shops on Saturday mornings."

"I'll call her," Della said, but her stomach knotted thinking what her mom would say about Della going against her dad's wishes and seeing her aunt.

Hanging up with Marla, Della called her mom.

It rang twice and her mom finally answered. "Hi, Della."

Her mom's voice didn't sound right.

"Hi, Mom."

"I told Marla to call you," her mom said. "Did she forget?"

"No, she called," Della said and tried to figure out a good reason for her to have visited her aunt.

"Look, Mom, I know you guys are upset—"

"I'm sorry I didn't call you back," her mom said. "We've been busy."

Della held tight to her cell. Her mom never beat around the bush. When there was a problem, she put it out there. And fast. So did that mean the problem wasn't that aunt Miao had spoken to her dad about Della's visit?

Relief filled her chest, but the next second, fear chased it away. If whatever was wrong at home wasn't about her, then what was it about?

"Mom, what's wrong?"

"Nothing . . . Della." Her mom's voice broke. Was her mom crying?

Hell, yes, she was.

"Mom, what's wrong? Just tell me what it is."

"I'm sorry, hon. This isn't something you need to worry about, okay? Chances are it's nothing."

"Are you sick or something, Mom?" Della recalled one of her friends' mom finding out she had breast cancer. "Did you find a lump or something in your breasts?"

"No."

"Dad? Is he—?" Her heart gripped.

"Nobody's sick. And you're just going to have to accept that I can't talk about things now."

"Mom, that scares me. If something is wrong, I need to know."

"Not now, sweetheart. You just concentrate on you." She paused. "I've got to go now. I love you," she said.

Tears filled Della's eyes. "I love you, too."

Then her mom hung up. Della sat down beside the tree and gave in. She cried about whatever was wrong at home. She cried because it felt like forever since her mom had told her she loved her. She cried because she didn't think she could save Natasha and Liam—and they would never get that apartment. All that love they shared would die with them.

She cried because she missed Chase.

After a good minute of letting herself go, she wiped her cheeks. She called Marla back and told her Mom wouldn't talk, but she made Marla promise she'd call her if she figured out what was wrong.

"Hang in there, okay?" she told her sister.

"I will," Marla said and she sounded alone.

"Why don't you go see your friend Mickie?" Della asked. "Get out of the house and enjoy yourself."

"I am," Marla said. "Her mom is picking me up in an hour."

"Good. Don't do anything I wouldn't do. No smoking, alcohol, or sex. French kissing's okay, even if it is gross."

Marla laughed and then said, "I miss you."

The swell of emotion hit tight. "I miss you, too."

Della hung up, the ache lingering in the pit of her stomach, and stared at the phone. The temptation hit. *Don't do it. Don't do it.*

She did it.

She hit dial.

"What's wrong?" Chase answered on the first ring.

"Why would you ask that?" she asked, holding her voice steady, remembering her mom's voice breaking up.

"Because you should be visiting with your family right now."

"Yeah, well . . . something came up."

"They didn't show?" he asked, sounding offended.

"No, but it doesn't matter."

"Sorry," he said and then, "Shit, did your aunt tell your dad you went to see her?"

"No. I thought it was that, but . . . I spoke with my mom and it seems like it's something else. I'm sure it's no big deal."

So why did it feel like it was?

"I was just thinking about Natasha and Liam," she said.

"Me, too. I've been searching the Internet for tattoos like they had. If I find the artist who did it, I thought it might lead us to them."

"That's a good idea," Della said. "Why didn't I think of that? I should get Derek to do it, too. He's good working with the Internet."

"Maybe he'll have better luck than I did," Chase said, sounding disappointed.

Della leaned back against the tree. "You know the first time I saw the tattoo, it reminded me of . . . something. Like I've seen the emblem before."

"But you don't remember where?"

"No."

There was a moment of silence and she knew they were both fearing the worst.

"I did a rough sketch of the tattoo," Chase said. "Do you want me to take a picture of it and send it to you so you can shoot it to Derek?"

"Yeah, that would be good."

A bird landed in the tree to her right. Della looked at it. "A red-headed woodpecker just landed," she told him, remembering him pointing one out yesterday on his porch.

He chuckled. "I'm making a birder out of you."

"Not on your life," she said, but she watched the bird gripping the bark of the tree and make knocking sounds with its beak. What was it that Miranda had said? Oh, yeah, watching birds lightens up your aura.

She supposed her aura could use some lightening.

"What are you doing now?" he asked.

"Talking to you. Watching birds."

"Besides that?"

"Nothing," she said.

"You want to go for a ride?" She heard the anticipation in his voice.

Her heart lifted. Then dropped. Burnett would be upset.

"Say yes." He sounded lonely. He sounded like she felt.

"Yes," she said, and then, "No."

"Which is it?" he asked, disappointment ringing in his voice.

"Yes, I want to go, but not just for a ride. I want to go to Uck's. See if maybe that were comes back."

"I'll be there in ten minutes . . . or less." She could hear the smile in his voice. And she could imagine it on his lips.

"Don't speed," she said.

"I'm not the speed demon," he said, chuckling, and hung up.

A minute later, she got the picture of the tattoo from him. She stared at it, and again got the crazy feeling she'd seen it somewhere . . . somewhere other than in the visions. But where, damn it?

She shot it to Derek and asked if he'd do a search on it. Then she got up to go find Holiday to tell her she was going out with Chase.

Knowing Holiday, she would probably make her go and tell Burnett, but right now, Della didn't care. She needed to see Chase. And she needed to do something, anything, that might help them find Natasha and Liam.

Della needed to stop thinking about problems at home that she couldn't do diddly-squat about.

She hadn't taken two steps when Burnett cleared the corner. Obviously, he'd come looking for her.

And the look in his eyes told her something else had happened. She recalled his phone call. She recalled thinking if it was news on Natasha and Liam, that it wouldn't be good.

It took everything she had not to turn and run. She didn't want to hear it.

Chapter Forty-one

"Your parents aren't showing?" Burnett asked.

Della prayed this was what he wanted, that his look was concern for her and not . . .

"No, there's something going on and they can't make it."

He exhaled, and that sad sound hit Della right in the gut.

"What is it?"

"They haven't identified anyone, but they have two African-American males and one girl who appears to be Asian. We don't have DNA from Natasha. But we're doing a DNA test to see if one of the males is Liam Jones. I've called in some favors and asked for them to do the test ASAP. I'll let you know as soon as I have something."

Della started shaking. She wanted to scream that it wasn't them. That they didn't know for sure that Natasha and Liam were at a junkyard. That it couldn't be. Tears filled her eyes, but she blinked them away.

She tilted her chin and met his eyes. "Chase is picking me up and we're going back to Uck's to see if the were is there."

Burnett's brows tightened as he frowned. He opened his mouth and she knew what he'd say. That she was wasting her time. That she shouldn't be with Chase. But then his gaze met hers right when a tear slipped down her cheek and he just sighed. "Fine. Don't be late."

She took in a stuttered breath and ran to the parking lot to meet Chase.

When Chase pulled up, Della could tell from his expression that Burnett had called him. Her throat tightened again, but she swore not to cry. Crying wouldn't help. She recalled a saying that her father had once translated from Chinese. *Crying does nothing but water the pain and allow it to grow.*

She didn't have room for this pain to grow.

Chase leapt out of his car and didn't open the door. He moved to her. "Did Burnett tell you?" she asked.

He nodded and pulled her to his chest.

She didn't fight him. Not even when some parents walked past to get to their cars. She held on. She'd never needed to feel someone's arms around her as much as she did his right now.

"Come on," he finally whispered in her ear. "Let's go to Uck's."

They both jumped into his car. She bit down on her lip and looked at him. "Are we wasting our time?"

"We don't stop looking until they have a positive ID."

She nodded. "I agree."

They drove off and the wind in her hair and just sitting next to Chase made some of that pain lessen.

When they arrived, they were the only two supernaturals in the place.

They sipped Cokes and chatted about the visions, trying to find anything that might help them.

"The place they're at—it doesn't look like a junkyard, does it?" she asked.

"I don't think so," he said.

"What kind of place could this be?" Della finally asked. "It looks like it's underground. It had block walls." She let the thought run through her head. "There're some underground tunnels in Houston. I know Kylie had a confrontation there a while back. Maybe this is something like that?"

He frowned. "I've been in those and it's not like that. This is like . . . a tomb or something."

She let go of a deep sigh and looked at the phone sitting on the table. Anytime now, Burnett could call and tell them it was over. That hurt like hell thinking about it.

Della went to refill her diet soda and got that first hint of . . . were.

She swung around and looked at Chase. He'd obviously smelled it, too, because he was already on his feet.

"Is that it?" he asked.

She inhaled again, waiting for her sensory bank to start pulling up old files. And then, bing. It hit. "That's it!" she whispered, and had to lower her upper lip to hide her extending canines. Not from danger, but from her determination not to lose the dog this time.

She started looking around. A group of three guys sat in one corner, all of them with hats on.

She moved closer to the three, checking if they were were. A noise suddenly clattered in the front of the restaurant.

"Where are you going?" someone called.

"What the hell did he run for?" someone else asked.

Della turned around and the closer she got to the chaos, the stronger the scent got. She arrived at the counter, and not willing to lose this creep, she leapt over it and shot between the fryers and grills, dodging several confused-looking employees.

She felt and heard Chase right behind her.

"You can't be back here," someone said, a manager-looking guy. A human manager guy.

She ignored him and followed her nose to the back. She went through a hall and then a prep room. She'd no more stepped foot in the prep room when a solid steel door leading outside slammed shut.

"Stop them!" yelled the manager dude.

Della surged forward, but about five Uck's Burgers guys surrounded her and looked eager to do as their boss ordered. Chase was suddenly at her back. "Too many humans to let our power show," he whispered in her ear.

Indecision boiled inside her. She wanted to barrel though them, yank that door from the wall, and see who'd just gone through it, but she knew Chase was right. Burnett had preached this lesson from the very beginning. Public displays of power were the biggest no-no.

She felt her eyes brighten and inhaled, thinking calming thoughts.

"Who just left here?" she asked.

"Who wants to know?" asked the manager dude. "I'll need to tell the cops when I call them."

"Don't worry, I'll call them for you." Chase grabbed his phone.

She thought he was calling someone from the Vampire Council. But then she heard Burnett's voice on the line. "What's wrong?"

"We need some assistance at Uck's. Someone just ran out the back to escape us and the manager and his employees aren't cooperating."

"I'll be there in five."

. . .

It only took three minutes. Burnett walked in, his badge promi-
nently hooked on his belt. He didn't ask permission to go behind
the counter. He didn't jump over it, but his demeanor wasn't any
less intimidating. He came to stand right beside her and Chase and
gave them a quick once-over.

"Who are you with?" the manager asked, gawking at the badge.

"FRU, an agency that works with the FBI for local cases."

"What the hell is the FBI doing here?" He kept on rattling
about how they'd lost a few customers due to the commotion.
Then he started in about past robberies.

Burnett ignored him and turned to Della and Chase. "What
happened?"

"We had a runner," Chase said. "I think he might have recognized Della and escaped out the back, and these guys didn't want
us to go after him."

"I have a safe in my office." The manager kept talking on and on.
"I can't just let anyone come back here. You should arrest them," the
balding guy told Burnett. "I don't think . . ."

Burnett swung around and faced the guy and gave him his best
glare. "Shut up!" he snapped. "One more word, and I'll have the
health department out here before you throw out that expired meat
you're cooking. And I saw about fifteen other violations just walking in here."

Chase leaned in. "That badge sure does come in handy."

Della looked over her shoulder at him. "I know." It was the first
positive thing Chase had said about the FRU, and she couldn't
help but wonder if he wasn't coming around.

Burnett didn't have to say anything else for Mr. Manager to
become cooperative. And after Burnett posed the question of who

had run out the back, he started singing like a happy bird. "It was one of my new employees. He came in, went to run the register, and the next thing we know, he's flying out the back so fast we barely saw him. Then these two jumped the counter like they're superhumans."

"Get me everything you've got on the guy. Now!" Burnett ordered when the man didn't move fast enough for him.

The manager tore off to his office. Before Burnett followed him, he came over to Chase and Della and in a low voice he said, "The DNA was negative on Liam."

Della wanted to kiss him. Hell, Chase looked happy enough to kiss him.

A feeling washed over her. A feeling she really, really liked. Hope. Natasha and Liam were alive and she was going to do everything in her power to make sure they stayed that way. Della had to swallow four or five times not to let the tears of joy fill her eyes.

When Burnett followed the guy into the office, Chase brushed the back of his hand against Della's. A gentle touch, but it spoke loudly. Chase felt it, too. Hope. Amazing how much one appreciated that feeling when it had been robbed from you.

"What did Red do?" one of the guys hanging in the back asked.

"Red?" Della asked. "That's his name?"

"That's what we call him. Red hair and all."

Red hair? Della's mind started playing connect-the-dots again and she found more dots than she expected. The last red-haired guy she'd encountered had been a were at the cemetery where Chan was buried. The cemetery where the security guards had worn uniforms. And on the uniforms had been a . . . cross emblem.

Suddenly, she heard Chase's remark from earlier: *This is like . . . a tomb or something.* She turned to Chase. "I know where they are."

Burnett came walking out of the office, looking surprised and somewhat content that he'd gotten something useful.

"He worked at the graveyard, didn't he? Evert something, right?" Della asked.

Burnett nodded. "How did you know?"

"They said they called him Red because of his red hair. And Natasha and Liam had tattoos—like a brand—similar to the ones on the uniforms of the security guards at the cemetery. They have them there, Burnett, in some kind of underground tomb."

He pulled out his phone. "We'll turn that graveyard upside down if we have to. I'll have some agents meet us."

It was dark when they got to the cemetery. Della glanced up at the moon, only a day from being full, which meant the weres would be at their most powerful. Not that it concerned her now.

They landed at the front entrance. The silver moonlight brushed against a rusty metal gate, baring the cross symbol. She could kick herself for not remembering it earlier. But she had no kicking time. Three other vampire agents showed up within seconds. Della inhaled and got hints of were just outside the gate. And Red was amongst them, too.

Burnett paired them up and sent them each to a side of the cemetery where they would enter. "Chances are the guards aren't cooped up in the office. They are probably walking the grounds. If we get the graveyard surrounded they'll have less chance of escaping. Let's get these guys," he said and glanced up at the moon. "Remember, they're at their most powerful right now."

Della and Chase went to the west side of the cemetery as Burnett had ordered.

Right before they leapt over the fence, Della got a strong scent of were.

Chase glanced at her, letting her know he'd gotten it, too.

He held up three fingers, and when the last one went down, they both bolted over the six-foot fence.

Midway over the rusty posts, Della heard the weres talking. They were close. Too close.

The sound of her and Chase's feet hitting the ground thudded in the dark.

The talking stopped. Silence echoed.

The guards either heard them or got their scent. Della didn't care. She was ready to kick ass.

Chapter Forty-two

There were five. Even in the dark, Della spotted them running full force at them.

Chase cut his eyes to her as if making sure she was ready.

Hell yeah. For Natasha and Liam she was ready to do whatever it took.

She kicked her foot out, hitting the first were right in the gut, and sending him about five feet in the air. A tree waited on him. He slammed against the trunk with an ominous clunk, then slid to the ground. His lack of muscle control told Della he was unconscious.

One down, four to go.

Nope. Make that three. Chase got in a right hook, and another were fell to the ground, out cold.

Two more came at Della . . . with knives. The silver of the blades reflected in the moon's glow.

Out of the corner of her vision, she spotted six more weres charging toward them. Damn, that made a whole pack of 'em.

Four surrounded Chase. And two came to join the other two circling her.

She went to kick one back to make it better odds, when another jabbed a knife into her arm.

She felt the pain.

Smelled the blood.

And just got plain ol' pissed off.

Chase's growl filled the night air. Fearing he was hurt, she cut her eyes his way.

His eyes glowed bright red, his fangs completely extended, but she got the feeling his reaction came from her injury. Not his own.

That one-second glance cost her. The weres now stood closer. Too close. Hands, feet, knives, they came at her all at once. But she moved with power, blocking, and even landing a few blows, as she moved.

She caught one were by the wrist, swung him around, and let him take the next few blows from his friends. He grunted, groaned as feet connected with his ribs.

When his friends stopped hitting him, she used her captive as a bowling ball. Chan, her champion bowler, would have been proud. He'd have called it a spare, because only one remained standing.

Just as she moved in to take him out, Burnett showed up. He caught the were by one arm and swung him into a tree.

Della turned to help Chase. But instead, she watched him take down his last attacker.

Burnett looked around. "Considering the odds, you did good." Then his eyes grew brighter as he moved closer to Della and smelled the blood on her shirt.

"It's okay," she muttered. Before Burnett could start coddling her, Chase shot over and did it for him. He ripped off her shirtsleeve to see the wound.

"It's not bad," she said.

Right then, the sound of fast-approaching footfalls sounded in her ear. All three spun around at the same time.

Della sucked air in her nose and caught the trace of one were. But he wasn't alone. He was being chased by several vamps—the other FRU agents.

Then the were scent found its way into her memory bank.

"I got this," she said and bolted forward.

In the silver light of the moon she caught sight of Red hauling ass toward her. He spotted her and turned his long-legged gait, moving fast back into the line of tall pine trees. But not fast enough.

"Girl Toy's baaaacccck!" Della seethed as she tackled him, pressing him into the layer of pine straw covering the ground.

She put her knee in his back. "Move and I promise I'll hit you where it hurts and you'll be talking like a girl for weeks."

When he didn't fight back, she rolled him over and looked him dead in the eyes. "Where are they?" Fear filled the were's eyes and for good reason. Della didn't plan on asking twice.

Red, along with all of the other weres told the same story. The owner of the cemetery, Ramon Henderson, had taken part in the underground fights. But when news came from Dallas that the FRU was on to them, he packed his bags, took his best men, and flew to Mexico.

They also admitted there had been several fresh turns kept at the cemetery, but all they knew was that they were kept in burial vaults. Mr. Henderson and his top men had been in charge of them, and they just assumed he'd disposed of the evidence.

There were six burial vaults on the property. Keys with numbers on them hung on the office wall.

The first four were empty. As she, Burnett, Chase, and two

other agents hurried through the cemetery to the fifth vault, she told herself not to panic. They were minutes from finding Natasha and Liam. *We're coming. We're coming.* She repeated in her head, somehow hoping Natasha and Liam could hear her.

The fifth vault proved difficult to open. Burnett rushed back to the office, found two sledgehammers in a storage room, and between him and Chase they brought the thick concrete door down.

And as soon as it crumbled, so did Della's heart. The strong smell of death whooshed out as if seeking escape. The two agents shot back.

Burnett, gritting his teeth, looked back at her and Chase with empathy. "You two stay here," he said as he stepped into the dark vault.

"No," she cried and tried to follow, but Chase grabbed her. "Let him check."

She fought Chase for a second, then she read the reasons in his eyes. If it was them, he didn't want her to see them like this. He didn't want to see them, either. Della leaned against Chase and fought to grasp tightly to her newfound hope. But the smell of death was so strong it threatened to destroy it.

In only a few seconds Burnett came out. He held his arm over the lower half of his face. His gaze went to Della and Chase. He lowered his arm and swallowed hard.

"Four bodies. Three male, one female. They are in too bad a shape to identify." His voice came out tight as if the sight sickened him.

"It's not them," Della said, her pulse racing so fast she felt it fluttering in her throat. "They were alone."

Burnett looked down as if seeking strength, and then up. "One female and male were alone in a room."

Della felt doubt cut through her heart like glass.

"There's still one tomb left."

Burnett nodded, apparently not throwing in the towel yet, either. He turned to the others and gave orders for someone to call for a van to take the bodies in.

He picked up the sledgehammer, Chase grabbed the other, and the three of them went in search of the last vault. The last one was half way across the graveyard. They didn't talk as they moved.

The moon gave off just enough light and turned some of the gravestones a milky white. When they came to the raised tomb, taller than Della, she didn't think her heart even beat. She couldn't seem to get enough oxygen into her lungs.

This was it. If Natasha and Liam weren't in there . . .

The key didn't want to turn the padlock that hung from the large concrete door. Burnett grabbed the sledgehammer and hit the lock and knocked it loose.

It took both her and Burnett to push the door open.

Darkness hung heavy in the tomb. Burnett switched on a flashlight. The beam of light moved left to right. Only a pile of concrete blocks filled the vault. No Liam. No Natasha.

Chase let out a breath. She felt him pull her closer, and they looked at each other. This near him she could see his eyes looked wet and hopeless. Frustration built up in Della so tight, she wanted to scream. She dropped to the floor, hugged her shins, and buried her head on her knees. They had failed. Della felt sick, her stomach heaved.

"Did you hear that?"

She recognized the voice and pulled in a shuddered breath. It wasn't Chase or Burnett.

"Hear what?" She raised her face, but saw only darkness.

"That noise," Liam said.

"They're burying someone else," Natasha said. "I don't want to listen."

"No, it was different. Listen."

"No, I'm tired, Liam. I want to go to sleep forever."

"Don't say that."

"They're here!" Another voice sounded, but distantly, and Della realized it was Chase. "They're here somewhere!"

"They're not," Burnett said. "We tried."

Della came out of the vision just in time to see Chase grab his sledgehammer. "Do you hear this?" he screamed as he slammed into the stone wall and knocked a hole in the tomb.

He must have been in the vision, too. And somewhere deep in her soul, she remained just enough in the vision to hear Liam say, "That? Did you hear it?"

"They can hear us!" Della screamed and jumped up. She turned in a complete circle searching in the dark for a door or entrance. None existed. Then her gaze fell to the pile of concrete blocks.

"There," she said. "Under there."

Burnett didn't look convinced, but when she and Chase started tossing the blocks to the other side, he helped.

Ten heavy blocks later, Della saw the metal latch that pulled up a steel door. Her tears of regret that had fallen were now followed by tears of joy.

It took all three of them to pull the door open.

Della jumped down into the small space. But she saw nothing but blackness.

Then she heard it. Breathing. She inhaled and caught the scent of vampires. Two.

"Natasha?" Della said. "Are you here?" Her vision cleared just enough to see another open doorway.

"We're here," Natasha said and it sounded as if she'd started crying. "We're . . . here. Right here."

Della ducked down to go through the doorway. A beam of light came behind her. She turned and saw Chase with a flashlight.

"We found them." She smiled up at him through her teary vision.

"I know." He handed her the light and came to stand next to her. His shoulder brushed against hers and she let herself savor that touch for one second. "Let's get them out of here."

Chapter Forty-three

Dr. Whitman and his family were on vacation, so Burnett had a different doctor meet them at Shadow Falls. He put the doctor and his patients in one of the bedrooms in an extra cabin. Della, Chase, Burnett, Holiday, and Hannah all sat in the living room. Miranda and Kylie had stopped in for support. Miranda hugged Della, Kylie just gave a thumbs-up, and then they went on their way.

Chase sat right beside Della, as if it was his place. She didn't argue with him. They had made a hell of a team. While her thoughts were mostly on the two behind the door, she couldn't help but think about Burnett's message about her and Chase: *After this case, if you continue to see Chase, your career with the FRU is over.*

Did she really have to make that choice?

She glanced at Chase and wondered what the chances were of him coming to work for the FRU.

From behind the bedroom wall, she could hear the doctor moving around and treating the patients. The first thing he'd asked for was extra blood. He'd brought some, but needed more. Burnett left and returned with four pints from his own reserves.

The doctor was going to let them feed and give it to them via

IV while he checked them. Finding Natasha and Liam alive had erased Della's panic, but seeing them so thin and weak brought some of it back. Both of them had been going in and out of consciousness on the way over here.

They looked like the old pictures of prisoners of war. The mood in the cabin now was cautiously optimistic.

Burnett stood on the front porch to make a few calls. Probably checking in to make sure things had gotten taken care of back at the cemetery.

Holiday, with Hannah in her arms, came over and sat beside Della and Chase. She offered Della a gentle, calming touch and then some words. "I'm proud of you. And you," she said, looking at Chase.

"Thanks," Chase said and Della saw a spark of pride in his eyes.

Hannah smiled up at Chase and flapped her arms.

"It appears my little girl already has good taste in men," Holiday said. "I'm afraid she's a big flirt."

After a second, Holiday continued. "And I'm a little disappointed in myself. I had serious doubts because I've never seen a case where the spirit was able to connect two live people, but I'm beginning to learn that nothing is impossible."

"I'm just glad it turned out okay." Della looked back at the bedroom door. "They're going to be okay, aren't they?"

"I'm not a doctor, but I would think so."

Della inhaled and breathed a little deeper this time.

"Did the spirit pass over?" Holiday asked.

Della looked back at Holiday. "I don't know."

"Oh, you'd know," Holiday said. "You'll see it. It's rather beautiful. A reward for all your work. And it's worth it." She got a gentle smile on her face.

"Then I guess she hasn't," Della said.

"Why would she still be hanging around?" Chase leaned in and asked.

"She might want to make sure they are okay. Or she might want something else."

Della recalled the bloody vision of her aunt, dead. And she knew from both Holiday and Kylie, that often what ghosts wanted was justice. But how could she offer that on a murder that happened so many years ago? And the thought of even trying to discover the truth when . . .

Holiday spoke again. "Did you ever find the connection of the ghost to these two?"

"She's Natasha's mother," Della said, but didn't add the fact that she was also her aunt. She knew that would lead Burnett to discovering too many truths. And before he went digging into her family tree, Della wanted to find the answers herself.

Holiday smiled. "I should have guessed." She bounced Hannah on her lap. "Maternal bonds are pretty powerful."

Della's thoughts went to her own mom and the last time she'd spoken with her. She could only hope whatever problem had arisen at home had decompressed. But as soon as she had a chance, she needed to call.

Voices echoed from the bedroom and she heard Natasha talking to the doctor.

Della wanted to talk to Natasha right away, but Burnett insisted they get them medical help first. And rightfully so.

Finally, the doctor walked out. Burnett moved through the door. Holiday, Chase, and Della all stood up. The doctor smiled, and suddenly the air tasted sweeter to Della.

"They're going to make it. I'm not sure how much longer they could have survived. It will take some time for them to get their strength back. They'll probably have more emotional scars than physical, but they'll be fine."

Della leaned her head back, closed her eyes, and said a prayer of thanks. Chase leaned in and whispered in her ear, "We did it."

She opened her eyes and smiled at him.

"The patients need rest," the doctor continued. "But if you'd like to visit with them, that's fine. Keep it low-key. One at a time and make it short."

Burnett inched forward and looked at Della and Chase. "I have to go to the office to fill out some paperwork. Why don't you two visit with them, and I'll do my interrogation later."

Della nodded.

"Oh," the doctor added, "I tried to convince them they would rest better in separate rooms, but they refused to be separated. Which isn't uncommon for victims who went through an ordeal together. I recommend letting them stay together for a while."

Della would bet that Natasha and Liam would be together longer than a while.

Chase's phone started to vibrate in his pocket. He pulled it out and looked up at Della. "It's the council, I should update them."

Della saw Burnett frown, but much to his credit, he didn't say anything. He kissed his wife and child and left.

After a few seconds, Chase went outside on the porch to take his call. Della heard him recounting what happened.

She looked back at the doctor. "Is it okay if I go in now?"

"Sure. But if they're sleeping, let them be."

"I understand." She started toward the door when Chase walked back inside. He moved over to her. "I need to go fill the council in on things in person. I shouldn't be too long."

"Good," she said. Before she knew his intent, he leaned down and kissed her. It wasn't a kiss full of sexual tension, just a simple good-bye from someone who cared about another person. It was, Della realized, very much like the one Burnett had just given Holiday.

He smiled and then passed his finger over her lips. "I won't be long."

"We need to talk," she said, prepared to tell him about the FRU ultimatum.

"That we do," he said, and she saw in his eyes how much he cared.

He turned to go, but she grabbed his hand and pulled him back. And she kissed him. This kiss lasted just a little longer. She knew Holiday and the doctor watched, but for once, she didn't care.

"Thank you," she said when she pulled back.

"For what?" he asked, smiling.

"For everything."

He gave her hand a squeeze. "I'll be back as soon as I can."

She smiled and watched him leave. When she heard him take a flying leap off the porch, she felt like a part of herself had taken off with him. It hit her then, somehow, someway, she wasn't going to stop seeing Chase. It didn't matter if her feelings were due to the bonding. She still felt them. And their being together was right. Like Natasha and Liam. Like Kylie and Lucas. Burnett and Holiday.

When she looked back, she saw Holiday's expression was less than happy. But Della refused to worry too much. Things would work out. She had to believe that.

"I'm going to check on Natasha and Liam," she said.

"You do that," Holiday said.

Della got to the door and paused. Taking a deep breath, and not completely sure what she was going to tell her cousin and her boyfriend, she eased open the door to their room.

. . .

Natasha and Liam were in separate twin beds, but someone had pushed them together. Each had an IV going into their arm. They both had their eyes closed.

Della paused at the door, her gaze going to Natasha. The doctor must have used a washcloth to at least get some of the dirt off her. She wore a gown, and Della suspected it was Holiday's. She almost turned around when Natasha's eyes fluttered open.

Della smiled at her, even though it hurt to see her with such dark circles under her eyes and her cheekbones so pronounced.

Natasha smiled back and sat up a little.

"Would you like to rest now? I can come back."

"No, please come in." Natasha motioned her in then checked on Liam, who was still asleep.

Della inched in. "I have doctor's orders not to stay long."

Natasha nodded. "I hear you and that guy who was with you are the ones responsible for finding us."

Indecision flipped around her head. Should she tell Natasha the whole truth about the ghost? Yes, Della realized. Natasha deserved to know. Della moved in and sat down in a chair beside the bed.

"Actually, we had a lot of help."

"The police, or . . . what do you call them? F something?"

"The FRU," Della said. "They're like the police to all the supernaturals."

Della saw Natasha squint to check out her pattern. "So you're vampire, too?"

Della nodded and remembered what she needed to tell the girl. "The FRU helped, but . . ." Oh, hell, how did she say it? "Actually, Natasha, your mom is the one who gets most of the credit."

"My mom?" Natasha's eyes grew wide. "But I thought . . . I was told she thought I was dead."

"No, not your adoptive mom. Your birth mother, Bao Yu Tsang."

Now tears filled her eyes and she touched her trembling lips. "I thought she was dead."

Shit! Della was screwing this up. "Yeah, well, she is. I'm sorry. But . . . she sort of hung around all these years, probably to look after you."

Natasha stared at Della as if she might need a shrink.

Della hesitated and then added, "I know it sounds crazy. Believe me, it kind of is." All of a sudden, cold filled the small bedroom, and Della knew her aunt was there.

"You're saying my real mom's ghost helped you find me?"

Della nodded. "Yeah, that's pretty much it in a nutshell." *Except that I was in your body when you and sleepyhead over there were doing the deed.* Maybe she shouldn't tell Natasha that part.

The girl looked down at her hands as if trying to come to grips with what Della had said.

Della let her take all the time she needed.

Finally, she looked up. "My first impulse is to say you're nuts. I don't believe in ghosts, but then . . . I'm a vampire, and I didn't believe in them, either, until I was turned."

"Yeah," Della said. "It kind of messes with your head, doesn't it?"

Natasha just nodded. "So, she told you where to find me?"

"Well, yeah, I mean . . . there's more to it than just that."

"What's more?" Natasha asked.

Della inhaled. "Can this part be just between us for a while?"

"What part?"

"I won't tell," a male voice said.

Della shifted her focus to Liam, whose eyes were open, and from the look on his face, he'd heard the ghost comment, too.

"Yeah, you can't tell, either," Della said.

"What is it?" Natasha asked, sounding leery.

"You and I . . . we're cousins," Della said in a low voice. "Bao Yu Tsang is . . . was my father's sister."

Natasha's eyes widened again. "You're Della? I should have recognized you. Your . . . I mean, our aunt, Miao, showed me pictures of you."

"Not the one where I was naked in the bathtub when I was three, I hope," Della said.

Natasha chuckled and tears filled her eyes at the same time. "Yeah, she showed me that one." She inhaled. "I can't believe I'm meeting you."

Della felt emotion tug on her heart. "I feel the same way. And it's not that I don't want people to know, but I'm trying to figure a few things out about our family, and until then, I just wanted to keep it between us."

"Is something wrong?" Natasha asked.

"Not anything you need to worry about now." Della felt the temperature dropping even lower.

Natasha pulled the sheet up higher and nodded. Then she looked like she was going to cry again. "When Chan died, I . . . I was devastated. We hung out sometimes. Went bowling. But his mom, Miao, was so crushed, and I felt bad going to see her because I felt like I reminded her of him."

Della started to tell her about Chan not being dead, and then dying, but it would take too much time and emotion. Later, she would tell her everything, just not now.

"The doctor said to keep it short. Obviously, I have a lot to tell you. But we'll have plenty of time."

Tell her I loved her.

Della fought the chill in the room. "Your mom, she loved you."

Suddenly, Della felt Natasha needed to hear more. "She wanted to keep you, but her parents were old-school and she didn't have a choice."

Natasha brushed a tear from her cheek. "I know. Will you see her again? My mom?"

"I hear her more than I see her. But I've seen her a couple of times."

"Can you tell her that I understand, and that I had a good mother and father? Tell her that I don't blame her. Miao told me what happened. How her parents and my father's parents wouldn't accept me. They wanted her to abort me, but she refused. Tell her thank you for giving me life. Oh, and for saving me now."

Della heard the ghost softly crying. "She can hear you."

"She's here?"

Della nodded.

"Thank you," Natasha said.

"Yeah, from me, too," Liam added and reached over and took Natasha's hand.

Chapter Forty-four

Della had no sooner walked out of Natasha's room, when her phone rang.

"Hey," Chase said, and Della's chest filled with warmth and wanting. "How are they?"

"Good," Della said though she heard some tension in his voice. "You okay?" she asked.

"Yeah, but I don't think I'm going to make it back there tonight. The council wants reports and all that stuff. Can you get away tomorrow?"

"Yeah," Della said, deciding to make it happen. She didn't care if she had to go against Burnett's wishes. "What time?"

"Nine in the morning? Or eight. I'll take as much time with you as I can get."

"Nine," Della said. "I'll want to check on Natasha and Liam again."

"Sure. And when we come back, maybe I can visit with them. It's weird, isn't it? I kind of feel like I know them."

"Me, too," Della said, thinking it would be nice having Natasha in her life.

Chase said good-bye and they hung up, hoping that tomorrow would end as well as today.

An hour later, Shawn, the agent who'd helped them with the case, showed up just to check in. Della, Holiday, and Shawn talked for a while, and then he and Holiday left.

After making sure Natasha and Liam didn't need anything and giving them her and Holiday's and Burnett's numbers, she left for her cabin. Miranda and Kylie were at the table again, with Diet Cokes.

Miranda had tears in her eyes. *Oh, crap.*

"What's up?"

Kylie appeared to wait to see if Miranda was going to answer, and when she didn't, Kylie did it for her. "Shawn dropped by and saw her."

"And?" Della asked and looked at the witch.

"I think he likes me and I don't know what to do."

Della dropped down at the table beside her friends. "You do what you want to do," she said.

Miranda shook her head and looked at Della. "Don't you feel at least a little bit guilty? You cared about Steve, and then bam, you just moved on to Chase."

Della swallowed. "Yeah, sometimes I feel guilty, but then I remember he left, I didn't. And he told me to find out what was between Chase and me." She looked at Kylie. "It's just like Kylie. Derek pulled away from Kylie, and she realized Derek wasn't the one. Lucas was." Della inhaled. "I don't want to hurt Steve, but whatever it is between Chase and me is bigger."

"But I can't say that," Miranda said. "And both of you said Perry felt like the right one for me."

Kylie nodded. "Maybe he was the right one for you then. I don't regret what I had with Derek. He was there for me when I needed him. I'll always care about him. And I think people come into our lives like that. Della needed Steve to help her move past her jerk of an ex-boyfriend, and you needed Perry to help you adjust to everything you were going through."

As much as Della normally hated Kylie's psychoanalytical crap, this made sense. She would probably always care about Steve.

Miranda turned the can in her hands. "I tried calling him, and he won't even answer. I mean, if he'd just call, I'd come out and ask if he was seeing other people, and if so . . . I'd hate him. And I'd probably eat ice cream for a week." She gave Della a you-won't-stop-me-this-time look. "But then I might give Shawn a chance."

The witch's expression almost got teary again. "Have you heard from Steve at all?"

Della recalled the one text, but afraid that would hurt Miranda, she lied. "No."

"How are Natasha and Liam?" Kylie asked, changing the subject.

"They're good," Della said.

"You should feel great," Kylie said. "You did it. Did you get to see the ghost cross over yet?"

Della shook her head. "No."

"That's odd," Kylie said.

"Not really," Della said. "I don't think she's through with me yet."

"What else does she want?" Miranda asked.

"To figure out who killed her." Just saying it made Della more certain. The ghost needed to know.

"I hate having to do that," Kylie said.

"Yeah, me, too," Della said, and got a flash of the vision and the man who looked just like her father standing over her with a bloody knife. "I think I'll go to bed."

Della fell asleep staring at the Smurfette. She thought about Chase. Then she heard Miranda's question: *Don't you feel at least a little bit guilty? You cared about Steve, and then bam, you just moved on to Chase.*

She shouldn't feel guilty, she told herself. Steve had known he was probably going to be leaving when he'd pushed his way into her heart. That was wrong.

Just wrong.

At six thirty the next morning, Della woke up to her phone ringing. Lordy, had she rolled over during the night? She didn't think so. She really must have needed the rest.

As she reached for her phone, she spotted the silly Smurf and smiled. When she saw the call was from Chase, her smiled widened.

"Hello," she said.

"Were you still sleeping?" he asked and his voice sounded raspy as if he'd just woken up, too.

"Yes," she said.

"Sorry, I just woke up and . . . I missed you. You want to meet me at seven instead of nine?"

She grinned. "No. I've gotta visit with Natasha and Liam, and then go tell Burnett and Holiday I'm going to meet you." And she wanted to call Marla, too. Just to make sure things at home hadn't gotten crazier.

He must have picked up on something in her voice. "Do you think they'll have a problem with it?"

"I'm not asking them, I'm telling them," she said.

"Because you don't think they'll let you come?" he asked.

"Let's talk about that later," she said. But they were going to have to. She closed her eyes. Would Chase decide to come work for the FRU? Dread spilled over her and her early morning good mood faded.

"Okay. Then nine," he said. "What do you want to do?" he asked.

She felt a tiny little tremble run through her. What did she want to do? Was she ready to let this thing between them go to the next level?

"Why don't we just play it by ear?"

"Sounds good." He got quiet. "I do miss you," he said.

She looked at the Smurfette. "Me, too."

Della got up to shower. She washed her hair, shaved her legs, and even put on a little makeup. Towel wrapped around her chest, she hurried through the living area to her room. Kylie and Miranda were still asleep and she preferred to leave before they woke up. Face it, she didn't want to fill them in on her plans, because she didn't know what those plans were.

Opening her underwear drawer, she found a black bra beneath her everyday white ones.

She pulled it out. The lacy piece of fabric dangled from her finger and she exhaled. Was she planning on Chase seeing that bra? Was she planning on Chase taking off that bra?

Oh, hell! She didn't know. But just because she wore it, didn't mean she would get naked. She slipped the bra on and then found a matching pair of black panties.

Out the door in fifteen minutes, she turned the corner in the path toward Natasha's cabin when her phone rang.

Thinking it would be Chase again, she eagerly grabbed the phone, but a quick check showed Burnett's number. "What now?" she muttered and prayed it wasn't bad news. Prayed it wasn't him reminding her that her time with Chase had ended.

"You up?" Burnett asked.

"On my way to see Natasha and Liam. Why?"

"Can you come to the office instead?"

"Why?" she asked.

"See you in a minute," he said, not answering her question.

Damn, damn, damn! Her gut said this wasn't going to be good.

Burnett waited inside Holiday's office. Holiday wasn't here, so maybe that meant it wasn't too bad. She'd noticed when things were gonna be bad, he had Holiday around to magically make bad news more tolerable.

Della had no more stepped into the room when she got Holiday's scent and she came stepping out of the bathroom. And she didn't look happy.

Della inhaled and sat on the sofa before they insisted she do just that. Holiday came and sat beside her.

"What is it?" Della asked.

Burnett picked up a big brown envelope and came and sat on the arm of the sofa.

"I told you I had my concerns about Chase."

So this was about her and Chase not seeing each other. But damn they weren't wasting any time.

"I know." Della looked from Burnett to Holiday and back to Burnett. "But we did this job and it went great. And I think . . . at least, I hope, I can talk him into maybe considering coming to work for the FRU."

Burnett stared at the envelope in his hands. "I had Hayden go invisible and hide out at Chase's cabin to see if he was up to anything."

Della frowned. "That wasn't nice."

"Be mad at me if you want. But I did it because I knew you weren't going to stop seeing him. And if I was going to let you continue this relationship, I had to be sure."

Della got a bad feeling. Why was Burnett telling her this? Did he think he'd caught Chase up to no good?

She looked at the envelope he held and knew it contained something bad. Something Burnett was going to try and use to keep her away from Chase. She wasn't sure what was in there, and she wasn't sure it would work.

"So what do you have?" she asked.

"Honestly," Burnett said, "I don't know, but it puzzles me."

"What puzzles you?"

When he didn't immediately start talking or hand over the evidence, she got a little pissy. She snagged the envelope.

He frowned, but she frowned right back.

"Della," Holiday said as if to try to calm her.

Della rolled her eyes at the fae. "He's going to show it to me sooner or later, right? Let's just get it over with."

Chapter Forty-five

They were photographs. Large eight-by-ten images. The first one was of Chase standing outside on his porch.

No incriminating evidence there.

Her hands shook slightly with fury at Burnett interfering with her life. She flipped to the next photo. Chase sitting on his porch with binoculars in his hands. Bird-watching. Oh, yeah, that made him a terrible person.

She moved to the next picture. Chase standing on his porch talking to someone. A man with his back to the camera, moving, so he was nothing more than a blur.

She flipped to the image behind that one. Her hands stopped shaking. Her heart stopped beating.

"I'm not sure what this means," Burnett said. "Does Chase know your father?"

"I . . . I . . ." She couldn't answer.

Della felt her chest grow heavy, and her sinuses stung, but not one tear dared to crawl up her nose and appear in her eyes. She was too busy studying the picture. Studying the man standing on Chase's porch. Staring at the look in Chase's eyes. He was angry.

Then she shifted her focus to the man. The same face as her father. The same height, but it wasn't him. Her father didn't have muscled arms; her father's gut, though not fat, was just a little paunchy.

This wasn't her father.

This was her uncle.

Emotion washed over her in waves of pain. Chase had lied. Had been lying to her from the start.

Anger.

Fury.

Betrayal.

And to think she'd worn her black bra. Had even considered taking off her black bra. She'd practically fallen . . .

No, she *had not* fallen. But, by God, he was going to fall. Hard. On his ass. And she was the one who was going to put him there.

"Are you okay?" Holiday asked.

"No," she said. Why lie? Burnett would know. But she said it in a low, quiet voice. "Can I have this?" She held up the photo and tried her best to sound pleasant.

Burnett nodded. "You're going to confront him?"

Or kill him. "I think that's a good idea." She stood.

"I don't think so." Holiday popped up and caught her arm. "You're too angry."

"She seems fine to me," Burnett said. "Let her go and get her answers. She deserves to know what kind of game he's playing. For all we know, her father wants Chase to find something bad to discredit the school."

My father's not doing anything. But Della didn't say a word.

Holiday continued to hold her arm and glanced at her husband. "Ever heard the saying, 'silence can be deadly'? Or 'the calm before the storm'?"

"I won't stay long," Della said. "I need to talk to him." *And more.*

"No," Holiday said with vigor. "Go take a walk or a run and then come back here in a few minutes and we'll reassess. When your emotions settle down, you can go talk to him."

Della wanted to explain that she wasn't going to calm down.

How could she? She'd been duped.

Played.

Nothing made her angrier than someone playing her for a fool.

And she'd been a fool all right.

"Give it ten minutes. Ten," Holiday said.

Della nodded. She pulled her phone out and snapped a picture of the photograph.

"Don't you leave until you come back to see me," Holiday said.

"I won't," she said and meant to keep that promise. Not that it would be easy, all she wanted to do right now was find the Panty Perv and tell him exactly what she thought of him. But like it or not, Holiday was right. She had to plan what needed to be said, because she didn't ever plan on laying eyes on him again.

Bonded my ass! How could he claim to be bonded to her, then do nothing but lie? The whole time, he'd lied. He knew about her uncle.

She suddenly felt sick. She walked out of the office and started toward her cabin, only to realize she didn't want to talk to Kylie or Miranda right now.

Right before she turned off the trail to head out toward the woods, she heard someone call her name.

Derek.

"Later," she said and started to take off.

"No!" Derek yelled out. "It's important."

She started to take off anyway, but words sounded in her head.

You need to hear this!

The cold surrounded her.

"Hear what? Why the hell should I listen to a word you say?" Della asked, speaking to a wall of nothing more than cold air. "Aren't you the one who put Chase and me together to work this case? I could've saved Natasha on my own. I didn't need him!"

She stopped and turned to face Derek, who she heard stop behind her.

"What did you say?" he asked.

"I wasn't talking to you. But since you're here . . . what is it?"

His mouth formed a tight line, concern filled his eyes. "I . . . shit, Della, I don't know how to tell you this."

"It's easy. You open your mouth and words come out," she said, her patience spent. "Try it."

He nodded. Exhaled loudly. "Remember when you asked me to check with the PI again about your aunt's case?"

She nodded.

"Since I didn't hear back from him, I called him again last night."

"And?" She motioned with her hands for him to continue.

"The detective called him back yesterday. He said after he looked at the files, he checked on what all they still had in evidence." Derek shuffled his feet a bit. "They ran some tests on some blood they'd collected. They weren't able to do that test back then, they didn't have the capability. The results came back." He hesitated. "They're going to make an arrest. They're going to arrest your dad, Della. I'm sorry."

She stood there for several seconds.

His words flew around her head. *Remember you asked me to check with the PI again about your aunt's case?*

Her father was going to be arrested for murder and it was her fault.

If she'd never asked Derek to look into it, the case would have stayed buried. Stayed cold.

She'd done this. Done this to her dad—an extremely private man, who didn't even want to think about the past. Now the whole world would know. There would be news reports, photos in the paper. Her father would be humiliated. More important than that, he'd be accused of murder. What if they convicted him?

She swallowed down the pain. Tears stung her eyes. If she hadn't disappointed him before, she'd really done it now.

Not just him this time, either. This wouldn't just hurt him, but her mom, her sister. It could destroy her family. Completely.

What the hell had she done?

Or a better question, how in the hell was she going to make it right?

Her phone rang. She pulled it out. Her sister's number showed on the screen.

Della answered the call. "Hey." Her voice shook with that one word.

"Della?" Her sister's voice came with the sound of tears—much like the ones running down Della's face. "The cops came . . . they took Dad." Marla sobbed. "They think he killed someone. Mom's so upset, she can't stop crying. You have to come home. You have to!"

Della heard Marla's request. But how could Della do it? How would she get blood if she was at home? How could she keep her secret from her family? How could she leave Shadow Falls?

Then again, how could she not go home and try to fix this, when she was the one who caused it?

"I'm coming," Della told Marla. "I'm coming home."

Yes, that was one hell of a cliff-hanger—and you won't believe what happens next!

Don't miss the final book in the
Shadow Falls: After Dark trilogy

Unspoken

where all will be revealed.

July 2015

Visit www.cchunterbooks.com for the latest news.

DON'T MISS C. C. HUNTER'S NEW SERIES

SHADOW FALLS:
After Dark

S
H
A
D
O
W
After Dark
FALLS

Reborn

NEW YORK TIMES BESTSELLING AUTHOR
C. C. HUNTER

BOOK 1

S
H
A
D
O
W
after Dark
FALLS

Eternal

NEW YORK TIMES BESTSELLING AUTHOR
C. C. HUNTER

BOOK 2

St. Martin's Griffin

Read the series that started it all

NEW YORK TIMES BESTSELLING SERIES

a shadow falls novel

c. c. hunter

Born at Midnight

Awake at Dawn
c. c. hunter

c. c. hunter
Taken at Dusk
a shadow falls novel

NEW YORK TIMES BESTSELLING SERIES
Whispers at Moonrise
c. c. hunter

NEW YORK TIMES BESTSELLING SERIES
Chosen at Nightfall
c. c. hunter

Available now.

St. Martin's Griffin